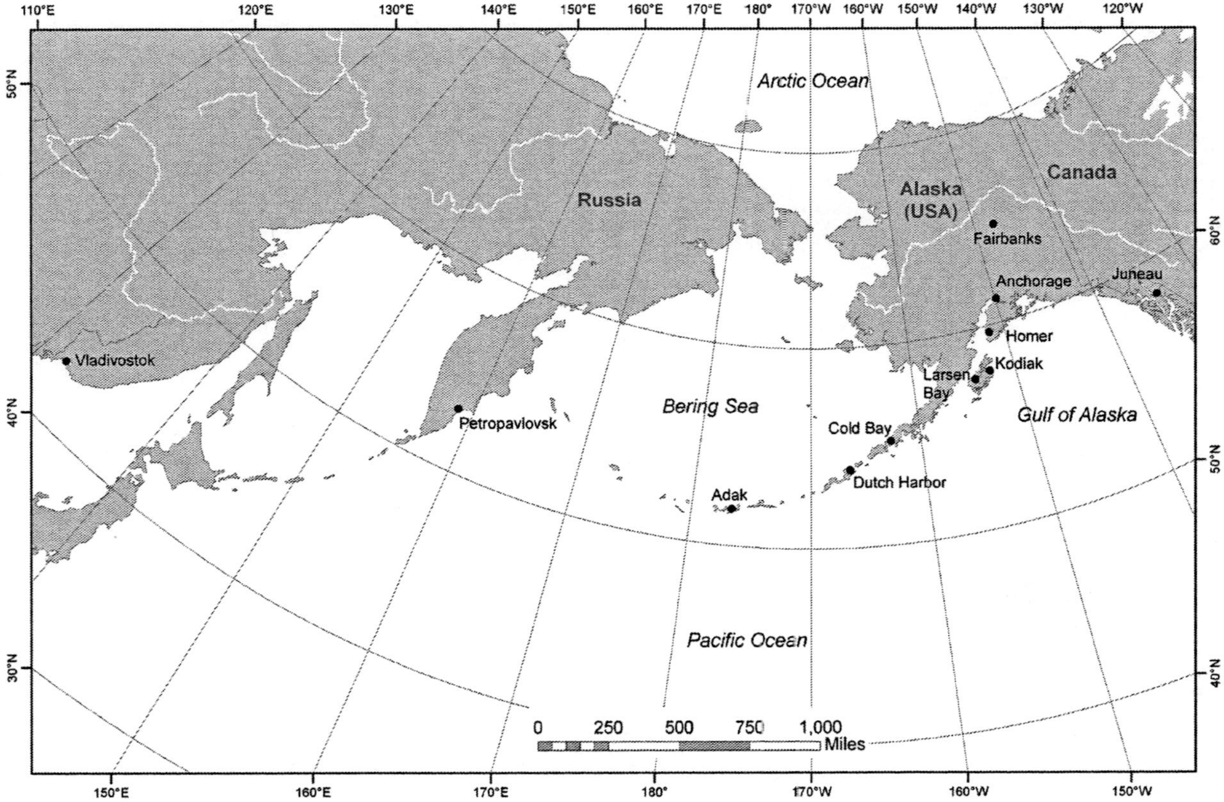

MW01640202

Arctic Ocean
Canada
Alaska (USA)
Fairbanks
Juneau
Anchorage
Homer
Kodiak
Larsen Bay
Gulf of Alaska
Cold Bay
Dutch Harbor
Bering Sea
Adak
Pacific Ocean
Russia
Petropavlovsk
Vladivostok
0 250 500 750 1,000 Miles
60°N
50°N
40°N
30°N
110°E
120°E
130°E
140°E
150°E
160°E
170°E
180°
170°W
160°W
150°W
140°W
130°W
120°W

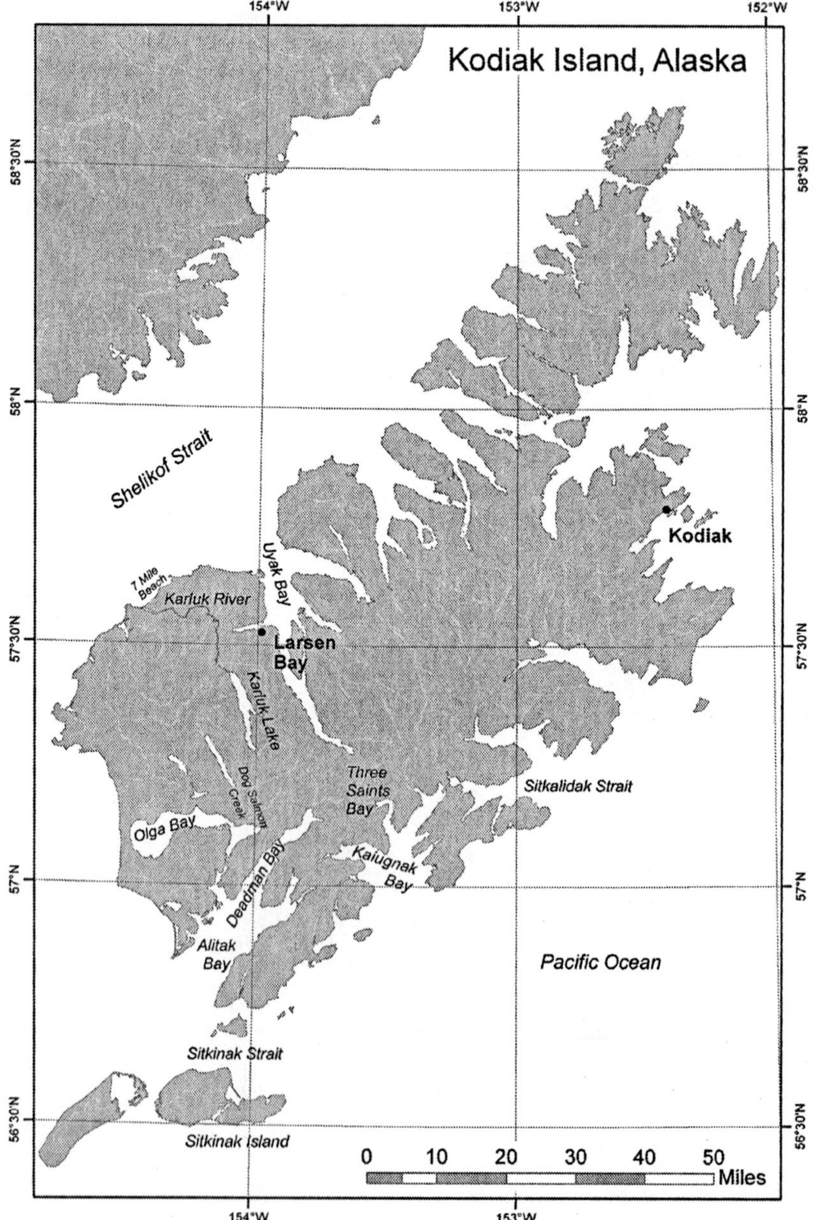
Kodiak Island, Alaska
154°W
153°W
152°W
58°30'N
58°N
57°30'N
57°N
56°30'N
Shelikof Strait
Uyak Bay
7 Mile Beach
Karluk River
Larsen Bay
Karluk Lake
Kodiak
Dog Salmon Creek
Three Saints Bay
Sitkalidak Strait
Olga Bay
Deadman Bay
Kaiugnak Bay
Alitak Bay
Pacific Ocean
Sitkinak Strait
Sitkinak Island
0 10 20 30 40 50
Miles

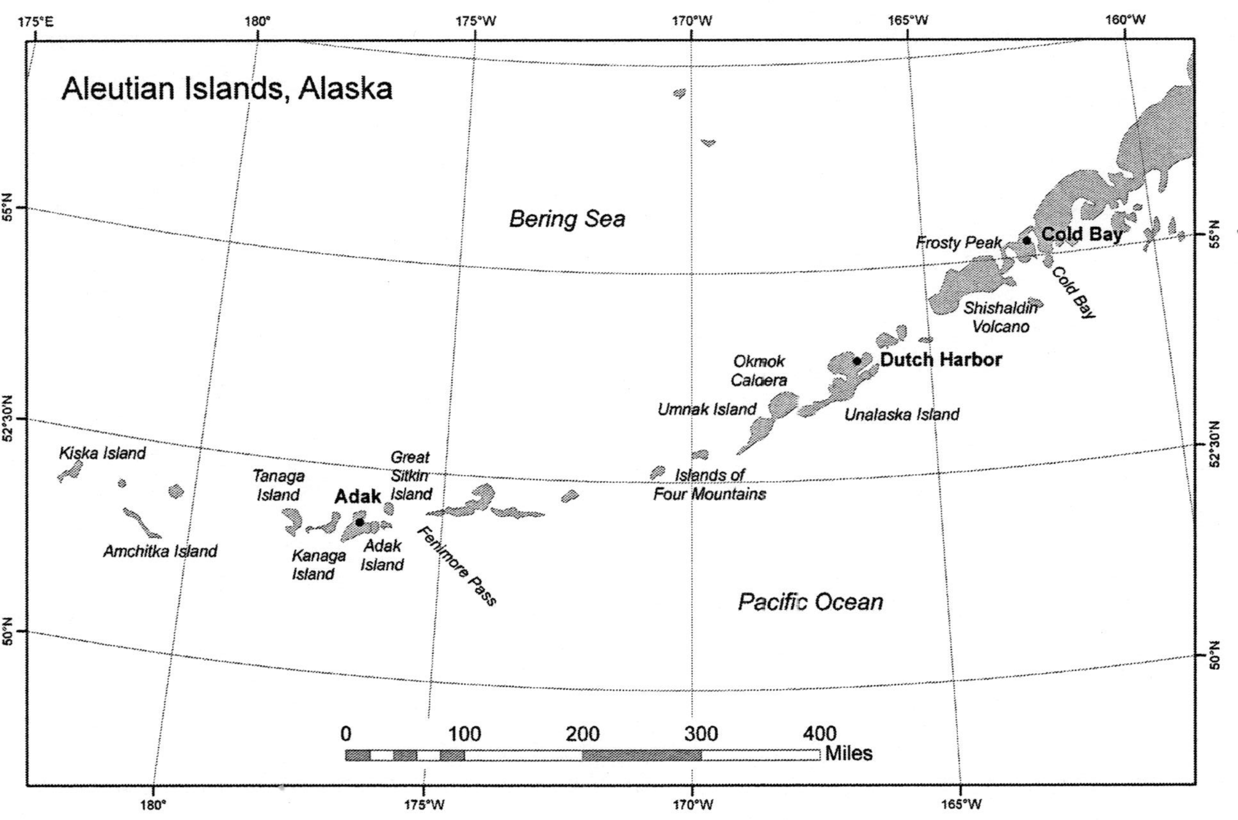
Aleutian Islands, Alaska
175°E
180°
175°W
170°W
165°W
160°W
55°N
52°30'N
50°N
Bering Sea
Pacific Ocean
Frosty Peak
Cold Bay
Cold Bay
Shishaldin Volcano
Dutch Harbor
Okmok Caldera
Umnak Island
Unalaska Island
Islands of Four Mountains
Kiska Island
Amchitka Island
Tanaga Island
Kanaga Island
Adak
Adak Island
Great Sitkin Island
Fenimore Pass
0
100
200
300
400
Miles

THE CHAINS OF OKMOK

Scott,

It was a pleasure meeting you. Good luck with your future. Remember that you can achieve anything if you are resilient and hardworking.

All the best.

[illegible]

6-2-06

THE CHAINS OF OKMOK

D.M. Stolworthy

Library of Congress Number:		2004195231
ISBN :	Hardcover	1-4134-8073-X
	Softcover	1-4134-8072-1

This is a work of fiction. Names, characters, places and incidents either are the product of the author's imagination or are used fictitiously, and any resemblance to any actual persons, living or dead, events, or locales is entirely coincidental.

This book was printed in the United States of America.

To order additional copies of this book, contact:
Xlibris Corporation
1-888-795-4274
www.Xlibris.com
Orders@Xlibris.com

27343

This book is dedicated to all those brave people who walk the most dangerous beat in law enforcement—our Correctional Officers and Probation and Parole Officers.

I want to thank everyone who contributed so much to the completion of this work and whose stories gave me the inspiration to write it. A special thanks goes out to Mike, Tom, Pam, George, Cyndi, Stu, and my beloved Kelley, who edited the manuscript several times, and Jax, who constantly reminded me to take a break and throw the ball.

DAY ONE

Russian Pacific Fleet Headquarters, Vladivostok, Russia

Those idiots, thought Admiral Voroshilov. He inhaled deeply on his cigarette making the end glow red. It had been three days since he'd last heard from Commander Ivanshenko. *Where the hell is he? He was supposed to have reported his arrival on station by this morning.* He exhaled the acrid smoke from his nostrils not releasing the cigarette from his taut lips.

Voroshilov stared out the window, thinking about the heated meeting he had attended in Moscow several months ago. When he first heard Admiral Bulgakov describe the plan, he thought everyone in the high command had gone mad. Didn't they know it was impossible to send a submarine out of Petropavlovsk undetected? Just how, he had argued, was his submarine commander supposed to shake off an American attack submarine? Pick your best commander and your best boat, Admiral Bulgakov had answered. *Fools!* He sucked hard on the hollow cigarette filter bringing the burning tip precariously close to his short graying moustache.

When he raised questions about trespassing into American waters, his objections were brushed aside. Didn't the Americans trespass into Russian waters all the time? When he tried cornering Bulgakov on just how he was to gain access to the target, he was told that the GRU (military intelligence) and SVR (Foreign Intelligence Service) had arranged everything. He didn't trust the

GRU or the SVR. He considered military intelligence an oxymoron and the SVR was no more effective than its predecessor, the now defunct KGB. Spy organizations, he heatedly reminded Admiral Bulgakov, were long on promises and short on delivery.

Unconsciously he rubbed the thin scar on his forehead—a reminder of how close he had come to being killed by a bullet in the 1967 Six-Day War. On that day the he had been standing on the banks of the Suez Canal with Egyptian troops after the initial invasion was launched against Israel. He remembered how the GRU had predicted an Israeli collapse in the face of the Egyptian onslaught. It only took the Israelis six days to prove the GRU wrong.

Just who was the American traitor that would assist them? The GRU and SVR refused to give up this information. *Funny*, he thought, *we risk our lives and the GRU tells us that everything has been arranged.*

He took a final puff on his cigarette before crushing it out in the brass ashtray sitting on the windowsill. *There are too many pieces to this puzzle*. With the instinctive skill of decades, he mindlessly pulled out another cigarette and lit it.

Out in the harbor a tugboat was pushing a guided-missile cruiser away from the pier. The rust running down the side of the once proud ship made him reflect on the current state of his fleet. He could remember when his fleet was more than a match for the Americans. He let his tired mind wander through memories of commanding anti-submarine warfare drills in the frigid waters of the White Sea. The visions of towering waves breaking across the clipper-bow of his cruiser during the seemingly endless games of cat and mouse with American submarines made his heart race. A small bead of sweat formed on his brow. *How I miss commanding a squadron at sea.*

"Admiral?" came the call from the outer office.

"Yes, Gromyko," he answered, somewhat annoyed at having his thoughts disturbed.

Captain Gromyko, dressed in his dark blue naval uniform, was holding a plate of food and tea, waiting patiently to be invited into the room.

Admiral Voroshilov invited him to come in and close the door.

"I thought you could use some lunch," said the blonde, blue-eyed captain. Setting the plate down on the large wooden desk, he said, "I know how you forget to eat when you are worried." After serving with Voroshilov for so many years, he knew his habits. And he had made a promise to the Admiral's wife of 30 years that he would make sure the Admiral at least ate regularly. She had given up on getting him to quit smoking.

"Correct as usual," answered a grateful Voroshilov. He walked over to the desk and poured himself a cup of tea. It was dark and steaming hot. Waving the cup under his nose, he took a deep breath. He loved his tea almost as much as his cigarettes. He walked back over to the window to continue watching the ships move around the harbor. "Any word from Ivanshenko?" he asked. He sipped the hot liquid gingerly.

"Nothing yet, sir," Gromyko answered.

"Do we know if he was followed coming out of Petropavlovsk?"

"Nothing has been confirmed Admiral. But since it's standard practice for the Americans to track every submarine we send out to sea, we must presume he is being followed." Captain Gromyko shared the Admiral's frustration over not having the resources to put more than one or two boats to sea at a time. He too could remember the days when several submarines a week sailed from Russia's harbors, making it harder for the Americans to track them all. For many years he had stood next to then Captain and then Rear Admiral Voroshilov on the bridge of the guided-missile cruiser Kiev during anti-submarine warfare maneuvers in the stormy North Atlantic. Now with so few deployments, the Americans had the advantage before the lines were untied at the dock.

"Do you think Ivanshenko can shake the Americans?" Voroshilov asked. He sucked on the cigarette filling his lungs with curling gray smoke before exhaling the remains into the already clouded air.

"Of course Admiral," Gromyko replied, trying to cheer the Admiral up. "Ivanshenko is our boldest commander. He has proven himself on numerous occasions. That's why you picked him for this mission. He'll make the rendezvous point and get Major Golkin's team onto the airplane."

Captain Gromyko knew the Admiral had been against this mission from the start. It was more than dangerous. It was foolhardy—and desperate. But now that the mission had begun it was too late to stop. He needed to boost the Admiral's confidence. If things went wrong, it would be Admiral Voroshilov and possibly his entire family who would pay the price.

Picking up some black bread and cheese, Admiral Voroshilov answered, "I suppose you're right, Alexander. Ivanshenko hasn't sent a message because he doesn't want to give away his position. Where should he be right now?"

"I was looking at the map just before I came in, Admiral. The Putin should be getting close to the Islands of the Four Mountains right now."

The food made Admiral Voroshilov think about the meeting in Moscow again. "Those idiots," he said cursing under his breath. *They're willing to risk an international incident just to keep the Army and the SVR happy. No American can be this important.*

But his warnings had fallen on deaf ears. The generals and admirals were all living in the past. And even his former classmate and friend, Prime Minister Kirov was unable to oppose the entire high command. To do so risked another military coup. Now his fate and the fate of the government rested in the hands of a few men sailing beneath the stormy waters of the North Pacific.

USS Hammerhead, 300 miles south, southwest of Adak, Island, Alaska

"Where the hell did he go?" Commander Jones barked at no one in particular. "How could we lose him?" he said angrily, brushing back his ball cap.

Jones's second-in-command was at a loss for words. Up until yesterday, the mission had been going perfectly. They had intercepted a Russian Akula Class submarine just as it exited Petropavlovsk and had been trailing it for three days as it sailed south, southeast towards the gap between Japan and the Aleutian Islands. And now it was gone.

"There's nothing out there Skipper," the sonarman stated conclusively.

"God damn it!" Jones spat emphatically. "Thompson, plot a direct course for Adak Island. Ten degrees up on the dive planes, let's get to the surface and send a message to CINCPAC. They aren't going to like this news."

Malloy Super Maximum-Security Prison, Adak Island, Alaska

Driven by hurricane force winds, sheets of rain and sleet slapped against the houses, tearing at the shutters shielding the darkened houses from the storm. The glow of street lamps shimmered in the inky darkness of early morning, illuminating the buildings in eerie, gusting shadows. With thunderous roars giant waves crashed against the harbor's breakwater throwing freezing spray high into the air and pulling against the rocks like so many angry green foaming claws. Fishing boats struggled against their moorings as the storm at one moment tried to pull them out to sea and at the next demolish them against the pier. The howling wind drowned out the violent orchestra of noise being played by the tugging of ropes and twisting of metal.

Out in Kuluk Bay, endless rows of white-capped waves continued their advance towards the rocky shoreline in an endless onslaught against the island.

Perched on the mountainside above the town, the dull-gray concrete monolith stood defiantly against the storm's fury, its glaring floodlights shimmering through gusting sheets of sleet and rain and its slit windows shining like an elaborately carved jack-o-lantern in the night. Poised high above the main complex, Lieutenant Carlos Banderas was standing watch in Alpha Tower, the main rifle tower, fighting off the urge to become hypnotized by the optical illusion of the rain shooting through the artificial light. Sipping his steaming cup of coffee he said to himself, "just another three hours until rotation and I can go home and crawl into my nice warm bed." Talking to yourself helped keep you awake during the 12-hour rotation.

Looking out over the prison grounds, Carlos let his mind wander over events he'd experienced in his career at Malloy Super Maximum-Security Prison—a 300-bed facility recessed 1,000-feet above sea level into the rocky slopes of Mt. Moffet. This storm reminded him of that wintry day ten years ago, when as a newly promoted corporal, he had first stepped onto the tarmac at Mitchell Field. He remembered how he had tried to ignore the pounding sleet in a vain attempt to show everyone he was impervious to Alaska's weather. In reality, all he had proven was his inability to button his raincoat in the raging wind and how to get soaked to the bone in a few minutes. It was hardly the impression he had planned to make, but he soon proved his worth as an officer. Today, he was still known as one of the best officers in the department. The only real difference was the patience he'd learned in the job and the gray streaks that now highlighted his jet-black hair.

"Ten years, hard to believe, ten years," he said to himself, "and here I sit, wondering why I'm enduring another month of graveyards." He rubbed his eyes to stay awake. Of course, he knew why he was there. He loved the money. With a wife and four teenage children, it was important to provide for them—officers working at Malloy earned an additional fifty percent in hazardous duty pay. Add in overtime and an officer could earn well over $100,000 a year.

But money wasn't his only motivator. He enjoyed his work and the responsibility. He enjoyed the challenge of trying to keep one step ahead of the prisoners. They were always planning an escape or an assault on an officer or another inmate. At Malloy you couldn't get away with coming to work and zoning out for 12 hours. You had to be on your toes all the time. The prisoners were far too dangerous to allow your routine to get sloppy. If you did, you could end up dead.

Carlos really liked his schedule of one month on and one month off. While working, he could hunt and fish on the island, and during his month off, he could spend a lot of time with his kids.

He was also a creature of habit. He liked the rhythm of the institution, its routines, and the staff.

"Alpha, Rover," came the call over the radio.

"Go Rover," Carlos replied.

"Yeah, I'm just pulling up to the South Outer Gate. It looks like we've got another intruder inside the fences," said Corporal Joan Steiger. She was assigned to Rover, the prison's 24-hour perimeter patrol vehicle. It was her job to drive around the outside of the prison to patrol for escaping prisoners or local citizens trying to throw drugs over the fences for the prisoners to pick up during outside recreation. Most of the time, however, her job entailed baiting foxes that managed to breech the outer fence.

"10-4 Rover," Carlos replied. "SS, you copy?"

"10-4 Alpha, SS copies," answered Captain Marc Anderson, the shift supervisor. Taking command of the situation, he ordered, "Rover, set some bait and see if our little friend won't follow the scent out."

"10-4 SS," replied Corporal Steiger. "Alpha, open South Outer Gate."

Covering seventeen acres, Malloy Super Maximum-Security Prison was surrounded by two 20-foot tall chain link fences. On the South side were the main gates, which accessed the prison complex. At the base and top of each fence was a coil of razor wire capable of cutting a person to the bone. Surrounding the perimeter fences was a dog run. Starting at the kennel next to the main gate, the dogs had access to the entire perimeter, except for the gates. At night, the dogs were let out of their kennels to patrol what the officers called, "No Man's Land."

Dogs were added to Malloy's security operations a few years after it opened. They had replaced the electronic proximity alarms, which were unable to distinguish between a man in the wire and a fox.

It was at the unpatrolled area at the main gates that Adak's fox population found access to a regular supply of mice and voles.

Screeching against the howling wind, the 20-foot tall gate stuttered open. Corporal Steiger steeled herself against the elements as she exited Rover. "Damn it's nasty out tonight," she cursed, pulling up her fur-lined collar and her winter hat down over her ears. Fighting to stay upright in the gusting winds, she made her way around Rover stopping in front of the truck's headlights. Opening the container filled with musk-scented, rotting flesh, she poured a small portion onto the ground. In a few moments the wind would carry the scent in the fox's direction. "Whew!" she said catching a whiff of the bait, "this is some vile stuff." Quickly, she resealed the container and scurried back inside Rover and out of the weather. "Why do I do this job?" she growled as she wiped the dripping rain from her forehead and nose. "Alpha, Rover. Bait set. Hope he likes it."

Shifting Rover into reverse, Corporal Steiger backed away from the fence and turned off the headlights. In Alpha Tower, Lt. Banderas watched the fox through his binoculars. He chuckled as he saw the fox catch the scent and begin trotting towards the open gate. *I think they know that if they can get inside the fences we'll feed them.* "SS, this is Alpha. Our little friend took the bait. Closing South Outer Gate."

"10-4 Alpha," replied Captain Anderson. "Looks like he'll be our only release this morning." With that comment, most of the prison's officers broke into smiles—a little drama in an otherwise dull shift.

Life at Malloy was a series of routines. Every day was the same. At 0600 hours the inmates were ordered out of bed to clean their rooms and prepare for inspection. At 0700 they were served a hot breakfast—cold breakfast if they failed inspection. At 0800 prisoners with jobs went to work, others went to classes or the law library, others to video visiting, and others remained in their cells. Lunch was served at 1200 hours and dinner at 1800 hours—hot if your cell passed inspection and cold if not. Six times a day, the entire facility came to a halt as the officers conducted formal prisoner counts to make sure no one had escaped. For criminals accustomed to the thrill of unbridled lawlessness, the routine at Malloy was almost as suffocating as the eight-by-ten cells.

Every aspect of a prisoner's life at Malloy was controlled. Cameras monitored every prisoner cell 24-hours a day. Officers searched their cells on a random, but frequent basis, escorted them to their work areas and back, and pat-searched them at least once a day. Officers also issued citations to prisoners, who broke minor rules or were disrespectful to staff or visitors. If a prisoner earned enough demerits through poor behavior they could lose their job, access to programs, television privileges, or outside recreation. Serious misconduct resulted in immediate solitary confinement and formal disciplinary sanctions, up to and including the loss of visitation for one month.

Dogs trained to sniff out drugs were part of the normal search routine at Malloy. The prisoners hated the dogs. Not only were they intimidating, but it was almost always the dogs that located a drug stash. Getting caught with drugs at Malloy meant an automatic 30 days in solitary confinement and a loss of privileges for 6 months. And life on this windswept rock without television or hot food was almost more than a person could endure. Still the allure of drugs to find escape from this concrete tomb was great enough that the segregation unit was always full.

After finishing his log entry about the fox, Captain Anderson returned to his computer to write his daily report. Over the past 12 years, he had completed so many reports he could almost write them in his sleep.

With a few last strokes on the keyboard, he emailed his report to the Superintendent's office and to the Commissioner's office over 1,300 miles away in Anchorage. As he waited for the message to complete its transmission, he thought about the incoming transport flight with the replacement shifts and two more prisoners. The two new arrivals would put his inmate count at 290. This would leave him only 10 empty beds in the event of a disturbance or large fight. He chuckled at this thought. "You're in the bad people business Marc," he reminded himself. He made a mental note to write a memo about the transport after inspection.

Anderson pushed back from the keyboard and stood up, stretching his tall, thin frame. It was time to conduct his last inspection of the prison before being rotated out for his month of leave. Since his office was in Main Control, he started there. With his hands crossed behind his back, he strolled around, observing the routines of the two control room officers.

The control room officers were responsible for controlling all staff and prisoner movement throughout the entire complex. From their enclosed bulletproof reflective glass fortress they could see the full length of all five main hallways, which radiated out from the control room. The only obstructions to their views down these expansive corridors were the heavy steel crash gates placed every 100 feet. In the event of a riot, the control room officers would be able to seal off an area and prevent the spread of the disturbance to other sections of the complex.

To supplement the control room officers' observations, the curved panel above their heads was packed with closed circuit television screens flashing with real-time images from numerous cameras strategically placed throughout the facility. At the officers' fingertips, were several computer touch screens, which they used to control movement through gates, doors, and hatches. To the right of each officer was a joystick, which they could use to control the movement and focus of any camera in the system. This gave the officers the unprecedented ability to observe and record the slightest activities of any prisoner. Not only did this capability make Malloy much safer, it virtually eliminated inmate appeals of disciplinary actions for misconduct.

Anderson never ceased to marvel at the technology arrayed before him. The computer screens were an intricate maze of colors and numbers, each one identifying the location and importance of a particular room, cell or door. When he had begun his career, the control room consisted of toggle switches and electronic breakers. Cameras had been a luxury.

Without a doubt, Main Control was the busiest post in the prison. That's why the selection of the officers was so important. These specialists had to be detail oriented and meticulous in their routines. In the event of an emergency, it was up to them to think and react quickly. It was their job to stay alert and isolate any area when trouble broke out.

Once an area was secure, the SS could order it flooded with paralyzing chemical agents that would immobilize everyone in that section in a matter of minutes. In the event of a power outage, the prison's computer system would bypass the island's main power grid and bring the backup generators online.

"Johnson," Captain Anderson said, "pan back to FP 15 (female pod, cell 15), I want to see what Lucas is up to." He had noticed that Prisoner Lucas was not feeling well at evening meal and just before the 2200 hour lockdown she had complained of abdominal cramps.

With a few quick keystrokes, the officer punched up FP 15's camera. Lying in a fetal position was Inmate Jenne Lucas.

Every time Anderson saw Lucas, he couldn't help but wonder how such a gentle looking, educated woman could have committed such a horrible crime. *What kind of jealousy would make someone condemn 144 innocent souls to their deaths?* He still remembered the headlines, "Jealous Flight Engineer Programs Airliner to Crash in Murder of Cheating Husband." He was surprised no one had made a movie about her crime yet. Perhaps it was because after arriving at Malloy, Lucas suffered a mental breakdown. Now she was under the care of the prison's psychiatrist.

Lucas's generally docile nature engendered sympathy for her condition from many of the officers. Sometimes they could hear her talking in rambling phrases. She said that dead people talked to her.

Watching Lucas through the camera it was obvious that she was in some distress. Anderson pressed the intercom button. "Lucas, are you feeling okay?"

"No. I don't feel good," she replied, glancing up at the smoky bubble protruding from the ceiling.

"What's the matter? Do you need to see the doc?" he asked.

"Maybe," she said, holding her arms across her midsection and grimacing. "It may just be cramps, you know, that time of the month, or maybe not. I don't feel very good."

"I'm going to put you down for sick call at 0730 just in case." He wrote Jenne Lucas's name on the sick call roster. He knew that she may be menstruating, but in a prison environment it was unusual for a female to have her period out of sync with the rest of the female population. Hell week, as the staff called it, had happened two weeks ago. He sensed that something else was wrong with Lucas.

"Okay Capt'n. Thanks," she replied before turning back over onto her side.

Anderson exited Main Control, heading off to complete his rounds.

The control room officer moved through her morning checklist. It was time to wake the prison's kitchen workers. Hitting the intercom button she ordered them to get out of bed. It was time to head down to the cafeteria to cook breakfast. The clank of tray slots being opened announced the arrival of officers on the floor for movement.

Inmate Toby Church covered his eyes as the lights came on in his cell. He cursed the arrival of a new day. He hated this place. He hated being ordered about. He hated not being in control of his life.

Pulling back his blanket, he swung his feet out from under the covers. Instinctively his feet found his foam slippers on the cold concrete floor. He shuffled over to the small shower to rinse the sleep off his body. He had to be fast. The water would only run for five minutes before shutting off automatically. This prevented prisoners from flooding their cells.

Retrieving the towel from the tray slot in his door, he dried off with the rough terry cloth. Inmates at Malloy were not allowed to keep extra towels or clothing in their cells.

Taking his toothbrush from its holder, he held it out of the tray slot. One of the post officers squeezed a dab onto the bristles. Prisoners were not allowed to keep toothpaste in their cells. Mixed with water, toothpaste is very corrosive. They use it to peel the paint off the walls. Church walked over to the stainless steel sink, where he brushed the morning scum off his teeth. Using the plastic, single blade razor that was handed out with the towel, he lathered up some soap and shaved the stubble off his face. Next he combed his thick brown hair and examined his appearance in the stainless steel sink. He didn't like to look messy.

Grabbing his orange pants and black-striped shirt, he got dressed. Slipping on his cloth rubber-soled shoes, he walked over to the door. Reaching out of the tray slot, he passed the towel, razor, comb, and dirty laundry to the officer, who checked them off his list. "Ready to go boss," he shouted from the behind the solid metal door.

The floor officer signaled for Main Control to open the doors to the kitchen workers' cells. With a clack and a whoosh, the pneumatic doors slid open.

Stepping out into the common area of the housing unit, Inmate Church took his position in line behind the other kitchen workers. With another whoosh, the doors slammed closed, their metallic clang echoing inside the concrete living unit.

"Move out," barked the officer.

Slowly, the prisoners walked into the 20-foot pod access sally port (the area between two solid steel mechanically controlled crash gates) and down the empty corridor towards Zone 4 and the kitchen. Walking at the rear of the line was an officer, who made sure everyone walked in single file between the red lines marked on the floor. Stepping outside the lines meant a 30-day loss of commissary privileges. The lines were used to keep a safety cushion between the prisoners and the staff moving in the hallways.

Keeping pace with the prisoners was another officer walking above them on a catwalk. He was armed with a shotgun. It was his job to deal with any outbreak of violence. In the event of an attack by one inmate on another or on an officer, he was authorized to use deadly force.

Church walked with his head held high. He knew the location of the lines by heart and to look down risked getting shanked by another prisoner. Survival in prison, he quickly learned after his arrival, meant staying alert and trusting no one.

After watching the fox gulp down his tasty treat, Carlos Banderas had returned to his vigil in Alpha Tower. His duties were to oversee the grounds of the complex, control the perimeter gates, and coordinate any shooting from the four other rifle towers—Bravo, Charlie, Delta, and Echo. All four towers were manned 24-hours a day by sniper qualified officers armed with .308 caliber rifles.

Looking down at his watch, Carlos noted the time. "Control, Alpha."

"Go Alpha."

"0515 hours, time to kennel the dogs." He wrote his log entry as he spoke.

Confined within their dog run, the two German Shepards were responsible for dealing with any prisoner, who managed to breech the two perimeter fences. Running in an area 10-yards wide and extending around the entire complex, they had free reign to attack anyone brave enough to take the chance. Only special K-9 officers could manage these dogs. Anyone else risked getting bit. During the day, the dogs were returned to their kennels for feeding and rest.

"Control, Alpha. Dogs are kenneled."

"10-4 Alpha. All posts, time is 0525 hours," announced the officer in Main Control. She entered the time in her logbook.

As Corporal Steiger drove around the perimeter, the other officers were completing their final entries in their post logbooks and checking on the prisoners in their dimly lit cells with flashlights. No prisoner ever got a full night's sleep at Malloy.

Back in his office, Captain Anderson was busy typing his briefing memo to the oncoming shift. Two high-profile prisoners were coming in on the morning flight from Anchorage. Extra security was on standby should the need arise.

As Bravo shift carried out the last of its duties within the quiet halls of Malloy, the cloak of night and the storm clung to Adak.

Out in Kuluk Bay, the white caps were still crashing onto the shore. Buttoned down against the weather, no one bothered to notice the seals and sea lions abandoning their haulouts and heading out to sea. No one could see the foxes, birds, and mice scurrying back to their homes. No one noticed the queer rhythm to the waves. No one knew that a whole new storm was approaching.

Malloy 1, Ted Stevens International Airport, Anchorage, Alaska

The Northern Lights danced in green-blue sheets of iridescent light obscuring the last traces of stars sparkling high above in the Arctic sky. Under the soft glow of the red cockpit lights, the pilot was reading through her pre-flight checklist, while her first officer was conducting his pre-flight inspection on the outside of Malloy 1—the Department of Corrections' aging, four-engine blue and gold Lockheed C-130 Super Max transport.

Malloy 1's pilot was a former C-130 pilot in the Air Force and then the Alaska Air National Guard. She enjoyed the challenges of flying in difficult conditions. And the Aleutian Islands were the purest definition of difficult flying conditions. Today's weather called for gale force winds enroute to Adak. She double-checked the flight engineer's fuel consumption estimates using the latest weather report of winds aloft.

With over 5,000 hours as pilot-in-command of a Hercules C-130 and with over 1,500 of those hours logged in Alaska, the pilot felt confident in her ability to handle almost anything thrown her way.

Joining her in the cockpit was the newest member of the aircrew, Flight Engineer Nikki Foster. This was Foster's second trip on Malloy 1.

"Foster," the pilot directed, "retest the hydraulic system again. I'm getting a peculiar reading on the pressure check."

For some reason, Nikki Foster gave her an uneasy feeling. He just seemed too ambitious, too quirky. He had passed his background investigation and had very good flight credentials, but still there was something weird about him. She shook off her feelings of uneasiness and went back to her checklist.

Nikki Foster wet his lips and wiped a small bead of sweat from his forehead. With a shaky hand he adjusted the hydraulic control valve. He hit the pressure test button. "Try it now Captain," he said, trying to hide the nervousness in his voice.

"Hydraulic pressure okay," she replied, after tapping the gauge one more time. Once again she went back to reading her checklist. In the dim glow of the cockpit, she did not see Foster reach inside his jacket and put his hand on his pistol to make sure the magazine was seated.

All his adult life, Nikki Foster had wanted to be rich. Despite growing up with a lot of opportunities, he had never quite succeeded. He knew it wasn't his fault. People kept getting in his way. A tense, shallow man, his massive ego and lack of diplomacy often put off those who were in a position to help him. It was only his skill as a flight engineer and his stepfather's connections in the government that had allowed him to continue to move up in the world.

Well, today my luck is going to change. Nikki Foster was living proof that anyone can pass a psychological examination.

Looking across the tarmac from Malloy 1, at the department's service hangar, the pilot could see the passengers for Malloy 1's monthly flight to Adak Island waiting for clearance to board. Among the passengers were 75 officers and staff. They were on their way to rotate out the other shifts. Standing on the other side of the hangar across from the employees were four prisoner transport officers (PTOs) and two prisoners secured by handcuffs, belly chains, leg irons, and electronic immobilization belts strapped to their waists.

"How you feeling boss," Brownie asked Harry.

"Fine," Harry lied without looking up at his giant friend. This was his first transport as the department's Chief Transportation Officer. Harry's throat was parched despite having just returned from getting a drink of water. Today, all eyes were on him to carry out the most important transport in department history.

Harry wondered what his parents would think of him now. Born in Kaktovik, Alaska on the Arctic Coast, Harry Ignustuk was the only surviving child of Betty and Robert Ignustuk. Harry's older sister and younger brother had drowned during a freak storm on the Arctic Ocean 15 years ago.

A quiet, sensitive man, Harry took the death of his siblings hard. As the last remaining child, he vowed to make his parents proud. When he was promoted to PTO V, Harry's parents flew almost 1,000 miles from Kaktovik to Anchorage to watch their son receive his lieutenant's bars—the first Eskimo to be promoted to lieutenant.

Follow the procedures, don't deviate from the routine, keep your guard up. Harry found it comforting to have his long-time partner and trusted friend PTO Sergeant Harold Powell with him on this transport. He glanced up to see if "Brownie" was nervous too.

Harold "Brownie" Powell was a mountain of a man. Thick from neck to waist, a little over six feet five inches tall and topping the scales at over 355 pounds, he was known affectionately by the other PTOs as "Brownie," because of his uncanny resemblance to a Brown Bear.

Quiet and thoughtful, Brownie said little. His sheer physical size elicited compliance from most combative or aggressive prisoners.

Harry smiled. Yes, he was glad "Brownie" was here with him.

Harry looked over at the two other transport officers assigned to his unit today—PTO Danny Sanders and PTO John Gregory. Officers Sanders and Gregory were two veteran officers. Harry had chosen them for his team, because he liked the way they paid attention to details. He especially appreciated Danny's habit of reading the complete histories of the super-max prisoners being transported. This helped everyone understand whom they were dealing with and often helped them avoid difficult situations.

While they waited for the pilots to clear them for boarding, Danny looked over at the prisoners, silently recalling the details of their crimes, which he had shared at an earlier pre-transport briefing. He liked to memorize the details. You never knew when this information would come in handy. Danny went over the facts in his mind again.

Ivan Lincoln had recently been sentenced to five life sentences for killing five women. He was a cold, calculating killer, who enjoyed terrorizing his victims before slaying them.

An Athabaskan Native, born and raised just outside of Fairbanks, he was adept at hunting, trapping, and ivory and bone carving. His preferred victims were middle-aged women. Frequenting area bars, he would offer them drugs or alcohol in exchange for sex. When a woman accepted, he would take her back to his cabin located far outside of town, get her high and rape her.

He would then hamstring his victim to prevent her from fleeing. Over the next few days he would repeatedly rape and torture her. Using his intimate knowledge of anatomy, he would cut and stab his victim so that she would slowly succumb to a loss of blood and shock. After the victim died, he would butcher her body, keeping only the bones. After boiling off the flesh, he would carve the bones into fish hooks, cribbage boards, and other items, which he would sell to tourist shops. His arrest and trial almost destroyed the curio industry in Fairbanks.

Ivan Lincoln made his mistake one evening when he picked up an undercover state trooper. Using a homing device hidden in her earring, the police were able to follow him to his lair. He confessed to the five murders that same evening.

Elizabeth LeDue stood in stark contrast to Ivan Lincoln. She was an elegant woman of 42, with long brunette hair, green eyes, and charm to match. She was the most famous prisoner in the United States. Formerly the Chief Biological Warfare Scientist for the Central Intelligence Agency, she now found herself at the low point of an otherwise stellar career.

A graduate of Harvard and MIT, Elizabeth LeDue had gone to work for a large bioengineering firm right out of college. Within a few short years, she had risen through the ranks of the company. Her skills and reputation led to her recruitment by the CIA, which was desperate to keep ahead of the Chinese and Russians in the area of biological warfare.

In just a few short years, Dr. LeDue had helped the CIA develop a genetically engineered biological agent that attacked with almost instant lethality. Her creation was virtually impossible to trace, because it dissipated within the matter of a few hours after application. It was a brilliant achievement. Following this success, the CIA rewarded her with a large bonus and the position of chief scientist. However, in their enthusiasm to keep ahead of the Chinese and Russians, they failed to pay heed to the warning signs in her personal life.

Raised in a proper Southern home, Elizabeth LeDue was cultured, well schooled and popular. What no one except her immediate family knew, however, was that card games and the rush a person gets from betting it all fascinated her. Coming from a privileged background, Elizabeth's father had always been able to cover her losses. But when his company went bankrupt, she was left to fend for herself, and she began to lose ground.

For a while she managed to cover her losses by selling personal jewelry and family heirlooms. But as time went on, these resources were exhausted. Even her hefty salary at the CIA could not keep up with her gambling habit.

It was only a matter of time before Russian agents from the GRU caught wind of her financial difficulties. Using one of their most skilled agents, the GRU drew her into their trap. Within a few weeks, he was sleeping with her. After a few months, he began blackmailing her for technical information.

By the time CIA uncovered her treason it was too late. The Washington media had picked up the story and it was national headlines. A sensational trial followed. Numerous high-level officials resigned. Dr. Elizabeth LeDue was sentenced to life without parole. And the CIA arranged to send her to the far ends of the Earth.

Danny wondered why fate had drawn together these two criminals. He was used to violent men like Lincoln, but the cultured LeDue was a whole new experience. He watched the tears running down her face.

"Okay, let's move out," Harry barked. He motioned for the prisoners to move toward the waiting transport.

Lincoln fell in between Officers Ignustuk and Gregory. He was used to walking in leg irons and had no trouble shuffling his feet to avoid tripping. LeDue on the other hand, was having a hard time getting the motion down. She kept stumbling along as she tried to take normal steps and the chains pulled at her ankles. Just as they crossed through the outer perimeter of shotgun armed officers and dogs, she tripped and fell down, scraping her hands and knees on the frozen asphalt. Brownie leaned over and picked her up with one hand.

"You okay?" he asked politely.

LeDue nodded her head 'yes,' but did not look up.

"Listen, you gotta learn how to shuffle your feet," he said, while demonstrating the hip-swaying short-stepped shuffle experienced prisoners used to avoid tripping in leg irons.

"Thanks," she said in a whisper, while picking the gravel out of her palm.

The prisoner transport team was always the last to be loaded. Entering through the hydraulic gate at the rear of the C-130, Harry and his officers escorted the prisoners down the cavernous interior to their hard-backed seats in compartment two.

"Brownie" Powell stood towering over the prisoners as he watched Harry chain them to their seats. PTO Gregory stood ready in the aisle, just in case a prisoner tried to break for the pilots. PTO Sanders stood at the rear of the plane in the event a prisoner broke free and ran for the exit. He also kept watch for intruders outside the aircraft.

Once the prisoners' legs were chained to the seats and their arms secured at their sides, the PTOs took their assigned seats—two facing back and two facing forward.

Harry started his pre-flight briefing. "In the event of an emergency landing, you will be removed from your seat, but will remain in your restraints. An officer will assist you in exiting the aircraft. Follow their instructions to the letter. Any deviation from his instructions will result in the application of force. You will not converse with each other during the flight. You will not converse with any of the officers during the flight. You may not use the restroom during the flight. In the event you become airsick, you will have to wait until our arrival at Malloy to receive treatment by the medical staff."

"What the hell do you mean, if I get sick, you won't help me," growled Lincoln.

"Quiet Lincoln," Harry said forcefully. "One more outburst and I'll tape your mouth shut." Harry reached over to his knapsack and pulled out a roll of duct tape holding in front of Lincoln's face.

Lincoln fought off the urge to spit on Ignustuk. He had no desire to ride for hours with his mouth taped shut. Pursing his lips, he looked away from Harry and scowled at PTO Gregory. *That pig sure doesn't act like an Eskimo*, Lincoln groused silently.

"Going to be a fun ride with that one," Brownie whispered to his boss.

"Got that right," Harry replied. "Let's just hope it's a smooth trip to Adak. The pilot says there's a gale blowing at Mitchell Field—65-knots from the southwest."

Seeing that Lincoln had settled down, Harry continued the pre-flight briefing. "In the event of an emergency ditching at sea, the officers will inflate rubber life rafts, escort you to the raft and proceed to the nearest shore. If you resist or try to disrupt the rescue, you will be shot." Harry always made sure to place particular emphasis on the last sentence. He sat down and buckled himself into his four-point restraint.

Ivan Lincoln sat stewing over the threat to tape his mouth shut.

Elizabeth LeDue fought back another outburst of tears. *Oh God, please forgive me.* She could feel the muscles in her throat constrict when she heard the gate at the rear of the aircraft close with a hollow metallic clang. Suddenly, the compartment felt much too small. Even though she could see her breath, she was uncomfortably hot. Thoughts of home and family flooded into her mind. She longed for the warmth of the Georgia sunshine. Her mind reached out in vain for some sign of familiarity and comfort. Never before had she felt so lost and alone.

As the rear door of the transport was closing, the pilot began her work. "Spin number one, spin number two, spin three, spin four. Anchorage Ground Control, this is DOC Super Max Transport Malloy 1, at DOC hangar 1, with ATIS Zulu, ready to taxi to active. Squawking code three three niner niner."

"Roger Malloy 1, you are cleared to taxi to runway two four right, winds two one zero at fourteen, visibility three zero miles. Ident three three niner niner."

The pilot hit the ident switch on her radio panel, sending a strong radar signal on frequency 3399 to the control tower. This intense burst of energy illuminated the aircraft on the radar screen, making it stand out from the other aircraft on the controller's radar. In the event of an emergency, they would "squawk" 3399. This "squawk" would pinpoint the aircraft for any search and rescue operation.

The pilot pushed the throttles forward and stepped on the rudder pedals, moving the big dark blue and gold transport down the taxiway to the active runway. She scanned the terminal and the other taxiways for ground traffic. There was no other activity except in a brightly lit hangar where mechanics were preparing aircraft for their early morning departures. The thrumming drone of the four turboprop engines pierced the air.

"Anchorage Ground Control, Malloy 1, holding short runway two four right."

"Roger Malloy 1, you are cleared for takeoff, two four right. Contact Departure Control on one twenty five point six."

"Copy, cleared for takeoff, two four right," she answered.

The first officer dialed in frequency 125.6 on the radio as the pilot steered with her feet taxiing the giant plane onto the active runway. She pushed the throttles all the way forward, making the C-130 roar ahead. Applying forward pressure on the yoke, she worked at keeping the airplane on the ground until she had enough airspeed to prevent a stall once they lifted off. Easing the pressure, she pulled back on the yoke. Slowly, the giant aircraft left the ground behind and climbed into the air. "Anchorage Departure Control this is Malloy 1, please activate our flight plan."

"Roger Malloy 1, you are cleared for a straight out departure to flight level one eight zero. Have a good trip."

"Thanks. Malloy 1 climbing to flight level one eight zero."

With condensed exhaust pouring from its powerful engines, Malloy 1 disappeared into the pre-dawn darkness. 1,300 miles to the southwest lay Adak Island.

Nikki Foster wiped his sweaty palms on his pants.

On the ground, the seismographs at the Alaska/West Coast Earthquake and Tsunami Warning Center twitched ever so slightly. Deep within the bowels of the Earth, trouble was brewing.

USS Billings, Amchitka Pass, Alaska

"Come about to course zero four five, speed 20 knots," ordered Lt. Commander Hastings. The helmsman turned the sleek fighting ship to a course that would take them north, out of Amchitka Pass and around Adak Island. Executing the turn exposed the frigate's port side to punishing 35-foot seas, making the narrow-hulled 445-foot ship roll violently. Sailors who had managed to wedge themselves into their bunks for some much-needed rest suddenly found themselves dislodged and hanging on for dear life. Sea spray flew over the superstructure, freezing in opaque white sheets on the flat surfaces and forming icicles on the antennas.

Under ordinary circumstances the Billings would have continued steering into the oncoming waves, making the voyage more tolerable for the crew, but new orders mandated a course change.

Lt. Commander Hastings picked up the internal phone, calling Commander Englemann in her quarters. "Skipper, this is Hastings, you're needed on the bridge."

Englemann loosened the straps holding her into her bunk and pressed the intercom button, "Why Brad, what's up?"

"We've just received a top priority message from CINCPAC."

Her tone told him that she was annoyed at being disturbed. She was probably pinching the bridge of her nose right now. She always did that when she was annoyed.

"Well Skipper, it would probably be better if you were to read it yourself."

"Very well," she said didactically, "I'll be there in 10 minutes." Englemann released the intercom button and prepared to get dressed while being pitched around her quarters. Timing her exit from the bunk, she stood up in rhythm to the swells and immediately wedged herself against the wall. With her free hand she buttoned her uniform and combed her short, copper-red hair. With one last look she checked her appearance in the mirror. Satisfied that she was neat, pressed and ready for duty, she opened the door and headed to the bridge.

Below decks, Marine Corps Lieutenant Vance Surin was struggling to keep from being tossed out of his bunk. "God damn North Pacific storms," he muttered bracing his arms and legs under the railings. Resting, let alone sleeping was almost impossible in these heavy seas. In the dim glow of the room's lights he could see that his two other comrades were having just as much trouble sleeping.

Being beaten against a bulkhead in a storm was bad enough. What made it worse was not knowing why they had pulled him from his Stateside duty station as an instructor and reassembled his three-man recon team. He'd already done his tour at sea. He was just getting settled into a routine with his new wife and their two sons. *Maybe I need to get out of the Marines.*

"Hey, Lieutenant," asked Sgt. Francisco Ramirez.

"Yeah, Ramirez, what do ya want?"

"Why are we here?"

"I haven't the foggiest, Ramirez. You know that if I knew I would let you know."

"Lieutenant?" piped in Sergeant Tariq Ali.

"Yes, Sergeant," Surin replied, slightly exasperated.

"Sir, when do you think they'll let us know the poop?"

"When they're good and ready, just like always."

"Figures," said Ali to no one in particular.

"Lt. Surin to the bridge," came the call over the intercom system.

Surin swung his feet out of his bunk and braced his hands over his head to prevent being thrown against the steam pipes running along the ceiling. On nights like this he didn't bother undressing for bed. All he had to do was put on his cap and boots, and try to make his way up the stairwell without getting a concussion. Keeping himself slightly hunched over, he proceeded down the corridor. Although only 5 feet 9 inches tall, the pipes overhead were uncomfortably close to the top of his head.

"Captain on the bridge!" barked the signalman.

"Okay Brad, what's this all about?" Englemann asked, as she made her way one step and handhold at a time to her chair.

"Better if you just read this communication, Skipper," he answered. He got out of her chair and handed her the message, while keeping an iron grip on the armrest with his free hand.

Ignoring the pounding seas, Englemann sat down and read the communication.

PRIORITY MESSAGE—TOP SECRET

TO: USS BILLINGS
FROM: CINCPAC

INFORMATION FROM POLAR-SAT SIERRA INDICATES PRESENCE OF RUSSIAN AKULA CLASS ATTACK SUBMARINE, LOCATED AT 170° 03' W: 53° 28' 33'' N; COURSE 095, SPEED 12 KNOTS. PROCEED BEST SPEED TO INTERCEPT. NOTIFY OF CONTACT.

Picking up her phone, Commander Englemann called the ship's Combat Information Center.

"Lieutenant, when do you expect this storm to break?"

"In about an hour Skipper. The system has almost passed over us."

"Then what?"

"Seas should subside to about 8 feet and then to about 4 feet after that."

"How long until the next blow comes in?"

"Hard to say Skipper, but we should have calmer weather for about 27 hours."

"Thanks lieutenant, let me know of any new developments."

She hung up the phone. "Helm, increase speed to 25 knots. Commander Hastings, man all stations, make way for a fast run in heavy seas. And get Lt. Surin up here on the double."

Before anyone could place another call to Lt. Surin, he arrived on the bridge. "You called for me Skipper?"

"Yes, Lieutenant. Come over here." She moved over to the chart table.

She directed Surin's eyes to a chart of the Andreanof Islands. Moving her finger across the chart she started her briefing. "We just received confirmation from CINCPAC of a Russian Akula Class submarine 10 miles north northeast of Carlisle Island. Command thinks this may be the start of the Russian operation to kidnap Dr. LeDue. I've ordered Hawk One on the ready pad for liftoff when the Alaska transport is two hours out. Here are your orders."

Surin took the envelope from Englemann's hand and opened it. A perplexed look crossed his face as he read his orders.

"What's the matter Lieutenant?"

Surin looked up from the paper. "This doesn't make sense, Skipper."

"What doesn't make sense?"

"My orders tell me that we are to deploy on Adak Island and cover Mitchell Field. You said the Russian sub is nearing Carlisle Island. If the Russians are planning to kidnap Dr. Elizabeth LeDue, what are they doing way the hell over there?"

Englemann nodded in agreement. "Good question Lieutenant. I have to admit that I'm just as perplexed as your are, but CINCPAC has a positive sighting. That leads me to believe the intelligence provided by the CIA is wrong. Maybe our agents missed some clue or the SVR or GRU was able to plant some misinformation."

"Any ideas Skipper?"

"Yes," she said matter-of-factly, "we will proceed with the confirmed intelligence we do have and prepare to intercept the Russians off Carlisle Island."

"Aye, aye, Skipper." Turning smartly, he left the bridge.

"Up and at em', it's showtime," Surin barked, entering the room.

Sergeants Ramirez and Ali swung from their bunks. In one smooth motion they went to work preparing their gear and checking their weapons. Being busy made them forget about the rolling nausea in their guts.

"Meet me in the mess in 15," Surin ordered. He grabbed his maps, pack, M-16 and AK-47, and headed out the door.

"Bring us about to course zero seven seven, increase speed to 31 knots. Ready the Seahawk, and hang on for a wild ride," ordered Commander Englemann. *This doesn't make sense.* "I don't like this one bit, not one damn bit," she muttered under her breath. "If this is a prelude to the Russian operation, why is their submarine over 250 miles from Adak? The CIA said the Russian operation to kidnap Dr. LeDue would take place on Adak." Either CINCPAC was wrong about the Akula's location or the CIA was wrong about how the Russians intended to kidnap the good doctor. She was betting that the CIA was wrong.

She decided to take matters into her own hands. "Commander Hastings. See if you can't get a message to the Hammerhead. Maybe they can pick up the Russian's trail again. We need more information about what's going on out there."

Akula Class Submarine Putin, 10 miles north, northeast of Carlisle Island, Alaska

The nuclear attack submarine Putin slid through the dark depths of the Bering Sea, heading almost due east in a giant circle just north of Carlisle Island—an uninhabited windswept rock two miles in circumference. For several days, the Putin had cruised at maximum depth out of Petropavlovsk—the main Russian submarine base in the Pacific. Commander Igor Ivanshenko knew that the longer he could stay undetected, the better the chances were for the mission to succeed. But as they approached their destination, even the brilliant Ivanshenko had to bow to topography. The shallow depths of the Bering Sea and his lack of charts for this area forced him sail closer to the surface.

He was counting on the deep cloud cover and tempestuous surface to obscure his submarine from the prying eyes of the American spy satellites or from any American warships that might be lurking about as he ordered the Putin to periscope depth. To further cloak his approach, he ordered the Putin to slow to a paltry 10-knots. This would prevent the American SOSIS nets, laid out on the ocean floor, from detecting the noise from the Putin's reactor pumps.

Igor Ivanshenko knew the dangers of navigating in uncharted waters. His memories of the sickening feeling in hearing the hull of K-276 crumple as it collided with a shoal near the Israeli coast were still vivid. Even after 10 years, his dreams were haunted with visions of his drowning comrades. He could still see his good friend, Peter Turgenev, drowning on the other side of the watertight hatch.

Trapped for two days inside the crippled hull of his submarine, then Lt. Commander Ivanshenko vowed that he would not make the same mistake as the commander of K-276. Riding a submarine to the bottom had taught him that indecision kills.

Igor Ivanshenko's tactical genius, tenacity, and ability to stay cool even under intense pressure made him an ideal choice for this assignment. Two days earlier he had managed to shake off an American Seawolf attack submarine, which had been following him ever since they had sailed out of Petropavlovsk. He had pushed his submarine and crew to their limits, using superior Russian metallurgy to defeat superior American electronics. He had lost the American sub by taking the Putin deep into the gaping Aleutians Trench—a 30,000-foot deep gash in the ocean floor. No American submarine could dive as deep or run as fast as a Russian Akula Class submarine.

Despite being somewhat of a maverick, Ivanshenko was widely recognized as Russia's most gifted submarine commander. That's why Admiral Voroshilov chose him for this mission—there could be no mishaps this time around.

In the forward torpedo room of the Putin, Spetsnaz Major Josef Golkin was briefing his team on their mission. This was the first time any of them had been allowed to know about the details of this assignment. He explained how all the training they had undergone over the last few months was to be put into play. Now they would understand why they'd spent so much time practicing getting into and out of a sinking airplane.

Major Golkin stood in front of the topographical maps obtained from an earlier expedition. "Okay men," he said in his raspy tenor voice, "Right now a plan is unfolding in the skies to the east of us. The GRU has arranged to have the American transport carrying the former CIA scientist Elizabeth LeDue ditch into the sea. Commander Ivanshenko will sail between Yunaska and Herbert Islands into Kagamil Pass. He will then bring us within three kilometers of Chuginadak Island. Once we see the transport in the water, we will deploy our inflatables from the rear hatch. We will proceed to the aircraft before it sinks and extract the prisoner."

He flipped through the charts and photos, stopping at aerial reconnaissance photos of the group of islands. "When the transport hits the water," he said, pointing to the narrow strip of water between Carlisle Island and Chuginadak Island, "some of the guards will probably escape. They will try to get onto life rafts. If our man has done his job, none of the life rafts will deploy. In these frigid waters, they should all drown in a matter of minutes. If not, we will have to make sure they drown before we leave the area. Remember—no witnesses!" He stopped talking and looked at each man to make sure they understood him. "Inside the aircraft, our man should have killed the pilots. We will kill anyone who remains, except the female prisoner. At this point, Timoshenko and Korkov will carry the prisoner back to the Putin. Team one will stay in its inflatable and provide covering fire if necessary. We will have 20 minutes from the start of the operation to complete the mission. Any questions?"

"What do we do with the GRU's man?" asked the giant Private Balzan.

"Kill him," Major Golkin replied without emotion.

Captain Petrov asked, "does the woman know we are coming for her?"

"No."

"What do we do if she resists?" He was concerned about having to struggle with someone inside a sinking airplane.

"Why that's why we continue to employ the mighty Balzan," replied the Major partly in jest.

F/V Neptune, Shelikof Straits, Kodiak Island, Alaska

Captain Alfred Lind was holding on tightly to the wheel with his feet spread out for balance as the waves pounded over the bow of the fishing boat. The windshield wipers slapped rapidly back and forth, trying to keep the window clear of ocean spray. The Neptune's floodlights illuminated the tops of the towering waves. He glanced out of the side port light to check on how much ice was forming on the rails. So far the temperatures were still warm enough to keep the railings fairly ice-free. If the temperature dropped, he would have to wake his crew and send them topside in this hellish storm with axes and hammers to break the ice loose. If too much ice built up on the superstructure, they would capsize. He checked the barometer next to his compass. *Holding steady.*

Piloting his boat through the predawn darkness, Captain Lind was heading for the rich fishing grounds of the Bering Sea. This would be his 25th season braving these tempestuous seas in the hopes of filling the holds with Black Cod and Pollock.

Ignoring the gale warnings, he had left Homer the day before. He had to get to the fishing grounds early. If he could beat the other boats, he might be able to catch enough fish to turn a profit this year. With four children, two of whom were in college, he needed to catch as many fish as possible. Kids cost money.

Sailing with Captain Lind were his 20-year old son Joseph, his crew foreman Roger Baker, and young Joy Frank, a 22-year old

New Yorker, who had come north to find adventure in the wilderness.

Based out of Homer, Alaska, the F/V Neptune was a classic steel-hulled trawler. 55-feet in length and powered by a single 750-horsepower diesel, the Neptune was a sturdy ship capable of holding her own in most North Pacific storms. But in these waters, even the biggest ship is vulnerable to Mother Nature's fury.

"Sure is nasty out tonight," Captain Lind said to himself. He tightened his grip on the wheel to avoid being tossed about the wheelhouse. "I hope we run out of this storm soon," he said, cursing and praying at the same time. Even after all these years, he had never gotten used to the up and down slamming of an angry ocean. He wasn't afraid, but in storms like these it took all his years of experience to keep him and his crew safe.

Down below in the forward compartment, Roger Baker and Joseph Lind were sleeping. Accustomed to the violent pitching and diving of the boat, they had strapped themselves into their bunks and nodded off earlier in the evening.

Joy Frank, on the other hand, was lying wide awake in her bunk. She concentrated on not vomiting. "What the hell am I doing out here?" she moaned under her breath. Her nausea was forcing a serious re-evaluation of the madness that had made her drop out of school at Columbia and head off to the Arctic. "Well, you wanted adventure and to experience the power of nature," she groused sarcastically. Every time the boat rode over a wave and came crashing down, she had to focus on something else besides her stomach. Unfortunately for her, the only thing she could focus on was the frightening sound of twisting steel beams. *Is the boat going to break apart? What is it like to drown?* Covering her mouth and holding her belly, she chastised herself, "and now you're getting to taste what Mother Nature has to offer."

Giving up on sleep, Joy swung out of her bunk. Pulling on her shoes and halibut jacket, she headed to the wheelhouse to join Captain Lind.

Joy tried putting on a smile as she hung onto the railings, climbing the short stairwell. "Morning Captain," she said unable to disguise her seasickness.

"Morning Joy. Couldn't sleep?" he replied. He couldn't help noticing the green tint to her complexion.

How can he be so damn cheery? "You could say that. I'm hoping that coming topside will make me feel better."

"Just keep your eyes forward and try to find the horizon. That should help."

Joy looked around. All she saw was towering waves illuminated by the boat's floodlights. "Any idea when we'll get out of this storm?" she asked. She hoped it would be soon.

"In a few hours. The Marine Forecast predicts the system will dissipate by mid-morning."

Doing a poor job at hiding her cynicism, Joy replied, "Wow, what a break. Only 5 more hours on this roller coaster."

Captain Lind didn't reply. He was used to greenhorns. Besides, Joy was too busy trying to locate the horizon to see the smirk on his face. *She's a lot like her dad,* he thought to himself, remembering how her father had come back from college with him in search of adventure. *He'd gotten seasick the first day out too.*

"Is the weather always this bad?" Joy asked. She didn't want to admit her dad had been right. He'd warned her that she wouldn't enjoy sailing in Alaska's waters. "Joy," she could still hear him say, "this isn't like sailing with Grandpa. Fishing in Alaska is the most dangerous job in the world. Remember how much you hate the roller coaster?"

"Not always. Sometimes it's worse."

"Worse?" She couldn't imagine how it could get worse.

"Oh hell yes," he said. "These are only 30 to 35 foot seas. In 25 years, I've seen them go well over 50 feet on more than one occasion." Captain Lind remembered when he was just a crewmember on his father's boat and asked almost the same question.

Suddenly Joy felt a strong urge to call her mom and ask to come home. Unfortunately, that was not an option. She was stuck in the middle of the North Pacific on a boat that suddenly seemed much too small. Looking out the starboard portlight, she watched the waves towering over the boat.

Fighting back her homesickness, Joy tried to get Captain Lind to teach her about the sea.

Always willing to talk about life on the sea, Alfred launched into several stories about all the storms he'd seen. He even told her about how her father had ended up working with him on his father's boat that one summer.

As the hours passed neither of them realized that a new kind of storm was coming and they were about to find themselves in the middle of it.

Umnak Island, Alaska

Jutting up out of the dark waters of the North Pacific, Tulik Volcano is one of hundreds of volcanoes that make up the Ring of Fire—a string of volcanoes that circle the Pacific Ocean from Chile to Indonesia. Part of the Okmok Caldera, Tulik Volcano rarely caught the attention of the villagers of Nikolski on the southern tip of Umnak Island. It was a quiet volcano that did not erupt very often and when it did it was not spectacular. Few people paid attention to it.

No one, not even the seismologists and vulcanologists in the Alaska Volcano Observatory and Earthquake Center, knew that deep beneath the surface of this grass and snow encrusted little rock, titanic forces were soon to be unleashed. Only the disappearance of the normal pattern of small earthquakes and tiny volcanic eruptions made scientists worry that a major geologic event was about to unfold.

Extending for thousands of miles, the American and Pacific Plates run from the surface to over 50 miles deep. Over the past few months, they had stopped grinding past each other. The result was a build up of tension in the subduction zones—the areas where one plate is pushed under the other. Thousands of kilotons of explosive energy were waiting to escape in one great convulsion.

Suddenly and with terrifyingly violent power, the two plates lurched past one another in one massive surge. All along the 30,000-foot deep Aleutians Trench, huge sections of the earth's crust were displaced up to 70 feet in the matter of a few seconds. Like a rubber band breaking, these displacements released multiple waves of kinetic energy. All along the trench, sections of the ocean floor became disjointed, shattering like glass being struck by a hammer. Entire sections of towering subterranean mountains broke free. Millions of tons of rock and mud rushed to the bottom of the Aleutians Trench in gargantuan landslides. Colliding with the ocean floor, these landslides triggered what scientists refer to as mega-tsunamis—giant waves that can reach to over 100-feet in height as they approach the shallower waters near islands and coasts. Radiating out in several directions, these waves would soon begin ravaging thousands of miles of coastline on both sides of the Pacific.

Registering 9.2 on the Richter Scale, seismic waves thundered across the Aleutian Islands, the Alaskan Peninsula, Kodiak Island, Prince William Sound, and Anchorage. In Dutch Harbor, just 70 miles from the epicenter, buildings were turned into rubble and docks collapsed, disappearing into the bay.

The seismic wave surged through the bedrock for thousands of square miles, making solid ground roll like the ocean, ripping open streets, shattering water mains and bursting pipelines. The earthquake ignited fires and sent water shooting through the air. Hundreds of people were killed in a matter of minutes.

In communities large and small, people clung to whatever they could find as the ground shook with terrifying ferocity. Cupboard doors swung and clapped wildly. Breaking glass and crashing dishes added to the frightful chorus. Dogs sat up, barking in agitation. Mighty spruce trees whipped back and forth. As the force of the shock wave increased, the air was filled with the sickening sound of snapping trees, telephone poles, and the metallic groan of collapsing towers.

Fishermen throughout the area watched piers, docks, and wharves disappear into the sea. Avalanches poured down out of their mountain hideaways, swallowing up anything or anyone standing in the way.

Rolling through the ground, the shock wave turned the airport runways at Sand Point, King Cove, Kodiak, Kenai, and Anchorage into asphalt jigsaw puzzles. Highways thrust up in topsy-turvy patterns. Collapsing bridges and overpasses crushed pedestrians and cars.

The earthquake split open the magma chamber deep beneath Unmak Island, setting free a giant river of molten rock. Racing to the surface, the magma exploded from the cone of Tulik Volcano. With a force later calculated to be greater than the pre-historic eruption of Mt. Mazama, Tulik Volcano obliterated the surrounding area. In an instant, the tiny village of Nikolski ceased to exist, buried under tons of rock, ash and molten boulders. Umnak Island became one massive crater.

A plume of flaming rock and ash belched up from the crater, surging high into the atmosphere. Roaring like a blast furnace, molten rock spewed thousands of feet into the air, vacating the space underneath the caldera's rim. With no support, the rim of the caldera came crashing down, opening a channel to the sea. Frigid seawater poured into the magma, which was still surging up from the Earth's core. The effect of thousands of tons of ice-cold water hitting molten rock set off a cataclysmic explosion. Hurling millions of tons of rock into the sky, the explosion generated a series of air pressure waves, which went racing out in concentric circles. Water molecules condensed along the front edge of blast wave. As more and more water condensed on the leading edge it became visible to the naked eye. The approach of this alien wave struck terror into the hearts of hundreds of survivors.

The pressure waves added to the carnage. Hitting land, they ripped already shattered structures from their foundations. Entire sections of forest were obliterated. Hundreds of acres of trees were slapped to the ground, marking the path of the blast wave.

With terrifying force, the pressure wave left thousands of dead animals and hundreds of humans in its wake. Only the sounds of fires and cries for help broke the eerie silence. In a few hours, the cacophony would be joined by the wail of tsunami warning sirens.

Shaking Alaska more than the Good Friday Earthquake of 1964, the Great Aleutian Earthquake and the Okmok Eruption turned major portions of Alaska into disaster areas.

Acting quickly, public officials implemented emergency disaster plans. However, it was soon apparent that they would be overwhelmed by the enormity of the catastrophe. Everyone knew that soon giant tsunamis would come crashing ashore, devouring everything in their path.

Over one thousand miles away in Juneau, the phone rang at the home of Governor Rick Malloy. "Hello?" he said wiping the sleep from his eyes.

"Governor, this is Dick Burke."

"Yeah, Dick what is it?"

"Governor, there's been a massive earthquake just off Unalaska! Anchorage, Kodiak, and several other communities have been destroyed."

"What!" Governor Malloy exclaimed sitting up abruptly. He rubbed his eyes, trying to shake off his sleep. Taking a deep breath, he took a few moments to gather his thoughts. "Okay, Dick, where are you?"

"At home."

"Call General Hornby. Get everyone together at the Capitol for an emergency briefing in 45 minutes."

"You got it Governor."

Malloy Super Maximum-Security Prison, Adak Island, Alaska

The earthquake announced its arrival with a thunderous crack. In a matter of moments dozens of houses collapsed into heaps of splintered wood. Those buildings that remained standing after the initial shock, swayed violently in tune to the harmonic rumbling of the ground. Windows exploded into shards, filling the air with lethal projectiles. Great tears in the ground opened up as the wave surged through the island. Vehicles parked along the darkened streets were swallowed by gaping maws in the earth. Mitchell Field's two runways were churned into blocks of asphalt rubble.

Annoyed at waking up before the alarm clock went off, Superintendent Jonathon Briggs was shuffling out to his kitchen to turn on the coffee pot when the first seismic wave hit Adak. With a violent lurch, the floor dropped out from under his feet leaving him airborne. Then just as suddenly, the wave thrust the floor towards the ceiling. He collided with it in a waterless belly flop. In a panic and with the wind knocked out of him, he scurried on his hands and knees under the kitchen table. His wife Darlene was still in bed. Jolted from her sleep as the earthquake hit, she opened her eyes in surprise just as the roof collapsed, killing her instantly.

Hearing the roof collapse, Jonathon rushed back towards the bedroom. The path was blocked by the debris. Frantically he began pulling boards and tiles out of the way. While he dug at the debris with his bleeding, splintered hands, he called out for his wife.

Jon and Darlene had been married for 25 years. With him less than 2 years away from retirement, they were looking forward to moving to Oregon, closer to their son. Now, Jon was digging with the strength of a man possessed. Wedging his feet against the frame of the door, he pulled with all his strength. Rushing into the littered bedroom he took the broken body of his beloved Darlene into his arms. Kissing her gently on the forehead, he clutched her in his arms, weeping.

The seismic wave roared through the concrete and steel of Malloy Super Max, throwing officers from their feet and tossing inmates off of their concrete bunks. Jagged cracks appeared in the walls as the air filled with the smoky white dust of concrete being pulverized. Throughout the complex, lights flickered on and off as the main power grid went off-line and the backup generators roared to life.

High above the complex, Lieutenant Carlos Banderas was taking the ride of his life as Alpha Tower swayed like a tree in a windstorm. Shards of glass flew from the shattering windows of Alpha Tower as it twisted like a corkscrew. Carlos was lying on the floor covering his head with his hands and jacket to prevent from being wounded by the flying glass.

Corporal Steiger was sitting in Rover, watching the last sea lions dive into the sea when the earthquake struck. The very next moment she was hanging on for dear life as the earthquake rocked Rover violently. She hung onto the steering wheel with all her might.

Passing through Main Control, the shock wave jerked the floor out from under Captain Marc Anderson. Finding himself suspended in mid-air, he reached for the corner of his desk trying to break his fall. Landing on his back with a thud, he heard the casing of his radio break. His handcuffs dug into the small of his back making him yelp in pain. "Son-of-a-bitch," he blurted out. Rolling over on his side, he rubbed the small of his back. He blinked to clear his vision, but there was nothing wrong with his eyes. The room was vibrating so violently that inanimate objects seemed to be alive.

Within seconds after the first shock wave, Malloy Super Max's computer set off the warning sirens, closed all sally ports and all cell doors, locking down the institution. Just before the earthquake hit, the dogs had started howling and barking in agitation. Now they were pacing back and forth inside their cages, whimpering in pain. The wailing siren hurt their ears.

The air was filled with the sounds of violent disruptions and chaos. The sharp boom of cracking walls was joined by a chorus of shattering glass and twisting metal caused by collapsing fences and pieces of the metal roof sliding to the ground.

Jenne Lucas stopped clutching her abdomen when she felt the building snap and then begin to shake. Rolling out of bed, she scurried under her desk for protection. The thundering noise was terrifying. The room seemed to be alive. The walls and doors and windows of her cell flexed under the strain. She watched her toothbrush rattle off its concrete shelf and fall to the floor. As the room began to shake even more violently, she watched water slosh out of the stainless steel toilet bowl.

Corporal Travis Nelson was sitting at his post in the control unit at the far end of the prison, writing a letter to his wife when he heard the clap of thunder echo through the building. Then everything began to shake. Jerking his head up, he clutched the edge of the control panel as rolling waves of energy pulsed through the prison. He found himself trying to equate the noise of the earthquake to that of a high-speed freight train rumbling through a small town.

Having grown up in Alaska, he was accustomed to earthquakes, but never before had he experienced shaking so fierce or long. He looked at the digital clock on the control panel in an effort to measure the time of the event. Reality slowly slipped away as the red numerals on the display became a harmonic blur.

Travis knew he should duck under the control panel, but he found himself transfixed by the ferociousness of the quake. For some reason his feet were unable to respond to his mind's command to move. It wasn't fear, but a fatal fascination with the reality of what was happening all around him. He'd been that way since a child. His wife said he had a streak of the daredevil in him. "Travis," she'd often chide, "your lack of survival instincts will be the death of you yet." Of course, it was just this sense of recklessness on his part that made her love him. He was fun and unpredictable.

Then suddenly and with just as little warning the shaking stopped. Travis reluctantly released his grip on the edge of the counter and looked around his post. To his amazement, the only signs of damage were a few cracks in the walls. He was sure the bulletproof windows would have cracked under the strain, but he was wrong. They were still intact and the lights on his control panel indicated all systems functioning.

Tentative at first and then with more confidence that the earthquake was over, the officers and inmates emerged from their hiding places. Inmates crawled out from under their beds and started picking up their rooms, while officers surveyed their posts for damage. Silence reigned. Everyone was reeling from the impact of what they had just experienced. To everyone's surprise the prison had suffered only minor damage. Malloy Super Max was intact—just as its designers had planned.

As he regained his footing, Carlos Banderas looked down on the crumpled perimeter fence. "SS this is Alpha Tower, fence is down, numerous perimeter breeches." He too was amazed that the complex was still intact and the floodlights were still operational. Carefully, he started brushing fine pieces of glass from his clothing as he waited for Captain Anderson to answer his report.

Captain Anderson didn't bother to respond directly to Carlos's radio call. He was too busy pulling himself to his feet. Next he brushed off his shirt and slacks and hobbled across the room to the main control panel. He stood behind his two officers, scanning the surveillance cameras and alarm systems for any sign of trouble. "Attention all posts, this is the SS. We have a fire in the cafeteria. Perimeter fences are down. All other areas appear secure. We are in lockdown."

Given the frequency of major earthquakes in Alaska and especially the Aleutian Islands, the architects had designed Malloy Super Max to withstand the impact of a 9.0 Richter Scale earthquake. To achieve this, they had used reinforced steel walls throughout the complex. They had also anchored the building's pilings deep into the bedrock.

Figuring that a major earthquake would trigger tsunamis, officials had insisted that the prison be located high on the slopes of Mount Moffet above the town of Adak. Unfortunately for the men and women at Malloy Super Max, not even the best-designed building is totally safe.

Inside the prison's cafeteria, the chief steward was supervising several inmates making breakfast when the quake struck. The prisoners from Alaska and California were the first to react. They quickly scrambled under tables. The remainder of the prisoners and the chief steward froze. Falling to the floor as the wave passed through the building, they covered their heads as the quake shook pots, pans, cups, and silverware from the cupboards and drawers in a chaotic symphony.

Beneath the building, the ground moved in a giant wave. The twisting and rolling action broke several of the gas lines behind the grill. An iron skillet falling from its hook hit the edge of a metal table. The resulting spark ignited the propane, which was spewing from the broken lines. Shooting from the broken pipes, the flames spread beyond the fire hoods, igniting everything flammable. With shocking rapidity, flames climbed up the walls across the ceiling of the kitchen. Within moments, bright orange flames had engulfed the entire cafeteria. The air was filled with toxic black and gray smoke.

The propane system had been designed with the automatic shutoff valves connected to the propane tanks. These valves were supposed to activate, cutting off the flow of gas to the building whenever an earthquake greater than 5.0 was registered on the prison's computer. Since earthquakes greater than magnitude 5.0 constantly rock the Aleutian Islands, the gas was continually being shut off. Out of frustration, the decision was made to disable the automatic shutoff valves. The maintenance chief had assured Superintendent Briggs he could shut the gas off in plenty of time to prevent an explosion in the building.

With the temperature in the room rising, the automatic fire suppression system sounded its alarm. The sprinkler system responded by spraying the room with water. The relief the men in the kitchen felt when the water came pouring out the sprinkler heads was soon replaced by terror as the spray of water sputtered before fading to a dribble. The quake had damaged the main control valve in the boiler room. Fire and smoke advanced into the dining hall.

Inside the cafeteria, panicking men rushed to the main entry door, which had automatically sealed when the quake hit. They pounded on the door, screaming for it to be opened. They could feel the heat on their backs. On the other side of the door, the officer tried to remain calm. His voice shook as he called for orders. "SS this is Post 7, I have a fire in the cafeteria. The sprinkler system has failed."

"10-4 Post 7. Stay calm and follow protocol."

"Dammit Captain, they're burning alive in there!"

"I know that Post 7, but you know the rules! Keep the door closed!" Captain Anderson cursed the department. *How many times had Superintendent Briggs argued with the commissioner for more officers? Post 7 was designed to be a two-man post.* Understaffing left him with no one to assist Officer Nikolaevich.

"What inmates are working in the kitchen this morning?" asked Captain Anderson.

Looking over the list, the control room officer answered, "Church, Jones, McIntyre, George, Sorrell, and Holland."

"Jesus," exclaimed Anderson, "it's like murder central up there."

"Sgt. Knight, SS."

"Go for Knight."

"We've got a fire in the cafeteria. Check your inmate worker list and get your security team ready. Proceed to the cafeteria as soon as you can." Marc Anderson was very worried. Toby Church was an intelligent and ruthless prisoner. Corbin Jones was a stocky powerhouse of a man, who was serving 150 years without parole for killing two State Troopers following a botched armed robbery. Although they had wounded him, he managed to run for two days before he was caught. McIntyre was a contract killer from Louisiana. Holland, George, and Sorrell had all been sent to Malloy after killing other inmates in prisons down south.

While the kitchen only employed inmates who had clean disciplinary records for at least three years, Marc Anderson knew that every man working up there wouldn't pass up the chance to escape. All of them were serving life sentences and had nothing to lose.

Ignoring department policy not to leave the command center, Captain Anderson ordered the control room officer to let him out. He raced down the hallway, cursing loudly. He hated waiting for each gate to slide open. For security reasons no two gates could be open at the same time in the same sally port. He looked at his watch counting the minutes go by.

Inside the cafeteria, the chief steward screamed for the Post 7 officer to open the door. He was a new father. Earlier in the morning he had been showing the pictures of his new daughter to his staff. "God help us! Open the door! I don't want to die! Not now, not now!"

The young officer raced through the emergency protocols in his mind. *In the event of an emergency fire and suppression systems have failed, keep the area secured and isolated from the rest of the building. All personnel and inmates in the area are expendable.* But he was a devout Russian Orthodox Christian. He crossed himself and prayed for guidance.

The chief steward was his friend. They often went fishing together after work. He had taught his daughter how to make cookies from scratch.

Opening the door control box with his key, the officer stared at the switches. One switch overrode Main Control's auto lock feature on the door. Another switch activated a ventilation vacuum pump designed to remove any oxygen from the room thereby robbing the fire of fuel.

Options raced through his mind. Saying a quick and silent prayer, he flipped the override switch. Rushing over to the door, he inserted his key in the deadbolt. With a push, he slid the cafeteria door open. Reaching down, he pulled the steward from the smoke-filled room.

After placing the steward against the wall, he raced back to the door to pull another person out of the room. He ignored the repeated radio calls to reseal the door.

As he stepped around the corner, the officer came face to face with inmates Toby Church and Corbin Jones. With a sickening realization of the error he'd just made, he felt a warm rush in his abdomen. Instinctively his hand gripped the shank as it entered just below his ribs. Jones twisted the blade as he grabbed the officer by the back of the shoulder, pushing it deep into his abdomen. He slumped to the floor, dark blood oozing from his wound and passed into unconsciousness.

Church and Jones worked quickly. Removing the officer's keys and radio they pulled him inside and slammed the door to the cafeteria shut. Wrapping damp rags around their faces to filter the choking smoke, they broke off a broom handle and jammed it into the rollers at the top of the door to slow down anyone trying to access the kitchen. Next they crawled on the floor to the loading dock elevator at the back of the kitchen.

Ignoring the choking smoke, Toby Church inserted the officer's key into the elevator door keyhole. Twisting to the right, then the left, and then right again, he waited for the door to open. With the last turn of the key, the elevator door should have opened, but it didn't. When the computer locked down the facility, it had disabled the elevators. "No time to panic," he said to himself. He was sure that was the sequence used to open the doors.

As Church thought about what to do next, Corbin Jones cursed excitedly, "Dammit Church, what's your plan? What are you thinking? We're gonna get caught if we don't get out now!"

"Shut the fuck up! I'm thinking," Church replied with a growl. Then he remembered that the steward had been working on a new bookshelf inside his office. "Get me the tool box out of the steward's office." He threw Jones the keys.

Rushing over to the office, Jones opened the door and grabbed the toolbox. He dashed back over to Church. "Here you go. What're you going to do?"

Ignoring Jones's annoying questions, Church unlocked the padlock with the master key and grabbed a hammer and a screwdriver before climbing up on the stool. Using a screwdriver as a chisel and a hammer, he chopped away at the security screws holding on the cover to the air circulation shaft. As the last screw fell to the floor, he slid the screwdriver into the seam of the cover and began prying it loose. It took only a few minutes before the cover clanged to the floor. Looking down at Jones, he said, "Give me a push up."

Grabbing Church's foot, Jones boosted him up through the hole. Bong! Church's head thumped against the airshaft entrance. "Fuck!" Church rubbed the top of his head. He knew Jones was strong, but he never really knew how strong. "Give me your hand," he ordered, reaching down from the shaft. With a tug he pulled Jones up into the shaft. "Follow me."

Using his knowledge of building construction, Toby Church moved through the smoke filled maze of sheet metal tunnels in search of an exhaust port on the roof. Corbin Jones was following right behind him. The acrid smoke made their eyes burn and water.

Captain Anderson sprinted the last few yards to the cafeteria. He found the door closed. The chief steward was lying against the wall badly burned. His clothes were charred and the smell of burned flesh permeated the air. Anderson felt nauseous. Hitting the vacuum switch inside the control box, he started the pumps built to suck the oxygen out of the cafeteria. He also ordered an officer to close the main propane valve to the building. This would starve the fire of its fuel. In a few minutes the lack of oxygen and fuel would extinguish the fire. Once the fire was out he would hit the override switch and open the door.

Anderson knelt beside the steward, put his hand on his neck and checked his pulse.

"Medical, this is the SS."

"Go for Medical," answered Nurse Evers.

"10-5 the cafeteria. We've got an injured man up here."

"10-4."

One by one, more officers arrived outside the cafeteria. While they waited for the cafeteria fire to die down, two of them administered first aid to the steward. He was in bad shape. His breathing was ragged and his pupils dilated.

"Medical, this is Corporal Nelson. We've got a badly burned man on Post 7. Get here as fast as you can."

"10-4 Corporal, I'm on my way," came Nurse Evers's exasperated reply. Things in the medical office were a shambles. Calls were coming in from all over the prison. When Captain

Anderson's radio call came she was busy reassembling her crash cart, which had been thrown to the floor by the earthquake.

As the last flames flickered out, Captain Anderson directed two officers to grab fire extinguishers and follow him into the room. Hitting the door override, he prepared to rush inside.

With a grinding screech the cafeteria door barely moved. "What the hell?" He hit the switch again. Nothing. *Why won't it open?* "Nelson," he called.

"Yes Captain?"

"Hit the override a couple of times."

Corporal Nelson flipped the switch back and forth. On the third try, the door slid open just enough for Anderson to see the broom handle jammed in the rollers.

Acting quickly, he called for maintenance to send someone to the cafeteria with a pry bar. Knowing that the door had been jammed on purpose, Captain Anderson took a few moments to brief the assembled officers. Something was wrong. Post 7's officer was missing and was not answering his radio. He warned his men to be alert. There was no time to put on stab vests and riot gear. They would have to count on their tactical skills if they had to fight inmates.

The maintenance man rushed up the stairs and handed the pry bar to Corporal Nelson. Using the bar, Corporal Nelson and two officers pushed with all their might. The door didn't move. Taking a different approach, they angled the bar up into the roller assembly and started working it back and forth. Several minutes later and with one last twist, they managed to break the broom handle loose. The cafeteria door rolled open. The bodies of the three dead prisoners and one assistant steward were lying on the floor next to the door—their faces charred into horrible masks. The smell of burnt flesh and charred paint mixed to create a most vile odor. Each man covered his nose and mouth with his hand in an effort to stem the stench.

Before entering the cafeteria, Captain Anderson made one last check to make sure the security team was ready. Led by Sergeant Knight, they were armed with pepper spray, batons, and electronic shields designed to shock with 50,000 volts of electricity. Around the room lay the charred bodies of two other kitchen workers. Back behind a dining table they spied the blood-drenched body of the Post 7 correctional officer—a shank sticking out from under his ribs.

In over 20 years in the department, Marc Anderson had never seen an officer killed. Seeing Officer Nikolaevich lying in a pool of blood made his heart ache. "Bill, Niko was murdered."

"Son-of-a-bitch," replied Sgt. Knight. He examined the trail of blood leading from the door to the table. "I think we've got an escape."

"Yes. Yes, so do I," Anderson said thinking about what to do next. "Okay, Bill you're in charge of this manhunt. You're responsible for capturing whoever did this to Niko."

Without saying a word, Sgt. Knight turned around and put his team to work.

Kneeling beside the slain officer, Marc Anderson thought about what he was going to tell Niko's wife. *If Niko had only followed procedures. But*, he reminded himself, *that was not Niko's way.* He was too kind hearted to leave a bunch of men to burn to death.

He closed Niko's eyelids. Anderson tried to come to grips with his grief and his anger. He wanted revenge. He blamed the commissioner for Officer Nikolaevich's death.

When Malloy Super Max was first proposed, there was a lot of opposition to the construction of such an expensive facility located in one of the most remote locations in the world. It was Governor Malloy, who countered the naysayer's arguments. He had proposed that the majority of the beds at the new prison be leased to states crippled by prison overcrowding and increasingly violent offenders. The concept was simple—offer other states a housing alternative for their most violent offenders and gang leaders.

At first, the opponents of Malloy Super Max were skeptical of Governor Malloy's plan. No state would sanction the $300 per day cost of housing an inmate. Surely, they argued, the courts would not allow an offender from another state to be housed in such a remote location in another state. They also argued that Alaska did not need a super max facility.

Ignoring the opposition, Governor Malloy pushed ahead with his concept. Much to everyone's surprise, several states jumped at the chance to remove their most troublesome inmates from their prisons. With state-of-the-art video conferencing for inmate visits, Governor Malloy squashed the argument that housing an inmate in the Aleutian Islands violated their rights to visitation. When a riot at the Anchorage Correctional Complex resulted in the deaths of several officers and an escape in the middle of the state's most populous city, all opposition to the new prison on Adak ceased.

But even running at almost one-hundred percent capacity and with over 75 percent of the beds leased to other states and the Federal Bureau of Prisons, the cost of running such an isolated facility exceeded all estimates.

The superintendent had warned every commissioner that in an emergency he would be short handed. He had told them Malloy was no ordinary prison and Malloy's inmates were not common criminals. Not only were they incredibly violent, but for the most part they were very intelligent. Unfortunately, he failed to convince them to staff his facility adequately.

Leaving the slain officer's side, Captain Anderson moved outside the cafeteria. He wanted to see how Nurse Evers was doing with the chief steward. Tears rolled down his face as he listened to the man's breathing become more ragged. He'd known the steward for almost 10 years.

Despite Nurse Evers's best efforts, she was unable to save her patient. With one great sigh, the steward gave up his fight. Anderson took Nurse Evers by the arm and motioned for two officers to remove the body from the area. He headed back to Main Control.

Cautiously working their way through the dining room, the security team moved into the kitchen. Smoke hung in the air, obscuring visibility. It was hard to see if any inmates were still in the room. The image of Office Nikolaevich's bloody body was stuck in their minds—no one wanted to be next. They were dealing with one or more desperate, unpredictable men. Having murdered one officer, they had nothing to lose by killing another.

Not finding any bodies in the kitchen, Sgt. Knight pulled out his count sheet. Running his finger down the list, he added up the numbers. "SS this is Security. We definitely have an escape in progress."

"10-4," responded Captain Anderson who had just returned to Main Control. Picking up the phone in his office, he called the cafeteria for an update.

Sgt. Knight briefed Captain Anderson. "It looks like two inmates have entered the air ventilation shaft above the kitchen. I don't know how, but it looks like they chiseled off the rivets holding on the screen covers."

Anderson hung up the phone and took a few moments to collect his thoughts. "Attention all posts—this is Captain Anderson. We have two inmates trying to escape from the kitchen through the airshafts. Towers watch the roofs, all officers on alert. You are authorized to use deadly force."

Lt. Carlos Banderas decided it was time to tell the Captain what was happening outside the prison. "SS this is Alpha Tower."

"Go Alpha."

"Captain, we have a lot of locals gathering outside the fence. I think they're looking for shelter from any tsunamis. I don't know if we have a clear shot."

"Roger, Alpha Tower. Rover, this is SS."

"Go for Rover."

"Can you get over to that crowd and move them back away from the perimeter fences?"

"I'll try Captain," replied Corporal Steiger. Putting her truck into gear, she started driving around the perimeter. She proceeded cautiously, because the earthquake had opened up huge cracks in the road.

Toby Church and Corbin Jones were crawling down the airshaft on their hands and knees. As they turned a corner they came to a horizontal shaft, which led to the outside of the building. Daylight filtered through the hole just ahead.

"Son-of-a-bitch," Church cursed quietly to himself. Directly ahead of them was a large motorized fan, designed to push air through the prison's ventilation system. It was blocking their way to the exit on the other side, although the earthquake had ripped it loose from most of its braces.

Looking over his shoulder, Church asked, "You think you can kick that fan out of the way if I can stop it from turning?"

Jones looked over Church's back to examine the large fan. After working in Leavenworth's metal shop, he knew how strong sheet metal rivets could be. His reply was anything but confident. "Maybe. That thing looks pretty solid."

"Well, you're pretty solid," said a smiling Toby Church.

Church crawled up next to the fan. Using the screwdriver he was carrying, he jammed it into the blades. With a snap, the fan jerked the screwdriver from his hands, slicing his forearm. He winced as the blade cut into his flesh. Sparks went flying.

Rotating with the fan, the screwdriver jammed against a brace holding the fan to the airshaft. The force of the impact cracked the blade. The fan ground to a halt, shearing off the two remaining bolts holding the frame inside the shaft.

Jones traded places with Church. Twisting around in the shaft so he could brace his back against one of the walls, Jones used his muscular legs to pound against the outer rim of the fan assembly. With each blow he could feel it coming loose. Sweating profusely, he grew more determined with each strike. Taking a deep breath and kicking with all his might he managed to dislodge the entire frame from the airshaft. Pushing it to one side, the prisoners crawled passed the obstruction. Jagged pieces of sheet metal scraped their arms and legs. It was a tight fit. They were lucky to be compact men.

They scurried to the end of the airshaft. Once again luck was with Toby Church. The cover plate on the outside of the building, designed to keep nesting birds out of the airshafts, had broken off during the earthquake. It was lying on the ground 15-feet below.

Peeking his head out of the airshaft, Toby Church could see Charlie Tower where a large section of fence had collapsed. Unfortunately, the razor wire appeared to be intact. A shiver ran down his spine. He hated the thought of getting cut on the wire. He couldn't tell whether or not the dogs were able to access the yard. If the dogs could get to them, they had no chance of getting out alive.

Retracting his head from the entrance, he took a few moments to collect his thoughts. During his 5 years at Malloy he had grown to respect razor wire. On one occasion he had been working as a janitor in the infirmary when they had brought in another prisoner who had tried to escape, but had become tangled in the wire. Church would never forget the sight of blood gushing from the man's thighs and arms. He could still see the bones showing through the shredded muscles. And he still remembered the stench of perforated intestines spilling their contents onto the floor.

Church shook his head to clear his thoughts. Feeling the warm blood seeping out under his sleeve, he tore the sleeve off his work shirt and tied it over the wound. "Well," he said to Jones, "we've got 50 yards to sprint, then we come to the first string of razor wire."

"How the hell do we get over that?" growled Jones.

"I'm open to ideas," Church replied sarcastically.

Annoyed at Church's sarcasm, Corbin Jones growled, "let me look." Despite the pen-ink blue lightning bolt and Death's Head tattoos emblazoned on his neck, Jones had no allegiance to Church, who was the leader of the prison's white supremacists. Jones' survival as a loner in prison was due to his well-earned reputation for strength and shear cold-bloodedness. A true sociopath, Jones hated just about everybody—Church included.

Moving around Church, he peered out into the yard. Looking straight down, he spotted several 8-foot sections of roofing steel laying along side the airshaft cover that had broken free during the earthquake. Grinning, he pulled his head back inside. Excitedly, he explained his idea. "There are several big pieces of the steel roofing laying just below us. Both of us need to jump down. We'll grab two pieces. We'll run holding them over our heads to the tower." He held his hands over his head to illustrate his idea. "Once we're at the wire, we throw down one piece to cover the wire and go over. Using the second piece as a shield, we run to the second wire. Once at the second wire, throw that piece down and run like hell." Smiling diabolically, he concluded, "besides that, once we clear the wire, there's a bunch of people gathered outside the fence so they won't be able to shoot."

Church was impressed. *Maybe Jones isn't such a simpleton after all.* "Damn Jones, that's good. But what about the dogs?"

Jones shook his head from side to side. He didn't have an answer. If the dogs could intercept them, their plan would come to an ignominious end. "Guess we'll just have to take our chances with the dogs," he said raising his hands in hopeful resignation.

Church nodded in agreement. They would just have to take a chance that the dogs would be cut off from the yard by all the fallen fence and tangled wire.

Both men knew that the other one would use them as bait for the dogs if it came to that. They eyed each other warily.

Corporal Steiger was standing outside her truck, looking at all the damage. Keying her radio, she called for Captain Anderson. "SS this is Rover."

"Go for SS."

"Captain, the road has collapsed in several places. I can't drive over to the crowd near Charlie Tower."

"10-4 Rover, hold your position." Anderson strummed his hand on his desk. He was studying the prison blueprints, trying to figure out just where the two prisoners would exit the building. He was sure they were trapped inside the airshafts. The blueprints showed fans blocking every exit. However, the next radio call destroyed his theory about the fugitives being confined in the ventilation system.

"Alpha, this is Charlie! Two 10-80s just dropped out the south air shaft, grabbed some steel roofing and are running towards my post."

Carlos Banderas surveyed the entire complex. Coming around the building were two men holding two large sheets of steel over their heads. "Charlie, this is Alpha, open fire! All other posts hold your fire!

Officer Ben Williams took aim at the steel plates and fired off three rounds. Sparks flew as the bullets ricocheted off the steel plates. The angle was too oblique. The men kept running. Ben fired two more rounds. Once again the bullets sent sparks flying as they failed to penetrate the roofing.

"Fuck that stings," hollered Church. The impact of the bullets made the steel vibrate and dig into his hands.

"Shut up and run, we're almost to the wire," cursed Jones.

Running up to the wire, Church and Jones slid the first piece off onto the top of the razor wire, which sprang like an accordion, entangling the edge of the sheet with its spikes. Crouching under the second steel plate, they crawled on their knees over the first razor wire barrier.

"All posts this is Charlie Tower, they're over the first fence and the man wire!"

Taking careful aim at the leg moving in and out from under the steel plate, Ben fired off another round. The sound of his rifle echoed through the early morning air.

Slamming into its target, the .308-caliber bullet penetrated Corbin Jones' right shin sending a spray of blood across Toby Church's face.

Despite being slammed to the ground by the bullet's impact, Jones managed to hold onto the steel plate. Grimacing at the pain, he got back to his feet and kept moving. Church was impressed.

Hearing Charlie Tower's radio call, Captain Anderson ordered the dogs released from their kennels. They only had a few minutes to react before the prisoners made good their escape.

Corporal Steiger ran back to Rover and grabbed the shotgun. She ran towards Charlie Tower leaping over the gaping cracks in the perimeter road. She could hear the dogs barking several hundred feet away. The fence had collapsed. The dogs were cut off from the prisoners.

Corporal Steiger never saw the hole in the ground. Suddenly the ground wasn't under her feet. Falling with the shotgun in her hands, she was unable to catch herself. She landed face first, right into a softball-sized rock. Blood oozed from the side of her skull, nostrils and the corner of her mouth. Her head was spinning from the impact. Before she could call for help on the radio, she slipped into unconsciousness.

Arriving at the outer string of razor wire, Jones and Church tossed down the last sheet of steel. They started over the top. The sound of their feet pounding over the flexing steel echoed across the prison grounds.

Ben Williams watched the prisoners scurry between the fences and throw down the second sheet of steel. He aimed carefully at the now exposed inmates. Keeping the crosshairs of his scope focused on the lead inmate, Officer Williams squeezed the trigger. The soft-tipped bullet found its mark in the middle of Corbin Jones' back, ripping through his flesh, shattering bones and shredding his heart. He was dead before he hit the ground.

Shifting his aim to the second inmate, he squeezed the trigger again. At that very moment, Toby Church cut to his left, heading for the crowd near maintenance shed.

Hair flew from the side of Toby Church's head as the passing bullet gave him a new haircut. He ducked instinctively. Stumbling slightly, he picked up his pace.

Before Ben could reload his rifle, Church was pushing his way through the middle of the crowd, running towards town.

"SS this is Charlie Tower, I've got one dead 10-80 in the wire and another escaping into town."

"10-4 Charlie Tower," replied Captain Anderson. He had been monitoring the escape over the cameras.

"Rover this is SS." No response.

"Rover this is SS?" he said more urgently. Still there was no answer. He called two more times for Rover. Each time his radio calls were met with silence.

Now that the shooting near Charlie Tower was finished, the officer manning Bravo Tower noticed the body of Corporal Steiger sprawled on the ground below his position. "SS this is Bravo Tower. It looks like Steiger is face down in a hole. She's not moving."

"Medical this is SS, get over to Bravo Tower and Rover now!" bellowed Captain Anderson over the radio.

Reacting immediately, the medical staff diverted from the dead inmate tangled in the fence near Charlie Tower. They rushed down the road towards Corporal Steiger.

Turning to his Main Control officers, Captain Anderson asked if anyone had heard from either the superintendent or the assistant superintendent. They said no. The phone lines were down and neither man was answering his radio.

"Get me the local PD on the radio," ordered Captain Anderson. "And issue an escape notice on that inmate that just went over the wire. Do we know who he is yet?"

"Yes sir," answered a soot-covered Sgt. Knight, who had just entered the room, "it's Toby Church."

"Church!" blurted Captain Anderson. "Aw, dammit, why did it have to be Church?"

DOC Transport Malloy 1, 18,000 feet over Shelikof Straits, Alaska

Malloy 1 was plowing into a fierce headwind just above the silvery cloud tops, its powerful turbine engines straining to move the ungainly aircraft forward on its lonely Aleutian migration. Bathed in the infrared glow of the cockpit light, the pilots were struggling to keep the aircraft level as turbulence buffeted them about the sky.

Nikki Foster stared at his instrument panel, rehearsing his traitorous plan in his mind. He licked his lips, trying to get rid of his cottonmouth. Beads of sweat were rolling down his face. His guts were churning as he tried to maintain his resolve to carry out his plan. He'd never killed anyone before.

Strapped tightly in their seats, Malloy 1's passengers were riding out the storm. Everyone was silent. Most of them were too busy trying to keep their minds off of vomiting to talk. In the front compartment, several of the more experienced officers ignored the violent tossing and swaying of the plane. This was old hat to them. They were sleeping.

The only thing that made the pilot uncomfortable about flying Malloy 1 in the perpetually violent weather of the Aleutians was the department's policy of maintaining secrecy about the exact flight route, altitude, and radio frequencies. Outside of the flight crew, only the commissioners of Public Safety and Corrections and the chief air controller in Anchorage knew Malloy 1's exact route. Secrecy made intercepting the flight very difficult. However, should anything go wrong, help could be a long time in coming.

Outside the cockpit dawn was breaking behind them, illuminating the tops of the clouds below them in shades of pink, red, and gray. "Sure is beautiful to see those silver linings, eh Captain?" the first officer commented.

"Yep, sure is pretty up here," the pilot replied absentmindedly. She was too busy battling to keep the airplane level in these violent winds to engage in any meaningful conversation.

The first officer looked down at his radar screen. A bright green line was approaching very fast from the west. "Captain," he said pointing to the screen, "what's this line on the radar?"

"Where?" she asked looking down at the screen.

She saw the bright green line moving towards them at amazing speed.

"Gotta be a glitch. Run a diagnostic," she ordered.

Looking back up, the pilot's mind froze in fear. Closing in on them at amazing speed was a pressure wave. Sunlight glistening off the condensation on the leading edge announced its approach. The churning clouds told her they were in trouble.

"Shit!" she exclaimed. She pulled back hard on the yoke. It was too late. The wave slammed into them with tremendous force. Hitting the wave in a nose up attitude caused the plane to pitch up violently. Struts inside the wings broke. Hydraulic lines split apart as the fuselage flexed against itself.

Malloy 1 was thrown onto its back by the blast before anyone in the cockpit could react. The wounded transport was inverted and falling in a death spiral towards the cold, dark waters of Shelikof Straits.

"Ugh! Whoof. Ugh! Whoof," the pilot grunted. She forced herself to breathe against the powerful G-forces pressing against her. She fought against becoming unconscious. Stepping hard on the left rudder pedal, she pulled on the yoke with all her might. She had to regain control of Malloy 1 or they would all die.

To her right, the first officer lay slumped over to one side. He had been knocked unconscious. Behind him, Nikki Foster was hanging on for dear life.

Harry Ignustuk thought someone had hit him in the chest with a sledgehammer when the pressure wave struck. With Malloy 1 spiraling towards the dark ocean, he felt like the G-forces would pull him apart.

Cursed by his massive size, PTO Harold Powell found himself airborne. The energy of the collision and his mass had torn him from his harnesses. He crashed down onto a bulkhead, his neck snapping on impact. A small trickle of blood dripped from his mouth, while the centrifugal force of the aircraft's spinning kept his lifeless body pinned against the wall.

The rest of the passengers were unconscious. They had either been knocked out by the initial impact or succumbed to the G-forces of the airplane's spin.

Malloy 1 gained speed as it plunged through the clouds. The pilot watched in horror as the airspeed indicator went into the red, Vne—never exceed arc. If she didn't regain control of the aircraft it would break apart. She fought against the G-forces pinning her to her seat. Stepping harder on the rudder pedal, she neutralized the aerilons. Slowly, the plane stopped spinning. Pulling back on the yoke and the throttles, she pulled Malloy 1 out of its screaming dive.

She sighed with relief as the plane leveled off. Looking right, she could see that the two starboard engines were out and black smoke was pouring from the cowlings. Hydraulic pressure was dropping throughout the entire system.

"Foster," she ordered, "get me a fix on our location and see if you can't stop this hydraulic failure. Bypass the main system."

"Yes, ma'am," he replied. He hit the reset button on the GPS and waited for it to download their current position. "We are at 154 degrees 30 minutes West and 56 degrees North."

"What's the nearest airport?"

"Kodiak at 57 degrees 47 minutes North, 152 degrees 25 minutes West."

"How far is that?" she asked. She didn't need coordinates. She needed information she could use.

"About 40 miles."

"We won't make it 5 miles," she said. They were losing too much hydraulic fluid. In a few minutes she would no longer be able to control the airplane.

Realizing they were about to crash in the middle of the wilderness, she initiated her emergency procedures. "Anchorage Departure Control this is Malloy 1, repeat this is Malloy 1. I am declaring a May Day." No answer. She didn't know that Anchorage couldn't answer. The main control tower had collapsed when the earthquake hit.

"Why don't they answer?" she asked. *Are the radios out? What's going on?*

She continued calling out her position in the off chance they would be heard. "We are over Shelikof Straits. Our position is 154 degrees 34 minutes West and 56 degrees North. We're going to ditch, repeat we're going to ditch." Turning the wounded transport towards Kodiak Island, the pilot hit the radar IDENT button set at frequency 3399. She said a silent prayer and prepared to ditch in the stormy waters below.

"Foster," the pilot ordered, "get your butt in the back, check everyone out and let them know we're going to ditch."

Nikki Foster didn't know what to do. Unbuckling his harnesses, he got up from his chair and moved quietly to the front of the cockpit. His heart was racing. This wasn't the plan, but he couldn't let her succeed in landing the airplane on Kodiak. He had to have that money.

Reaching inside his jacket, he pulled out his semi-automatic pistol. He screwed on the silencer, took aim and pulled the trigger. The pilot never knew what happened. The bullet's impact jerked her head back, splattering her brains all over the windshield. Foster fought back the urge to vomit as the smell of death filled the cockpit. His legs went limp as he watched his victim convulsing in her seat.

Recovering quickly, he pulled the pilot out of her seat. Taking over the controls, he turned the transport into the wind. He was going to set it down in the rolling seas. In his panic, he never thought of letting the pilot ditch the airplane and then killing her.

Malloy 1 began breaking apart as it skipped over the waves. The entire aircraft shuddered with each impact. The tail section broke away first, showering the sea with officers still strapped to their seats and cargo bound for Adak. Struggling against the elements, a few of the officers not killed on impact managed to get free from their seats and swim free of the wreckage. Their efforts were in vain. Within a few minutes they succumbed to hypothermia. The weight of their water-soaked clothes pulled them beneath the waves. The howling wind drowned out their cries for help.

Shaking off the pain of his broken ribs and bleeding nose, Harry Ignustuk released himself from his four-point restraint. Making his way past Ivan Lincoln and Elizabeth LeDue, he checked Officers Sanders and Gregory for signs of life. Sanders was still alive, but Gregory's head hung at an impossible angle. His neck had been broken. Harry closed the dead man's eyelids.

Harry roused Sanders with a sharp slap to his face. They didn't have much time. Seawater swirled about his feet. It was getting deeper by the minute. Wrestling the inflatable rubber raft from its container, he swung it out of the gaping hole in the side of the cabin. Luckily for him, Foster had disobeyed the GRU's orders to disable all the rafts. Foster wasn't stupid. He was hedging his bets that the GRU would leave him behind to drown inside the plane.

Lashing the raft to one of the exposed ribs of the airframe, Harry pulled the cord and inflated the raft. He took two oars from under the seats and tossed them into bobbing raft.

Grabbing Danny Sanders by the back of the coat, Harry climbed through the jagged hole into the dark, freezing water, Danny in tow. He swam with all his strength as he tried to save his friend. He hadn't been there to save his brother and sister. He wasn't going to let Sanders drown. Stroking with one arm and kicking with his legs, Harry dragged Sanders behind him to the raft. He tried to time the waves, waiting for a swell to lift them up above the bouncing raft. Pushing with every ounce of strength, he shoved Sanders into the bright orange life raft.

Exhausted, but still determined to do his duty, Harry swam back towards the mangled hulk of Malloy 1. He needed to retrieve his prisoners, whom he could hear screaming for help inside the sinking wreckage. But the jagged edge of the C-130's fuselage was climbing higher into the early morning light. The hole from which he and Sanders had just swum was now beneath the waves. It was too late.

He swam back to his raft, pulled himself in and cut the line to Malloy 1. Each passing wave pushed them further and further away from the crippled aircraft.

Inside the sinking fuselage, Ivan Lincoln had regained consciousness. Water was swirling around his waist. He shouted for help, struggling against the chains holding him in his seat. "Hey! Hey! God damn it! Somebody get me the fuck out of these chains!"

Lincoln's rantings brought Elizabeth LeDue back to full consciousness. Her head hurt. It took a moment for her to realize where she was. Water was rushing in around her waist and chest.

She panicked. "Oh God, oh God, somebody help me!" she screamed.

In the front half of the plane, Nikki Foster was still sitting in the pilot's chair, struggling to free himself from the vise that held him. Blood soaked his pant legs. In a karmic twist of fate, when Malloy 1 hit the water, the impact had crushed the nose of the plane, bending the metal of the instrument panel over his waist. He was stuck.

He cried and pounded on the instrument panel, wrestling to free himself as the nose of the plane began to plunge into the depths. The jagged edge of the panel cut into his thighs. Blood ran from the now exposed muscle as he wiggled desperately. But no matter how hard he tried, Malloy 1 held on to him. In his mind, he heard a voice proclaim that a captain always goes down with his ship. He resorted to screaming in vain for help.

Nikki Foster could feel the pressure increasing as the front section of the plane sank deeper into the black depths. He was drowning. He struggled one last time to free himself from his trap. With each exertion his thrashing slowed until he slipped into unconsciousness.

Thousands of feet below the surface, the crabs and sea lice were waiting to feast on his flesh.

Harold Powell's body was floating next to Ivan Lincoln. The water was now at chest level and he could feel the fuselage beginning to settle by the tail. A set of cuff keys was hanging from Powell's duty belt. Grabbing the dead man's body with his teeth, Lincoln pulled the corpse over to his hands and unclasped the cuff keys from Harold's duty belt.

With the nimble fingers of a taxidermist, who was used to threading needles, he inserted the key into Elizabeth LeDue's right hand cuff unlatching the double lock. With a twist to the right and then the left, he unlocked it. Her hand slid out.

"Here bitch, take the key and unlock me," Lincoln commanded. He put the key in his mouth and passed it to her.

Without thinking about the danger of what she was doing, Elizabeth unlocked Lincoln's left handcuff. Jerking his hand free from the cuff, he grabbed her right hand and snatched the key back from her.

The water was like ice. He was shivering. Moving quickly, Lincoln unlocked his right hand, took a deep breath, stuck his head under the water to unlock his leg irons. "Fuck, that's some cold water. Let me tell you." he said coming to the surface.

"Aren't you going to uncuff me?" Elizabeth pleaded. "I don't want to die."

Lincoln stared at Elizabeth's chest. The ice cold water had made her nipples stand erect under her jumpsuit. Leaning over, he unlocked her other handcuff and belly chain. "Yeah, I guess I'll take you with me, I might find a use for you," he said in a low menacing tone.

Lincoln's words filled Elizabeth with dread. The last time she'd felt that alone was when she had been robbed at knife point in Washington, DC. It had been a cold, rainy night in April, when she had left the restaurant to walk back to her car and he had intercepted her and drug her into a dark alley. She had been fortunate that all he had wanted was her money.

Taking a deep breath, Lincoln stuck his head under the water and unlocked her leg irons. She was free. The urge to run away from Lincoln was overwhelming, but this wasn't some dark alley in the capital, it was the middle of a freezing liquid wilderness. She had to wait for a better opportunity to escape the clutches of this maniac.

The rear section of the airplane was now riding in the water at almost a 90-degree angle. They had to stand on the seat backs while the water swirled around them at their waists. Directly above they could see the stormy sky. Below them the water was climbing rapidly. Lincoln pulled Powell's body over to him and took his pistol from its holster. He put it inside his coveralls along with handcuffs and a key.

Strapped to the inside of the fuselage was another life raft. He pulled the raft from its container and inflated it. Climbing into the raft, he pulled Elizabeth onboard.

Just as she rolled into the raft, the rear section of the plane slid out from beneath them and disappeared into the murky depths. They now found themselves surrounded by mountainous waves rolling in an angry tempest.

Taking insulated, waterproof blankets from the raft's survival kit, Harry covered Danny. They would have to ride out the storm. Harry ran his survival training drills through his mind—*survey the gear, get a bearing, treat the injured, keep warm, and most of all stay calm.*

At the same time he was watching the horizon. He thought he'd seen another raft inflate outside of Malloy 1. But the churning seas prevented him from getting a long look in any one direction. *It must have been your imagination. No one else could have gotten out of the aircraft. Your mind's playing tricks on you.*

Harry could see the snow-capped mountains of Kodiak Island dominating the morning skyline several miles to the south. Within a few hours, the roaring winds would blow them ashore—if they didn't capsize first. He took out the oars and began rowing towards the mountains in the distance. The exercise would help keep him warm. And with a little luck it might keep them from being blown out into the vast expanses of the Pacific Ocean.

Danny started wheezing and coughing up seawater. "Thanks Harry. I owe you one," he said in between convulsions.

"No problem, glad I could help," Harry replied nonchalantly. He didn't want to make a big deal out of it. This was no time to get emotional. "It looks like we're about 10 miles offshore of Kodiak Island."

"Well, that's good, I guess," Danny answered. He placed his hand over his heart, concentrating on slowing his pulse.

"How're you feeling Harry?"

"Not bad."

"Do you think they know we're missing?"

"Hard to say," Harry replied in his typical low-key tone. He knew that only a few people had information about their exact route.

"Guess, we'd better figure on surviving for a few days," Danny said trying to lighten the conversation.

"Yep," said Harry nodding his head in agreement. "Kodiak's a lonely place. It might be some time before they find us." Harry kept his eyes the horizon. It helped him from getting seasick and it hid his tear-swollen eyes from Danny.

"What happened? Who else made it?"

"I don't know," Harry said with an edge in his voice. "We've got to concentrate on the here and now." Harry fought off the urge to cry. He was thinking of his good friend 'Brownie' and all the other officers who had just perished.

Danny nodded in agreement. He lay back down on the bottom of the raft and covered himself with the blanket. He didn't have the strength to help Harry row the boat, but he could serve a purpose by becoming the ballast they needed in these heavy seas.

Further west, Ivan Lincoln was rowing in the opposite direction using a piece of Malloy 1's outer skin, which he had bent into a crude paddle.

After almost two hours on the raft, Dr. Elizabeth LeDue was coming to her senses. The world around her no longer seemed so surreal. She watched Lincoln row with steady strokes. The sea seemed to be calming down. *Or maybe,* she thought, *I'm getting used to the rolling motion.* She could see mountains looming in the distance.

Elizabeth was afraid. Thoughts about the danger she might be in flashed through her mind. *Is he going to rape me? Is he going to kill me?* The fact that Lincoln was a psychopath was finally starting to dawn on her. His seething anger combined with calculating control told Elizabeth that he was a dangerous man.

Recalling a television show she'd seen on hostage situations, she decided she would use the theory about trying to make yourself familiar to your captor. If her memory served, experts said that a kidnapper is less likely to harm someone they know. *What was that called?*

All her life Elizabeth had been able to charm people with her witty conversation, good looks, and intelligence. Lacking any other alternatives, she decided to try her proven techniques for getting to know people.

"Where are we going?" she asked politely.

"Shut up bitch," Lincoln snarled. "You do exactly as I tell you, get it?" He glared at her coldly.

"But,"

"Shut up!" he growled. He took out Officer Powell's pistol, brandishing it in front of her face. "You do exactly what I say, keep your BITCH mouth shut, and I may let you live."

Elizabeth pulled as far away from him as possible. She huddled up and prayed for this nightmare to end.

F/V Neptune, Shelikof Straits, Alaska

Captain Lind's thoughts about a bountiful harvest in the Bering Sea evaporated the moment he heard the news about the earthquake broadcast over the marine radio. The fishing season was over. He would have to worry about paying his bills later. Right now he had to get home. He sent Joy below to fetch Roger and Joseph while he turned the Neptune around.

Filled with worry, Captain Lind fought against the raging sea to keep a steady course. Outside the pilothouse, darkness clung to the world. Only the Neptune's lights glaring from the masts defied the night's attempt to crush all hope. All alone, on the vast raging sea, Captain Lind and the Neptune charged ahead clinging to faith and the promise of a new dawn.

Steadily Captain Lind drove his boat up and over the giant waves. One moment, he was guiding his vessel as it climbed up the back of a green liquid monster. The next moment he was staring out into space as the bow surged over the top of the wave. With each crest, the boat's floodlights lit up the bottom of the low scudding clouds, causing the driving rain to sparkle like diamonds against a velvet curtain, and then with a sinking feeling he would watch the powerful beams illuminate their path down into the shimmering green-black chasm.

Captain Lind scanned his surroundings, ever vigilant for that rogue wave that would swallow them and drag them down into the unforgiving deep.

Everyone on board was sick with worry over what might have happened to the Lind family back in Homer. All attempts to reach Alfred's wife on the radio had been futile. They didn't know the volcanic ash surging high into the atmosphere was making electronic communication all but impossible.

Giving up on the radio, they all sat silently in the wheelhouse staring out at the churning sea. The dawn was breaking, but Homer was two days away. Listening to the desperate radio traffic from quake-ravaged communities like Larsen Bay only increased their desire to make it home as soon as possible.

The lightening sky revealed their position in the middle of Shelikof Straits. To the south they could see the shadows of Kodiak Island's forbidding mountains obscured through the mist. Ahead and behind them were the seemingly endless rows of rolling seas, each one breaking with a spray of white foam.

As he was looking over his shoulder, Roger Baker caught sight of a wall of condensation racing over the water. He blinked. He thought his eyes were playing tricks on him. He looked again.

Stretching from the surface of the tempestuous ocean into the clouds, the blast wave was heading straight at them. By the time he realized they were in trouble it was too late. The pressure wave from the Tulik eruption slammed into the stern of the Neptune before he could shout a warning.

Shuddering under the collision, the steel-hulled trawler lurched down by the bow, and the stern was shoved high into the air. Overpressure outside the cabin caused the wheelhouse windows to implode. Glass flew across the backs of the crew. With the boat's propeller spinning free and the rudder out of the water, the wind shoved the Neptune sideways.

As the Neptune skidded by the bow across the heaving seas her crew was being thrown about the cabin. Joy felt herself suspended in mid-air as she screamed and reached for a handhold. Joseph was slammed forward and came to rest under the dash. Roger, who had been quicker, had managed to get his arm around a railing and had ducked his head to avoid the flying glass and rock-hard water.

As she fell towards the front of the wheelhouse, Joy could see the gaping maw of the icy green depths waiting to swallow her should she crash through one of the windows. Luckily for her, she was small and the wheelhouse strong. With a bone-crushing thud she landed flat against a window frame knocking the wind out of her.

Captain Lind gripped the wheel, fighting against the centrifugal force trying to pin him to the wall. He had to get control of the Neptune or they would founder in these heavy seas. Summoning all the strength he had, he pulled himself upright.

Released from the grip of the wind, the Neptune's stern slapped down into the sea. Waves surged through the shattered portlights. Joy was thrown to the floor. In an instant she was bathed in frigid seawater. Ignoring the shock of the ice-cold water, Joy reached out and grabbed hold of a brass foot rail. She could feel the Neptune sliding sideways over the waves.

The force of the wave had turned the Neptune broadside to the sea—a very precarious situation. While Captain Lind fought to turn the boat back around into the advancing waves, the rest of the crew hung on for dear life.

With a sudden burst of superhuman strength, Captain Lind twisted the wheel and righted the Neptune before she could founder. "All right folks, we're in the clear. You can get up now," he said with relief.

The Neptune's wheelhouse was in good condition, except for the broken windows. The radio antenna was still in place. So were the masts and all the fishing gear.

"Is everybody alright?" Lind shouted above the howling wind. He couldn't let go of the wheel to check them physically.

No one answered. Joy wiped the trickle of blood from under her nose—the result of her impact with the window. Joseph was rubbing the knot on the back of his head and Roger was rubbing his jaw.

"Joy," he commanded, "come and help me steer the boat. Roger, you and Joseph check the damage."

Joy walked over and stood next to the Captain, while Joseph and Roger carried out their orders.

"Looks like we're still in one piece," Roger reported. Wiping the rain off his face, he asked, "What the hell happened?"

"Haven't got a bloody clue," replied Captain Lind.

Joseph Lind returned from the engine room, reporting that other than a lot of seawater in the bilge, they were in good shape. "I started the bilge pumps and checked the oil. It looks like the engine is no worse for the wear and tear, although we may want to check the propeller shaft when we get back home. Being jerked out of the water like that allowed it to over-rev."

"Thanks Son." Captain Lind turned to Joy and ordered her to get some plastic from the storage locker and cover the portlights. "You'll find duct tape there too." Finally, he breathed a sigh of relief. *We're okay. No one was hurt badly. Thank God the boat is still in one piece.*

Removing the seat cover, Joy took out the supplies, and set to work sealing up the wheelhouse. Using a towel to dry the inside of the wall before applying the duct tape, she made quick work of her project. A few minutes later she was sitting next to Joseph. She found his presence comforting. He was handsome, intelligent, and patient with her inexperience. It didn't take a genius to know he liked her too.

Captain Lind glanced over his shoulder. Joseph was examining Joy's slightly swelling nose. But it was no ordinary seaman's examination. Joseph was being much too attentive for such a small injury. He was even checking to see if Joy's pupils were reacting. Alfred smiled. *I thought there was something between those kids.*

Absorbed in conversation about the phenomenon they'd just experienced, no one heard the roar of the C-130's engines as it dove out of the clouds. Malloy 1's sudden arrival over the Neptune made everyone duck.

"Son-of-a-bitch" blurted Roger as he held his hands instinctively over his head.

"What the?" cried Joseph as he watched the giant blue and gold aircraft wobble through the sky. The smoke trailing from its engines contrasted sharply against the gray overcast.

Pulling herself up from the crouch she'd taken when the airplane shot overhead, Joy grabbed the binoculars from their case. She watched the wounded aircraft slowly disappear over the horizon. "It's a four-engine plane. Big. Looks like it's in trouble. I think it may crash into the sea." She swallowed the lump in her throat.

"Joseph," ordered Captain Lind, "get on the radio to Coast Guard Station Kodiak. Give them our position and report what we just saw."

"Yes, sir," he replied. Joseph grabbed the radio microphone. "Coast Guard Kodiak, Coast Guard Kodiak, this is the fishing vessel Neptune. Over."

No reply.

"Coast Guard Kodiak, this is the fishing vessel Neptune. Over."

Again, no reply.

Joseph continued calling on the radio, giving their position and a description of the crippled airplane they'd just seen. He didn't know the Coast Guard could not answer.

On the south side of the island, the community of fishing town of Kodiak lay in ruins. If they could have responded, the men and women of Coast Guard Station Kodiak would have come to the rescue. But all their radio towers had been destroyed by the earthquake and the pressure wave. And they were all rallying to care for the town's 5,000 citizens.

All over the base, buildings, homes, and aircraft hangars had collapsed, trapping victims beneath the rubble. Buckled runways had swallowed two of the three Dauphin helicopters along with both of the white and orange C-130 Hercules. Search parties were rushing from location to location hunting for survivors. Working against time and the elements, they removed debris and pulled people from the rubble. Those found alive were transported to a triage center that had been set up in the local high school gymnasium.

On the hillsides above the base and in coves scattered all over the island, radio towers and satellite dishes had been reduced to heaps of useless metal. Coast Guard Station Kodiak was going to be "off-line" for more than just a few hours.

After several minutes, Joseph Lind gave up trying to raise the Coast Guard. "No answer Dad," he said hanging the microphone on its hook.

Captain Lind didn't really expect an answer. He had figured Kodiak had been hit pretty hard by the earthquake. But still he instructed his son to continue in his efforts. "The earthquake may have destroyed their radio towers. Keep sending a message about our position, the approximate position of the plane, and let them know we are proceeding to the area to conduct a search."

Captain Lind put aside his concerns for his family back in Homer for the moment and altered course. The mariner's code required him to sail after the stricken plane. Praying silently, he asked God to watch over his family while he went to the rescue of these unknown airmen.

Following their Captain's lead the crew set to work getting the boat ready to take on survivors. No one spoke. Even the good-natured bantering about what the "greenhorn" was going to learn that day was absent. It was one thing to tease Joy about how to bait a hook or gaff a fish and quite another when the catch of the day would be human.

As she was putting on her rain gear, Joy was thinking about how she'd left home on the spur of the moment in search of adventure. Never in her wildest dreams did she ever think she'd be caught up in a life-or-death rescue effort in the frigid North Pacific. It had been a rainy day in New York City, when she told her best friend Molly about her decision. She recalled Molly's concern about her jetting off into the great wilderness. "But you don't know anything about fishing or Alaska," Molly argued. "You could get lost at sea. I saw a TV show once that said fishing in Alaska is one of the most dangerous jobs in the world!"

Joy had countered every argument Molly had made. Those were just sensational television shows, she told Molly. "Besides," Joy reminded her friend, "my Dad went to college with the owner of this boat. It's really big and made of steel. My Dad used to show me pictures. He even went up there for a few weeks of fishing. Made a lot of money too."

Unwilling to concede her point, Molly spent the next few days trying to pry this insane idea out of her best friend's head. The memory of hugging Molly at the airport made Joy smile.

Roger brought Joy back to reality when he slapped her on the shoulder. He was heading back to the bridge. He leaned over and shouted above the wind into her ear, "Get your butt in gear, girl. This is going to be messy and damn dangerous." She'd never seen him look so serious.

Joy took a deep breath, reminding herself to pay attention to Roger's instructions. She'd never been in seas this big or had to work on a cold, slippery deck with waves trying to wash you overboard. Weekends spent in your grandpa's boat sport fishing off Montalk Point on the Hudson River didn't count. She finished buttoning her slicker and headed topside to join the other crewmembers. Suddenly her Dad's stories of killer seas didn't seem so far-fetched.

Adak Island, Alaska

Toby Church ran at breakneck speed, working his way down the hillside in the early morning light. His heart was pounding in his chest and his legs felt like lead, but he knew that he couldn't stop. If he did he'd end up back in his concrete hell. The rain was beginning to let up and he knew that soon he would be spotted moving through the town.

At the far end of the street he could see the boat harbor filled with small boats and skiffs. He ducked into the splintered remains of a house to rummage through drawers and closets. Stepping through the rubble and over the bloody bodies of a mother and her two children, he grabbed a coat, a pair of insulated boots, a pair of gloves and a wool cap. Moving into the kitchen, he found a plastic milk crate, which he loaded with canned goods, bread, matches, and a jug of water. He found several knives in one of the few drawers not spilled by the earthquake. Satisfied with his new stash of supplies, he resumed his journey to the boat harbor.

As he moved through the shattered streets of Adak, he tried to blend in with the shadows as he sprinted from one scene of destruction to another. Oblivious to the death and destruction around him, his only concern was when the guards would catch up with him. He wasn't an idiot. As soon as they got things under control at the prison, they'd send search parties out for him.

Until then, he didn't have to worry. Both of the town's police officers were dead—crushed under the debris of the police station. And every available officer at the prison was busy making sure no one else escaped.

Arriving at the boat harbor, Church saw that the main pier had collapsed, cutting off access to the floating docks, where the larger boats were moored. He looked around for another way over to the big boats. Nothing. Only the imposing spikes of the shattered pilings remained standing defiantly above the sloshing waves. Scurrying around the dock he managed to locate two jerry cans of gasoline and headed off down to the beach where the skiffs were stored. "Doesn't anybody around here have a boat with a cabin," he cursed under his breath. Only two skiffs were available. He took the larger of the two—an aluminum 19-footer.

Untying the rope attached to the now shattered piling he shoved the boat into the surf. Carefully, he crawled into the boat and started the engine by pulling on the starter rope. It wouldn't do to fall into these freezing waters. Twisting the throttle, he swung the skiff's bow away from the beach and headed northeast out of Kuluk Bay. Several miles ahead lay the open ocean and freedom. A smile crossed his face. It'd been a long time since he'd felt the wind in his face like this.

Reaching up to pull the wool cap down over his ears, Church took a deep breath of the cold fresh air. It made his face sting. Feeling blood running down his arm again, he slowed down and locked the throttle on the outboard engine. He pulled up his coat sleeve, took out the first-aid kit, and dressed the wound. The cut was not very deep, but it was long. It would take some time for it to heal. Luckily for him, it had missed any major arteries and the muscle was intact. His biggest danger would be infection.

Finding a survival blanket in a small locker, he wrapped it around his feet. The floor of the aluminum boat was cold. He set course for the large island on the eastern edge of the bay.

Church was about three miles out into open water and in the trough of a swell when the volcano's blast wave thundered over him. He was lucky. Being in a trough in a low-profile boat saved him from being skipped across the water like a flat rock. But he wasn't out of danger. Just as in a nuclear blast, he found himself victim of what is called overpressure—a condition where the intensity of the wave passing overhead causes an intense increase in air pressure on the surface.

When the blast wave roared overhead, the overpressure slapped him to the floor of the skiff. His jaws clacked together as the back of his head hit one of the braces. Clutching his ears, he screamed as his left eardrum ruptured and blood poured from his nose.

Wiping the blood from his nose and ear, Church sat up and took a few minutes to regain his composure. *I gotta get outta this God-forsaken place.*

Resuming his position at the back of the skiff, he twisted the throttle, and headed once again towards the rising sun. He planned to navigate from island to island since he was unfamiliar with the area. Hopefully, the weather would hold so he could keep his bearings. Great Sitkin Island, with its 5,770-foot peak stabbing into the glowing overcast would serve as his first steer point.

For the first time in a long time Toby Church allowed himself to think of the past. He was pleased with himself. He had just done what they said couldn't be done—escape from the most secure and remote maximum-security prison in the world. He grinned at his luck and ingenuity. *Another chapter for my book.* In a few days he would once again dominate the headlines.

All across the country newspapers and magazines would once again tell his tale. The son of modest suburban Chicago family, who had grown up in what many would define as classic Middle America. Following his graduation from High School, where he lettered in football, was vice-president of his class, and one of the most popular boys in school, he had headed off to a nearby state university. It was during his sophomore year, after failing to make the varsity football team that he had found himself drawn to neo-nationalist movements. He started by participating in gatherings and protests. At the end of his junior year, he dropped out of school and headed to the Pacific Northwest, the base of several hate groups and anti-government factions.

Within a few years, the leaders of these groups recognized his gift for leadership. They began grooming him for special assignments. Unfortunately for them, they failed to appreciate his ambition. It only took him six years to move aside the president and founder of the neo-fascist group, Reich America—one of America's most radical and violent of the neo-fascist groups.

Reich America's goal was the overthrow of the United States Government, NATO, and the United Nations, and for the deportation of all "non-white" peoples. Under Church's leadership, Reich America became an even bigger threat to society. Not only did his organization sponsor terrorism against minorities and US Government installations, he recruited disaffected computer programmers, who managed to disrupt the financial sector with false stock headlines, phony deposits, and fake banking transactions.

After moving his base from Northern Idaho to the backwaters of Montana's Bull Mountains, he recruited ex-military specialists. He wanted an organization capable of challenging the FBI, ATF, and even the US Army. He made it a habit to join in on all the training and became a wilderness survival expert.

It probably would have been some time before he was apprehended, if he had avoided playing the field with the ladies. Nothing is more dangerous than a woman betrayed—someone who knows the most intimate details of your nightly forays and wants to get even.

His arrest and trial were national news. Always one to revel in the limelight, he took the stand at the trial. Although he did not deny his actions, federal prosecutors were unable to link him directly to any of the terrorist attacks that had rocked the nation. Church's followers were intensely loyal. None of them would turn state's evidence.

Because no one would betray their leader, prosecutors were unable to get the judge to sentence him to the death penalty. However, once he was turned over to the Federal Bureau of Prisons, officials there made sure he disappeared from public view. After a few weeks in Malloy Super Max, he was forgotten for more sensational headlines. Malloy Super Max was a great "out of sight, out of mind" dumping ground.

As his boat raced over the pounding waves, Church realized that he would need all his skills to survive. This wasn't Montana or Idaho. The sea was an alien environment to him. He was trained to survive in the forest and mountains. But even if he had grown up on the sea, he still wouldn't have noticed the unusually large wave pass under his skiff on its way into Kuluk Bay.

Malloy Super Maximum-Security Prison, Adak Island, Alaska

It was a beehive of activity as personnel entered and exited Captain Anderson's office adjacent to Main Control. Seated behind his desk, Marc was busy issuing directives, marking tasks off his checklist, and listening carefully to the constant flow of radio traffic among the officers. His primary task centered around getting the island's survivors into the gymnasium where extra beds and tables had been set up to accommodate the townsfolk.

High above the complex Lieutenant Carlos Banderas was working diligently to get things in Alpha Tower back in order. He picked up his lunch bucket, coffee cup and broom. Shattered glass was lying everywhere. He swept the shards into the corner. He hadn't been able to find the dustpan. Setting down his broom, he cupped his hand to his ear. Far in the distance he could hear the thundering of a helicopter approaching from the west. *What is a helicopter doing out in this part of the world?*

The SH-60 Seahawk dropped out of the clouds just over Mt. Moffet and thudded overhead. It was heading towards Kuluk Bay. As he watched the helicopter fly by Carlos saw the wall of condensing moisture racing towards the island. Stretching from the surface of the ocean into the overcast sky, the pressure wave plowed through the clouds. It was closing in on the island at frightening speed. He shook his head and rubbed his eyes in disbelief.

"All posts this is Alpha Tower, I think we're about to get hit with a big shock wave!" Carlos shouted over his radio. He lay down on the floor and covered his head with his hands. Before he could lace his fingers together, the blast wave slammed into the island.

Ripping through already devastated structures and debris, the hellish wind turned ordinary objects into lethal projectiles. Cars, boats, and planes flew through the air. Small fires burning since the earthquake were blown out as the overpressure created a vacuum in its wake. When oxygen rushed back into the void, hot embers exploded into flame igniting the remains of the town's wooden houses and storefronts.

As it slammed into the prison, the blast wave made quick work of the already mangled fences and damaged roofing. Once rigid steel was corkscrewed into ribbons of unrecognizable confusion. Rover was tossed into the air. Tumbling end over end it came crashing down onto the road—totally destroyed. Inside the facility, people covered their ears as the air pressure suddenly increased. Some of them screamed in pain. But no one could hear their distress over the howl of the wind.

Only the prison's concrete and steel construction and its lack of large windows saved it from further damage.

Marc Anderson got up from the floor, brushing off his clothes. So far this had been one hell of a day. "What else is going to happen?" he lamented.

"Captain?"

"Yes Johnson, what is it?"

"Do you think anyone is left alive in town?"

"Probably not Sam." The earthquake had just been too massive and now with that freak wind, he was sure no one could possibly still be alive in town. But still, deep inside, he prayed for a miracle for his good friends Jon and Darlene Riggs. And he knew that soon, tsunamis would begin ravaging the coastline.

USS Billings, 80 miles west of Adak, Alaska

The Great Aleutian Earthquake hit Alaska just as the Billings was turning east. She was running at flank speed in a following sea near the north end of Amchitka Pass. After being pounded for the past few hours by the heavy, quartering seas the crew was grateful for the course change.

"Skipper?" the Ensign called over the intercom, "a message has just come in over the wire."

"Go ahead Mister, what's is it?" she answered perfunctorily. She was still trying to unravel the mystery of the Russian submarine's last reported position.

"We've just received a priority message from CINCPAC. They're reporting a massive earthquake and volcanic eruption have hit the Aleutian Islands. Intelligence satellites report a massive heat signature rising from Umnak Island."

"Is that report confirmed Ensign?"

"Aye, Skipper. Confirmation code Zulu One One Echo Niner."

This was disturbing news. Carefully laid plans would soon be made moot by geologic events. Margaret Englemann walked over to the chart table. Flipping through the charts, she opened them to the middle and eastern Aleutians. "Brad, come over here for a look.

"Brad, here is Adak," she said pointing to the small island on the map, "and here is Umnak Island. And here are the Islands of Four Mountains."

"Yes?" He wasn't sure what she was trying to point out.

Noticing his confusion, she continued. "This earthquake is not well-timed for the Russians. This volcano is pretty darn close to the Islands of Four Mountains. If I was flying that prison transport, I'd turn back and wait for a better delivery date."

"And your point Skipper?" Hastings asked still somewhat confused.

"My point Brad," she said with some irritation, "is that we may not have to intercept that sub right now. I think we should stand down and prepare to conduct search and rescue operations."

"Well, that would make sense," he replied with some hesitation, "but I think we should see if we can get a status report on the airfield on Adak and on the flight path of the transport first."

"I agree. You follow up. I'm going to the CIC to see what other information has come in over the satellite."

"Captain off the bridge!"

Hastings began issuing his orders. "Helm. Maintain course, slow to 20 knots, and see if we can't raise Adak Island on the radio."

"Sir," interjected the radioman over the CIC intercom.

"Yes sailor, what is it?"

"Sir, if that quake is as big as they say, I'm betting their communications will be down. Wouldn't it be better to dispatch the SH-60 for a visual?"

"Good idea, sailor. But first," he said, "try and raise them on the radio."

As he flipped through the channels, the radioman scanned his book to make sure he didn't dial in the wrong frequency. After several minutes of futile effort, he informed Lt. Commander Hastings he was unable to raise Adak on the radio.

Hastings picked up the phone. It was time to implement phase two of the operation to contact Adak. "Lt. Chu, this is XO Hastings."

Lt. Chu was in his quarters, studying for his upcoming check ride. Pressing the intercom button, he answered, "Yes, sir?"

"Lieutenant, I want you to warm up Hawk One and get ready to conduct a visual over Adak. Meet me in the flight operations room for a briefing."

"Aye, aye, Commander" he replied. Lt. Chu put down his book and headed down the gangway towards flight operations room.

Next, Lt. Commander Hastings called the Combat Information Center. He informed Commander Englemann of his decision to have Hawk One conduct a visual over Adak since they had been unable to raise anyone on the radio. Hanging up the phone, he headed below decks to brief Lt. Chu.

Following the mission briefing, Lt Chu and his co-pilot Lt. Allen picked up their gear and headed towards the helo pad on the aft deck of the Billings. It was time to get airborne.

Methodically the two pilots worked through the pre-flight checklist, preparing to launch from the rolling deck of the frigate. Chu looked around the flight pad, making sure the area was clear of all personnel before shouting "clear" from his side window and hitting the ignition button. With a whine, the turbine engines of the SH-60 began spinning. Igniting after a few seconds, the engines roared to life. Lt. Chu twisted the throttle. The once sagging rotor blades became a spinning blur slicing at thousands of revolutions per minute just feet above the flight deck. Twisting the throttle to full thrust, Chu lifted the helicopter off the flight pad into the howling wind. 110 miles to the east lay Adak Island.

Lt. Allen checked his watch. They would be over the island in less than an hour.

Cruising just below the low scudding clouds, Lieutenants Chu and Allen ignored the violent updrafts and downdrafts. They were accustomed to rugged flight operations. Both men were veterans of search and rescue and anti-submarine warfare operations and had spent their fair share of time flying in the North Pacific. Despite the bumpy air, this was an easy mission—fly over Adak and make sure everything was still in one piece. A check of the flight computer showed that despite the wind they were making good time and would be over Adak Island in less than five minutes.

They planned to come in over the island from the east, and pass over Malloy Super Max before flying over the town. Up ahead, sunlight filtered through the clouds. Below them they could make out Malloy Super Max. Large sections of the perimeter fence lay in disarray, but the buildings appeared to be intact.

Descending closer to the ground, they saw devastation that had once been the town of Adak. "My God," moaned Lt. Allen into his headset, "do you see that?"

Chu shook his head in silent reply.

"Chu," said Allen touching his partner on the shoulder, "look over there." He pointed in the direction of a small boat heading out to sea, its florescent wake glowing in the dim morning light.

"Let's see what's up." Chu put the stick over, banking the SH-60 hard to the left.

"Hey Lieutenant!" exclaimed Allen, pointing to the radar screen. "What's that line moving in on us fast?"

Lt. Chu looked down at the monitor. *What the hell is that?* A bright solid line was moving straight for them. Lt. Allen looked out the windshield. He tapped Chu on the shoulder. In an instant they both realized they were in big trouble.

Barreling directly at them was the condensation barrier on the leading edge of the blast wave. Behind the barrier was an invisible wall of wind. Before they could react, the wave crashed into the helicopter, tossing it like a rag doll through the overcast sky.

Tumbling wildly through the air, the SH-60 lost power due to the sudden disruption of airflow to the turbines. Chu's head snapped back from the impact. He fought for consciousness, struggling to regain control of the chopper.

Hawk One's crew chief never knew what hit him. He was thrown face first into the floor of the helicopter as the blast tossed the flimsy craft on its back. Blood poured from his nose.

Spinning and fluttering, the SH-60 left a trail of dark gray smoke as it fell from the sky just south of Church's position. Accelerating out of control the helicopter careened into the side of Great Sitkin Island shattering into sections and bursting into smoldering flames. Thick black smoke billowed into the crisp morning breeze.

Lieutenants Chu and Allen were killed on impact. The crew chief had been thrown clear of the wreckage. He was alive—barely. His skull had impacted an exposed rock and one of his lungs had been punctured. The plume of smoke rising from the wreckage marked its location.

"Skipper!" shouted the radarman, "I've just lost Hawk One!"

"Come again?!" Englemann replied in disbelief.

"Yes, ma'am. One minute she was there, just over Adak, then poof, she was gone!"

Englemann slammed down the receiver and rushed down the gangway to the CIC. *How could that be? This was just a simple reconnaissance flight. Surely the Russians were not in Kuluk Bay. This didn't make sense.*

Commander Englemann arrived at the CIC slightly short of breath and red-faced. She asked Lt. Commander Hastings for a briefing. Had they received any communication from the helicopter before it disappeared from radar?

"Not a word Skipper," he replied.

Englemann went into action. "Helm, come to flank speed, and set course for Adak.

"Brad, I want you to gather Lt. Surin and his squad. Prepare to conduct a rescue operation for Hawk One."

"Aye, aye," he replied while choking back his emotions. He'd flown with both Chu and Allen on many flights.

"And Brad," Commander Englemann said, "it's not your fault." Her thoughts turned to the lost crewmen. *How am I going to tell their families?* She'd never had to write a death in the line of duty letter.

"Skipper?" interrupted the young Ensign.

She looked in his direction, waiting for him to continue.

"Skipper, I have a fix on the Emergency Locator Transmitter for Hawk One. They crashed on Great Sitkin Island, just across Kuluk Bay from Adak."

"Very good, Mister Merriwether, very good."

"And ma'am," he stuttered before correcting himself, "uh, excuse me, Skipper, I've just intercepted a radio message, which may be of interest to you."

"Yes?" she said trying not to vent her frustration on the young officer. He was brand new to this duty and he just getting used to referring to her as skipper.

"Well, it appears to have come from the prison transport over Shelikof Straits."

"Yes?" she asked again. She sensed the young man was reluctant to give her the news.

"I'll read it to you. Anchorage Departure Control this is Malloy 1, repeat this is Malloy 1, declaring a May Day. We are over Shelikof Straits. Our position is 154 degrees 34 minutes West and 56 degrees North. We're going to ditch, repeat we're going to ditch. End of transmission."

Englemann did not reply. She was in a dilemma. Somewhere on Great Sitkin Island she had three crewmen who were either injured or dead and now she knew that the object of her mission had crashed into Shelikof Straits off Kodiak Island, over 1,100 miles to the east.

"Helm, adjust your heading to zero one zero. All ahead full. Lt. Commander Hastings, come with me to the bridge!" she ordered. If the Billings had intercepted the May Day from Malloy 1, so had the Russians! Dr. Elizabeth LeDue must not be allowed to fall into enemy hands. Lieutenants Chu and Allen would have to wait. Right now she had to catch that Russian sub before they could get to the good doctor.

Great Sitkin Island, Alaska

When Toby Church first heard the pounding of the Seahawk's rotor blades, he figured it was the Department of Corrections looking for him. But the heavy ocean swells prevented him from locating the approaching helicopter.

When he was slapped to the floor of his boat by the blast wave he missed seeing Hawk One fall from the sky and hit Great Sitkin Island. But it wasn't too long before he saw the column of black smoke rising from the crash site.

Now he faced a dilemma. At the crash site he might be able to retrieve valuable items, like weapons, rations, clothing, and maybe even a radio. However, if the crew was still alive, he might be apprehended. If they were dead, it would be easier, but surely help would be coming and he might get caught on the island.

"Life is full of risks," he said to himself. He turned his boat toward the island. The chance of finding valuable survival items at the crash site outweighed the risk of getting caught.

Malloy Super Maximum-Security Prison, Adak Island, Alaska

After picking himself up off the floor of Alpha Tower, Lt. Carlos Banderas searched the sky for the helicopter. Through his binoculars he could see a ribbon of black smoke rising from Great Sitkin Island.

"SS, Alpha Tower."

"Go Alpha."

"Captain, are you available to call my post?"

"10-4 Alpha, I'm heading to my office now," answered Captain Anderson. He put down his coffee cup, walked into his office and picked up the phone.

Carlos described what he had seen just before the blast wave hit the prison. Now, he said, the helicopter was no longer anywhere to be seen and smoke was rising from Great Sitkin Island.

"A Navy chopper? Are you sure?"

"Yep, I'm sure. I used to be crew chief on one before I came here."

"Where would it have come from?" asked Captain Anderson. The Navy regularly conducted maneuvers in the area, but it was still early in the year. They usually waited until summer.

"Well Captain, I would guess that it's either off a carrier, a cruiser or a frigate somewhere to the west."

Anderson agreed with Carlos. "I'll assemble a rescue team. Maybe we can find a boat and get over there to see if there are any survivors."

Akula Class Submarine Putin, Islands of Four Mountains

Commander Igor Ivanshenko was surveying the horizon through the periscope when the earthquake hit.

"Conn, sonar. We've just picked up a tremendous explosion southwest of our position!" the sonar man exclaimed.

Ivanshenko jerked his head back from the periscope. "What kind of explosion?"

"I don't know Commander. But the computer says it's geologic. An earthquake, I think. And if my guess is right there may have been a volcanic eruption too."

An earthquake and volcano did not particularly bother Ivanshenko. He knew the Aleutian Islands were very geologically active, with hundreds of earthquakes and several eruptions occurring every year. Besides, his submarine was the safest vessel around. He continued patrolling at periscope depth just north of Carlisle Island.

But still, such an event could alter our plans. He turned to his second-in-command, Lt. Commander Vatutin. "Vatutin, increase monitoring of civilian and military radio traffic, just in case some important news is broadcast."

"Yes, Commander." After serving with Ivanshenko for so many years, Vatutin had already anticipated his orders and dialed in new frequencies. He ordered the communications officer to make himself comfortable and monitor radio traffic.

For over an hour, the communications officer sat at the radio, growing tired of listening to static. *Why did Vatutin give me this duty? I'm wasting my time. I should be standing at the periscope, learning how to command a submarine.* Just then he picked up a faint message.

Listening to the mayday changed his mind about the importance of his job. His complexion grew ashen. He translated the message into Russian, pushed himself back from the communications console, and walked over to Ivanshenko, who was deep in thought and looking very intense.

"Commander," he said quietly, "I just intercepted a message. It may be very important."

"Go on," said Commander Ivanshenko as he turned to face the young Lieutenant, his blue eyes flashing as he flipped up the periscope handles. "Up scope." The young officer was not the first person to be intimidated by Ivanshenko's presence. Matter of fact, it was a fairly normal reaction for people unaccustomed to his fiery personality and keen intellect. His habit of staring at whoever was talking to him merely added to his aura of invincibility.

"Sir, I think there may be a problem with the American transport plane. This is what I picked up over the radio. I've already translated it." He handed Ivanshenko his note and waited for a reply.

"Are you sure you translated this correctly?" Ivanshenko asked raising an eyebrow and glaring coldly into the Lieutenant's eyes. The young man's lack of confidence was troubling. A submariner had to be confident at all times. A lack of faith in one's abilities could lead to disaster if you ended up questioning your decisions.

"Absolutely," he replied quickly.

Ivanshenko read the note several times, flashed the officer a quick smile and walked over to the chart table. "Shelikof Straits. Ah yes, here it is. Just off Kodiak Island." Grabbing his plotter, he marked a course to the last known position of Malloy 1. "Vatutin? Any sign of that American submarine? No? Good. Take us down to 50 meters and increase to flank speed. Bring the reactor up to full power. Have Major Golkin meet me in my cabin in two minutes."

Major Golkin arrived outside Commander Ivanshenko's cabin door. He knocked on the door softly, "You called for me Commander?"

"Yes, Major, please come in and sit down." Ivanshenko motioned to the small table at the back of his cabin. "It seems we have a slight change in plans."

"What do you mean sir?" Golkin replied, his curiosity piqued. He turned sideways to enter through the narrow door into the cabin all the while holding Ivanshenko's gaze.

"Sonar reported a major earthquake and volcanic eruption to the east of us. Then we intercepted a May Day radio call from the American transport saying they were ditching in Shelikof Straits."

"The Shelikof Straits?" Golkin asked no one in particular. He didn't like the thought of trespassing further into American territory. They were already pushing the limits of international espionage. His years of experience in clandestine operations had taught him to be skeptical about the loyalty of his superior officers when things went sour. Admiral Voroshilov was an exception and would stand by his men, but the rest of those political vipers in the Kremlin were shifty—he didn't like spineless politicians.

"The Shelikof Straits separate the Alaska Peninsula from Kodiak Island, here," said Ivanshenko pointing to the map. He glanced up, making sure Major Golkin followed his hand. "Based on the last known position of the aircraft, the closest landfall is Kodiak Island. If the prevailing winds hold true, and if the currents are as our charts indicate, any survivors should end up on Kodiak."

"Do we abort the mission?" asked Major Golkin. He *really* didn't enjoy the thought of trespassing so deep into American waters. It was one thing to engage American Special Forces in Vietnam or Afghanistan and quite another to do it on their native soil.

"No. This is our best chance to nab that young woman and this may be even better for us." A self-assured smile flashed across Ivanshenko's weatherworn face.

"What do you mean better? How can it be better?" Golkin growled.

Ivanshenko noticed that Golkin didn't seem to have any problem voicing his opinion. This was a rare quality in a former Red Army officer, especially one attached to the GRU.

Stocky and built for endurance, Joseph Golkin was a career officer of the Spetsnaz—Russia's elite special forces. His mustache was cropped short, like his sandy blonde hair. His flashing blue eyes made his stern appearance even more intense. Killing was his business and he took it very seriously. He didn't like unnecessary complications. In his business patience was a virtue. His guts told him it was time to head home. Instinctively, he rubbed the star-shaped scar underneath his shirt where the Northern Alliance bullet had gone through him during an ambush in the middle of the night in the Khyber Pass.

"Think about it Major," continued Ivanshenko in his most soothing tone. "We're no longer on a covert operations mission. We just happened to be patrolling in the Bering Sea when we intercepted a distress call. We merely responded to their call for help. Of course," he said pausing for effect, "we found no survivors." He leaned back in his chair and took a sip of his tea.

Major Golkin perused the charts, while he considered Ivanshenko's idea. He had no idea Ivanshenko was so cold-blooded. "That's pretty good Commander. Pretty good," he replied. The thought of having to execute innocent civilians didn't bother him. His many years in the Spetsnaz had taught him how to emotionally disengage from his moral struggles. This was his job, period. Sitting back in his chair, he poured himself some tea. "You wouldn't happen to have any vodka to make a toast to your new plan would you?"

Reaching under the cushion of his bench, Ivanshenko pulled out a small bottle of vodka and poured two glasses. He also pulled out a carefully hoarded stash of imported chocolate to sweeten the celebration. He found his hypocrisy over murdering innocent civilians disgusting, but if he didn't succeed his good friend Admiral Voroshilov would probably pay with his life. He owed the man too much to let that happen.

Governor's Conference Room, Capitol Building, Juneau, Alaska

"Good morning everyone," began Governor Malloy taking his center seat at the large conference table. His cabinet was assembled around the table. Clasping his hands in front of him, he looked around at each person before speaking. "As you all probably know by now, there has been a catastrophic earthquake in the Aleutians. And to make matters worse there has also been a massive volcanic eruption. Commissioner Burke would you begin?"

Dick Burke rose from his chair and moved to the front of the room where a large map of Alaska was hanging. Using a wooden pointer, he said, "At approximately five-thirty this morning an earthquake measuring 9.2 on the Richter Scale hit the Aleutian Islands and all of South-central Alaska. We have received reports of extensive damage all along the chain, the Alaska Peninsula, Kodiak Island, the Kenai Peninsula and the Anchorage Bowl. Radio communications have been disrupted all over the region."

He made a sweeping pass with his hand over the map. "My troopers are still trying to gather more information."

Pausing for a moment to see if anyone had a question, he continued with his briefing. "Compounding the earthquake is a report of a massive volcanic eruption on Umnak Island. Satellite radar shows that Umnak Island has disappeared from the face of the earth. A plume of volcanic ash is pouring into the upper atmosphere. The National Weather Service reports the plume reaches over 60,000 feet into the atmosphere."

All around the room people began whispering and chatting nervously as the reality of what was happening sank in.

"Quiet people!" barked General Hornby, "let's finish this briefing, then we can all get to our jobs. Now is not the time to panic."

"Thanks General," said Burke before continuing. "It gets worse folks. We have unconfirmed reports of a tremendous blast wave that was generated by the volcano when it exploded. Eyewitnesses report this wave has leveled what remained of already shattered communities."

At the back of the room, the Governor's Press Secretary raised his hand.

"Yes John," Commissioner Burke said, gesturing for him to speak.

"Commissioner. What are the predictions for a tsunami hitting the area?"

"My people are trying to get in touch with the Alaska/West Coast Earthquake and Tsunami Warning Center right now. Given the nature and size of the quake, I think we can pretty much figure on one or more tsunamis hitting the coasts of Alaska, British Columbia, Eastern Japan, Kamchatka, and Hawaii. Who knows, they may even hit the coasts of Australia and all of Pacific Asia."

"Dick," interjected General Hornby, "if I may?"

A dynamic and animated speaker, General Hornby began pacing at the front of the room. "We have every confidence that our tsunami sirens have alerted citizens in all our coastal communities. They should be heading to higher ground at this very moment. The State Troopers are busy restoring order to our major towns and villages. I have an order sitting on Governor Malloy's desk authorizing the deployment of the National Guard. I have aircraft, vehicles and personnel all around the state gearing up to handle this emergency. The Division of Emergency Services is in the process of setting up incident command centers for each area. DES will coordinate responses throughout the state. But make no bones about it. This is big—very big. And I think we are going to be in bad shape for the next several weeks."

This dire news made everyone anxious. Once again the room erupted in chaotic chatter. People were scared. They needed to talk.

Governor Malloy rose from his chair at the head of the table. Displaying a confidence he didn't really feel, he tried to calm the fearful and motivate the hesitant. This was a far cry from the corporate boardroom. "Okay, everybody," he said motioning with his hands for everyone to be quiet, "we know we've got a major crisis on our hands. What I want now is for each commissioner to give a short status report on their department's condition and plan of action. Let's start with Transportation." Governor Malloy gestured towards Commissioner Murphy.

Not bothering to lift his rotund frame, Joe Murphy cleared his throat before speaking. "Well, as best I can tell, it's not good. I have reports that the airports at Dutch Harbor, King Cove, Sand Point, Kodiak, Kenai, and Anchorage are all out of service. My people tell me that the control tower at Anchorage has collapsed and the runways have been turned into rubble. In the Anchorage area, numerous bridges and overpasses have collapsed. The ferry terminals at Dutch Harbor and Kodiak are out of service. I have crews out right now with orders to give me complete reports by 10 am."

Governor Malloy pointed to his Health and Social Services commissioner gesturing for him to give an update. "Commissioner Lundgren?"

Adjusting his glasses in a nervous twitch, Dr. Robert Lundgren took his cue. "Right now, I am mobilizing a team to gather additional medical personnel and supplies, blood, and safe drinking water. I will be in a better position to give a realistic update this evening."

Turning his gaze to the far left end of the table, Governor Malloy gestured for his new Department of Corrections Commissioner Michelle Dornier to present her update.

Michelle Dornier was a veteran corrections administrator from New Jersey, where she had built a reputation for controlling prison costs. Since arriving in Alaska, she had been overwhelmed responding to legislative inquiries into the massive cost overruns within the department. As a result, she had not been able to visit any of the outlying institutions. This left her without any hands-on knowledge of the department's facilities. And like most newcomers to Alaska, she had yet to fathom the great distances between communities and the brutal nature of the environment. Furthermore, she had never worked in the security end of an institution. Her entire career had been spent in administration and budgeting.

She stood up from the table and began her briefing by pulling out her notes on each institution. "Right now, I don't have a lot of information. I have been unable to contact my Director of Institutions. However, I have put the entire department on emergency alert. At this time, it appears that all the institutions in the Anchorage Bowl are secure. The Anchorage jail is without water, but they are coping with the situation. All of the prisons, except for those in Juneau and Fairbanks are locked down.

From here it appears to get worse, although I do not yet have complete reports. Wildwood in Kenai had one dormitory collapse and is reporting casualties. Spring Creek in Seward has held up well, but I understand the access road has buckled and the prison cannot be reached except by helicopter."

Growing impatient with Dornier's book report, Burke growled, "what about Malloy Super Max, dammit?!"

Taken surprise by Dick Burke's outburst, the diminutive Dornier responded flatly, "there are no reports out of Malloy. The satellite communications system is down." She could feel her face turn red as she tried to maintain her composure.

Seeing the flushed look on Commissioner Dornier's face, Governor Malloy stepped into the conversation to give her a little time to think. "How far away from Adak was the epicenter?" he asked.

"About 90 miles," responded General Hornby.

"Given the location of the quake," she said, thankful for the Governor's intervention, "I think it's safe to assume that Adak and Malloy Super Max have been hit pretty hard. However, we put the damn thing out there so if someone did escape it would be incredibly hard to escape very far. And I know Jon Briggs. He's the best we've got and so is his crew. I'm sure the situation is under control."

"What's the word on today's transport?" asked the prickly Burke.

Dornier replied, "That's the worst of it. We have not heard anything out of Malloy 1 since it lifted off from Anchorage before first light this morning."

"Son-of-a-bitch," cursed Burke. "Governor, I think we need to convene in your office immediately!" He glared at Dornier.

"Agreed Dick. Okay, everyone. Go to work and be prepared to give me updates every four hours. Burke and Dornier in my office. Everyone else—we will meet again at one pm."

Governor Malloy turned to his Chief-of-Staff, George Roberts, and ordered, "Call Admiral Rourke at the Coast Guard. Ask him to meet me in my office in one hour."

Dick Burke followed Governor Malloy down the hallway into his office. He was seething at what he perceived was Michelle Dornier's lack of leadership and inability to comprehend the gravity of the situation. He closed the door behind him, immediately launching a verbal attack on Dornier. "Dammit Michelle, we're in one helluva pickle if Malloy 1 has gone down!"

"Don't you think I know that?" retorted Dornier. Although only five feet two inches tall, she stood her ground with Burke. She didn't like a bully and she was beginning to think Dick Burke was a bully.

"Both of you, quiet!" shouted Governor Malloy. "Michelle why don't you tell us what's up and what your plan is."

As he entered the Governor's office, Chief-of-Staff George Roberts instructed the governor's secretary to get Lieutenant General McCarthy, the head of the Alaska Command, on the line. Sensing the tension in the room, he found a neutral corner from which to observe the conversation.

Dornier stood next to the wall-size map of Alaska hanging in the corner. "As you all know, Malloy 1 took off this morning with Dr. Elizabeth LeDue and the notorious murderer Ivan Lincoln. When the quake hit, Malloy 1 was somewhere over Cook Inlet. If the reports of the blast wave are true, and if the transport got caught in it, then it probably went down somewhere here." She pointed to Katmai National Park. Since the chief air controller in Anchorage was now dead, she didn't know that the fierce weather had made Malloy 1 deviate from its course in an attempt to find smoother air.

"What are the chances they would survive a crash?" asked Governor Malloy.

"Hard to say Rick," Burke interrupted, trying to take over the conversation.

Dornier wasn't going to let Burke bully his way into taking over the situation. She cleared her throat, staring at him with her most menacing look. Much to her surprise, he yielded the floor, allowing her to continue. Unfortunately, her ignorance of Alaska geography was haunting her.

"I must assume they landed at an alternate airport. There have been no reports of an emergency locator transmitter beacon going off anywhere in that area."

Burke shook his head in disgust, walking over to the map. "Noooo. Any idiot can see that there are no cities around there." He made a big circle with his hand around where she'd been pointing. "If you understood anything about Alaska you'd know that there are no major airports within 300 miles of Katmai. It's obvious," he said in his most sarcastic tone, "just because we don't have an ELT signal doesn't mean they didn't crash. Those things are damn unreliable." He had little patience for anybody who didn't understand Alaska, let alone some foreigner from New Jersey.

"Okay Dick that's enough," interjected George Roberts. He could see that the conversation was degenerating. "Sarcasm will get us nowhere. We need to come up with a plan."

Quietly opening the door and sticking her head inside, the Governor's secretary announced, "Governor, I've got General McCarthy on the phone from Elmendorf Air Force Base."

"Very good Kerri. Thank you."

Hitting the speaker button on the phone, Governor Malloy said hello to his long-time friend and former college classmate.

"Hello, Governor."

"How are things in Anchorage, General?"

"Pretty bad I'm afraid. I've only got one operational runway for my fighters. And I don't expect to have a runway long enough to launch my heavy aircraft for hours."

"How about casualties?"

"Hard to tell. As you know our housing is pretty old and some of the buildings have collapsed."

"General, we have a situation here and we need your help."

"I can't make any promises Governor. But I'll give you whatever help I can."

"This morning DOC transport Malloy 1 took off from Anchorage with two prisoners—one of whom is Dr. Elizabeth LeDue. We've lost contact with Malloy 1 and we're pretty sure it's gone down somewhere over the area around Katmai National Park."

The Elizabeth LeDue? General McCarthy took a moment to absorb this disturbing information. *The President is going to be pissed.* "Okay, Governor. How can I help?"

"Could you launch a couple of F-15s to fly over the last known flight path of Malloy 1 and see if there is any sign of wreckage?"

"I'll check into it, Governor. My intelligence reports an ash cloud spewing out from the Okmok Caldera to an altitude of 65,000 feet and tracking on an east, northeast course towards Kodiak and the Kenai Peninsula. I'm pretty sure I can help, but it'll be a few hours before I can be sure. I'm short of pilots and I've got to provide air cover for the base."

"Thanks, General. I know you'll do your best."

Governor Malloy hung up the phone, turning to Burke and Dornier. "I want regular updates on this situation. I'm going to call the President." With that he dismissed them from his office.

Rick Malloy rubbed his temples. He needed to take a few minutes to vent his frustration at Burke's clumsiness and Dornier's total lack of understanding of Alaska. He knew Burke was rough around the edges, but he had never seen him so condescending before. As for Dornier, maybe she wasn't tough enough to lead a department. These were the times when he wondered why he'd ever wanted to run for governor.

George Roberts, who had been watching the whole scene in silence, knew what the governor was thinking. He reminded him again that he had wanted the take on the challenges of leading the state. Smiling, Roberts got up from his chair, and said, "Now's your chance Governor." He exited the office before Rick Malloy could respond.

Sitting down at his desk, Governor Malloy placed a call to the White House. After several minutes on hold, his call was transferred into the Oval Office.

"Mr. President?"

"Yes, Governor Malloy. I've been told that you've got quite a situation on your hands. What can I do for you?"

"Well, Mr. President, as you know by now, we've just had a massive earthquake and volcanic eruption in the Aleutian Islands. There is a lot of damage and it looks like we've got hundreds of casualties. I'm preparing to declare a state-wide disaster."

"I understand. I've got the head of FEMA getting on a flight right now headed your way."

"Thank you very much, Mr. President."

"No problem Governor."

"Mr. President," Malloy couldn't think of a good way to pass this information on, so he just blurted it out, "the airplane carrying Dr. LeDue to our Super Max Prison on Adak is missing. We believe it's gone down somewhere in the wilderness west of Anchorage."

"*Dr. Elizabeth LeDue*?" asked President Bainbridge. He hoped he had heard wrong.

"Yes sir, the very same."

"Well this isn't good news Governor. What are your people doing about it?"

"We are trying to mount a search, but all of our airports are crippled. I've asked General McCarthy to launch F-15s to fly over the last known flight path of the transport."

President Bainbridge strummed his hand on the corner of his desk. "Governor, I may have worse news for you. Right now the Chief of Naval Operations and the Director of the CIA are headed to my office for a briefing. I will call you in 45 minutes. Be available."

Life Rafts, Shelikof Straits, Alaska

As the tiny raft carrying the two prisoners from Malloy 1 rode the swells, moving inexorably toward the emerald shores of Kodiak, Ivan Lincoln tried to get a good look at what appeared to be a valley to the southeast. He was rowing with long steady strokes, adjusting his course to allow the wind and the waves to push him towards the shore. The storm was abating making life on board a little more tolerable, but not by much.

Elizabeth was huddled at the other end of the raft, trying to fathom the situation in which she now found herself. She was wet and cold. She was scared. Whenever Lincoln looked at her she was afraid. Her eyes were sore from crying and she had to keep swallowing the lump in her throat.

Further to the northeast, Harry Ignustuk and Danny Sanders traded rowing duties as they made their way over the 15-foot swells towards Kodiak Island. The wind was still howling, blowing spray off the tops of the waves.

"How much further do you think it is?" Sanders bellowed over the wind.

"Don't know," shouted Harry, "10-15 miles maybe. With this storm and the currents, I think we'll have to find some sheltered water before we can land."

"How long until they notice we're missing?"

"Probably 8 hours or more," Harry answered. "When we don't show up over Adak they'll know something's wrong."

"Any idea how long it'll take them to find us?"

"Days. Weeks," Harry said flatly.

"Why do you think we crashed?"

"Your guess is as good as mine," Harry said shrugging his shoulders. "Could have been anything. It was like we flew right into a mountain."

F/V Neptune, Shelikof Straits, Alaska

Joseph Lind stood at the helm, steering the Neptune on a course south, southeast to where he saw the airplane disappear over the horizon. The heavy seas were hitting the boat at an angle, causing it to pitch and roll violently. The wiper blades slapped back and forth rhythmically almost in keeping with the boat's surging over the waves.

Joy and Roger were up on the flying bridge, hanging on for dear life, searching the horizon for some sign of wreckage. Their rain suits kept them dry, but all the ocean spray shooting over the railings made the footing slippery. Joy had forgotten about being seasick and was longing to be back in her home in Connecticut. Roger was thinking about the two times he'd had to abandon ship in the Gulf of Alaska.

Inside the wheelhouse, Captain Lind was reading the charts. Now was not the time to hit any rocks or reefs as they plowed through the sea.

"Debris in the water off the starboard bow!" shouted Roger thrusting his arm in the direction of the flotsam.

Captain Lind looked up. He could see a large section of the airplane bobbing in the waves. He also saw several other objects, which looked like bodies still strapped in their seats. "Come right five degrees," he ordered.

Joseph turned the wheel, watching the compass as he steered the Neptune on a new course.

Captain Lind left the wheelhouse, climbing the ladder to join Roger and Joy on the flying bridge. "See any survivors?"

"Don't know Captain. Looks like bodies and maybe a piece of the tail section."

Within a few minutes the Neptune was circling around several bodies strapped to flotation seats. The crew had descended from the flying bridge and was now standing at the rear of the wheelhouse.

"Get'em on board," Captain Lind ordered.

Roger looked around the deck for a place to put the bodies. In these pitching seas, they couldn't leave them topside. He lifted the hatch covering the refrigerated hold. It was their only option. Handing Joy a gaff, he showed her how to wrap a leg around the rail and reach over the side to hook a body. She felt nauseous. Together they began the grizzly task of gaffing dead bodies, pulling them onboard and lowering them into the fish hold all the while struggling to stay upright and on board.

Having spent most of his adult life on the sea, this was not the first time Roger had retrieved a dead body. He had spent ten years as a crew chief on a crabber out of Dutch Harbor. He had pulled more than his share of drowned sailors from the icy grip of the Bering Sea. Roger turned off his emotions and set to work with relative calm.

Joy, on the other hand, was new to this aspect of life. The strain of gaffing and handling the cold stiff bodies was terrible. Despite the frigid ocean spray, she was sweating under the rubber suit. With a lunge she'd reach out just as a body came up on a wave and sink the hard steel point into the corpse's ribs. Joy winced at the hollow thudding sound this made. With all her might she pulled the body over and grabbed an arm or leg, wrestling them onto the deck. With a push of her foot, she slid them over to Captain Lind, who was spilling them into the hold.

As she dragged body after body on board, Joy couldn't help but notice that some of the bodies had been shattered by the aircraft's impact. Heads hung at unusual angles, jaws were dislocated, and arms and legs were bent unnaturally. Further adding to her dread was the dark blood that painted the hook's point. Most of the corpses eyes were dark and fixed. A few of the faces were frozen in agonizing death poses. She had to fight off the urge to get sick. Never before had she met death on such intimate terms. Sure, she'd been to several funerals, including her Grandmother's. But this was different. Standing on the pitching deck in the middle of a heaving sea made death very real. There was no music, no crying, no comforting hugs from grieving relatives. This was death on its purest level—cold, harsh, and gruesome.

"Dad," Joseph shouted, "I think I see a life raft off the stern. About two miles away."

Captain Lind grabbed his binoculars. As he struggled to keep his eyes fixed on the horizon, he caught a brief glimpse of a life raft going over the top of a swell. There were two people on board—a man and a woman.

At this moment Roger caught sight of another life raft several miles away off the port bow. He tapped Lind on the shoulder and pointed.

"God dammit," Captain Lind cursed, "this is a helluva fucking mess." He was faced with a choice of which raft to rescue first. The Neptune wasn't a fast boat. It would take hours to get to one raft and then to the other. He needed to do two things at once or risk losing sight of one of the rafts.

"Roger!" he shouted above the wind and the drone of the throbbing diesel engine, "get the inflatable down off the wheelhouse and get over to those people." He directed Roger's eyes to the raft rolling over the swells far behind the Neptune. "Take Joy with you. I need Joseph at the helm. We'll head over the to the raft ahead of us. After we get those survivors on board, we'll get over to you as fast as we can."

Roger put down his gaff hook and went to work with the small crane and wench unloading the rigid inflatable over the side of the Neptune. This was dangerous work and Joy was precious little help. He shouted instructions to her above the howling wind. She was doing her best to comply, but with the wet deck and the Neptune rolling in the 20-foot seas, she soon regretted not having a more padded butt.

"Well, Joy, you wanted adventure and now you've got it," she cursed under her breath. "I wonder what my Mom would think of me now!" she shouted over the waves to Roger. He just smiled. *Quiet fellow.*

Lashing the inflatable to the Neptune, Roger motioned for Joy to climb down into the tiny craft.

Joy felt a rush of fear as she looked around at the seas dwarfing them. Grabbing hold of the rail, she timed her jump as the inflatable came closer to the side. She sprang over the side of the steel-hulled Neptune into the flimsy boat. This was exciting, but not in a fun way.

Roger started the motor and told Joy to untie them. With a mighty push, she shoved them away from the steel-hulled Neptune. A few moments later they were speeding across the rolling sea.

Roger ignored the spray hitting him in the face, instructing Joy on what to do when they came along side the raft.

In the meantime, Joseph Lind was driving the Neptune at full speed towards the other raft on the distant horizon.

Life Raft, Shelikof Straits, Alaska

For the last thirty minutes Lincoln had been watching the activity on the green and white fishing vessel. He was suspicious. He watched the crewmen use the crane to lift the small boat over the side, deducing they had been spotted. The fishermen were coming over to rescue them. He reached inside his coat, gripping the 40-caliber pistol he had taken off the body of Harold Powell. "Hope the powder's dry," he said under his breath. Menacing

Elizabeth with another look, he growled, "You do exactly as I say if you want to live."

Elizabeth recoiled in fear, nodding her head in understanding. She had no doubts that Lincoln would carry out his threat. The look in his eyes reminded her of the man, who had robbed her in the subway five years ago—his eyes were cold and calculating too.

As Elizabeth watched the approaching boat, she tried to think of a way to escape this madman. *Maybe I should leap into the sea? No, the water is like ice.* She was a poor swimmer, and if she didn't drown she would soon succumb to hypothermia. *Maybe I should try and jump from the raft into the boat before they can actually link up. No, there won't be time to tell them to get out of there before he shoots them.* She was stuck.

The waves pounded the inflatable as Roger and Joy drew closer to the raft. Roger slowed down, timing the waves. He was being patient. Docking with Lincoln's raft in the pitching seas would be difficult. With all the bucking and the howling wind, he barely took notice of the red jumpsuits the two people were wearing. It was an unfortunate oversight on his part.

As the boats got closer, Joy tossed a line over to Lincoln.

Lincoln caught the rope and began pulling the rubber boats together.

Roger concentrated on keeping the two boats next to each other so the survivors could climb into the Neptune's inflatable.

"Come on," Joy shouted holding her hands out to help Elizabeth into the boat.

Elizabeth was too afraid to move. Without thinking Joy jumped over to the raft. Grabbing Elizabeth by the hand, she steadied her as they jumped back into the inflatable. Sensing her opportunity to warn Joy and Roger, Elizabeth tried to tell them Lincoln had a gun. But she was too afraid to speak. All that came out was a little squeak.

As Roger and Joy held onto the raft, Lincoln crawled across into the front of Roger's boat. He sat down and looked out over the ocean, away from the group.

Roger Baker never saw Lincoln pull the pistol from his coveralls.

Wheeling around, Lincoln pointed the pistol at Roger. Two shots rang out over the waves. Blood spurted from Roger's chest as the 40-caliber hollow point bullet shredded his coat and exited out of his back. Stumbling backwards, he tumbled over the side. Joy screamed.

Moving quickly, Lincoln took control.

"Don't get cute or you'll end up dead like your friend," Lincoln shouted, pointing the pistol at Joy. Turning the throttle, he powered up the outboard engine. They raced off towards the shore.

Roger was left floating on the surface, a trail of blood oozing from his body. His eyes were fixed wide in surprise. The bullet had shredded his heart, killing him instantly.

F/V Neptune, Shelikof Straits, Alaska

"What the hell is going on out there!" exclaimed Captain Lind. He had been watching the progress of Roger and Joy as the Neptune headed in the opposite direction towards the other raft. As he watched his inflatable turn away from the Neptune and head towards the island he said in disbelief, "Where are they going? Where is Roger?" He had a bad feeling.

"Want to follow them Dad?"

"We can't. I think I saw Roger fall overboard. We've got to go look for him."

Joseph pushed the throttle forward and swung the Neptune back around. If Roger was still alive they needed to get to him as quickly as possible. Even in a survival suit, he wouldn't last long in these frigid waters. It was slow going as the Neptune plowed into the charging waves.

"There he is!" Captain Lind yelled. He could see the bright orange suit riding over the tops of the waves.

As Joseph steered the Neptune alongside Roger's body, Captain Lind snagged one of the straps on his suit with a gaff. As he pulled Roger onto the boat, he could see that his friend was dead. He reached down and closed Roger's eyes. *What the hell is going on? Why did they shoot Roger?* He was going to get that son-of-a-bitch. His mind flashed back to the memory of pulling his father's frozen body from the clutches of the Bering Sea some 10 years ago. *How am I going to tell Trudy?* Roger was like a member of the family. Alfred's wife was going to be devastated.

"What are we going to do now, Dad?" Joseph shouted over his shoulder through the open wheelhouse door.

"Damn It!" Captain Lind cursed in frustration. Whoever shot Roger now had Joy. But he had no options. The Neptune wasn't fast enough to catch the escaping boat. He tried to come up with a plan as he slid Roger's body into the refrigerated hold. "Let's get to that other raft. Maybe they know what the hell is going on."

Once again Joseph pushed the throttle forward, making the Neptune's engines roar to life. Soon the 55-foot trawler was churning ahead through the following sea.

F/V Neptune Inflatable, Shelikof Straits, Alaska

Lincoln continued to steer towards shore. Up ahead he could see the faint line of Sevenmile Beach. Far in the distance were the shadows of Kodiak's snowcapped mountains. Running at full throttle, the little skiff pounded across the waves. Several times it bounced completely out of the water.

Joy and Elizabeth sat in the front of the boat, hanging on for dear life.

About 50 yards from the beach, Lincoln gunned the engine, making the boat skim over the churning surf. The sound of the inflatable's rigid bottom grinding against gravel announced their arrival on shore. He had managed to drive the boat completely out of the water.

Waving the pistol in the air, he ordered the women to get out of the boat. "Get out now and lie face down on the ground."

Joy and Elizabeth stepped onto the beach and lowered themselves to the ground. They were shivering from the cold and damp, their hearts pounding.

After making the women lie down, Lincoln gathered supplies out of the bottom of the boat. He grabbed a fillet knife, matches, tarp, some rope and a few other items.

"Get up!" he shouted. "Get up, grab some drift wood and get moving." He pointed with the pistol away from the beach and towards the distant mountains.

With the wind at their back they began hiking up the Karluk River Valley. Ahead of them lay the untamed wilderness of Kodiak Island.

F/V Neptune, Shelikof Straits, Alaska

Just as the skiff landed on Sevenmile Beach, the Neptune came alongside the life raft carrying Harry and Danny. Wedging his foot against the side of the boat, Captain Lind tossed a line over to the small rubber boat. He had a pistol in his waistband, just in case there was more trouble. When Harry caught the rope, he braced himself and pulled.

After securing the rope to a cleat, Captain Lind extended his hand out to the blue-shirted officer. Gripping Danny's hand, he jerked him on board. He repeated the drill for Harry.

"Thank you, thank you very much," wheezed Danny, who was now kneeling on the pitching deck. He didn't have the strength to stand up.

"Sure am glad you came along," Harry shouted above the howling wind. "Thanks for saving us." Like Danny, Harry was spent from all they had just gone through. He sat down heavily. He didn't care that the deck was cold and wet.

"You're welcome!" replied Captain Lind. He was hungry for answers. "What the hell are you guys doing out here? Who are you? Who were those other people in their raft? They murdered my crew chief!"

What other people? Harry saw the pistol under Captain Lind's belt. "I'm Prisoner Transport Officer Harry Ignustuk. This is officer Danny Sanders."

"I'm Alfred Lind, owner and captain of the fishing vessel Neptune. Did you just say you're a prisoner transport officer?"

"Yes sir," Harry shouted above the howling wind. "Can we go inside?"

"You bet!" answered Captain Lind. He gave them a hand up.

As Captain Lind closed the door, Harry recounted their tale. "We were on our way to Adak with two prisoners, when suddenly our plane was knocked from the sky. It crashed into the sea. We barely made it out alive."

"Then those people in the red suits in the other raft, who were they?" asked Captain Lind.

"Red suits? How many red suits?" Harry asked in alarm.

"Two. A man and a woman."

"Oh God," moaned Danny.

"What do you mean 'Oh God'?" Captain Lind didn't like what he was hearing.

"Those two were our only prisoners. They are very dangerous. You said you saw them in the other raft?" Harry asked again. The irony that the prisoners survived while so many officers perished was not lost on him.

Captain Lind became even more upset by the news that two prisoners had murdered his friend and now they had his longtime friend's daughter. He tried to maintain his composure as he described what had taken place earlier.

Harry looked hard at Captain Lind. "You've got to get us over to where your boat went ashore. We have to capture those prisoners right now. If Lincoln makes it into the forest, we'll never find him."

"No can do," replied Captain Lind, "there is no moorage at Sevenmile Beach. We'll have to drop you off at Larsen Bay."

"How long will that take?" asked Danny. He was sipping the warm cup of coffee Joseph had given him. Even wrapped in a blanket, he was shivering.

"About an hour and a half," Captain Lind replied. He ran his finger along the chart to show Harry the planned route.

"I don't want to frighten you," Harry said looking Lind right in the eye, "but your friend Joy is in serious danger. I need you to loan me your rifle, some food, rain gear, and survival gear. And," he said while writing down a message, "I need you to radio this message to the Coast Guard."

Harry slid the piece of paper over to Captain Lind. "Urgent. Repeat, urgent. Malloy 1 has ditched in Shelikof Straits. Four survivors are Officers Ignustuk and Sanders and prisoners LeDue and Lincoln. Prisoners have escaped onto Kodiak Island. Have female hostage. Prisoners landed in the vicinity of Sevenmile Beach on the north side of Kodiak. Ignustuk and Sanders in pursuit. Prisoners still dressed in red jump suits. Send help. Harry Ignustuk, Chief Prisoner Transportation Officer."

Captain Lind agreed to send the message as soon as he was able to raise the Coast Guard on the radio.

Joseph Lind pushed the Neptune hard. He had to get Harry and Danny to Larsen Bay as quickly as possible. He couldn't lose Joy—he needed to tell her he loved her.

Malloy Super Maximum-Security Prison, Adak, Alaska

In deep water, tsunami waves are virtually undetectable. However, as the ocean floor rises and the water becomes shallow, compressing the wavelength and causing them to grow to tremendous heights. Arriving on shore, they hit like a giant wall, obliterating everything in their path.

Not since 1946 had such great waves struck the Aleutian Islands. That year witnesses on Unimak Island reported the wave to be over 150 feet tall. The lighthouse located on the southern coast was washed away without a trace. In 1960, after the great earthquake off the coast of Chile, a tsunami over 50 feet in height ravaged the town of Hilo, Hawaii. And after the Good Friday Earthquake in 1964 in Prince William Sound, Alaska, tsunamis swept away the towns of Valdez and Seward.

Carlos Banderas was exhausted from the day's events. First the earthquake, then the escape, then the blast wave from the Okmok eruption. "Boy, when it rains it pours," he said to Officer Thurston, who had just arrived to relieve him in Alpha Tower. He tried to steady his nerves with a cup of coffee. "I sure hope the tsunami misses us."

"Me too," replied Thurston. Thurston had grown up in Kodiak and still remembered the tsunami that had flooded the town in 1964.

With a sudden sense of dread, Carlos grabbed his binoculars. "Hang on to your britches," he said, putting his hand on Thurston's should and directing him to look out to sea.

"Speak of the Devil," whispered Thurston.

"Here it comes! All posts this is Alpha Tower," Carlos said over his radio, "we've got a tsunami rolling in from Kuluk Bay."

Already numb from the morning's events, Captain Anderson didn't want to believe what he was hearing. Surely the world was coming to an end. Responding with more confidence than he felt, he replied, "Alpha, SS. Keep us informed of what you see."

Carlos watched the water retreat away from the shore, exposing the mud flats. He never realized how many reefs existed below the frigid waters of Kuluk Bay. With terrifying speed, the wave grew in height, advancing like a mindless green monster towards the helpless community. "Here it comes!" he announced excitedly. Despite his fear, he was mesmerized by the scene unfolding below him.

Within the institution, everyone listened in prayerful silence to Carlos's description of the newest disaster to hit them.

"It's growing. Maybe 20-feet tall. Still growing. No wait, it looks to be more like 30-feet. It's going to hit shore! Holy Jesus," he moaned. He watched the wave swallow the remains of the pier, tearing great timbers loose from their pilings. Next the wave consumed the debris of collapsed buildings and vehicles, pushing it along in a frothy, boiling mass. He was glad they were over 1,000 feet above sea level at the prison.

As they listened to Lt. Banderas's words, the officers and townspeople lost all hope that anything would be left of Adak. Some of them cracked under the strain of the day's catastrophes, weeping silently for lost loved ones, homes, and prized possessions.

Safe and dry in Alpha Tower, Carlos watched the tsunami swamp the town, wreaking wholesale devastation on a once-proud Naval base and Aleut community. Rivers of seawater ran down the streets, gathering up debris along the way. Parts of houses, cars, children's toys, shattered fishing boats, airplanes and other unidentifiable objects were swept along with the current as the wave headed back out to sea.

Believing that the worst was over, Carlos was horrified by what he saw next. While the initial tsunami retreated back out to sea, the level of the bay continued to drop precipitously. The shoreline receded almost a mile from the pier. Scattered along the now uncovered mud flats were the stranded hulks of old shipwrecks.

Carlos watched in awe as a giant wave formed along the leading edge of the water. Growing taller by the moment, the main tsunami wave charged in towards the shore. Adak lay helpless before it.

"Everyone, this in Alpha again. Another wave is forming. It looks bigger than the first. I bet the damn thing is over 200 feet tall!" *My God! What a monster.* Carlos felt his knees shaking as he watched a giant wall of water rise high above the shoreline. His thoughts turned to his wife and children in Anchorage. He hoped they had been spared the tsunami.

The main tsunami thundered ashore, consuming everything in its path. The wave was so large that it didn't break until it was well inland. The sound was deafening. With incredible power the wave surged up the hillside reaching out for the prison perimeter with its foaming liquid fingers. For a moment Carlos thought it would breech the perimeter fence of the prison almost 1,000 feet above sea level.

Then as quickly as it had come, the wave raced back towards Kuluk Bay. The town of Adak had ceased to exist. Only the foundations of houses remained—silent victims of nature's wrath.

Carlos continued reporting, "All posts this is Alpha, the town is gone. There's nothing left. And you won't believe this."

Every person in Malloy Super Max turned his or her attention to his next words. Banderas was looking at a pile of rubble stretched out in an arc before the prison fence.

"The wave has swept a small airplane and a skiff up against the perimeter fence. They look like they hardly have a scratch on them. I'll be damned."

Like a tornado that destroys one house but leaves another untouched, the giant tsunami had spared two items desperately needed by the survivors of Adak. It was as if the hand of God had reached down, and gently plucked them from the jaws of destruction.

Great Sitkin Island, Alaska

Toby Church was in his skiff, skimming across the waves on the eastern side of Kuluk Bay, watching in disbelief as the massive green wave climbed into the air and surged up onto Great Sitkin Island several miles away. The raw power of nature made his heart skip. He could hear the roar of the wave slamming into the island. "Jesus Christ!" he exclaimed. Thoughts of abandoning his salvage plan raced through his mind. He didn't want to get caught in another of those killer waves. "No dammit, you need those supplies and weapons," he said to himself.

He slowed down, talking to himself, trying to build up his courage. "You just need to get up to that chopper and back to your boat in a hurry. You can do it."

It took almost ten minutes for him to restore his own confidence. By then the hull of his skiff ground to a halt on the gravel beach. He'd made a good choice for a landing site. Only a small cliff blocked his access to the field where he could still see smoke rising from the crash site. He tossed out the anchor, grabbed some gear, and started walking up the rocky cliff. The terrain was slippery, but not too steep. Small streams of seawater were running back down to the beach and into the bay.

As he came to the top of the cliff, an incredible sight greeted his eyes. Two hundred yards up the hill lay the mangled shell of the SH-60. Strewn along the path to the wreckage were carcasses of dead marine animals that had been washed ashore by the gigantic wave. Foxes, Norway Rats, and birds were already feasting on the dead.

Church took note of the largest carcass. About the size of a Volkswagen Bus, the Stellar Sea Lion was big enough to feed an entire army of small scavengers. "Doesn't look like I'll go hungry," he said, walking up to the sea lion. He shooed away the scavengers. Pulling the fillet knife out of its sheath, he cut off several large pieces of blubber and muscle. He packed his sack with enough food for several days and went back to his original task—retrieving equipment from the helicopter.

At the crash site, he came upon a grisly sight. Charred by fire, the broken bodies of Lieutenants Chu and Allen lay inside the shell of the smoldering helicopter. He could feel the heat of the melted aluminum on his hands and face. He watched the pilots for a few moments to make sure they were dead. Mercifully, they had died on impact. A few feet away, he heard a groan.

Quickly, he grabbed the pistol from Lt. Chu's charred holster and ducked behind the helicopter. *How the hell did someone get here? Who else could possibly be on this desolate rock?*

Cautiously, Church crawled around the side of the wreckage. The groaning was muffled and growing weaker. Then he spotted the source.

Lying face down in the grass was Hawk One's crew chief. He had been thrown from the helicopter when it hit the ground. Although severely wounded, he had managed to crawl away from the smoldering fuselage. But with numerous broken bones and internal injuries, he was unable to move very far.

Church walked over to the wounded crew chief. He aimed the pistol at the back of the wounded man's head and squeezed off a round. The bullet made a hollow sound as it shattered the chief's skull. Dark blood oozed out onto the marshy ground. The pistol's report echoed among the rocks.

Unfazed by his crime, Church walked back to the wreckage to scavenge supplies. He took a survival suit, the first aid kit, Lt. Allen's pistol, which was still warm to the touch, and two loaded ammunition magazines. Rummaging through the center console, he found a large knife and a navigation chart for the Western Aleutians. The chart was singed where it had been touching the sides of the console, but it was still legible.

Just inside the broken windshield was the best prizes of all—the helicopter's magnetic compass, which had broken off its mounting in the crash. Because the dashboard was still hot to the touch, he did not try to remove the radio.

Wanting to get back into the boat and as far away from Adak as possible, he moved swiftly back down the hill. After piling his prizes into his boat, he took a few moments to grab some driftwood in case he decided to build a fire at his next stop. He shoved his boat back into the surf and started the engine. Turning the nose of the boat towards open water and using the compass and the navigation charts, he set off on a course to the northeast.

Church was heading around Great Sitkin Island, while talking to himself about the best escape route. "You've got to get yourself to shelter for the night. You've got to throw them off the trail. And you've got to make it to the mainland so your people can rescue you."

Studying the charts, he concluded that if he continued on his present course, it would not be too long before he was caught. "You idiot," he said chiding himself, "they'll be expecting you to head to the nearest large town. You've got to be smarter than that."

A smile spread across his face as he formulated what he considered to be a positively brilliant plan. He turned the rudder and set a course south—southwest back into Kuluk Bay towards Adak Island.

Malloy Super Maximum-Security Prison, Adak Island, Alaska

Carlos nodded to the two officers as he entered Main Control. He'd been summoned to Captain Anderson's office located in the back of the room.

He stopped in the doorway. "Lieutenant Banderas reporting as ordered."

Captain Anderson looked up from the map and waved him into the room. "Good Carlos you're here. Come in. Sergeant Knight and Corporal Nelson will be here in a few moments." Turning back to his map, he said, "Help yourself to some coffee and food."

"Thanks Captain." Carlos walked over to the food tray and made himself a sandwich. His instincts told him he was about to "volunteer" for a mission. The routine was too much like his Navy days.

"Officers Knight and Nelson reporting as ordered."

"Come in," Anderson said without looking up from the map. "Like I told Carlos, get some coffee and some food. You're going to need the energy."

"What's new, Captain?" Carlos asked while catching the crumbs from his cookie in his free hand.

Anderson walked across the room and closed the door. Turning to his men, he motioned for them to join him at the map table. "As you all know, we've got quite a mess on our hands. First," he said holding up his finger to emphasize the point, "Toby Church, our *survivalist* has escaped. He has a boat and was last seen heading north out of Kuluk Bay. Second," he said holding up two fingers, "our perimeter fence is down. Third," he held up three fingers, "maintenance reports that it will be at least 8 hours before communications with the outside world can be re-established. Fourth, Corporal Steiger is seriously injured. No one has heard from Doctor Quincy and Inmate Lucas is very ill. Fifth, we've got a gymnasium full of refugees who require food, shelter, counseling. Sixth, most of Alpha shift has perished. We've lost so many." His voiced trailed off as he thought about all the people who had died. He felt overwhelmed. He hesitated to go on with more bad news. Even a life-long career in law enforcement had failed to harden his emotions and he had to choke back the lump in his throat.

Never one to be subtle, Sgt. Knight blurted out, "Do we know if Superintendent Briggs or Assistant Super Wellington made it?"

Anderson tried to hide his grief over losing his good friend Jon Briggs. "They didn't make it. If either one of them had survived they would have been here by now."

"Damn," Corporal Nelson lamented quietly.

"Doesn't seem fair," said Carlos. The sorrow in his voice validated what they all felt—both Briggs and Wellington were close to retirement.

Bringing them back to the task at hand, Captain Anderson motioned for everyone to take a seat around the map table. "I need ideas, gentlemen, and I need them fast."

Now that he was second-in-command, Carlos took the initiative. "Our first and foremost priority is to reestablish communications with the outside world. Then I think we focus on Corporal Steiger. So many have died already, we don't need to lose another one. The refugees are a lower priority. We can house them pretty well and if we ration the food we can get by for ten days or more. Getting the perimeter fences back up is necessary, but we can keep the inmates locked down until further notice. The nursing staff will just have to cope with Lucas. And then comes Toby Church." He moved his hand over the map, speaking deliberately, "Toby Church is our biggest problem."

"Go on?" encouraged Captain Anderson.

"Well, one of the reasons they put this prison out here was in case there was an escape. Everyone figured it would be damn hard to get very far without dying of hypothermia, starving, drowning, or getting lost in some nasty storm. But Church is a skilled outdoorsman. If anyone has a chance to make it out of here alive, it's him. But I still think we have a few hours to assemble the right team to hunt him down—he can't get too far in a day. Besides, it will take us several hours to get ready anyway." Carlos pushed back from the table and took a drink of coffee.

Sgt. Knight nodded in agreement, his blonde flattop haircut glistening in the artificial light. "I agree with the Lt. Banderas. We need to be sure of what we're doing before we go after Church. If we send the wrong people or go off half-cocked, we'll lose him."

"SS, this is medical," came the urgent call over the radio.

"Go for the SS," responded Anderson.

"Captain, we need you in the emergency room right away." It was Doreen Evers.

"I'm 10-19," answered Captain Anderson rising from his chair. As he headed out the door, he turned around and said, "Carlos, I want you three to come up with a plan to get us on our feet. Choose a team and figure out how to track down Toby Church. I'll expect to see your plan in writing in one hour." He exited his office, walking out of Main Control and down the corridor to the Medical Department.

"Captain," greeted a relieved Nurse Evers, "thank you for coming so quickly." She noticed his bloodshot eyes. Obviously, he'd been crying.

"Your welcome, what's up?" he said, trying to get his throat to loosen up. He couldn't get the image of Jon and Darlene Briggs out of his mind.

"I have a situation on my hands," she said, "as you know the doctor is missing and . . ."

Anderson could tell she was about to launch into one of her famous long-winded explanations. He cut her off before she could give him a blow-by-blow description of all the events since the quake. "Just get to the point Evers. I've got a lot of problems to solve in very little time."

By the way she glared at Anderson before continuing, it was clear he'd hurt her feelings. "Corporal Steiger is critically ill. X-rays show she's suffered a skull fracture. There is bleeding in the brain. If we don't get her to a surgeon within the next 24 hours, she will probably die."

"You know that we are cut off from the world," he snapped. He started pacing around the room to help ease some of the pressure he was feeling. "Just how am I supposed to get a doctor out here, or her to a doctor?"

"I don't know," Evers retorted bristling at his sarcastic tone. She didn't have any ideas either.

Anderson took a deep breath before speaking. He didn't want to alienate Evers too much. It wasn't her fault. "You'll just have to do the best you can." He headed for the door. But before he could exit, she delivered more bad news.

"Captain?"

"Yes, Evers, what is it now." He was getting angry. *Is it me? Or does she really sound like she's whining all the time?*

"Sorry to add to your burden, but Inmate Lucas is suffering from an acute appendicitis attack. If she doesn't get an appendectomy in the next 24 hours, she will probably die too."

Anderson suppressed the urge to yell, "Screw Lucas. Just deal with it." Instead he cursed, "Ah, for the love of God!" and ran his hand through his hair. "Okay, okay. I'll come up with something and get back to you in a little while." *Is there anything else that can go wrong today?*

Instead of returning to his office, Captain Anderson headed down the hallway. Walking helped him think. He needed to burn off some the stress. *What am I going to do?*

As Anderson walked back into Main Control, he was met by Corporal Nelson.

"Glad to see you're back Captain," Nelson said smiling.

Carlos motioned for Captain Anderson to take his seat. He was anxious to present their ideas. It had been an open, and at times volatile, debate. But in the end they had managed to sketch out a contingency plan, which they felt would handle all the challenges being faced by the officers of Malloy Super Max on this most tragic of April days.

Carlos passed a copy of the plan to Anderson, commenting, "I think we've come up with a fairly good plan. Instead of trying to prioritize each and every project, we decided that all of them needed to be addressed to some degree right now. We worked out a flow chart of the various priority projects and allocated resources to handle them. Take some time and read what we put down."

Anderson nodded his head in appreciation as he read down through the list.

A smiling Marc Anderson delivered some well-earned praise, "Good work fellas. I like it. Drinks are on me when we get out of this hell. But," he said leaning back in his chair, "we've got another problem to take care of."

"What's that?" Sgt. Knight asked, eyebrow cocked.

"Nurse Evers has just informed me that Corporal Steiger and Inmate Lucas are both in serious condition and without a doctor, neither of them will live much longer."

"For the love of Pete," blurted Corporal Nelson. He couldn't believe that so much could go wrong in one day.

Carlos was silent. He was trying to come up with an idea. Then it dawned on him. "Hey, Captain, why don't we have young Blaine Smith fly Steiger and Lucas over to Dutch Harbor? They have a small hospital and several doctors."

"Smith?" asked Anderson skeptically. Smith was the youngest officer at Malloy and Anderson wasn't sure he was up to such a dangerous mission.

"Yes," Carlos said confidently. From the first moment he'd met Blaine Smith he had been impressed with the young man's intelligence and drive.

"What will he fly? That 180 sitting next to the fence?" Sgt. Knight asked sarcastically. He really didn't believe the plane was airworthy after taking a saltwater bath.

Carlos nodded his head. "Yep, that's the one. I bet if we clean it up, it'll fly just fine."

"Are you sure?" Anderson asked Banderas firmly. The side windows were broken and there was seaweed hanging from the propeller, wings and landing gear.

"No, but what options do we have?"

Anderson had to admit that Banderas was right. He leaned back in his chair with arms folded over his chest and said to Sergeant Knight, "Well Bill, I guess you and I better get busy telling everyone the game plan."

"I imagine so."

Anderson exited his office and walked over to the public announcement booth located just to the left of the main control panel. He sat down in front of the remote closed-circuit camera. With a flick of a switch, his message was broadcast to television screens in every post, cell, and room in the facility.

Speaking calmly and deliberately, he announced he was instituting food rationing and ceasing all non-critical inmate movement. Father Androvsky would provide grief counseling to those in need.

To no one's surprise, there was grumbling among inmates about the suspension of their privileges. They were especially upset about the reduction in medication rounds. The officers ignored the bitching. They were used to prisoners complaining about being inconvenienced.

While Captain Anderson broadcast his message, Sergeant Knight visited each post. He ordered those officers working non-critical posts, to go to the exercise room for a shower and some sleep. They would be back on duty in 6 hours, when the new 12-hour rotation would begin. Next he visited the kitchen, where he briefed the food service staff about the food rationing. His final visit was with the maintenance workers, who he gave a list of projects to complete in the next three days.

After completing his prison broadcast, Marc Anderson returned to his office to implement the other pieces of the plan.

"Officer Blaine Smith, this is the SS. 10-5 my office in 15."

"Copy SS."

"Bravo Tower. 10-5 SS's office in 30 minutes."

"10-4," Ben Williams answered. His stomach turned over. *Am I in trouble for missing Toby Church?* He was still mad at himself. Ben prided himself on being the best shot in the department. All morning he'd been trying to figure out how he'd missed hitting Church with that last shot.

Blaine Smith wondered what Captain Anderson wanted with him. *I hope I'm not in trouble.* He couldn't think of anything he'd done wrong. This was only his third rotation.

Traversing the entire length of the prison took some time. Blaine hated waiting to be cleared through each gate by the post officer. When you were in a hurry, it was a real pain trying to get down the hallway. On the upside, it did give you time to think.

He was nervous. He couldn't imagine why Captain Anderson wanted to see him. He hadn't done anything wrong. Everyone told him that he had a bright future ahead of him in the department. He was the first officer to be assigned to Malloy Super Max with less than five years service.

Arriving outside Main Control, he looked up into the surveillance camera so the control room officer could clear him into the room. With a familiar "clunk, clack" the outer door latch popped open allowing him access to the sally port between the doors. He pulled the heavy solid-steel door open. It swung closed behind him with a loud metallic thunk. Once inside the sally port, the control room officer released another electronic door lock, allowing him into Main Control and Captain Anderson's office.

"Officer Smith reporting as ordered."

"Come in Smith," greeted Captain Anderson.

Lt. Banderas was sitting on the couch. Corporal Nelson and Nurse Evers were standing along the window looking into the control room. "What's up Captain? Am I in some kind of trouble?"

"No, no, no. Not at all," Anderson said reassuringly. "Have a seat next to Lt. Banderas. I want to ask you a couple of questions. I have a very important assignment for you."

"Go ahead sir, I'm ready to do whatever you need," Blaine replied without thinking.

Anderson smiled at the young man's enthusiasm. He reminded him of his youngest brother—the eager beaver of the family.

"I hear you have your private pilot's license?"

"Yes sir. Got it four years ago in Anchorage. Logged almost 150 hours now," Smith said with pride.

"Good, good. What kind of planes can you fly?"

"Well, I'm rated for single-engine land aircraft."

"Like a Cessna 180?"

"A tail-dragger?" Smith replied with some consternation. All his time had been in tricycle gear airplanes. Tail draggers were very different. He understood the theory, but the practice was another matter.

"I take it by your response that you've never flown a Cessna 180?" Anderson asked again with more authority. He cocked his head slightly to emphasize the question.

"No sir. I've never flown a tail-dragger, but I'm familiar with the principles."

Anderson noted Smith's less than confident reply and asked again, "Do you think you could fly a 180?"

"I believe so—yes." Smith could see the doubt in Captain Anderson's face. He didn't want to lose this chance to prove himself. "A Cessna is a Cessna sir. Once you've flown one, you've flown them all. I'm sure I can get it off the ground and back down again without killing anybody."

"We are going to have to have faith that your theory is pretty good. Do you know Corporal Joan Steiger?"

"Yes sir. Pretty well, matter of fact." Steiger had befriended Smith soon after his assignment to Malloy. He was young enough she didn't have to worry about him hitting on her, but old enough that hanging out with him wouldn't look queer.

"Nurse Evers is worried that Steiger will die from her head injury if we don't get her to a doctor. And if that's not enough, Inmate Jenne Lucas has appendicitis. She could die if we don't get her help too."

"What do you want me to do Captain?"

"I need you to apply your theory, grab your courage, and fly Nurse Evers and our two patients to Dutch Harbor."

Blaine Smith took a moment to think about the mission. This was a tall order. Flying in the Aleutians was dangerous. But he didn't have any doubts about his abilities. "You got it Captain. Where's the plane?" he said standing up.

"Sitting on the slopes of Mt. Moffet, right next to our perimeter fence," Carlos answered. "Ever do a tundra takeoff?"

Suddenly Blaine didn't feel so confident. "No sir, but it sounds like these ladies are dead if I don't get them off this rock. If we get off the ground, then they may live. And if we don't then nothing will have changed." He felt his stomach tighten. The risk he faced was beginning to sink in.

Captain Anderson rose from his chair. "Then it's decided. Officer Smith will lead the mission to save Corporal Steiger. Good luck," he said gripping the young officer by the shoulder and shaking his hand. "Get with Nurse Evers and make your plans. And remember that you are also responsible for making sure Lucas is kept in restraints in her hospital bed and for guarding her." As he led Smith out of his office, Anderson noticed just how young he really was.

"Officer Williams reporting as ordered."

"Come in Ben," said Carlos patting the chair next to him. "Have a seat." Carlos liked Ben. They had worked together almost 7 years. He trusted him.

Ben Williams had been with the department for over 26 years. He was an outstanding officer—solid, reliable, and calm. He made his decisions without consideration for promotion. Carlos never understood why this powerful, quiet, intelligent man never tried to make Sergeant.

And Ben never felt compelled to explain his reasons to anyone, including his wife and two children. His father had taught him that Tlingit warriors did not have to explain their reasons. He was happy with his life. His work as a Correctional Officer allowed him to earn a good living, spend time with his family, hunt in the fall, fish in the summer, teach his son the ways of the Tlingit people, and relax all by himself whenever he wanted. When you became a Sergeant or Lieutenant, you had to boss people around, do a lot of paperwork, and get called at home to answer stupid questions.

Carlos put his hand on Ben's shoulder, and looked into his eyes, "you okay after killing Jones?"

"Yeah, I'm fine. Terrible thing to have to kill a man, but I had to do my duty. Still angry I missed Church."

"Got your incident report written?" Anderson asked returning from the restroom.

"Yes sir. It's in your inbox," Ben replied pointing to the desk.

"Don't worry Ben," said a smiling Carlos, "we're going to give you another chance to stop Church."

"Good!" Ben exclaimed forcefully. He wanted a chance to redeem himself.

Pointing to the other officers in the room, Carlos continued, "You, me, and Corporal Nelson are going to hunt Mr. Church down. I want you and Nelson to get that remaining skiff set up with supplies, food, clothing, overnight gear, rifles, ammo, night vision goggles, and some of those Tlingit prayer beads of yours. Then we'll all sit down to go over possible routes he may have taken. We'll set out for him tomorrow morning."

"We're on it," Ben and Travis replied simultaneously. They exited the room. Ben was excited about getting another chance to nab Church. Travis was anxious. This was no drill.

Kuluk Bay, Alaska

While the officers of Malloy Super Max were putting the emergency plan into operation, Toby Church was carefully working his way due south across Kuluk Bay towards Little Tanaga Island.

He was trying to preserve his fuel by taking his time navigating between the small islands. Luckily for him the storm was subsiding. He was no longer fighting a headwind and the waves were no longer white capping.

To maximize his energy and conserve his food, he disciplined himself to take small bites of food every hour. He couldn't afford to waste supplies nor could he afford to become hypothermic. The survival suit he'd found in the skiff's footlocker was keeping him quite comfortable despite the biting ocean spray.

As he passed the Eastern shore of Little Tanaga Island, he swung his boat to the west and headed back towards the southern shore of Adak Island. Reasoning that the authorities would expect him to put as much distance as possible between him and them, Church was doing just the opposite. He was going to hide right under their noses just like an elk did when being pressed by hunters. Tomorrow at first light he would head west instead of east. But for right now, the South coast of Adak would be a good place to spend the night.

Watching seals and sea lions returning to shore was a reassuring sign that the danger of any more earthquakes or tsunamis was over.

Malloy Super Maximum-Security Prison, Adak Island, Alaska

It took a couple hours for Blaine and his helpers to clean the airplane and replace the side windows with plastic and duct tape. Seaweed had to be pulled from the flaps, the cabin, and the inside of the engine compartment. They had to use a blow dryer on the coil, distributor, the instruments, and the radio. After pouring water out of the carburetor, Blaine had wanted to change the oil just to be sure that no water had gotten inside the engine, but the tsunami had made sure that there wasn't any extra oil to be found among the debris. He would have to trust that everything would be okay.

As he prepared the aircraft for flight, he drained the water from the bottom of the fuel tanks until it ran blue into the test tube. Next he climbed up on a strut and checked the tanks. He had more than enough fuel to reach Dutch Harbor.

In order to get Nurse Evers and her two patients in the Cessna 180, they had to remove three of the four seats. Luckily, both Steiger and Lucas were small women. They could lie with their feet toward the narrower rear section of the cabin and still allow Nurse Evers room to kneel between them.

Blaine Smith was worried. He had never flown a Cessna 180 before. Compared to what he'd been flying in Anchorage, this plane was a dinosaur. It didn't even have a Global Positioning System (GPS) navigation system. It was only equipped with a compass and an Automatic Direction Finder (ADF). ADF's were so old that he'd never seen one outside of a book. If he got airborne, he would have to fly by compass in a region laced with large magnetic variations and notorious for poor visibility.

"You can do it," Blaine reassured himself. He read over the pre-flight checklist.

"What'd you say," asked Evers.

"I said we're gonna do it."

Pushing in the mixture, setting the brake, grabbing the throttle, and saying a little prayer, he turned the ignition key. Saltwater shot out of the exhaust as the engine coughed and wheezed before roaring to life. The entire airplane vibrated violently as the engine purged the seawater from its exhaust.

Blaine sighed with relief. He checked his gauges making sure he had oil pressure and that all the cylinders were working. He would have to trust the engine would hold out, because there was no place to do a full throttle engine check on this rocky hillside.

Slowly, he moved the throttle forward and released the brake. The airplane lurched ahead. Moments later, the plane was bouncing over small rocks and tufts of grass. This was the roughest takeoff he'd ever done. "Full throttle, move the yoke forward until the rear wheel is off the ground, apply neutral yoke, gain airspeed, and pull back on the stick," he said, talking himself through the procedures.

He prayed as he pulled back on the stick. Instead of becoming airborne, however, the plane bounced into the air and back down to the ground. A sickening feeling washed over him. The payload was too heavy and there wasn't enough room to stop. He could see a ditch up ahead. They weren't going to make it! Blaine made a desperate decision. He applied full flaps. Suddenly the plane jumped into the air. Cheering and arm waving erupted among the small group on the ground—a small victory in a day of defeats. He smiled over his shoulder at Evers.

Turning east, he set course for Dutch Harbor. Blaine's adventure had just begun. Now he had to navigate across 450 miles of the North Pacific in some of the most dangerous flying conditions in the world.

Karluk River Valley, Kodiak Island, Alaska

Ivan Lincoln was walking just behind his hostages as they moved inland along the grass and gravel strewn valley floor. He was intent on reaching the mountains looming in the distance before dark.

Lincoln was relying on the skills first learned as a boy in the wilds of the Alaskan Interior. He knew how to live off the land and how to avoid detection in the wilderness. For him, freedom was living in the wilderness. Unlike most people, who would follow a river or a creek to the shore and locate a town, Lincoln planned to disappear deep into the rugged mountains of what he believed was the Alaska Peninsula. The constant rain and large population of game would make it impossible for the police to use dogs to track his scent. And once secure in a hideout, he would formulate plans for making his way to an even more remote location—somewhere they would never find him.

Joy Frank and Elizabeth LeDue, only weeks removed from the hustle and bustle of the Eastern United States, tried to keep up the pace. They were out of shape and completely out of their element.

Even though Joy had come north to challenge the wilderness, this was not what she had in mind. The mountains towering in the distance no longer looked inviting and peaceful. They represented toil and hardship. The romanticism of experiencing the raw power of nature had lost its allure. She longed for the comfort of her Connecticut home with its crackling fireplace, welcoming hardwood floors, and comfortable quilts.

Elizabeth had always hated the outdoors. The cold biting wind sweeping down the valley only served to remind her of how much she hated being outside. Outside was for hippies, beggars, and elitists, who didn't have a real job. To fight off her misery, she turned her thoughts to happier days—when she had been the center of attention in the biology department. Memories of the dinners, the stimulating conversation, and the warm fires in cozy New England homes came flashing back.

Hours passed as they trekked along the banks of the rain-swollen Karluk River.

Joy was thinking of a way to escape from this hell into which she had suddenly been thrust. She recalled her mother saying, "You're a strong girl, with a good head on your shoulders. Be brave, trust your instincts, and don't be afraid to come home." Her chest felt heavy. She missed her family, she missed her friends, she even missed her biology class at college. She wondered whether she'd live through this ordeal. *Will I ever see Joseph again?*

After being locked in a cell for 22-months, Elizabeth was completely soft. She was growing more weary with each passing mile. She was sweating and her heart was pounding. She had to concentrate on every step to keep from falling down. The melting snow had soaked her shoes, and despite the exertion, her feet were numb from the cold. Pulling her feet out of the sucking mud and snowdrifts was exhausting. She slipped on yet another mossy rock, falling face first into the mud.

"Get up!" Lincoln shouted. Shoving Joy aside, he grabbed Elizabeth by the hair and jerked her to her feet. "Get up! You worthless Bitch! I oughta just fucking kill you right here and now!"

"I can't," wheezed Elizabeth. "I have to rest. My feet are frozen, I'm cold, I'm hungry." She didn't care if he killed her. She was too exhausted to go on.

Lincoln shoved the barrel of the pistol into her temple and said, "Start moving, Bitch or all they'll find is a corpse."

Somehow Elizabeth found the strength to start walking again. She wasn't ready to die. Her legs trembled at the effort, but one thing Elizabeth LeDue did have was willpower.

Joy knew they were in deep trouble as she watched Lincoln hold the gun to Elizabeth's head. But somehow she knew he wasn't ready to kill them. The delight registering on his face told her he was hatching some horrific plan. She didn't plan on asking. Instead she kept thinking about how to escape.

F/V Neptune, Shelikof Straits, Alaska

Captain Lind steered the F/V Neptune around Harvester Island and into Uyak Bay. In a few miles they would turn into Larsen Bay and land at the small community bearing the same name.

Joseph was still trying to raise the Coast Guard on the radio.

Coffee cups in hand, Harry and Danny were studying maps of the area.

Harry had a plan to recapture the convicts. "Lincoln knows how to survive in the woods," Harry said in a whisper, without looking up from the map. "If he hasn't killed the women already, they should slow him down." Harry knew he had to anticipate Lincoln's moves. Harry closed his eyes thinking of the time he'd been with his father tracking a Polar Bear. "Remember son," his father had said, "the bear is a ruthless hunter. The bear knows that we are hunting him and will wait for us in the snow. He is not afraid. He knows how to hide and how to stalk his prey. If we do not respect the bear, we will become the hunted." Harry opened his eyes and smiled. He would not forget to respect Lincoln's ability to survive the hunt.

"If he stays true to form, he'll move deep into the mountains and try to disappear," Danny said.

"If he's going to disappear into the wilderness, why did he kidnap Joy and take that other woman?" Joseph asked. It wasn't logical for someone trying to escape to drag along hostages.

How could they tell this young man that the girl he loved was in grave danger? Harry and Danny looked at each other, waiting to see who would answer this most difficult question. Danny was the first one to come up with an answer. "He might figure we'd be right on his tail so he'll want hostages if he has to negotiate." Danny didn't like lying, but he didn't have the heart to tell Joseph the truth about Lincoln.

"Oh, well, yeah, that makes sense," Joseph replied. He didn't quite buy this story, but he wanted to believe it, so he let the matter drop. He let his mind wander back to the day when he first saw Joy step out of the airplane at the airport in Kenai. *She was so beautiful.* The moment he saw her, he felt attracted to her. She had a friendly smile. She was not particularly curvy, but she did have a long, slender body. Naturally shy, he had avoided approaching her directly. Instead, when his father asked him if he wanted to teach Joy about her duties, he jumped at the chance. Roger was more experienced and probably a better teacher, but Alfred Lind was not blind. He could see the attraction was mutual.

Harry and Danny sighed with relief when the younger Lind didn't probe any further. They didn't have the heart to tell either Lind that Ivan Lincoln was a cold, calculating killer.

"What the hell?" said Captain Lind. *Why are we slowing down?* He pushed the throttles all the way forward. The Neptune's propeller churned the sea into foam.

As the Neptune moved backward everyone ran to the side of the boat to look over the side. The waters of Uyak Bay were retreating towards Shelikof Straits like a river flowing to the sea.

"I've never seen a tide this hard before," said a puzzled Captain Lind. He backed off the throttle to ease the strain on the engines.

Danny asked the question that was in everyone's mind. "Would a tsunami make the water leave the bay?"

Everyone knew he was right. No one said anything. They braced themselves for what they believed would be a giant wave. Luckily for them, Danny was only partially right.

As the main tsunami wave raced northeast up Shelikof Strait, centrifugal forces were pulling the waters of Uyak Bay out, making the tide run harder than normal. Fortunately, Uyak Bay sits perpendicular to Shelikof Straits. The tsunami never entered the protected waters. A stroke of geographic luck had spared Larsen Bay and the Neptune.

Within a few minutes the waters had calmed down and the Neptune continued towards Larsen Bay.

"Harry?" asked Danny.

"Yeah?" Harry replied. Danny's habit of always asking questions never ceased to amuse Harry.

"Do you think Lincoln will try to stick to the shore and find a town?"

"It wouldn't be like him," Harry replied trying to figure out where Danny was going with this thought. "Why? What're you thinking?"

Danny threw out his idea. "Lincoln is pretty smart. He knows we know he's a skilled outdoorsman. He might figure we'll begin searching for him in the interior of the island. He might think he can fool us by doing the opposite of his pattern and head to shore."

"Interesting," Harry said, "but I think we shouldn't try to outsmart ourselves. Lincoln is an Athabaskan. He's not used to the ocean or beaches. He probably doesn't even know he's on an island. My guess is that he's planning to disappear into the wilderness."

"What makes you think that," Joseph scoffed. He had been following their conversation closely and was frustrated at not being invited to join the rescue team.

Harry answered sharply. "A Polar Bear never wanders far from the ocean. He doesn't go to Anchorage to hunt." Harry's outburst was uncharacteristic. Danny looked at him hard.

Harry turned back to his maps. "I think he'll try to move into the high country so he can get a better view of the terrain. Once he does that, he'll head for the forests on the eastern shores." The thought of having to track this madman was wearing on Harry's nerves.

"Forests?" asked Danny. He wasn't sure why that was important.

"Yes, forest. Remember he's an Athabaskan," Harry said curtly.

Danny nodded in agreement. That made perfect sense. Ivan Lincoln would seek out the terrain in which he was most comfortable. Danny was betting that Harry's life on the treeless North Slope would even the odds with Lincoln—if they could catch him before he made it to the forested eastern side of Kodiak. But by the stern look on Harry's face, Danny could tell that Harry was worried about their chances of success.

Harry looked up at Danny, running his finger along the map of the Karluk River Valley. "He'll head up the valley to Karluk Lake and then cut up over the mountains. He'll head east in the expectation of finding forest." He thumped his finger down on the blue color denoting Karluk Lake. "We'll move 16-hours a day and catch him before he can get over the mountains. The women will slow him down. That's our advantage."

The Neptune's passengers were shocked at what they saw as the boat pulled alongside the remains of the collapsed pier. Larsen Bay lay in ruins. The town was empty. Everyone had run to higher ground when the tsunami warning sirens had sounded. Several dogs were barking and jumping at the ends of their chains.

After unloading their gear, Harry and Danny bid farewell to Captain Lind and his son. Joseph was struggling with his emotions. His heart was divided between concern for his mother and siblings and those for Joy. *Should I return to Homer or should try one more time to talk Harry and Danny into taking me along?*

"Dad," he pleaded, "I know Joy. She'll be scared."

Alfred Lind understood his son's feelings. He also understood the impulsive nature of young men. He listened patiently to his son's arguments as to why he should accompany Harry and Danny on the manhunt. "I understand your concerns Joseph, but I need your help getting the Neptune back to Homer. And besides, I don't think these two gentlemen need you tagging along."

Overhearing their discussion, Harry took the initiative. He walked over to the Neptune. "Young man," he said with authority, "I understand your concern over Ms. Frank, but in all honesty, this is an official operation. I cannot allow you to come with us."

"But," Joseph began to argue.

Harry cut him off before he could launch into a debate. "No," he said holding up his hand, "this is not open to discussion. PTO Sanders and I are trained for this kind of work. I give you my word that we will bring Ms. Frank back to you safe and sound. Your father needs you in Homer and we need to get to work."

Harry pivoted smartly, walking away before Joseph could muster another argument. He smiled at the young man's devotion to this young woman. It was obvious he loved her. Harry intended to keep his promise. He hadn't been there for his brother and sister—he didn't intend to let another mother grieve over a child.

Throwing their gear over their shoulders, Harry and Danny started walking through the shattered remains of Larsen Bay. Several miles to the west lay the Karluk River Valley.

"Watch out for bears," shouted Alfred.

Harry put his hand to his ear shouting back, "What did you say?"

Cupping his hands to his mouth, Alfred repeated his warning, "Watch out for bears! It's about time for them to be coming out of their dens. And they'll be hungry and aggressive!"

"Thanks!" Harry shouted waving goodbye. "You know Danny, he's right."

"I forgot it's time for them to come out of their dens," Danny answered.

Anyone who'd lived in Alaska for any length of time knew that Kodiak Brown Bears were the largest and most aggressive species of grizzly bear in North America.

Harry and Danny would have to stay on their guard all the time. They would have to sleep in shifts and move slower than expected. This was no time to be surprised by a hungry grizzly bear.

Karluk River Valley, Kodiak Island, Alaska

Traveling with two hostages was slowing Lincoln down. After walking all day, they had only covered 17 miles. Their slow pace made him angry. If he'd been alone, he probably would have covered twice that distance. Daylight was fading. They would have to stop at the base of the 2,000-foot mountains on the southwest shore of Karluk Lake.

"We'll stop here for the night," Lincoln said, motioning for Joy and Elizabeth to put the driftwood down next to a large alder tree.

The women dropped the wood and slumped to the ground—totally exhausted from the day's march.

Elizabeth's feet were frozen. She pulled off her prison issued tennis shoes and socks. Her toes were blue from the cold. They ached. She rubbed them, ignoring the burning, tingling pain of the blood rushing back into her frozen feet. Her hands hurt from crashing into stones whenever she had lost her footing during the muddy march. Her thigh muscles were cramping from too much exercise and no water. Adding to her exhaustion was her fear of the night to come. All day long she'd listened to Lincoln ranting about being railroaded by the criminal justice system and how women were evil. Shudders ran up her spine when he talked about his crimes.

Joy had never been so tired or so afraid. She struggled to unpack the food. She was too tired to run. Now was the perfect opportunity. Lincoln was busy cutting willow branches and pulling up grass for a bed. But she was simply too exhausted to try. Her teeth chattered and her body shook from being so cold. Like Elizabeth, she was dreading the night.

Lincoln watched the women out of the corner of his eye. *They are probably planning an escape. That's the problem with women—they're always trying to deceive you. It doesn't matter whether it's your mother standing by while your uncles rape you or your girlfriend sleeping with your buddies for a swig off the bottle. Women are evil.* He found satisfaction in making them suffer.

Lincoln decided to use Elizabeth for his evening's activities. She was older and less likely to survive the grueling pace. *I'll have to kill her first,* he decided with finality. She was pretty and the transport officers called her Doctor, so she had to be educated. She represented the worst of the female race—pretty, smart, and criminal.

He walked over to Joy and Elizabeth, threw down the grass and willow branches, and told them on how to make a bed. "Put down these branches and then spread a layer of grass over them. It will get you off the ground and provide some insulation." He loved to get his victims to drop their guard. Being nice would confuse them.

As he walked away, he pulled out the small hatchet and dug a shallow depression in the ground. Next, he shaved small pieces off the driftwood the women had carried from the beach. Using some paper and a match, he lit a small fire. He sat down on a rock motioning for the two women to come closer to the fire.

Joy and Elizabeth scurried over to the flames, extending their hands and feet to absorb the warmth. Lincoln opened the rations. He tossed a few morsels in their direction, watching in satisfaction as his captives lost heart at the small portions.

Despite the meager portions, they divided the food equally. Hungrily, they devoured their shares. Lincoln, however, knew better. He ate his food slowly, giving it time to fill his stomach. He heated some water in a tin cup and drank the hot liquid. It would help keep him warm during the long night.

Looking up at Lincoln, Joy asked, "I've got to go to the bathroom. Is it okay if I go over there?" She pointed to a hill about 25 feet away.

A shiver shot down her spine as she looked into his cold eyes. "Sure," he said with a grin, "but first I'm going to tie your legs so you can't run."

"I won't run, I promise."

"My way or no way," he replied pulling a piece of rope from a bag.

Resigning herself to the situation, Joy sat down and let Lincoln hobble her. She struggled to her feet and shuffled over to the rocks to relieve herself.

While Joy was away from the camp, Lincoln bound Elizabeth. Tying her hands behind her and her feet together, he cinched the ropes tightly, cutting off the circulation. She pleaded for him to stop. He ignored her pleas. Grabbing her by the legs, he dragged her over to her bed of willow branches. Flipping her onto her stomach, he completed his work by hogtying her hands and feet behind her back.

Joy watched Lincoln bind LeDue. She froze in place when he grabbed another piece of rope and headed towards her. "What are you going to do?" she pleaded. There was no reply.

Without saying a word, he spun her around, tying her hands behind her back. Pushing her down, he dragged her over to her sleeping place. The rough, wet terrain scratched her stomach and chest. The stinging caused by the scraping was soothed by the wet mud soaking her shirt front. Pulling her legs up into the air, he hogtied her just as he had done Elizabeth. The ropes burned as they dug into her flesh. She could feel her fingers and toes growing numb. As a final insult, Lincoln reached down, grabbed her by the crotch and squeezed while shoving the material of her panties into her vagina with his finger. Joy bit her lip as he fondled her through her pants. Then suddenly, he stopped, got up and walked away.

East Side, Karluk River Valley, Kodiak Island, Alaska

All through the day, Harry and Danny had been working their way up the east side of the Karluk River Valley. Harry had been unable to pick up any sign of Lincoln's group. In the marshy terrain, it would have been pretty easy to see footprints or other marks made by three people. "I'm wondering if they're on the other side of the river?" he said, looking across the rain-swollen torrent.

"Could be," Danny replied. "We've been moving all day in this terrible slush and muck. Surely they would have left some sign." Danny had done enough hunting near his home on Moose Pass to know how to spot footprints.

Harry stared at the river, trying to figure out a way to get across. His instincts told him they were getting close. *Lincoln will be following the river.* But with evening approaching, it was too late to attempt a crossing. "Let's put up camp for the night," he suggested, propping his rifle against a tree and sitting down on a rock.

"Sounds good to me," sighed Danny. He was exhausted, not only from hiking in a zigzag pattern across the valley all day, but also from surviving that horrible plane crash.

As he unloaded his gear, Danny asked, "who's got the first watch?"

"You take first watch. I'll take second watch in four hours," ordered Harry. He cut some willow branches for a bed. It was important to stay off the cold ground. Spreading out his poncho, he curled up on the cushiony bed and drifted off to sleep.

Amukta Pass, Aleutian Islands, Alaska

Since intercepting the distress call from Malloy 1, the USS Billings had been running at flank speed through the cold, rolling waters of the Bering Sea on a course for the Gulf of Alaska. Ocean spray was flying over the ship's superstructure as the Billings' clipper bow cut a frothy swath through the dark waters. Below decks, sailors fought to keep from being thrown from their bunks as they tried to get some sleep before returning to duty.

Commander Englemann was meeting with her officers in the Ward Room. They were upset over her decision not to launch a rescue for the downed Seahawk. "I know you're all upset that we haven't launched a rescue for the crew of Hawk One. However, we are on a priority mission—a matter of national security. I cannot send the second Seahawk to search for wreckage and risk losing it or losing precious time."

She pounded her fist into her other hand and said, "We must catch that sub! We cannot let the Russians get their hands on Dr. Elizabeth LeDue." The mission to stop the Russians was their priority. Commander Englemann knew that the families of the downed airmen would be upset that she hadn't launched an immediate rescue. This was something she was willing to face. It was part of being in command. She might even end up being the scapegoat for the Navy. But if the mission failed, United States's national security would be seriously compromised.

"*The* Elizabeth LeDue?" an officer exclaimed.

"The very same," replied Lt. Commander Hastings.

Her junior officers were taken by surprise. Until now, none of them had known this information. All they had known was that they were on a very covert operation to intercept a Russian submarine.

She continued her briefing. "We have to get within range of that Akula. Then we'll launch Hawk Two with Lt. Surin's team to fly over the last known location of Dr. LeDue's transport. If there are survivors, they will initiate a rescue. If no survivors are found, Hawk Two will conduct an area-wide sweep and put Surin's team onto Kodiak Island."

Raising his voice above the din, Lt. Surin interjected, "if Dr. LeDue has survived, my men will find her. Then we can go back and rescue Chu, Allen, and Murphy."

Someone asked, "And what if the Russians get her before we do?"

"My orders are to sink the submarine," Englemann replied flatly.

Startled glances were exchanged between the officers. Now they finally understood the gravity of the situation.

"Meeting adjourned, gentlemen. Return to your stations. The information about Dr. LeDue is classified, but I want your men to know this is not some glorified drill."

As the officers filed out of the room, she touched the young Ensign lightly on the shoulder, signaling for him to remain behind. Closing the door, she said quietly, "Mister Merriwether."

"Yes Skipper," he responded nervously.

"I need you to send a priority message to Lt. General McCarthy at Elmendorf Air Force Base in Anchorage. Give him the last known coordinates of Malloy 1 and ask him to launch an air search."

"But Skipper, that means we'll have to break radio silence. It's against orders," the Ensign whispered loudly.

"I know that Ensign," she said staring at the young officer, "but don't you think with all that's happened in the last 10 hours, radio silence is the least of our worries? Besides, it might be to our advantage if the Russians know we're on their tail. Might make em' nervous." Her confident smile let him know she was fully aware of what she was doing. With a wave of her hand, she sent him to do her bidding.

"Margaret," she said to herself, "you'd better be right on this one."

Returning to her cabin, Commander Englemann removed her khaki shirt and splashed water on her face. She brushed her teeth, combed her hair, and donned a clean uniform. With one last check in the mirror she headed back to the bridge. In a world dominated by men, she had learned that not only did her performance have to be superior, but at all times she needed to look more composed too.

Arriving on the bridge, she summoned the Engineering Officer.

"Lieutenant," she said, "what's the status on the repairs to the ship following that hellish wind that hit us?"

The Lieutenant replied thoughtfully, "Well, Skipper, the starboard radar array is a mess. My men have already replaced most of the damaged wiring. And with some creative bypassing on my part, I've got the radar operational, although ghosts do appear on the displays. We were lucky to be heading almost directly into that wind when it hit."

"Any other damage?"

"Just the nerves of the crew, Skipper."

His comment made her curious. Leaning over her armrest, she asked, "What do you mean?"

Pursing his lips, he spoke his mind. "That wind that hit us was nothing like I've ever seen Skipper." He looked around to see if anyone was eavesdropping. He leaned closer to Englemann and whispered, "That wind looked just like those winds caused by a nuclear explosion. Matter of fact, scuttlebutt has it that a nuke went off somewhere near here."

Englemann leaned back in her chair and shook her head. "No Lieutenant, that was no nuclear blast. Intelligence reports a volcano on Umnak Island exploded. What hit us was the blast wave from that eruption."

"I'll be damned," he replied shaking his head in disbelief. "Mind if I say something Skipper?"

"Go ahead."

"I think it might be a good idea if you let the whole crew know about that volcano."

"Good idea. I'll brief the crew. You make sure this ship holds together. I need her to make top speed for the next 25 hours."

The officer turned smartly and exited the bridge and headed for the engineering section.

Englemann followed him off the bridge. She was going to the Combat Information Center and inform the crew about the eruption on Unmak Island.

Inside Hawk Two's cockpit, Lt. Cowdrey was reading over his pre-flight checklist, making sure everything was in order. He'd just lost two good friends in a freak storm. He didn't want to lose any more.

The side door slid open. Lt. Surin's team loaded their gear into the helicopter. The crew chief helped them stow their supplies. It was rough work on the rolling and pitching deck, but everyone was glad to be busy. It had been a bizarre day. Hopes were running high that life would soon return to normal.

Entering the bridge, the Ensign called out excitedly, "Skipper?" He was holding a note in his hand.

"Yes, Ensign, what is it?"

He held out the note. "We've received a reply from General McCarthy."

TO: USS BILLINGS
FR: LT. GEN. MCCARTHY, ALASKA COMMAND

MESSAGE RECEIVED. COPY COORDINATES OF MALLOY 1. AREA DEVASTATED. UNABLE TO LAUNCH PATROL FOR SEVERAL HOURS. COAST GUARD STATION KODIAK DESTROYED. CINC WARNS INTRUDER IN THE AREA. KEEP ME ADVISED.

She handed the message to Commander Hastings, closed her eyes, and pinched the bridge of her nose to subdue her frustration. "We're on our own for the next few hours, Brad," she said with resignation. She had been hoping the Air Force would be able to give her a jump on the Russians by telling her if there were survivors in the water.

Hastings frowned too. "Sounds like the whole state got pounded. Anchorage must be a mess if they can't send us a C-130 to patrol the area."

"Anything else Skipper?" the Ensign asked. He was waiting to be dismissed.

"No," she said shooing him away. "Helm, what's our speed?"

"31-knots, Skipper."

Englemann stood up and turned command over to Hastings. "Brad, you have the bridge. I'm going to my cabin."

South of Whalebone Cape, Unalaska Island, Alaska

Igor Ivanshenko strummed his fingers on the chart table in frustration. Having to sail southwest through Samalga Pass was costing him precious time. But it was the only way he could obey his orders. Admiral Voroshilov had made it quite clear. Under no circumstances was he to risk being seen by anyone. This included fishing boats and beachcombers. Samalga Pass was the only route in the area without any villages on the coast. Adding to Ivanshenko's stress was the fact that somewhere out there an American submarine was still searching for him. If the Americans managed to intercept him again, the game would be up. There wouldn't be enough time for him to dash back out to the Aleutians Trench to elude the Americans one more time.

Even though he had managed to shake off the Americans, he was still nervous. These were unfamiliar waters and he was having to rely on the Putin's inertial navigation system and sonar to avoid running aground. Running aground was the one thing Ivanshenko feared most. His dreams were haunted by visions of being grounded at a depth not deep enough to crush the hull, but too deep for the men to escape without a rescue submarine. Yes, he feared a long, excruciating death of cold and suffocation. Too often of late he had bolted upright from his bed bathed in sweat after dreaming about being trapped in his escape suit, unable to breath, the crushing weight of the ocean's depths squeezing his chest. While not a superstitious man, he wasn't so sure that such vivid dreams could be discounted offhand. He knew of too many people who had dreamed something before it happened. These dreams always seemed to be in color and were very realistic—just like his.

Ivanshenko knew that he couldn't let his fears control his actions. His men were depending on him. Looking around the control room, he watched each sailor concentrating on his respective tasks. He wiped the sweat from his brow, cleared his mind of these troubling thoughts, and walked back over to the sonar station.

The sonar man was complaining about all the background noise obscuring the readings as they sailed farther into the pass. The noise was so continuous and loud that the sonarman said it was impossible to make an accurate sounding.

Ivanshenko took the headphones from the sonarman and listened to the rumbling and grinding and roaring noises that poured in over the sonar system. His attempts to filter out the noise were futile. The sonarman was right. There was too much background noise to make the sonar useful.

He handed the headphones back to the sonarman and ordered the helm to bring the Putin up to periscope depth. If he couldn't sound his way through the channel, he would have to risk running on the surface.

Ivanshenko surveyed the surrounding waters through the periscope. Pulling back from the lenses, he rubbed his eyes. He'd never seen anything like it. Shaking his head, he put his face back to the periscope.

To the northeast he could see a huge pillar of volcanic smoke and ash billowing into the overcast sky. Even though it was midday, it was dark. Molten rivers of lava were running down the slopes of the jagged remains of the Umnak Island, casting an eerie red glow on the base of the clouds. Molten rock was pouring into the sea, making it boil. Great clouds of steam rose into the sky. Igor Ivanshenko had seen many things in his years at sea, but nothing like this.

Summoning Lt. Commander Vatutin and Major Golkin to the periscope, he urged them to take a look at this incredible display of nature. The first thought Golkin had peering through the lens was of Dante's Inferno. Vatutin shuddered at the thought of what must have happened to the island's residents.

The Putin's men understood what it was like to live in a volcano's shadow. The naval base at Petropavlovsk sits in the shadow of a volcano.

Even though he was awestruck by what he saw, Commander Ivanshenko did not stop to gawk at the sights. He didn't have time. He wanted to get to the crash site before everyone else. Slowly he walked around in a circle, peering at the outside world through the magnified lens of the periscope. There were no surface contacts.

Figuring that this massive eruption would blind any spy satellite and ground all aircraft, Ivanshenko ordered the Putin to the surface.

"Commander," the radioman called out walking over from his communications panel, "we've intercepted a message from a US Navy ship."

Ivanshenko held out his hand. He sipped his coffee as he read the intercepted communication between the Billings and Lt. General McCarthy.

"Vatutin, come over here," he said putting down his coffee cup.

Ivanshenko handed him the message. "Looks like the US Navy is out and about. Look up the USS Billings. Triangulate their position and tell me what we're facing?"

Lt. Commander Vatutin read the message. Pulling out his vessel identification references, he scanned the section on the US Navy. It only took a few minutes for him to find information on the USS Billings.

"Commander," he said reading from the book, "the Billings is a Fast Frigate, Anti-submarine warfare vessel. 4,100 tons, 445 feet long, capable of 30 knots. Two SH-60 Seahawk helicopters, rapid fire 5-inch cannon, Phalanx Anti-missile Gatling Gun, and Mark 46 torpedoes."

"SH-60 Seahawks?" said a troubled Ivanshenko. He didn't like this news. "What type of torpedoes are they carrying?"

"They are equipped to carry either the Mark 48 or the new Mark 50, with a speed of over 40 knots."

Ivanshenko whistled. They would be put to the test if the Billings located them. Matters were getting complicated. *Do the Americans know about our plans?* Being tailed coming out of Petropavlovsk was normal. But having the Billings in the area was more than coincidence. *Did I really manage to shake the American submarine? Or are we being driven into a trap? Does Admiral Voroshilov know about the American frigate? Surely he would know about the crash of the American transport by now? Is Moscow trying to issue a recall order?* There was no way to tell. He couldn't risk sending a message. If it were intercepted, he would give away his position.

Daring to ask the obvious, a junior officer piped up, "Commander?"

"Yes Lieutenant?"

"What will the Americans do if they find us?"

Now was not the time to tell the whole truth. Ivanshenko lied. "Hard to say. They may just shadow us. They may try to keep us from surfacing. The only sure thing is that they will harass us and try to drive us out into the Gulf of Alaska." He didn't want to frighten the young Lieutenant. He wasn't so sure the Americans wouldn't sink them.

Ivanshenko gave the young man an assignment. "Lieutenant, go forward and make sure our torpedoes are in working order."

Picking up the intercom phone, Ivanshenko ordered his engineering officer to bring the reactors to 110 percent. He needed to widen the gap between the Putin and the USS Billings. By his calculations, the Americans were only four or five hours behind. This was a race for a great prize. Igor Ivanshenko had no intention of losing it.

Swallowing hard, he accepted the inevitable fact that the Americans knew about their plans. He ordered the Putin to dive. He had to risk running aground. The chances of being spotted running on the surface were too great.

Pacific Fleet Headquarters, Vladivostok, Russia

Admiral Voroshilov inhaled deeply on his cigarette as he waited nervously for the arrival of General Chuchenko. *Chuchenko must have very important information. Otherwise the message would have been sent via teletype or courier.* The fact that the information was being personally delivered by the head of the Air Force in the Far East was a portent of bad news.

Voroshilov looked out his office window at the dark waters of the bay. The lights of the harbor and city reflected off the gentle waves. Normally, he loved his job. But at times like these he hated it.

He watched the Chaika limousine pull up in the front of the building before going over to the cabinet to pour a couple cups of hot steaming coffee. It was far too late at night to be dealing with such momentous issues. They needed to keep their wits about them. He pressed out his cigarette in the ashtray and waved the smoke away.

"Welcome General. It's good to see you again," greeted Admiral Voroshilov extending his hand. In traditional fashion, he kissed his good friend on the side of the face.

"You too Valentii," replied General Chuchenko.

"So what brings you to my office at so late an hour? You should be home with mama snuggling in bed."

General Chuchenko opened his briefcase and handed over the report from his intelligence section. "We just picked this up from American radio traffic in Alaska."

As he read the note, Voroshilov's hand began to shake so much he was forced to put down his cup of coffee. With each passing sentence, the crease between his eyebrows grew deeper and the corners of his mouth turned further down. He rubbed his arthritic elbow out of habit.

Watching and waiting for his comrade to finish reading the communiqué, General Chuchenko stated the obvious, "This is most disturbing news. The American transport has crashed somewhere near Kodiak Island, deep in the heart of American territory. And we have been unable to communicate with the Putin."

"I can see that, Georgii," Voroshilov replied more testily than he intended. He smiled to take the edge off his abrupt reply. He walked over to the map on the wall and plotted the last known position of the Putin and the reported location of the American transport. "If I know Ivanshenko, he intercepted this distress call while waiting for the rendezvous. Since we haven't heard from him, I must presume he is heading to the crash site right now."

A look of disbelief washed over General Chuchenko's leathery face. "Surely, Commander Ivanshenko would not be so foolhardy?"

Seeing the look on his old friend's face, Voroshilov explained, "Think about it Georgii. Ivanshenko's orders are to capture the American scientist after a plane crash. He will not differentiate between the GRU's orchestrated plane crash and the real thing. He will simply conclude that his orders stand and proceed to the crash site. I trained this man. My guess is that right now he is making his way into the Gulf of Alaska. Once he gets into deeper water, he will turn east and make a hard run to Kodiak Island."

"There's something else you should know, Valentii," Chuchenko added sullenly.

"Yes?" Voroshilov asked raising an eyebrow suspiciously.

"Our satellites have picked up an American warship in the area. We presume she is making way for the crash site too. If our intelligence is correct, then Ivanshenko may have more to deal with than just an American scientist." He passed over a satellite photo of the Billings.

Admiral Voroshilov lit up another cigarette as he pondered this new information. Staring at the map, he made some quick calculations in his head. At top speed, the American warship was about four hours behind the Putin. Smiling with a confidence he truly didn't feel, he said, "If my calculations are correct, the Putin will be on station long before the American warship can reach the crash site. By the time the Americans arrive, Ivanshenko will have searched the area. He will either have Dr. LeDue in his possession or will have discovered she is dead."

Georgii Chuchenko had known Valentii Voroshilov far too long to doubt his friend's calculations. But this affair wasn't just about calculations. Ivanshenko was brilliant, but even he couldn't overcome impossible odds. He took a deep breath before breeching the most uncomfortable of subjects. "Do you think we should inform Moscow of this information?"

That is a serious question, Voroshilov thought for a moment. He recalled how poorly Admiral Bulgakov took bad news and this news would send those rats at High Command scurrying for political cover. Most likely it would be him and his long-time colleague Georgii Chuckenko who would pay the price for this fiasco. Even their friendship with Prime Minister Kirov would not guarantee their safety. Given the enormity of this gamble he had no doubts they would be offered up as a sacrifice to the public to deflect criticism of the High Command. And in Russia, scapegoats could still face a firing squad.

Many times he and General Chuckenko had faced danger together on the river systems of North Vietnam. But this type of danger was very different. This type was like a silent poisonous spider biting you in your sleep. The results were the same, but there was no honor in a poisonous death.

For the next hour, the two veterans discussed the merits of whether or not to inform Moscow about the crash of the American transport. Without knowing exactly what Commander Ivanshenko was doing, it was impossible to predict all the variables. Informing

Moscow of these developments ran the risk of compromising not only the secrecy of the mission, but also the Prime Minister's ability to deny any knowledge of the operation if things went wrong. American listening posts and communication spy satellites constantly monitored their communications. The only sure way to inform the Kremlin without compromising the mission's secrecy was for one of them to fly to Moscow and brief the PM in person. But the departure of a senior officer to Moscow so close to the disaster might tip off the CIA that Dr. LeDue was their target. It was too early to get the High Command involved. Besides, with the Putin submerged, there was no way to abort the mission. Better to wait for a little while and see if the bold and daring Ivanshenko could pull off another covert operation right under the Americans' noses.

Raising snifters of cognac, both men toasted their country and prayed their luck would hold. If not, their careers, and maybe even their lives, would be in jeopardy.

Governor's Office, Juneau, Alaska

The call from the president had been delayed for several hours. Things in Washington were hectic. The Great Aleutian Earthquake was making work for President Bainbridge on several fronts. The Joint Chiefs of Staff were pressing him to expand the military operation to recapture Dr. LeDue. Calls were pouring in from civil defense authorities all over the West Coast as reports of approaching tsunamis generated panic. And the media was pressing him for answers to the reports about Dr. LeDue's disappearance—nothing was secret in Washington.

The phone rang. Governor Malloy answered, "Hello Mr. President. Thank you for taking the time to return my call."

Joining the president in the Oval Office were the Chairman of the Joint Chiefs of Staff, the Director of the CIA, the Chief of Naval Operations, and the Attorney General.

President Bainbridge began, "Governor, I've got several key people in my office right now. Everyone is anxious to hear about what information you have on the downed prison transport?"

"No news, Mr. President," replied Governor Malloy with candor. "I'm afraid we still don't have communications throughout most of the Gulf Coast region. And as you are probably aware, we have been unable to raise the Coast Guard Station on Kodiak."

"Governor, this is CIA Director Colin Clarke."

"Yes, Mr. Clarke?" Governor Malloy hoped the CIA's presence in the Oval Office wasn't a prelude to worse news. He knew the CIA was keenly interested in the fate of Dr. Elizabeth LeDue. The agency had pushed hard to get the Federal Bureau of Prisons to agree to send her to Malloy Super Max.

"Governor, we have a report that there is a Russian Akula Class nuclear submarine heading at full speed towards the Shelikof Straits. We think the Russians are trying to nab Dr. LeDue."

Rick Malloy rubbed his hands over his face. He looked to Commissioners Burke and Dornier for reassurance. *Why would a Russian submarine be sailing towards Shelikof Straits? How can Clarke sound so calm? A Russian submarine deep inside Alaska waters is not a trivial matter.*

Burke and Dornier returned the Governor's stare. They were perplexed too.

"Governor, this is Admiral Quinn, Chief of Naval Operations."

"Hello, Admiral, I hope you have better news for me than Mr. Clarke."

"Yes, Governor I believe I do. But before I begin, is there anyone else listening to this conversation?"

"Yes Admiral, I have the head of the Alaska State Troopers and the head of the Department of Corrections here in my office. I've got you on the speaker phone."

"Very well." Admiral Quinn continued in his rich baritone voice, "Right now, I have a fast frigate in hot pursuit of the Russian sub. Margaret Englemann is in command. She is the best anti-submarine warfare tactician in the fleet. I also have a special operations team on the ship. They are ready to move in, if Dr. LeDue is still alive."

"Sounds good Admiral, but . . ."

"Furthermore Governor," interjected the Chairman of the Joint Chiefs-of-Staff, I have been informed by General McCarthy at

Elmendorf that he has been contacted by the USS Billings. We have dispatched several F-16s from Eielson to free up his F-15s, so they can conduct an aerial reconnaissance over the last known position of the transport."

Dick Burke bolted up from his chair, cutting in excitedly, "You mean to tell me that you have the last known coordinates of Malloy 1!"

"Who's talking?" demanded the President.

"Dick Burke, Mr. President. Commissioner of Public Safety."

"Well, Commissioner Burke, we do," President Bainbridge responded heatedly. He was annoyed by Burke's gruff interruption. "And we will fax them to you in a few minutes."

Governor Malloy motioned angrily for Burke to sit down and be quiet. "Is there anything we can do to assist the Navy, Mr. President?" Malloy asked, trying to smooth ruffled feathers.

"Other than keeping us informed of any new developments, Governor, not really."

"Admiral Quinn, this is Corrections Commissioner Dornier."

"Yes Commissioner?"

"Admiral, would you be kind enough to keep me abreast of the situation as you receive information?"

"Yes, Commissioner, I think that can be arranged."

"Thank you," she said. She enjoyed showing Dick Burke how to handle people. *He may know Alaska, but I know how to play politics.*

"Admiral, this is Public Safety Commissioner Dick Burke."

"Yes Commissioner, what can I do for you," Quinn replied coolly. He was used to hotheads and by the sounds coming from the other end of the telephone line, he was pretty sure Burke was a hothead.

"Why wasn't my department notified of this information when it became available?"

Before Admiral Quinn could respond to Burke's challenge, Governor Malloy took the situation in hand. Raising his voice, he again motioned angrily for Commissioner Burke to take his seat, "That's enough Dick! This is the time for cooperation, not recrimination! Sit down!"

Grumbling under his breath at the rebuke, a sulking Burke reluctantly sat down.

"Stay in touch Governor and let me remind everyone that the information we just discussed is confidential. That means no leaks and no press," said President Bainbridge concluding the conversation.

"Yes Sir. Thank you Mr. President."

As soon as the call was disconnected, Governor Malloy started in on Burke. "Dammit Dick, the last thing we need is the feds stonewalling us on this situation!"

"Aw bullshit, Rick!" Burke responded heatedly. "You know the feds treat us like poor stepchildren. They're always interfering in our affairs. They should have had the courtesy to let us know they knew the location of Malloy 1."

Dornier was shocked at Burke's manner. She didn't know the two men had been friends for years.

"That's beside the point and you know it Dick!" Governor Malloy countered.

Their argument was interrupted by a knock on the door. The Governor's secretary stuck her head in, waving Dornier over to take the note from her hand.

> TO: CORRECTIONS COMMISSIONER DORNIER
> FR: COAST GUARD COMMANDER ADMIRAL RALSTON
>
> RADIO MESSAGES RECEIVED FROM THE F/V NEPTUNE OPERATING IN SHELIKOF STRAITS. DOC TRANSPORT AIRCRAFT DITCHED IN SEA, TWO INMATES SURVIVED, HAVE FEMALE HOSTAGE AND HAVE MADE LANDFALL IN THE KARLUK RIVER VALLEY ON KODIAK ISLAND. F/V NEPTUNE DELIVERING CORRECTIONAL OFFICERS IGNUSTUK AND SANDERS TO LARSEN BAY. OFFICERS SEARCHING FOR ESCAPED PRISONERS.

The note brought a smile to Michelle Dornier's face. *Good news at last!*

Across the room, Governor Malloy and Dick Burke were waiting anxiously for her to finish reading the message. The smile spreading across her face raised their hopes that the whole affair was over. Were Elizabeth LeDue and Ivan Lincoln back in custody?

She read the note.

This was some good news—finally. However, the part about the hostage was troubling. Was the hostage was a civilian or a correctional officer? If civilian, the search would take on a whole new dimension.

Never one to be shy, Dick Burke opened the conversation. "Well, at least now we know where the prisoners are. This is good."

Again revealing her ignorance of Alaska geography, Dornier said, "Maybe we can assemble a team and fly to Larsen Bay in DOC's other C-130 to help with the manhunt."

Burke rolled his eyes in disgust. "For God's sake, you can't do that!"

The puzzled look on Dornier's face only encouraged him to continue with his criticism. "Larsen Bay is a tiny community on the northwest side of Kodiak Island. They don't have an airport big enough to handle a C-130."

Unwilling to concede her point, Dornier made another proposal. "Okay, that makes sense. So why don't we fly into Kodiak and set out from there?"

Dick Burke struggled to maintain his composure. Grabbing her by the arm, he pulled her over the map on the wall. He stabbed at the map with his finger, detailing the stupidity of her proposition.

First he showed her the distance and terrain between the town of Kodiak and Larsen Bay. Next he showed her that there were no roads on the island and that much of the terrain was covered by rugged snow-capped mountains.

Listening to this bickering irritated Governor Malloy. He interrupted their argument. "Dick, I want you and Michelle to take DMVA's King Air to Elmendorf. From there I want both of you to fly out with a search team and a couple of EMTs to Larsen

Bay. You are to establish a command post and coordinate the capture of these two criminals."

"What about the Navy and the Russians sir?" Burke asked raising the obvious dilemma.

"Fuck the Russians!" barked Governor Malloy, startling both his commissioners. "If they interfere, arrest them or stop them with whatever force is necessary. As for the Navy, try and work with them, but if not, I want us," he said, looking intensely at both of them and thumping himself on his chest, "to bring these two back into custody. I don't want any black eyes on this one. Do I make myself clear?"

"Clear as day, Governor," answered Burke. He'd never seen Rick Malloy so forceful. He liked it. Burke led Dornier out of the governor's office and down the hall to his waiting trooper escort.

Cessna 180 Flight for Life, Aleutian Islands, Alaska

Blaine Smith sighed with relief as the plane continued climbing on its flight away from Adak. Taking off down a rocky hill was an experience he would not soon forget. According to the owner's manual, the plane never should have gotten airborne. But here they were, climbing steadily over the broadening expanse of water.

The turbulence was terrible as they headed east out across Kuluk Bay and over Great Sitkin Island. Nurse Evers was concerned. The rough air was aggravating her patient's condition. "Officer Smith," she said tapping him on the shoulder and speaking into his ear, "can you find some smoother air? All this pounding is making Corporal Steiger worse."

Blaine thought back to the day when he'd been caught in ferocious turbulence over Prince William Sound, remembering his instructor's admonition to climb above the clouds to search for smoother air. "The air is probably smoother above the clouds," he answered. "I can climb through them, but I'm not instrument rated. We could get lost." He hoped she understood the dangers of flying without any landmarks.

"If we continue this pounding, it won't matter if we get lost. Steiger will die." Evers knew Smith was a young pilot. But they didn't have many options.

Blaine swallowed hard and added power. The aircraft climbed into the clouds.

Flying in Alaska is tricky business, but flying in the Aleutians is the toughest flying in the world. Most of the time the sky is a solid mass of gray. Billowing overcast driven by violent updrafts and downdrafts punishes any aircraft that braves the perils of this forbidding environment. The islands are rugged, the ocean waters freezing cold. A lost aircrew has but the slimmest chance of surviving an emergency landing.

Like every Alaskan pilot, Blaine Smith knew the dangers of flying in the Aleutians. He just hoped his luck would be with him today.

Blaine kept his eyes roving over his instrument panel to avoid getting vertigo. It took all his strength to keep the Cessna on a steady climb through the gray mist as the winds buffeted them violently.

At 6,000 feet, the sky suddenly opened up. Sunshine filled the cabin. The air became smoother. Nurse Evers relaxed.

Now that he could hold the plane steady with one hand, Blaine took out his sectional charts of the eastern Aleutian Islands and plotted a course to Dutch Harbor. He set his watch. He needed to time how long it would take them to get there. He was guessing he had a tail wind of more than 20-knots, but without radio communications, he couldn't be sure. The plane's lack of a Global Positioning System added to his troubles. Navigating by compass in the wildly fluxuating magnetic environment of the Aleutians was tricky business even for an experienced pilot. He was being forced to dead reckon in one of the most treacherous airways on earth.

Without any landmarks, he was calculating his airspeed by the number of hours they'd been flying. At 130 miles per hour, he figured it would take them about three hours and 45 minutes to fly the 450 miles to Dutch Harbor. It was a rough calculation, but it was better than nothing. *We should be coming up on Dutch Harbor in about an hour.*

Up in the distance soaring above the clouds, Blaine saw the volcano's plume of smoke and ash dominating the horizon. He rubbed his eyes to make sure he wasn't seeing things and looked again. He reached around, tapping Evers on the shoulder and pointing out the window.

"Oh My God! What is that?" she exclaimed. She couldn't believe her eyes. The ash cloud mushroomed high into the stratosphere.

"Looks like a volcano erupted out here. A big one."

"Which one?" she asked.

"My guess is it's the Korovin Volcano," he replied pointing to the map.

Her eyes followed his fingers to the spot on the map a few miles west of Dutch Harbor.

"I can't fly through the stuff. I'm going to have to try and swing around it," Blaine said nervously. "The spreading cloud is blocking a direct approach to Dutch Harbor." He looked at his charts for an alternative route.

"Be careful," Evers cautioned. "I read once that volcanic clouds generate lightning."

"Great," Smith snarled under his breath. He was getting in over his head. Beads of sweat formed on his brow. But they were too far out to turn back.

After changing course to avoid the lethal ash cloud, Blaine flew on for several more hours with his precious cargo. He did not realize that ever since leaving Adak, the tailwinds had increased his groundspeed by over 60 miles per hour. They were already well east of Dutch Harbor when he'd spotted the volcano. Now they were even farther east.

Blaine saw the brilliant glimmer of a symmetrical volcano mountain jutting above the clouds up ahead in the late afternoon light. Puzzled, he looked for this mountain on his chart. Nothing. Desperately, he looked all over the map of Unalaska Island for any mountain that would be sticking several thousand feet above the clouds. Still nothing.

He flipped to the other side his chart, trying to locate this mountain. A lump formed in his throat as his finger came to rest on Shishaldin Volcano on Unimak Island, 140 miles northeast of Dutch Harbor. He had missed his destination completely.

He tried to hide his rising panic. He searched the chart for a town and airport. His hopes rose when he located airports at False Pass and Cold Bay on the Alaska Peninsula. "I'll try for Cold Bay," he told himself, "they probably have a doctor there."

Blaine eased back on the power, initiating the plane's descent into the unbroken blanket of clouds. He prayed under his breath that his guess about his location was right. "We're headed down now," he informed Evers, who was wiping sweat from the face of Inmate Lucas.

Preoccupied with her patients, she did not respond.

Upset by his navigation error, Blaine compounded his mistakes. He forgot to pull on the carburetor heat. Ice built up in the manifold intakes of the engine. As they emerged from the base of the clouds he added power. A loud explosion rang out from in front of the firewall, startling him. He checked his instruments and gauges. The manifold pressure was dropping rapidly. Even more distressing was the sudden loss of oil pressure.

"What was that!" cried a surprised Evers. The explosion made her bolt upright.

"I don't know," came Blaine's worried response. "We're losing oil and manifold pressure. I . . ."

Before he could finish speaking, the engine seized and the propeller came to an ominous stop. The cabin grew very quiet. The only sound was the wind whistling through the wing struts. Doreen Evers watched the color drain from Smith's face.

Blaine went through his emergency procedures. Slowing the aircraft to about 90 miles per hour, he extended his glide path in an effort to make it to Cold Bay. He could see the jagged summit of Frosty Peak directly ahead. Without airspeed he couldn't risk turning out of the way—he was really regretting having too much weight on board. He was hoping an updraft would catch them and lift them over the top of the peak. If he could clear the mountain, he would be able to glide into the airport on the other side. But he was losing altitude too fast.

Realizing that they wouldn't clear the top of the peak, he took the chance he could swing the plane out and around the summit. "Hang on," he yelled to Evers, "I'm going to try and glide around the mountain. If we stall, we're going to hit the ground hard."

Blaine turned the yoke to the right, trying to gently nudge the plane around the south side of Frosty Peak. But it was impossible. The moment he began turning, the airspeed bled off and the Cessna stalled. With a shrill wail, the stall-warning indicator sounded its alarm. The nose of the plane pitched up slightly and the whole plane shuddered. Before Blaine could react, the plane nosed over and fell in a lazy spiral into the rocky slopes of Frosty Peak.

Slamming into the ground, the fragile plane cartwheeled down the mountainside, breaking the left wing off the fuselage. Inside the cabin, Blaine held onto the yoke with all his strength, as Doreen was thrown about the cabin. Crashing into a boulder, the windshield shattered. With a haunting groan the twisted metal hulk came to a halt up against a large moss covered rock. Smoke poured from the engine.

Blood oozed from Blaine's chest. The shaft of the yoke was sticking out of his back. His breathing was labored. Slowly the essence of life faded from his blue eyes.

Coming to her senses, Evers ran her hand over the very large bump on her head. She shook the dizziness from her brain and pushed the cabin door open. With a shriek of pain she grabbed her left collarbone and rolled onto her side. It was broken. She could feel a numb, piercing sensation in her left side. She ran her right hand down her torso. With a grimace she stopped her hand at the small piece of metal protruding from her abdomen. "Don't panic Doreen," she told herself, "keep your cool. You're alive. You can survive. Check your patients, and then take care of yourself."

Carefully sitting up, she checked her patients' vital signs. She breathed a sigh of relief. Both of them were still alive. She thanked her good senses to have their stretchers strapped to the cabin floor before they took off from Adak.

Twisting around, Evers saw the shattered body of Officer Blaine Smith. He wasn't breathing. His eyes were fixed and a small trickle of blood was running down his chin. It wasn't fair. Tears formed in the corners of her eyes and she fought back the urge to sob.

Evers pulled herself to her knees with her good arm and fashioned a sling for her broken collarbone. Next she packed some cloth around her abdominal wound. Sweat rolled down her cheeks from the exertion and the pain. She was dizzy.

The touch on her arm startled her. Inmate Lucas had sat up. Evers protested that she should remain resting and tried without success to get her to lie back down.

Ignoring Nurse Evers's instructions to remain in her stretcher, Lucas silently went to work sealing up the fuselage with pieces of cloth and metal. Night was falling. She covered Steiger and Evers with blankets and fabric from the torn interior. Finding the water canteen inside the survival kit she gave each of them a small drink. She examined Evers' wound—dark blood oozed around the edges of the metal. Evers told her not to remove the metal.

Lucas dabbed the sweat from Evers' face, elevated her feet and lay down next to Steiger. It would be impossible to walk off the mountain in the dark.

The three survivors settled in for a long miserable night on the windswept slopes of Frosty Peak.

South Shore, Adak Island, Alaska

Toby Church came around the southernmost tip of Adak, heading due north into the Bay of Waterfalls. True to its name, the bay was bordered by low cliffs laced with tumbling waterfalls spilling off the dark rock faces into the greenish blue ocean. The remote beauty of the location was not lost on Church. Even though he was from the Midwest, he had grown to love the rugged outdoors.

According to his map there were several cabins located at the head of the bay, which were used by the residents of the island for hunting and fishing and shelter from the constant storms that rake this region of the North. He was betting that the remote nature of the bay had protected it from the tsunami's destruction. He was shivering from the cold evening air in his face. He had to find shelter for the evening. He needed to eat a warm meal and get some rest. Directly ahead he caught sight of a moss-covered roof.

As he neared the shore, Church saw that his guess about the tsunami missing this bay was only partially correct. While the tsunami had missed the bay, its sucking action had caused a higher than normal tidal surge, which had washed away several pilings. The front of the cabin had partially collapsed. However, most of the building was still intact and would provide him with shelter for the night. A stovepipe chimney was sticking out of the roof. He could gather some driftwood and build a fire.

Church drove his skiff up onto the beach. Grabbing his pistol, he climbed out of the skiff and searched the area around the cabin. Once he was satisfied the area was safe, he unloaded his supplies.

After hauling his food and survival gear into the cabin, he stepped back outside. He inhaled deeply, savoring his newfound freedom. To the west, the clouds parted, letting the sunset's evening rays stream through onto to his face. It felt good to be free, even if he was on the run.

Church set off to gather driftwood from the shore. He was looking forward to sitting by a fire, eating a tasty meal, and sleeping in the great outdoors. The silence surrounding the bay was bliss. For the first time in years, he could enjoy the sound of the ocean lapping on the shore and sea lions barking in the distance without the ringing of prison movement bells.

With his arms full of wood, he returned to the cabin to build a fire. Soon he was sitting in his underwear next to the dancing flames. Even with the partially collapsed wall, the small woodstove soon heated the room to a toasty temperature.

Toby Church was beginning to realize just how lucky he'd been. He'd managed to escape the most secure prison in the United

States. He'd found a boat. He'd missed being killed by a tsunami. He'd found a compass, pistol, charts, and meat.

He used a stick to stir some chunks of meat and fat on top of the stove. The aroma of food filled the air. He smacked his lips in anticipation of a hot meal. The last time he'd enjoyed a meal cooked over an open fire was in the woods the day before his arrest in Billings.

Leaving the meat to simmer on the stove, he went outside to get some water. Dipping a small pan he'd found inside a cupboard into a nearby stream, he collected some water for drinking, cooking and bathing. He returned to the cabin and put the pan on the stove. He was being careful to sterilize his drinking water. He could not afford to get sick. With his meat cooked and his water boiling, he sat down to a real survivalist meal. The seal lion blubber would give him energy and the sterilized water would keep him hydrated.

The lack of seasonings and side dishes did not diminish the pleasure of this meal. He knew he should eat slower, but he couldn't control himself. He was famished. *I'll make sure to eat slower from here on out.*

After he finished his supper, Church started worrying about the possibility of another earthquake and tsunami. While it was unlikely that another catastrophic event would occur so soon after the first, he could not shake the thought of a repeat. *Will I be safe in the cabin?* "Nonsense," he said out loud, "you had no choice. You had to find shelter for the night." His survival depended on it.

Dismissing his fears of destruction in the middle of the night, he turned his thoughts to one of his biggest problems—fuel.

He studied the navigation charts. The nearest potential fuel depot looked to be on Tanaga Island at Cape Amagalik. Although there were no villages anywhere near this location, the map indicated the existence of an airstrip. "If my luck holds out, I'll find some fuel in drums or abandoned tanks."

He used his knife blade to measure the distance. It was just over 50 miles to Cape Amagalik. He could make the airfield by tomorrow afternoon.

From Cape Amagalik he marked out the distances to Amchitka Island, Kiska Island, and Shemya Island, the site of a US Air Force

Base. He thought about his plan, ticking off the steps: *first to Tanaga Island, find some fuel, then to Amchitka Island where I might be able to steal a bigger boat, and then to Shemya, where I can stow away on a transport.*

He was pleased. For the most part everything was going smoothly. His only frustration was the lack of towns in the area. He needed a bigger boat. *Surely*, he thought to himself, *somewhere in these islands is a fishing trawler?*

Malloy Super Maximum-Security Prison, Adak Island, Alaska

By evening, the stress of the long day's events was showing on everyone. It was most evident in the townsfolk, who were housed in the gym. Some were quietly sobbing. Others milled about aimlessly.

The officers of Malloy Super Max were more fortunate. They were busy with the routines of keeping post log notes and inspecting cells. However, for those officers with orders to get some sleep, it was tough. Most of them were lying on their bedrolls, staring at the ceiling, quietly reflecting on the day and worrying about loved ones back on the mainland.

Marc Anderson stared at a broken ceiling tile, praying that his wife was okay. Feeling a touch on the shoulder, he turned his head. Kneeling beside him was the prison's head of maintenance.

"Captain, I've got communications restored. We're trying to raise Anchorage or Juneau right now."

Anderson sat up and smiled at the balding foreman. Patting him on the shoulder, he said, "Good work Jeff. Let's hope somebody's home to take our call."

Anderson gave up on rest. He could rest later. He walked next to the foreman down the corridor steps towards Main Control. When they reached the cafeteria, he ordered him to get some food and rest. Tomorrow would be another busy day.

Anderson went right to work as soon as he entered Main Control. "Sergeant Knight, have you managed to raise anybody on the phone yet?"

"No sir. I've tried to call both Anchorage Central Office and Juneau Central Office. Maybe the lines are down? All I get is ringing. Not even an answering machine. Now, I'm trying to get in touch with the Trooper detachment in Juneau."

Anderson motioned for Sgt. Knight to follow him into his office. "Sit down Bill. Give me a status report."

"Well, Captain, we're running on our main power system. Amazingly, the earthquake didn't knock out our geothermal generators. Maintenance should have the outer perimeter fence back up sometime tomorrow. All the inmates are in their cells and behaving surprisingly well. The good Father has exhausted himself counseling people in the gym. I've got the food rationed to last 15 days. Lt. Banderas's team is catching some shut-eye. They'll head out at first light."

"Good work Bill. Go get some rest, while I try to raise somebody in Juneau," Anderson said, shooing Sgt. Knight out of his office. He stood in the doorway for a moment watching Bill Knight exit into the main sally port. Even though Knight's Marine Corps habits got annoying, Anderson had to admit that the man was rugged and reliable. He was glad to have him right now.

Returning to his desk, he picked up the phone and dialed his home phone number in Anchorage. "We're sorry, all circuits are busy," came the annoying recording. "Figures," he said putting down the receiver.

Just then the phone rang, making him jump. "Hello, Malloy Super Max, Captain Anderson speaking."

"This is Trooper Hollings in Juneau. I have a message from a Sergeant Bill Knight to call you guys."

"Thanks for calling Trooper Hollings. How're things in Juneau?"

"Fine. We never felt a thing."

"That's good. I'm sure you know by now that we've suffered a catastrophe out here. I need to talk to someone in authority—either the Commissioner of Public Safety or Corrections or the governor."

"Commissioners Burke and Dornier are with General Hornby on the King Air flying to Anchorage. I'll call the governor's house and ask him to give you a call."

"Thanks a million. How long do you think it will be?"

"Hard to say. If he's home, he will probably call right away. If not, I'll head over to the Capitol and track him down."

"Thanks again. I'll stand by." Anderson felt a little better. Only in Alaska would a state trooper feel comfortable calling the governor. Maybe in a few minutes he'd be able to tell someone about what had happened on Adak. He tried his home phone number in Anchorage again. He got the same recording.

Governor Malloy and his Chief-of-Staff George Roberts called within a few minutes of the trooper's call to the Mansion. "Captain Anderson?"

"Yes, this is Captain Anderson."

"Captain, this is Governor Rick Malloy."

"Hello Governor, thank you very much for returning my call," he said. Anderson was nervous. He'd never talked to a governor before.

"Captain, my Chief-of-Staff George Roberts is with me. Can you give us a status report?" Governor Malloy asked politely. He was sensitive to the tremendous pressure Captain Anderson must be feeling.

Unsure of just where to begin, Marc Anderson described the day's events: the earthquake, the escape, and the tsunami. He paused briefly to answer the governor's questions and then briefed him on the current condition of the prison and the emergency plan. He also took a few minutes to explain the plan to recapture Toby Church. Anderson was amazed at how well informed the governor was and how well he reacted to the news of Toby Church's escape.

When Governor Malloy explained what was afoot with the loss of Malloy 1, Marc Anderson understood why the governor was undisturbed by Church's escape—he had bigger fish to fry.

"Captain," said Governor Malloy in his most matter-of-fact tone, "as you know your commissioner is on her way to Anchorage. I have ordered her and Commissioner Burke to Kodiak. They will coordinate the search for Lincoln and LeDue. It sounds like you have your situation well in hand. We will pass this news on to Commissioner Dornier. My chief-of-staff will contact the Troopers in Dutch Harbor. He'll order them to dispatch a vessel to your location with food and supplies. I will call the Japanese Consul General to see if we can't get them to send a supply ship from Hokkaido. And finally, I will call General McCarthy to see if he can't launch a C-130 loaded with supplies from Eielson to do an air drop over Mitchell Field."

"Captain, this is George Roberts. Fax me a list of the supplies you need and I will get it to General McCarthy."

"Yes sir!" came the relieved reply. Anderson smiled for the first time in two days. After thanking the governor profusely for all his assistance, he put down the receiver, ordered an officer to fax a list to the governor's office, and immediately dialed home.

"Hello?"

"Cathy?" he asked hopefully. Although he recognized her voice, he wanted assurance it was really her.

"Yes," came her excited reply, "is that you Marc?"

"It's me baby. Are you alright?" Relief surged through him. She was alive!

"Yes, I'm fine. Everyone's fine. We are all safe and sound. Anchorage is a mess. We heard over the radio that the Aleutians were hit by a huge tsunami. I was so worried!"

"We're all fine. We're far enough up Mt. Moffet to have missed it. Must've been 200 feet tall," he replied. He used his hands to show the wave even though he knew she couldn't see him through the phone.

"Thank God you're safe. When're you coming home?" she asked hopefully.

"Don't know. Pretty messy here. Probably won't be home for a couple weeks at least. Now for the bad part baby," he said lowering his voice, "Jon and Darlene were killed sometime during the quake or tsunami. So were the assistant superintendent and about 15 officers."

Cathy covered her mouth, fighting back tears. She tried to comfort her husband, "I'm so sorry Marc. I'm so sorry." But her effort was futile. She broke down crying.

Listening to his wife cry was too hard. He cut the call short. "Gotta run honey, be safe and I'll call you in a couple days. I love you." With a click the conversation was over. Anderson wiped the tears from his eyes before walking out into Main Control. "Notify all posts that when they are relieved from duty they may use the phones to call their families. Calls are limited to 5 minutes each."

Anderson exited Main Control to do a walk through of the institution. It kept his mind off of home.

Dragon Flight, Shelikof Straits, Alaska

Cruising 1,000 feet above the choppy waters of Shelikof Straits the two pilots of Dragon Squadron's F-15s searched in the fading light for signs of Malloy 1. On their flight down they had noticed dozens of fishing trawlers churning through the choppy seas, heading back to Cook Inlet—fishermen pushing hard for home, desperate to see their families again.

The flight leader eased back on the throttles, slowing his sleek fighter to 250 knots. He flew in slow wide-arcing turns over the last known location of Malloy 1, hoping to catch even a glimpse of floating wreckage. But all he could see was the vast expanse of the dark unforgiving ocean.

"Latchkey this is Dragon One, repeat, this is Dragon One."

"Dragon One, this is Latchkey, go ahead."

"Latchkey we are over the search area. No sign of debris or survivors."

"Dragon One this is Dragon Two."

"Go Dragon Two."

"I see debris about 6 miles offshore of Kodiak Island. There are a couple of Mae Wests in the water, but no bodies, repeat no bodies."

"Copy Dragon Two. Do you copy Latchkey?"

"We copy Dragon Flight. Go down for a closer look, get a positive ID on the debris and return to base," crackled the mission commander's voice over the radio.

Extending their aircrafts' speed brakes, the pilots of Dragon Flight slowed their normally agile fighters to a lumbering pace. Weaving back and forth to cover as wide a search area as possible, they dropped to 100 feet off the surface. Bobbing in the heaving seas were several empty life vests, seat cushions, and partially submerged sections of Malloy 1's fuselage.

The flight leader held his thumb up, signaling to his wingman. It was time to go home. With a hard pull on their sticks, the pilots of Dragon Flight accelerated back up to 400 knots. They sped from the scene, climbing through the clouds, heading back to Anchorage.

DMVA King Air 200, 21,000-ft over Gulf of Alaska—Enroute to Anchorage, Alaska

"Instead of viewing Alaska as a state, like New Jersey, you need to think of it as a country," argued Major General Hornby, Commissioner of the Alaska Department of Military and Veterans Affairs (DMVA.) He moved his hands apart like someone showing a fish. He stared at Commissioner Dornier, speaking in his animatedly passionate manner. "Hell, if you were to cut Alaska in two, Texas would become the third largest state."

Dick Burke jumped into the conversation. "It's obvious you haven't had time to travel around the state and get a feel for the country. From Anchorage to Juneau it's over 600 miles. From Anchorage to Kodiak it's over 250 miles. And from Anchorage to Adak, it's over 1,000 miles!"

Dornier listened patiently to the lecture on the immense size of Alaska, but the lack of diplomacy made it hard not to argue. Still, she reminded herself their hearts were in the right place. They were trying to educate her in a hurry. She decided to put her ego aside and accept their help.

"I hear what you're saying gentlemen, but I think you can appreciate it's pretty hard to visualize what you're describing without ever having seen it."

General Hornby smiled. "Give yourself some time. It'll take you weeks to visit all the places you need to go. We've been in the air 45 minutes and we're not even half way to Anchorage yet. And when we get to Anchorage, it will be another two hours to Kodiak on the Jet Ranger."

Dornier still couldn't understand why they couldn't load up the King Air in Anchorage and fly to Larsen Bay. "I'm still not clear on why we can't use your plane to take us to Larsen Bay General."

General Hornby went to the cockpit and returned to the table with the navigation chart for Kodiak. He opened the map. Pointing to Larsen Bay, he said, "Here is Larsen Bay—population 127. Setting—on the shore of a narrow fjord. Runway—3,000 feet of gravel, probably unusable after the earthquake."

He ran his finger along the blue line marking the Karluk River. "This is some of the most difficult terrain in the world.

You will have to set up a command center in this tiny town. You'll have to send out teams to find two escaped prisoners, one of whom is a skilled hunter and outdoorsman. At the same time you'll have to maintain contact with your search teams in very mountainous terrain."

Dick Burke threw in his two cents. "And not to put too a fine point on it Commissioner Dornier, if Ivan Lincoln gets deep into the mountains of Kodiak, we will probably never find him."

Thinking Burke was exaggerating, Dornier replied skeptically, "I think with infrared technology and a good plan we should be able to locate him in a few days."

General Hornby shook his head trying not to laugh. "That's all well and nice in a place without any wildlife or caves. But Kodiak Island has one of the largest populations of bears and deer in the United States. Infrared technology will provide us with heat signatures, but we won't be able to tell if they're bears, deer, or humans."

Unwilling to concede her point, she defended her concept. "But we know he's got two others with him. When we find three heat signatures, then we know we've got him and Dr. LeDue too. Surely, the bears won't be moving in threes?"

Dick Burke was surprised by her insight. He validated Dornier for the first time in the last twenty-four hours. "Very good Commissioner. Of course, if he kills LeDue and the hostage, which is very likely, we will be at square one again."

General Hornby held up three fingers and said, "Let's not forget that sows generally have two or three cubs, so keying off three heat signatures isn't a sure thing."

The three commissioners sat back in their seats, satisfied they'd solved all the issues they could at the particular time.

Burke began mulling over how best to ensure his department could assist with rescues, stop looters, manage traffic in the cities and larger towns, and respond to emergencies. General Hornby was thinking about the upcoming meeting with the Director of the Division of Emergency Services and Brigadier General Smith of the Alaska National Guard to make sure their efforts were being coordinated with Public Safety and the US military. Dornier was worrying about going on her first field assignment. *I'm an administrator, not a tactician.* However, she had to swallow her fear and doubt. Governor Malloy had been quite clear. She was to be on the scene with Commissioner Burke. *I have to follow through, not only for the governor, but to prove to the crusty Burke that I'm up to the task of running my department. I'm not going to give him any more ammunition to criticize me.*

Michelle Dornier gazed out her window at the ice-encrusted tops of Canada's Mt. Logan and Alaska's Mt. St. Elias jutting above the sea of clouds. The setting sun reflected hues of pink and silver off their glistening glacier encrusted slopes. The scene was magnificent. Memories of sunsets shared with her father on the Atlantic Coast flooded her mind. She thought fondly of how her father would love to see the mountains sparkling in the evening light.

Michelle adored her father. He was her inspiration. And he had been her biggest cheerleader. Her mind drifted off to memories of how she ended up in Alaska.

Over the years she had earned a reputation as an organizational genius. A graduate of Princeton, she had taken her talents and applied them with patience and fortitude, gradually rising to the top of New Jersey's correctional system. Adroit at making people feel good, she had excelled in the political world. This ability had drawn the attention of Governor Malloy's wife, who had come from a prominent New Jersey family.

It was at a cocktail party at Drum Thwacket that Michelle Dornier had been introduced to Rick Malloy. They had struck up a conversation and soon discovered they shared many of the same convictions. A few weeks later, Michelle Dornier found herself sitting before the Alaska State Legislature in a confirmation hearing.

Governor Malloy had given her a chance to make a name for herself in the world of corrections. She would be in charge of the world's most secure super maximum-security prison. She wanted to experience the great outdoors. She also was hoping to put her painful divorce behind her. Maybe Alaska would her heal her broken heart.

She had arrived in Juneau at the end of January. It was clear and cold. She had been mesmerized by the crystal blue skies and the Northern Lights. This, she thought, was paradise. Of course, within a few days, the skies grew overcast and the snow began to fall—then the rain. It only took her a few weeks to appreciate the t-shirts saying, "Juneau Rain Festival January 1-December 31." But still she liked Juneau.

Even though her job kept her busy, she had managed to meet a few eligible bachelors at the many receptions hosted by the Governor and First Lady during the Legislative Session. Things were looking up. She had managed to get control of the department's runaway budget, winning her allies in the halls of the Capitol. But her decisions were controversial among the department's veterans. They felt she was compromising safety. They did not care what the studies said. They were worried about maintaining the integrity of the system.

Michelle Dornier was seen as an up-and-coming political star. She was cultured, pretty, and smart. Stay in Alaska, the powerbrokers told her, and you'll go far.

Standing in stark contrast to Michelle Dornier's refined nature and political savvy was Dick Burke. He viewed the scene outside not in terms of beauty, but with a respect for the awesome power of nature. To him the mountains jutting high above the clouds represented the unforgiving nature of his home state. The mountains represented majesty and mystery. The sea below represented bounty, solitude and danger. Life on the sea had taught him that what was beautiful one moment could be a living hell the next.

It was the untamed wildness of Alaska that held his heart. He often found himself telling people how Alaska was an icy mistress that lured men to her bosom with her beauty and then kept them in her cold embrace never to let them go. Alaska was inside you as much as it was around you.

A 22-year veteran of the Alaska State Troopers, Richard "Dick" Burke was born in Seattle. His parents had moved to Ketchikan when he was just a boy. They were commercial fishermen. Alaska's abundant waters promised a better life for them and their three children.

Working with his father on the boat in the summer and fall had taught him the hard lessons of the sea. Coiling rope and pulling nets made you tough. Working on a slippery deck in a churning sea taught you respect for nature.

He had joined the troopers at age 21, graduating in the middle of his class. He wasn't the best at taking tests or book learning, but he was good at reading people and taking command of situations. Over the next 19 years, many a criminal discovered that even though he was of slight build, Dick Burke was one tough hombre.

As Commissioner of Public Safety, he led his department with a firm hand. This earned the respect of his employees, but it also managed to irritate a lot of people in the political arena. On more than one occasion, Governor Malloy had rescued him after one of his infamous outbursts.

Everyone's thoughts were interrupted when they descended through the clouds above Anchorage. Fires were burning all over town. The city looked like a war zone. All three commissioners swallowed lumps in their throats as they stared out onto the nightmarish scene.

As they taxied up to the hangar at Elmendorf Air Force Base, Michelle Dornier saw Lt. General McCarthy waiting by his staff car. "Welcome to Anchorage," greeted the amiable McCarthy. "We've got private quarters set up for you on the base. Unfortunately, travel along the streets is almost impossible at this time."

"What about getting me to my office?" Burke asked.

"Your helicopter should be here any minute now Commissioner. It will take you there."

General McCarthy turned to Dornier, handing her a note. "Governor Malloy called with a message about the situation at Malloy Super Max. He wants you to give him a call." He gestured for everyone to get into his car.

After arriving at General McCarthy's office, Dornier called Governor Malloy and then Captain Anderson at Malloy Super Max. It was time to retire for the evening. Tomorrow would be a big day.

Karluk River Valley, Kodiak Island, Alaska

The sleeping bag donated by Alfred Lind was dry and warm. Tucked safely inside, Harry Ignustuk was sleeping soundly.

Danny Sanders maintained his vigil in the darkness, listening intently to the wind rustling through the alders. He was keeping his guard up against the approach of Ivan Lincoln. But, he was also concerned with the very real possibility of having a hungry Brown Bear just a few days out hibernation stalk into camp in search of food—Kodiak Brown Bears fear little and they have a reputation for hunting the hunters.

Danny gripped the shotgun he had rummaged from the ruins of a house on his way out of Larsen Bay. Hopefully he would have enough time to fire a couple shots before a bear could get on top of him. In the pitch black of night he would have little warning of an attack. Luckily, both he and Harry were skilled outdoorsmen. They knew to keep their camp free of food and garbage that could attract a marauding bear.

As he sat quietly in the dark, Danny thought about their plans for tracking down Ivan Lincoln and Elizabeth LeDue. Lincoln was evil incarnate. He kept hearing Joseph Lind's plea to bring Joy back safely. Danny could feel the anger well up inside him. He despised people like Lincoln—cowards that preyed on the weak and vulnerable—criminals who terrorized the innocent. He wondered what Lincoln would do if he had to face a man.

Suddenly the hair stood up on the back of his neck. Danny stopped thinking about the hunt. He cupped his hand to his ear, straining to hear through the sound of the wind moaning in the alders. He could hear something—far in the distance. *It sounds like a human voice. Is someone crying? Surely, we're not that close to Lincoln's camp? There it is again. Sometimes bear cubs sound like a crying human. What am I hearing?* It was so hard to tell. If it were a bear cub, then a sow would not be too far away.

After several more minutes, Danny gave up. The sound had stopped. *It was probably just the wind whistling in the brush.* He shrugged his shoulders, dismissing his fears as figments of his imagination.

Shortly before Danny had heard LeDue's screams, Ivan Lincoln had been plotting his assault. He tingled with anticipation. The small fire was casting twisted shadows across his face. Slowly, he ran his eyes up and down the sleeping figure of Dr. Elizabeth LeDue. She looked so innocent and vulnerable laying there, her figure illuminated by the dull glow of the fire. Shadows flickered on the alders behind her.

Rising from his squatting position, Lincoln walked over to where Elizabeth was sleeping. She was so exhausted; not even being hogtied had stopped her from dropping off into a deep slumber. Lincoln untied the ropes and lowered her feet to the ground. Unlocking the handcuffs, he rolled her over onto her back. Trying not to wake her just yet, he looped the handcuffs behind the base of a small bush. With patience and a gentleness that belied his evil intent, he took his time cuffing her hands again.

He quivered with excitement as he unbuttoned her jacket. Moving his hands over her torso, he slowly unzipped her prison jumpsuit. He slid his hands over her breasts. Elizabeth's eyes snapped open. In a world of half-sleep, half-consciousness, she screamed, "Stop! What are you doing? Get off me. Help!" She thrashed from side to side, attempting to throw him off her.

Grabbing her by the throat with one hand, Lincoln held the fillet knife above her face menacingly. He leaned close to her ear, threatening, "Quiet bitch! You scream again and I'll cut you from ear to ear. Understand?" He applied just a little pressure, running the knife blade across her throat, leaving a thin line of blood marking the knife's path.

Elizabeth felt blood trickle down her neck. She stopped resisting.

Lincoln could sense her fear. The smell of blood made his heart race. He became more excited. Twirling the point of the knife on her sternum, he said, "you don't know who I am do you?"

Elizabeth shook her head no.

With the fire casting shadows across his chiseled face, he held the knife up and said in a sinister tone, "Well, I've been sentenced to life in prison for kidnapping, raping and killing a *lot* of women. What do you think of that?"

Elizabeth was silent. Fear clouded her eyes. She wanted to cry, but couldn't.

Lincoln bent down and ran his tongue over the lobe of her ear as he spoke softly into it, "and then I cut them up into little pieces and make trinkets of their bones."

Elizabeth closed her eyes as Lincoln violated her body. His methods were brutal. His attack seemed to last an eternity. In reality, it was over in a few minutes.

Completing his rape and sodomy, Lincoln ordered her to perform fellatio—the final humiliation. He'd humiliated her like he'd been humiliated as a boy.

On the other side of the fire, Joy was praying. *He's going to kill us.* She'd never been so scared. Deep in her heart she knew she'd be next. *I have to escape from this madman.*

Joy was horrified as she watched the beast complete his torture by cutting a small piece of flesh from Elizabeth's neck. She fought back the urge to vomit at the smell of blood and sex.

Following the assault, Elizabeth was unable to close her eyes. Her insides hurt. And the blood from the cut on her neck ran down her shoulder forming a sticky film. She looked up at the clouds highlighted by the moonlight, cursing God and everything she had once held dear.

DAY TWO

Frosty Peak, Alaska Peninsula

The intense cold of the night woke Jenne Lucas up. The cloth cover over the hole in the fuselage was snapping in the light wind. She could hear the faint howl of wolves far, far away. She lay there, savoring the moment. For the first time in years her mind was no longer haunted by the ghostly chanting of voices. Perhaps the trauma of the accident had snapped her out of her delusions? It didn't matter. It was wonderful to think clearly.

Lucas ignored the stabbing pain in her abdomen and her fever. Slowly, she turned over and got to her knees. She set to work trying to keep Corporal Steiger and Nurse Evers comfortable. Pulling on the tattered fabric from the aircraft's interior, she once again sealed off the gaping hole in the fuselage, which had been blown open during the night by the wind. Grabbing another seat cushion, she used a piece of sharp aluminum to cut the fabric off and covered the tops of the heads her two patients so they would better retain body heat.

While searching through the tail section, she found some crackers, canned tuna, water, a coffee can and a candle with some matches. After placing the candle inside the coffee can she lit the wick. In a few minutes, the metal sides of the can were radiating heat. It wasn't much, but it helped keep the inside of the shelter a more tolerable temperature. With the shelter getting warmer, she turned her attention to Joan Steiger. She tried to get her to take small sips of water and tried to get her to talk.

Next she turned her attention to Doreen Evers, who was lying next to Corporal Steiger. She was suffering from a severe case of shock and her stomach wound was still bleeding. Lucas dabbed the sweat off her forehead, squeezed some water across her parched lips, and adjusted her blanket. Evers groaned and her head moved from side to side, but she did not wake. Lucas worried that the nurse never would regain consciousness.

Her work done for the moment, Lucas crawled back beneath her coverings. At no time did Jenne Lucas consider escape. Something inside her was keeping her there. Perhaps it was her belief that by helping these two injured women she would find redemption after all these years of anguish. Perhaps it was a sense of decency eating at her conscience. Whatever the motivation, she had a useful purpose and she found solace in the work. She pulled some fabric over her legs and drifted back off to sleep.

The light of dawn breaking over Shelikof Straits woke Lucas up. She exited the makeshift shelter, hiking through a newly fallen snow over to a rise on the side of the mountain. Several miles down the mountain to the east, she could see the shimmering lights of Cold Bay. She smiled. She was proud that she had managed to keep them all alive throughout the night. She tried to ignore the body of the young officer, lying a few feet away. She had dragged him free of the airplane right after the crash. She had been unable to sleep next to a corpse.

Should I leave the nurse and corporal? Or should I try and figure out a way to get them off the mountain and into town? If I leave them and head down the mountain alone, they will be sheltered, but medical aid will have to come to them and they will be stranded on the mountain for several more hours. If I try to fabricate a sled and pull them down the mountain, the rough ride might kill them. She flexed her bicep, rethinking that option. She was not very strong.

Climbing back into the plane, Lucas awakened Evers. "Nurse, nurse, are you awake?"

Doreen Evers slowly opened her eyes. She was groggy and it took a few minutes before she knew where she was. "Yeah, I'm awake." She reached down to feel the piece of metal protruding from her abdomen. Rays of light were streaming through openings in the cockpit. She asked, "Is it morning? Are we alive?"

"Yes, it's morning and we're alive," Lucas replied cheerily. She wiped the sweat off Ever's face and filled her in on the situation. "I can see a town about 15 miles away down the mountain. I'm going to leave you with the corporal and try to get to town as fast as I can."

Knowing Lucas was suffering from appendicitis, Evers said with concern, "You're sick. Do you think you can make it?"

"We don't have any options," replied Lucas, staring directly into the Ever's eyes. "If I stay we all die. If I try and take you with me, I probably won't make it, and we all die. If I go alone and get to town as fast as possible, I can send help and none of us die."

As she listened to Lucas's plan, Evers considered the very real fact that Jenne Lucas was a murderer. As a DOC employee, she was obligated to ensure that a prisoner was never out of custody—even if that meant no one lived. It was a harsh policy. If she broke it, she would lose her job. But she had no options left. She wasn't ready to die.

Before setting off down the rugged mountainside, Lucas gathered some supplies for Evers. "Here's some more food and water and some cloth to use as a wick for the melted wax in the coffee can. Make another candle. It'll help you stay warm."

Kneeling over, she hugged Evers before exiting the plane. From the ridge, the terrain looked pretty good—flat and treeless. Little did she realize it was going to be one of the toughest hikes of her life.

Bay of Waterfalls, Adak Island, Alaska

Toby Church was up and about before first light, making preparations for his departure to the west. He could hardly believe his luck. He'd found an almost full ten-gallon can of gasoline, left no doubt by someone who frequented the cabin. He looked up at the fading stars in the morning sky and thanked his good fortune. *Gasoline and a nice day in the Aleutians! It doesn't get any better than this.*

Gathering his supplies, including all the canned goods stored in the cabin, he loaded his boat before pushing off the beach and starting the engine. With a twist of the throttle, he swung the bow around and headed south towards the entrance of the bay. For the first time since his arrival in the Aleutians, he could appreciate the beauty of the area—a beauty he had overlooked behind the intimidating razor wire and bars of Malloy Super Max.

High above him several flocks of geese and ducks honked. They were heading north to their breeding grounds. Nearer the boulder-strewn shore, small seabirds skimmed the glassy surface, searching for fish and other delicacies in the early morning. It was wonderful to be free after so many years in prison.

After exiting the Bay of Waterfalls, Church turned west towards Cape Amagalik some 50 miles distant. Several hundred yards off his port bow, a pod of Dall porpoises surfaced and began pacing his skiff. Unfamiliar with the sea, he was nervous at first as the swift porpoises darted around his boat. Their speed was impressive. In a few moments, however, he relaxed. He smiled as they frolicked in front of his boat. Far off to his starboard a flock of Eiders were flying in a v-formation on their way to Kanaga Island—its snow-capped volcano shimmering in the early morning sun.

Looking west, he could see the snow-capped summit of Tanaga Volcano jutting above the horizon. The sky was so clear, he was sure he could see steam rising from the volcano's cone. *On a day like today, 50 miles will be a piece of cake.*

Kuluk Bay, Adak Island, Alaska

In stark contrast to the day before, the waters of Kuluk Bay lay still as the first rays of dawn painted the horizon in varying hues of pink and bright red. The beach was littered with debris of what was once the town of Adak. Boats and cars and pieces of houses were all jumbled together in a melee' of chaos. Seagulls and rats were feeding on the bloated bodies. The stench of death hung over the town.

Groups of townsfolk were moving silently among the ruins, searching for relatives and loved ones lost in the disaster. With plodding determination they sorted through the shattered buildings and twisted rubble. Pulling bodies from the rubble was a grisly task. These people weren't strangers. They were family and friends. As the young men stacked the bodies in a pile, the older men placed them on a makeshift wagon to be taken to the high ground above the airport. On the hillside above the remains of the town, Father Androvsky was administering the last rights to the dead. After each ceremony, burial teams buried the dead in mass graves on the side of Mt. Moffett.

No one liked the idea of piling their loved ones and friends in this manner, but there simply wasn't enough time to dig individual graves. The survivors couldn't risk the outbreak of disease.

Off to the side of the grave, several village elders were combing through a pile of personal items, making notes. Families would have to be notified. Many of the people killed in the earthquake and the subsequent tsunami had been washed out into Kuluk Bay, never to be seen again.

Inside Malloy Super Max, Captain Anderson inspected the kitchen repairs. Satisfied that everything was in working condition and safe, he opened the cafeteria. The stewards began preparing the prison's first hot meal in almost 24 hours—until further notice, no prisoners would be allowed to work in the kitchen. Officers would deliver food trays to inmates in their cells. The institution was still locked down.

Marc Anderson couldn't stop thinking that if the kitchen had been staffed by correctional officers, an officer wouldn't be dead and Toby Church would still be in custody. But the commissioner had ignored Superintendent Briggs's warning that staffing the kitchen with inmates wasn't safe. Her only concern had been to save money—prisoners were paid fifty cents an hour versus $30 per hour for a correctional officer. *That's what you get when your leader has never walked the floor.* He sighed heavily and headed to the gym.

In the gymnasium, people were making small talk. Their chatter filling the room. Several people talked about the strength of the quake and size of the tsunami. Others reminisced about lost friends and colleagues.

Captain Marc Anderson moved from group to group. Without drawing attention to himself, he deftly joined a group, stopping to listen to a conversation, touching a shoulder in sympathy, or warming a heart with a sincere look from his grey-blue eyes.

Meanwhile, the Marine-tough Sergeant Knight was working to keep the prison's operations running smoothly. Moving from post to post, he reminded staff that everything that could be done for their loved ones back on the mainland was being done. He also inspected post logbooks to make sure the officers were staying vigilant.

Bill Knight's gift for gab, his toothy smile and bold manners helped buoy the officers' spirits. His forthright manner also helped placate the inmates. The institutional lockdown was just a matter of security. Within a few days everything would be back to normal. They were not being punished.

After completing his inspection, Knight went to his office to call in some favors. He picked up the phone and called his good friend and former shipmate at the Trooper Detachment in Anchorage to ask him if he would let the officers' families know they were okay. As for those officers killed in their apartments by the earthquake and tsunami, he planned on notifying their families in person.

After finishing his rounds in the gymnasium, Captain Anderson headed down the corridor to Main Control. Last night had been rough and he was thanking his lucky stars for Bill Knight. Without him, things might have gotten out of hand.

Anderson looked through the camera at Cell C-1. Inmate Speer was sleeping soundly. He didn't seem any worse for the wear and tear. This was good. Carl Speer was one of Malloy's most violent prisoners.

After receiving his sack lunch, Speer had decided there was no reason he should not be fed a hot meal. He had reached through the tray slot, grabbed the control unit officer and wrenched the officer's elbow. After the officer pulled himself free, Speer had kicked on his windows and rammed himself against the walls.

Under ordinary circumstances, Anderson would have let Speer act out and after he had exhausted himself, gone into his cell, restrained him, stripped him and placed him in "the chair" for several hours while the Thorazine took effect. However, this was no ordinary time at Malloy. His yelling and screaming agitated the other inmates. With less than a full compliment of officers it was necessary to stop his tantrum before more inmates decided to act out.

Sergeant Knight had led the extraction team into the cell behind a cloud of pepper spray and the electronic immobilization shield. Speer screamed from having the pepper spray in his eyes, nose and mouth. He did not see the officers rush him with the EID shield. He only heard the door slide open.

With its electric probes sparking blue, the EID shield hit him with 50,000 volts of electricity. The electric pulses short-circuited his nervous system. He dropped to the floor in the fetal position. Several officers pressed him flat, while the others cuffed his legs and arms before dragging him out of his cell for decontamination.

Within 20 minutes, Carl Speer was naked, washed, and sitting in the restraint chair while the nurse administered a dose of Thorazine.

Anderson left Main Control, heading down the corridor to the female pod. It had been an exciting night there as well.

Following lights out at 2200 hours, Inmate Anna Harvey had decided to set a fire in her room. She thought it would be funny to make Anderson, whom she despised, evacuate the female unit. What she didn't count on was Sergeant Knight's decision just to open her cell and wash it down with a fire hose—without removing her first.

A strip and cavity search revealed she had managed to sneak tobacco and matches into her cell via her rectum. Never one to submit quietly to a search, Harvey spent the rest of the night, naked and in her damp cell under a shred-proof suicide blanket. By morning she was ready to comply with staff instructions to remain calm, eat her breakfast, and clean up her room.

"Morning Harvey," said Captain Anderson pressing down on the intercom button outside her cell.

"Morning Captain," she replied rather sheepishly.

"I take it that you're feeling better today?"

She nodded her head 'yes' and got out of bed and walked over to the door. "Do you think the doc could look at the bump on the back of my head?" she said respectfully. She rubbed her hand over the back of her head. She had hit her head against the wall when Sgt. Knight had sprayed her with the fire hose.

"You going to behave?" asked Anderson. He wanted to make sure she wasn't going to start another ruckus if he had the nurse come down to check on her.

"Yes, Captain," she replied.

"Okay, but I'll have to send a nurse. The doctor was killed in the tsunami."

Captain Anderson called on the radio, instructing the medical staff to add Harvey to their list of patients. He headed back to Main Control.

Several hundred yards down the beach, away from the bulk of the debris, Lt. Banderas, Corporal Nelson, and Officer Williams were loading their supplies into a salvaged 17-foot skiff. Despite the cool temperatures, they were sweating. Thirty miles to the east, they could just see the top of Great Sitkin Island's volcano. The bright red dawn was painting the snow-encrusted summit in innocent shades of pink. Looking out over the now glassy waters of Kuluk Bay it was hard to believe that it had been only yesterday when the sea had unleashed its fury on the island.

They worked silently. Each man was thinking about his responsibilities and duties on this mission. Corporal Nelson double-checked the food supplies and the radio. It would not do to run out of food or to lose touch with Captain Anderson. Officer Ben Williams checked the rifles and the ammunition. He sorted through each box, making sure everything was in working condition. He took out the night vision goggles, checking and re-checking them to make damn sure they were working. He reached inside his jacket and pulled out his bear claw necklace, carefully placing it around his neck—for good luck on the hunt. Carlos Banderas walked around making sure everything was in order. They were in for what promised to be several grueling days of man hunting. Experience had taught him that life was much easier when you were prepared.

Better than anyone on this team, Carlos knew this was going to be a difficult and dangerous mission. "Okay guys, let's get this show on the road," he barked while helping Corporal Nelson push the boat into the surf. They jumped in as it floated free.

Ben Williams pulled on the rope to start the engine. With a twist of the throttle, he swung the bow around from the beach. He pointed the bow east. Soon the skiff was zooming across the surface of the glassy waters of Kuluk Bay.

Travis Nelson and Carlos Banderas pulled their coats up around their necks and their caps further down over their ears to ward off the biting chill of the morning air.

They searched the horizon with their binoculars, trying to make out even the faintest sign of another skiff in the area. The only thing of interest was a pod of Orcas patrolling the north end of Kuluk Bay. The whales cruised just beneath the surface, searching for seals and sea lion pups. The mist from the whales' blows sparkled in the early morning light, marking their position. The faint "whoof" of their breathing resounded across the bay, bringing a smile to everyone's face.

"Carlos, I think the Orcas are coming our way," Nelson said, shouting and pointing at the approaching whales.

"Probably after seals," Ben replied. He had grown up around Killer Whales in Southeast Alaska. He knew their hunting patterns. "Keep your eyes on them, we might get to see quite a show."

Pointing excitedly, Carlos shouted, "There they go!"

The Orcas accelerated with amazing speed, closing in on a point between the skiff and Great Sitkin Island. Their sleek dorsal fins knifing through the water added drama to the moment. Like an orchestrated ballet, the pod surfaced, blowing mist into the air, and then dove. It was race between predator and prey. Somewhere below the surface, seals were swimming frantically to escape to the safety of the beaches on Great Sitkin Island.

According to Ben, two large whales—probably the alpha male and alpha female—were leading the pod. He identified them by the size of their dorsal fin and by their willingness to separate from the pack. Two smaller whales surfaced behind the skiff, herding the prey into the jaws of the other whales up ahead.

Carlos motioned for Ben to slow down. His heart raced in anticipation of the events about to unfold before them. Suddenly the ocean erupted around them. The surface boiled red as Killer Whales broke the surface with seals in their mouths. Twisting above the surface, the whales tossed the helpless seals high into the air. The air reverberated with the sounds of bodies slapping against the mirror-like waters. The cries of the wounded seals echoing across the waves sent shivers down Carlos's spine. Then, as if nothing had happened, everything was calm. The only evidence for the massacre they'd just witnessed was the small flock of seagulls and kittiwakes skimming over the waves, feeding on severed bits of carcasses. Several hundred yards away the pod had resumed formation, renewing its stealthy patrol of the feeding ground.

Understanding the brutality of nature didn't make it any easier for any of the men to accept the slaughter they'd just witnessed. And the fact that they'd been witness to an incredible spectacle was not lost on them. Each man tried to rationalize the brutality of the hunt.

Travis Nelson was speechless. He was wondering if what they'd just witnessed was an omen of things to come.

The cacophony of barking seals from the beach broke the silence. Chancing nothing, the seals had raced from the water up onto the shore. The Orca pod was still out there and they knew it. They were heading for higher ground, their sleek bodies undulating in the morning light.

Carlos turned around to face Ben and told him to head to the beach several hundred yards from the seal haul out. He had no intention of further upsetting those animals that had managed to escape the morning's carnage. They deserved a rest. And if Church was on the island, they didn't need their arrival announced.

Ben gunned the engine one last time, sliding the skiff up on the rock beach. As soon as they were clear of the deeper surf, Carlos and Travis jumped out, grabbing the bow and pulling the boat further up on the beach. Ben held his rifle at the ready, eyeing the treeless tundra for any sign of a would-be sniper named Toby Church.

Carlos secured the boat to a large boulder. He tested the mooring line and ordered Ben and Travis to grab their weapons, the radio, and a small pack of food. He also took the precaution of removing the spark plugs to prevent someone from stealing the boat while they were gone.

"Ben? Which route looks the best?" Carlos asked. He knelt beside his men keeping an eye on the cliffs above the beach. Together they surveyed the cliffs leading up to the treeless, grass-covered tundra that characterizes the Aleutian Islands.

Pointing to his right, Ben replied, "Over there is a small trail. It looks like it winds up off the beach. It should give us a good field of vision if Church is up there."

"Very good," Carlos said nodding his head in agreement. "Okay gents," he said confidently, "Let's head up the trail. Keep yourselves spaced at 20-foot intervals. Remember, give Church an opportunity to surrender. If he refuses to surrender, deadly force is authorized." It was important to stress the need to give Church a chance to surrender. Carlos didn't like it, but as a professional he had to set aside the murder of Officer Nikolaevich and follow procedures. There wasn't an officer at Malloy or on this mission that didn't want to make quick work of Toby Church, him included. But his commitment to following the law was what set him and his fellow officers apart from murdering scum like Toby Church. He motioned for the group to set off towards the middle of Great Sitkin Island. They were alert. Church could be hiding anywhere on the island. No one wanted to be shot.

Coming over a rise, Ben Williams caught site of the SH-60 wreckage. He raised his hand in a closed fist, signaling everyone to stop. Taking out his binoculars, he lay down on the grassy slope and surveyed the area around the mangled helicopter.

Carlos dropped to his belly and slithered up next to Ben.

Whispering, Ben said, "Look down there Lieutenant, about 300 yards. It's that Navy chopper."

"I see it," Carlos replied. He ordered his men to fan out and approach the wreckage from three directions.

Carefully, the three officers approached the downed aircraft. If Toby Church were still on the island, he would have his best opportunity to ambush them as they crossed this grassy meadow. Even though it took only a few minutes to traverse the short distance, to Ben it seemed like an eternity. The anxiety of not knowing whether or not Toby Church was lying in wait to ambush them was hard to handle.

Half way across the meadow, Ben noticed footprints in the mud and trampled blades of grass. He knelt down to examine them. He retraced their path. As he followed the tracks over a small rise, he came upon the now scavenged carcass of the sea lion. Next, he noticed the trail in the grass leading to a small cliff down to the beach where the seals were now sunning themselves. Church had been here, but it was obvious that he was long gone.

Ben slung his rifle over his shoulder and hiked back up to the crash site. "He was here alright. Probably yesterday," Ben called out, while motioning to the beach behind him. "My guess is that he saw the chopper go down, beached to scavenge the wreckage, and headed back out to sea. It looks like he took some meat from a dead sea lion just down the trail."

Rising from one knee, where he had been carefully sifting through the remains of the pilots and the SH-60, Carlos agreed with Ben's assessment. "Sounds about right. By the looks of it he took one of the pilot's 9mm pistols and ammo, some navigation charts, and the compass."

Travis Nelson lifted his cap and ran his fingers across his brow, commenting on Church's ingenuity. "This guy sure knows his stuff. He knew exactly what items he needed. Didn't waste any time."

"Damn right, Corporal," Carlos said. "Church knows his stuff. This is not going to be easy." He wiped the sweat off his brow. He never could understand how it could get so warm when the sun came out.

Thinking out loud, Ben Williams interjected, "He may not have much gas though. And if he's low on fuel he'll need to find some quick."

Nelson pulled out the maps and a thermos of coffee. While Carlos spread the map out on a piece of metal, Travis radioed Captain Anderson at Malloy. After finishing his report to Captain Anderson, he pulled the charred bodies of the pilots from the wreckage. He dragged them a few yards away from the crash and covered them with debris and stones. It wasn't much of a burial, but it would help stop some of the scavengers until the Navy could send a retrieval team to the island. Using some dark volcanic stones, he finished their makeshift graves by lining out a cross on the top of the mound. Bowing his head, he removed his cap and said a short prayer.

Next Travis walked over to the crew chief's body. He knelt down to examine him. The back of the dead man's head was soaked in blood. The ground under his face was dyed reddish-gray. Taking a deep breath, Travis gently rolled the chief over onto his back. He almost vomited. The entire front section of the chief's skull was missing. He'd been shot in the back of the head—executed. "Lieutenant!" Travis shouted out.

"Yeah Nelson, what is it?"

"Lieutenant, it looks like the chief was alive when Church found him."

"What?" said a confused Carlos. He'd assumed the chief had been killed on impact. He walked over to take a look for himself.

Seeing the chief's shattered skull left no doubt. Church had executed the poor man. "That Motherfucker! That lousy son-of-a-bitch," Carlos cursed. It was one thing to kill somebody while trying to escape, but quite another to kill a helpless man.

Turning around, Carlos kicked at a clump of tundra. "Bury him Corporal. We can't do anything for him now," He was fuming. Only his years of training kept him from taking an oath to kill that lousy pig. But it didn't stop him from visualizing how he would avenge himself on Church. Shaking his head, he walked over next to Ben.

They stood together looking out to sea. They were at a loss as to which direction Church may have headed.

"Ben, I don't think he would have headed west," Carlos argued. "He can't have much fuel. I think he's heading towards Atka Island where he can steal a bigger boat."

"What you're saying makes sense," Ben answered thoughtfully, "but Church is a hunter and most smart animals, like a bear, deer or elk, will circle back on you when they're being hunted." He used a stick to illustrate his point in the mud. "I think Church is doubling back on us. I'm guessing he's sitting right under our noses on Adak Island. In one of those cabins on the south side of the island."

Ben had a good argument, but Carlos didn't want to get too cute in trying to second-guess Toby Church. The largest population centers were to the east. And even if he did head west, he'd never be able to cross the North Pacific in a skiff.

"You've got a point Ben, but I think we'd better play the odds." They would head east across Fenimore Pass to the village of Atka on Atka Island.

Ben was unwilling to concede his point completely. He continued advocating for his theory all the way back to the beach.

Ben's insistence was uncharacteristic and several times Carlos almost gave in, but he couldn't overrule logic with a hunch. Finally Carlos agreed to radio Captain Anderson and ask him send a team to check out the cabins on the south side of Adak.

Exasperated, Carlos said, "Now can we get in the boat?"

Ben didn't reply. He just nodded his head and flashed his disarming smile.

They loaded back into the skiff. They were going to sail around the north tip of Great Sitkin Island and into the choppy waters of Fenimore Pass. Eighty miles away, on the other side of the pass lay Atka Island.

Karluk River Valley, Kodiak Island, Alaska

Slowly, Joy opened her eyes. Her muscles burned and her body ached all over after spending the night hog-tied and sleeping on her belly. Once she was untied, needles of pain shot through her shoulders, arms, thighs and calves as the blood rushed back into them with a vengeance. The circulation returning to her cold hands and feet made tears well up in her eyes. Never before had she felt such pain. Ever so gently, she stretched her arms and legs one at a time. It took all her willpower to raise up on her hand and roll over onto her butt. Her head throbbed. She massaged her temples. Her stomach growled. She was desperately hungry.

Elizabeth yelped in pain as Lincoln untied the ropes and dropped her feet and arms to the ground. Pain knifed through her limbs as blood raced back into her muscles and tissue. She felt dirty and violated.

Joy's touch startled her. But when Joy began rubbing her legs, she managed to flash a brief smile of thanks. She sighed with relief as Joy manipulated her joints. Soon her muscles and tendons were loose enough for her to stand up.

Joy pulled Elizabeth's shirt away from her neck, examining the wound where Lincoln had cut her following the rape, and applied some antibacterial cream from the survival kit. Grateful for Joy's ministrations, Elizabeth touched Joy's arm, silently expressing her deepest thanks.

In the meantime, Lincoln had returned from relieving himself. Reluctantly, he passed out a small ration of food to his hostages. "Eat your food and grab the gear. We've got a long day ahead of us and I want to get out of here," he growled.

Joy and Elizabeth glanced at each other. Looking south they could see the steep mountains and were overcome with a sinking feeling. Their legs ached just at the thought of the climb. The sight of cloud wisps sweeping away at the peaks made them shiver. It was going to be a long day indeed.

"Okay bitches," Lincoln slurred with a lecherous smile, "let's get this show on the road. Keep your mouths shut and don't get any ideas about escaping. I feel like killing somebody today." He racked the slide on the pistol, making sure both women understood his intentions.

With that last menacing threat, the trio set off up the steep slopes of the mountains on the west side of Karluk Lake. High above them, blue skies were breaking through the overcast.

Throughout the morning they struggled over the wet grass and moss-covered stones. Sometimes they found themselves on all fours struggling towards the 2,000-foot summit. Sweat poured from their brows despite the cool morning air.

Luckily for Joy, she was in better shape than Elizabeth. Not only was she younger, but she had spent the winter playing intramural volleyball with her friends at Columbia University. She moved her feet in a steady rhythm, trying to keep her bearings. She was waiting for an opportunity for escape to present itself. When it did, she was going to run for it. She didn't care that she knew nothing of wilderness survival. Her instincts were telling her that Lincoln was only biding his time before he killed them both.

All her life Elizabeth LeDue had been a pampered woman. Outside of an occasional game of golf or tennis, she had rarely done more than walk to keep her trim figure. Furthermore, she had just spent the last 22 months in jail awaiting trial. She was tired. Only her willpower kept her going. "Must keep going," she murmured under her breath, "must keep going or he will kill me."

Ivan Lincoln was following his hostages, cursing their efforts under his breath. "Worthless fucking bitches," he growled, "get your asses moving or I'll kill you both." *I should leave them both behind. But I can't. I'll make that bitch beg for her life yet.*

As for this young blonde, well now there is a prime filly. Tall, young, and pretty. Lincoln relished the thought of terrorizing her. *Maybe she'll beg for mercy? Yes, this young one is going to be fun. After a few days of pushing up and down these mountains she'll be in no condition to resist.*

Stumbling over the rocks, the women came to a halt. It had taken them hours just to cover a few miles. Now they stood on the summit, towering 2,000-feet above the mirrored waters of Karluk Lake. Lincoln allowed Joy and Elizabeth a small break to drink some water and share a candy bar. A few feet away lay the carcass of a winterkilled mountain goat. Taking out the fillet knife, he carved some fat and meat off the partially decomposed animal.

Lincoln motioned for his hostages to sit down, took a long drink of water, and scanned the surrounding mountains for any trace of pursuit. Without binoculars he had to rely on his not-too-good eyesight. It was frustrating, but in this open terrain, it would be pretty easy to spot someone following him. Sooner or later someone would be coming after them. But he was sure he had a good head start.

Far to the south and west he could see the ocean. Although he could not see over the mountains to the east, experience told him that he would find the safety of the forest in that direction. He picked his next route—a course over the ridges and down the slopes to the shores at the head of Karluk Lake. There they would cross over and make for the interior.

Across the valley, on a ridge 2,800-feet above Cottonwood Creek, Harry Ignustuk and Danny Sanders were watching the fugitives scramble to the top of the ridgeline. Wiping sweat from their foreheads, they took a few minutes to catch their breath. They had been going hard since before dawn and they still had a long day ahead of them.

They had set out just before dawn. It had been a treacherous climb in the dark, but Harry was determined to be on the high ground before Lincoln could move his group from their camp, which he had guessed to be located on the other side of the Karluk River.

Harry was a patient tracker. He wasn't going to try to cross the river and chase Ivan Lincoln. Crossing the rain-swollen Karluk River would be dangerous for them and setting up a hot pursuit could endanger the lives of the hostage. Harry planned to intercept Lincoln by cutting across his path and surprising him in an ambush. He was operating on a hunch that Lincoln would circle the lake and make for the deep interior of the island.

"Do you think they've seen us, Harry?"

"Hard to say, but it doesn't look like it," Harry replied calmly. "If Lincoln had seen us, they'd be heading off the other side of that ridge."

Harry had to guess correctly. The fate of two women rested on his ability to anticipate Ivan Lincoln's moves.

"Today," Harry said to Danny, "we'll shadow Lincoln. We need to determine their exact route. I'm figuring Lincoln will hike to the end of the valley and cut across the east—towards the interior and away from the sea. Once he cuts down the slopes we'll pick up our pace and pin him against the shores of O'Malley Lake."

"They're on the move again Harry," Danny said, pointing to the far ridge.

"Yep," confirmed Harry. He watched the trio heading south along the ridgeline. "Let's pick up stakes and keep just behind them. Remember to keep on the back side of the ridge so he doesn't see us when he turns around."

Submarine Putin, 55 degrees North; 158 degrees West, Gulf of Alaska

The nuclear submarine Putin was charging through the water at over 35-knots, increasing the distance between itself and the USS Billings. It was rapidly closing in on Shelikof Straits and Kodiak Island.

Commander Ivanshenko was resting in his quarters, thinking about the upcoming mission. Life aboard a submarine was fraught with peril. Crushing depths, uncharted reefs, undersea mountains, sticky valves, questionable reactors, other submarines, and surface ships all posed hazards. But a sailor ate well, enjoyed good pay, didn't have to get seasick during storms, and got to travel. And if a commander was skilled and daring, he almost always had the advantage in a fight. But Ivanshenko harbored no illusions. The Americans would try every trick in the book to stop him. The clandestine nature of this mission meant that all bets were off. *The Americans might even use force. I, on the other hand, do not enjoy the luxury of being able to shoot back if the Americans decide to play hardball. If I damage or sink an American ship, I can be sure that the US Navy will announce the "unprovoked attack" around the world with pictures and sound bites. Furthermore, the Americans can fire on, damage or sink my boat and the only people to know what happened will be a few select people in the Kremlin and the Pentagon. No press releases about an "unprovoked attack" will be sent from the Russian Admiralty. Once again, a brave Russian crew would "disappear" somewhere in the North Pacific for unexplained reasons.*

Ivanshenko picked up the intercom phone. "Get me Vatutin."

"Yes Commander?"

"How much further to the entrance of Shelikof Straits?"

"About eight hours at current speed. Why?"

"I have a hunch the Americans will try to intercept us before we can enter the area." Pausing for effect, Ivanshenko said, "Somewhere far out to sea where there will be few witnesses." He wanted to have a plan of attack if they did.

Vatutin noticed the dark tone in his commander's voice. "What's your plan if they do, Commander?" He felt uneasy about this whole operation. He was a man of concrete thoughts and actions. He didn't like ad-libbing things.

"Gather up Golkin and come to my quarters." Ivanshenko wanted to have a private discussion—away from the prying eyes and ears of the crew.

Golkin and Vatutin arrived a few moments later. Ivanshenko invited them to sit down and offered them tea and bread.

Pulling out his charts of Shelikof Straits and Kodiak Island, Ivanshenko began the discussion. For the next thirty minutes they discussed all the possible ways the Americans could try to prevent them from entering the straits. They discussed whether or not to abort the mission. If they returned, they could not be blamed for a natural disaster downing the American transport plane and foiling the GRU's plan. However, this mission was vital to their country's security. If the mission failed, Admiral Voroshilov would lose his job and maybe even his life. But more than anything, they did not like to admit defeat; especially when there was a chance they could pull it off. They were in this business because they enjoyed defying the odds.

Intelligence reports from the last satellite pass before leaving Petropavlovsk indicated the US Coast Guard had a cutter stationed at Kodiak, along with several SH-60 helicopters and two C-130 Hercules. These forces might be deployed to place sonobuoys and harass the Putin to prevent her from surfacing and launching her Spetznaz team. He was sure the US Navy had also intercepted the Neptune's radio report about the location of the fugitives.

The USS Billings carried two SH-60 Seahawk helicopters. These helicopters could be used to harass the Putin until the Billings could come on station and drive them out of the straits.

Ivanshenko slapped his hand down on the table bringing the discussion to an end. "Then we are agreed. We will dive to 150 meters—just below the layer of cold, dense water, slow to 20 knots, and go to silent running in an effort to throw off any sonobuoys. We will launch Major Golkin's force under the cover of darkness."

He pulled out a bottle of vodka and poured each man a small shot of the powerful liquor. Raising his glass, he offered a toast for good luck. The vodka burned all the way down.

USS Billings, 150 miles west of the Putin, Gulf of Alaska

"Lt. Commander Hastings," said Commander Englemann summoning her Executive Officer. "Raise Admiral Brower in Honolulu on a secured line. I want to confirm my orders concerning that Russian sub." She was contemplating just how she was going to stop the Russians from entering Shelikof Straits. Even running at flank speed in calm waters the Billings would be unable to catch the Russians—if the Russians were running at top speed too. She was sure the Russians were opening the distance.

"And Brad, see if CINCPAC can't identify which sub it is and who her Commander is."

Hastings left the bridge for the Combat Information Center. As soon as he arrived he sent an encrypted message to headquarters. It took only a few minutes to make a connection. Soon he was talking to CINCPAC over a secured satellite communications link. He notified Commander Englemann over the intercom that contact had been made.

"Skipper, I've got Admiral Brower on the line."

Picking up the phone, Margaret Englemann discussed the situation with the admiral. After a few moments, she put down the receiver, took a long sip of her coffee, and ordered her officers to assemble in the wardroom in 20 minutes.

"Ensign?" she said.

"Yes Skipper?"

"Admiral Brower says the Akula Class sub we're chasing is most likely the Putin under the command of Igor Ivanshenko. Gather what information you have on the boat and its commander. Be prepared to give a short briefing in 15 minutes."

She headed to the wardroom. She needed a few minutes alone. Throughout her career she had participated in dozens of naval exercises and countless simulated attacks on submarines. But never had she really been in combat. She hoped that this would not be her first time. However, Admiral Brower had been clear. The Russians must be stopped at all costs. She had a free hand to take any course of action she felt necessary. This was no war game.

The soft knock on the door broke her concentration. She welcomed her officers, directing them to take seats while the officer prepared his briefing.

A short, rather studious looking man, this ensign did not cut the figure of the classic naval officer. His dark-rimmed glasses and freckled face belied his analytical prowess. This was his first deployment at sea. Commander Englemann could make or break his career. His palms were sweating.

He cleared his throat before speaking. "According to the latest intelligence reports, the Russian submarine is the Putin out of Petropavlovsk. She is an Akula Class nuclear attack submarine. Her keel was laid in 1993. She is 362-feet long, displacing 12,770 tons. She is manned by a crew of 73 officers and men. She is capable of making 35 knots or more when submerged. Her maximum dive depth is unknown, although it is believed to be in excess of 2,000 feet. She carries the latest in Russian torpedo technology. These new torpedoes come equipped with proximity warheads. They are reported to have speeds of up to 51 knots and ranges over 3 nautical miles."

He stopped to see if there were any questions, then continued. "The Putin is commanded by Commander Igor Ivanshenko. He is a graduate of Leningrad State University with advanced degrees in military history and mathematics. He is a survivor of one submarine sinking. In this accident, he was the executive officer on a Delta Class submarine that struck a reef off the Israeli coast. The collision killed most of the command crew. It was Ivanshenko's cool head, quick decisions, and bravery that led to the escape of 20 of the crewmen. For his bravery, he was made a Hero of the Soviet Union."

Seeing that her young ensign was almost finished, Englemann helped him conclude his briefing by asked a very important question. "Thank you Ensign, but what is Ivanshenko's reputation as a commander?"

The ensign removed his glasses. "Commander Ivanshenko is known as one of the most daring and decisive submarine commanders in the Russian fleet. He acts on instinct and is known to be a skilled tactician. As the commander of an Oscar class submarine, he disobeyed a direct order not to rescue the crew of a Swedish destroyer that had collided with a Soviet spy submarine in the waters off Stockholm. His actions almost cost him his career, but it was then Rear Admiral Voroshilov who saved him from court martial."

Commander Englemann stood up and addressed her officers. "Well, as you've all just heard from Ensign Taft, we are facing a formidable adversary. He has a reputation for skill and bravery. He commands one of the fastest and deepest diving submarines in the world. We are under orders to prevent the Russians from capturing Dr. Elizabeth LeDue. I am open to suggestions on how we accomplish our mission without too much bloodshed."

She had learned long ago that to make the best decisions you needed as much information as possible. It was Admiral Quinn who had taught her to seek the input of her officers whenever the situation allowed it. Her subordinates appreciated her inclusive style.

The officers of the Billings understood they could well find themselves in a shooting war with an enemy submarine. Several of the more junior officers cleared their throats or squirmed in their seats. The reality of what was about to happen in the next few hours was beginning to sink in. The discussion proceeded as ideas were traded back and forth. Englemann sat back and listened.

As the conversation wound down, Englemann cleared her throat. "Okay, gentlemen, I've heard enough. Mr. Lewis, get me a detailed weather report for the next 24 hours. Lt. Commander Hastings, get back up to the bridge and tell engineering that I expect 31 knots out of our engines. Ready the crew to go to general quarters on my orders. Lieutenants Cowdrey and Martin, I want you to get Hawk Two fired up and ready to launch. Lt. Surin," she said with special vigor, "get your men ready and load up on the helo—I want you on Kodiak Island as soon as possible."

In closing, she tried to instill calm and confidence for the upcoming events. "Everyone listen to me. I want you to remember we have the advantage. The Russians will be reluctant to attack us, because they cannot afford to be exposed. However, we are about to try and corner a very dangerous animal, and cornered animals are unpredictable. You are all professionals. Go out there and do your best. Dismissed."

The wardroom was silent as they filed out into the corridor. As soon as the room was empty, Lt. Commander Hastings closed the hatch and turned around, "Skipper?"

"Yes Brad?" she replied. After all these years of serving together, she knew he was about to ask a very pointed question.

"What are your orders if the Putin continues into Shelikof Straits or manages to put men on the island?" he asked respectfully.

"Sink her."

Cold Bay, Alaska

Despite being racked by spasms of pain in her abdomen, Jenne Lucas pressed on towards the lights of Cold Bay shimmering in the distance. The terrain leading down from Frosty Peak was a maze of bogs, trenches and small mounds of lichens called Tussocks. Outfitted with rubber soled, cotton slip-on shoes, she was stumbling at almost every step. And whenever she slipped off a tussock, she would break through the icy surface, soaking her feet in the spongy terrain. Her fingers were frozen from being soaked in the mud whenever she fell. Her only salvation was the warmth of the winter coat she had taken from the nurse. She had given Evers the fur-lined parka worn by Officer Smith.

From her perch on Frosty Peak, the path to Cold Bay had looked relatively flat. In reality, it was a seemingly endless stretch of undulating hills laced by glacial streams. She struggled to keep going as the pain clouded her mind. Her feet were freezing and her head burned with fever. She was shivering. The only thing keeping her going was her determination that this would be her chance to right some of the wrongs she had done so many years ago.

As she came over a rise, she spotted a gravel road. "Thank God," she said falling to one knee to catch her breath.

Forcing herself to get to her feet she started to walk down the gravel path towards town. She froze in fear as she rounded a small hill. Ambling down the middle of the road was a bear! "Oh Jesus," she moaned.

Unsure of what to do, Lucas began screaming at the top of her lungs. "Get out of here! Scram! Ahhhhhh!" She started throwing rocks.

Taken by surprise, the young bruin rose up on its hind legs and swayed its head back and forth trying to get a good look at the creature blocking his path. Having recently gorged itself on a walrus carcass, the young bear simply barked a soft whoof, turned around and trotted back down the road on all fours.

Jenne laughed nervously in relief. *Thank you God!* She resumed walking down the road—this time more carefully.

Just outside of Cold Bay, Lucas spotted a group of people huddled around a small cabin. Following the earthquake and the tsunami warning they had evacuated their homes to seek shelter several hundred feet above the town. With the break of day and no sign of an approaching tsunami they were gathering their belongings and chatting nervously about when would be the best time to return home.

A young boy blessed with sharp eyes was the first to spot Lucas coming down the road. "Look over there! It's a lady. She looks hurt!" he shouted pointing excitedly.

Several people in the group turned to look. It was a female in an orange jumpsuit and mud-encrusted coat stumbling down the hill. She had her hands pressed to her belly.

They were unsure of what to do. Why would someone be dressed in hunter orange this time of year? Only when Lucas stumbled and fell, did several people break ranks, rushing up the hill to her aid.

Lucas fought to remain conscious as she saw people running towards her. "Help, help," she cried in a feeble voice. She rolled onto her side, fighting against the burning pain in her side. *I made it.*

The owner of the local cafe was the first person to reach her. "Are you all right? What's the matter?" she asked. A mother of five, she knew how to extract information from an injured person. God knows she'd spent enough of her time mending her kids whenever they'd gotten hurt.

"Please help us," Jenne begged in a raspy voice. The elderly woman lifted her head and placed it on her lap. "Our plane crashed on the mountain. The pilot is dead. There are two other women still alive."

"She says that she's from a plane crash up on Frosty Peak and that there're survivors," she announced to the gathering crowd. "Somebody get a blanket so we can carry this poor woman down to town. She's burning up with fever."

Lucas tugged on the lapel of the old woman's coat, pleading, "Please, you've got to go save the nurse and the officer."

Noticing for the first time the numbers printed on the left breast of the orange jumpsuit, the woman rolled her over. Stenciled across the back were three rows of words "Prisoner—Malloy Super Maximum Security Prison—Alaska Department of Corrections."

"She's a prisoner from that prison on Adak," she announced to the group. Everyone fell silent. Then they began murmuring among themselves, speculating about how a female prisoner from Adak got to Cold Bay in an airplane.

"Maybe she escaped!"

"No, she looks sick, I bet it was a rescue flight!"

"Well, only the most dangerous people are taken there, so we'd better be careful when we get to that plane."

Knuckleheads, the old lady thought, *always looking for the worst.* She took control of the situation, dowsing the idea of a major prison escape by pointing out in a rather shrill voice that this woman had just told her a nurse and officer were still in the plane. "Furthermore," she said defiantly, "this particular prisoner is burning up with fever." There was no escape, she told everyone with confidence. This had to be a medical evacuation gone terribly wrong.

Running up, blanket in hand, the sharp-eyed boy beamed at his speedy response to the request for a blanket. He handed it to one of the men in the crowd, watching with satisfaction as several people laid it out on the ground and placed the prisoner in the orange jumpsuit on the makeshift stretcher.

"Let's get her down to town and to the clinic," ordered the manager of the local mercantile. Six men grabbed the edges of the blanket and set off with their mystery guest back to town.

In the meantime, a group of several young men and women were already jogging up the road. They were toting blankets, food, water, and firearms. Pointing to the top of the peak, the old woman instructed them to follow the prisoner's footprints up to the crash site. She made sure that one of them had a portable radio. Confident they had the necessary supplies to execute a rescue, she sent them on their way.

Lucas was hallucinating. Being juggled along the bumpy trail to town wasn't helping either. Racked by pain, she began vomiting.

The litter bearers quickened their pace. Despite the cool ocean breeze, sweat poured off their faces and soaked their clothes.

The local priest had grabbed his coat the minute he heard the news of a stranger found on the side of the mountain. Jogging up the trail to meet the group, he was gasping for air when he intercepted them. "How is she?" he asked one of the litter bearers.

"Not good I'm afraid Father," the man replied. "She's hardly breathing and she's been vomiting something awful."

"Put me down, please," Lucas asked in a weak but firm voice. "Put me down and let me die."

The exhausted litter bearers came to a halt, gently lowering her to the ground.

The priest knelt beside her and looked into Jenne Lucas's pale and pain etched face. "Tell me child," he said holding her hand and stroking her forehead. "Is there anything you'd like to confess?"

Jenne gazed into the priest's kind eyes. "I murdered my husband and 144 other people. I hope God will forgive me." Convulsions racked her body as she coughed violently. Squeezing the priest's hand, she pulled him closer. "Father, do you think God will forgive me?"

"Yes, my child," he said smiling compassionately, "I do. May God have mercy on your soul." With those words he felt her grip go limp and watched the life fade from her eyes. Jenne Lucas's long torment was over.

Solemnly the litter bearers resumed their journey. They would keep this poor stranger's body frozen until the authorities arrived to claim it.

The men from Cold Bay had been following Lucas's footprints for hours. It had been an arduous climb up the icy slopes, but they were all determined to save the survivors of the plane crash.

Coming over a rise, the group leader spotted the mangled fuselage of the plane. "There it is!" he shouted, pointing excitedly.

"Looks like one helluva crash," said another.

"Don't see how anyone could survive that," the youngest of the group said.

Scowling at his companions, the group leader said, "Think positive you guys. Hell, that little gal survived the crash and hiked all the way down the mountain. Let's quit talking and get over to that plane."

Despite appearing fairly close, it took the rescuers another 30 minutes to hike over the rough terrain to the wreckage.

"Hello," the youngest called out.

There was no reply.

"Hello!" the group leader yelled with his hands cupped to his mouth.

Silence.

Walking up to the remains of the plane, the group leader reached out and pulled off the piece of metal covering the opening. He knelt down next to the woman dressed in a nurses' uniform. Her eyes were fixed and dead.

Looking to his left, he saw the body of a corrections officer lying under a blanket. Her eyes were fixed and dead too. The rescue had come too late. Both Doreen Evers and Joan Steiger had succumbed to their wounds and hypothermia. The rescuers grew silent as they prepared to carry the bodies of the dead off the mountain. Even though they did not know any of the victims of the crash, they all felt that human connection that touches a soul in the face of death.

Using tubing from the fuselage of the Cessna, the rescuers built makeshift litters to transport the bodies off the mountain. Gently, they loaded the corpses of Corporal Steiger, Doreen Evers and Blaine Smith onto the litters. Even though they were dead, they solemnly covered them with coats and blankets.

Hoisting the litters to their shoulders, the rescuers headed down off the mountain. It was a long way back to town.

Malloy Super Maximum-Security Prison, Adak Island, Alaska

Captain Anderson had just received news that the community of Dutch Harbor had been obliterated. The airport had been destroyed. There were no reports of any airplanes landing or crashing anywhere near the town.

Anderson's heart sank at the thought of more deaths. *Where are Smith and Evers?* Desperate to find an answer, he started plotting every possible route. It was an exercise in futility. *Are they lost at sea? Have they crashed on some remote island? Are they marooned on some desolate island waiting for a rescue that may never come? Or have they made it to an airport and help?* He had no idea. He wanted to believe they were all right, but in his heart of hearts he knew they were gone. He clung to the hope that they weren't lost. Knowing they were dead was easier to handle.

Picking up the phone, he placed a call to Juneau. He needed to inform the governor he had three more people missing, including another murderer.

Cook Inlet, Alaska

Michelle Dornier had slept restlessly. She was exhausted after the previous day's events and the hectic night spent at Elmendorf Air Force Base. She gazed out the side window, watching the other Bell 206 Jet Ranger pacing them in the rough air. Even with a lid on the coffee cup, she was having a hard time taking a drink, let alone not spilling it all over her blouse.

She felt nauseous. But it wasn't the rough air making her queasy, it was the upcoming mission. She was totally out of her element. *Do I have the strength to deal with this crisis?* She was a city girl. *What can I possibly do to make things better in a small village on some island in the middle of the Pacific Ocean?* She didn't like the idea of spending the next several days cooped up with grumpy old Dick Burke, listening to him criticize her every move. *I should have stood up to Governor Malloy and stayed in Juneau, where I could oversee the big picture.* Years ago she'd made the decision not to go into the field. *Why did I let Governor Malloy push me into this insane assignment?* She knew why—when the governor gave you an order, you obeyed.

Dick Burke was staring out the window at the plumes of smoke rising from the endless forest along the Kenai Peninsula—fires caused by the earthquake. He wondered if his friends in Homer and Kasilof were okay. Up in the distance, he could see the symmetrical cone of Mount Augustine towering above the sea. It reminded him of how vulnerable they all were. He pulled out his maps of Kodiak Island and traced possible routes for tracking down the fugitives. Even though it had been years since he'd been in the field, he still remembered how difficult manhunts could be and how important it was to have a plan.

Flying in the second chopper was a team of four state troopers and prisoner transport officers, who, once an operations center had been established in Larsen Bay, would set out in search of Inmates Lincoln and LeDue. Two EMTs accompanied the group to provide emergency medical care to the injured.

Led by Alaska State Trooper Major John Calhoun, a 14-year veteran with experience in Western Alaska, the team was equipped with the latest in night vision equipment, weapons, and communications gear.

Joining Major Calhoun on this mission were: Trooper Jason Abelsen, the department's best sniper, PTO Karen Marston, a tough little gal transplanted to Alaska from Wyoming, and PTO Kent Price, a former US Army communications specialist.

Major Calhoun was concerned. This team had never worked together before. He knew very little about any of the officers.

Reading a biographical sketch was not very useful—especially when you were about to embark on a manhunt in a harsh wilderness. *Oh well, it's too late to worry about that now. This is the team and we'll have to work things out.*

Price and Marston were assigned to the prison in Kenai. Both of them had reputations for being avid hunters and crack shots. Trooper Abelsen was selected because he had been posted on Kodiak Island the year before. He knew the Karluk River area intimately. For three years he had led a sting operation into bear poaching in the valley. His hard work had uncovered an international conspiracy of killing and smuggling which led all the way back to some of the most powerful people in Korea and Taiwan. Bear gallbladders are highly prized in Chinese medicine. The political fallout from his investigation resulted in him being transferred to a more sedate post in Anchorage.

Flying over the Kenai Peninsula and Afognak Island opened Dornier's eyes. The vast expanse of forest and mountains stretching before her made her realize that tracking down a man like Lincoln would not be easy. *They don't call it the Last Frontier for nothing.*

Burke broke her concentration. "When we get to Larsen Bay, we will probably be accosted by the townsfolk. I will take care of them. You need to take the team to a building where we can set up a command center. Set up the radios and get in touch with General McCarthy's people in Anchorage."

"Then what?" she asked. She tried not to bristle at his presumption of assuming command. This was to be a joint operation. He didn't outrank her.

"By the time you set up, I should have figured out what supplies need to be sent to help cover the next few weeks. We can call for supplies and get the people busy rebuilding their lives. In the meantime, we launch the search."

Reaching down to his ankle, Burke pulled his 40-caliber pistol from his ankle holster, ejected the magazine from the grip, pulled back the slide, and ejected a shell onto the floor. He held the pistol in front of her. "You ever shoot a gun?"

What is he doing? Why is he pulling out his gun inside the helicopter? She was stunned. "No, I haven't," she said uncomfortably.

Burke shook his head in disbelief and tried not to laugh. "Well, don't go wandering too far from me or one of our troopers."

She didn't understand. "Why would I need a gun?" she replied somewhat puzzled and annoyed. "I'm not going after these prisoners."

"It's not for the prisoners," he yelled over the pounding of the rotor blades. "It's for the bears that are sure to come into town when they start smelling all the garbage and waste that's going to pile up over the next few days. I'd give you a shotgun, but we don't have any spares right now."

As he showed her how to load and unload the pistol he said, "Just keep your finger off the trigger until you are ready to shoot and know what you're shooting."

Bears? She hadn't thought of bears. "What kind of bears?" she asked trying to act nonchalant.

"Big, hairy, and mean," he said. Burke took delight in Dornier's discomfort. He didn't like outsiders.

Dornier tried not to let Burke's warning upset her. Most of all, she didn't want to let him know that she really couldn't comprehend the true nature of what he was telling her. Wild bears were not a major issue in New Jersey and in downtown Juneau the bears were more of a garbage nuisance than a predatory threat.

Reluctantly she took the pistol from Burke immediately noticing how small it was—it fit her petite hand very well. Inserting the magazine into the grip, she slid the slide back like he'd showed her, chambered a round and put it inside her coat pocket.

Coming around the Northeast corner of Uyak Bay, the two AST helicopters descended below the surrounding mountains to get out of the blustery winds that had been pounding them the length of Shelikof Straits. Larsen Bay was visible in the distance. Even from this far out, everyone could see the damage caused by the earthquake. The cannery had collapsed into the water. Jagged pilings stuck up above the water like broken matchsticks.

They could see people searching through the debris for cherished items and lost loved ones. Visions of old television disaster reports flashed through everyone's mind.

The noise of the helicopters flying down the bay and over the town attracted everyone's attention. In one great herd, the survivors moved in the direction of the airport, abandoning their efforts for the moment. Help was on its way!

Kicking up small rocks, the two helicopters came to a bumpy stop on the gravel pad of the Larsen Bay airport. No sooner had the rotor blades slowed down than shell-shocked survivors surrounded both helicopters. Burke opened the door and tried to move the crowd back from the helicopter. It was futile. Dozens of voices clamored for answers to their questions. When would their town and their lives be restored to normal? When would supplies and medical personnel arrive?

Resigning himself to the fact he could not out shout dozens of anxious people, Burke plunged into the midst of this chaos. He shook hands, gave hugs, and patted people on the shoulder and took command of the crowd. Slowly, he moved them away from the helicopters. With a patience that belied his nature, he answered their questions. He did not, however, tell them the exact nature of the mission—no need to panic them right now.

Using Burke's diversion, Dornier and Major Calhoun loaded up their supplies onto a four-wheeler, which was sitting outside a small hangar. Dornier thought it odd that there were no cars around. She didn't know that the favored mode of transport in the Bush was the versatile four-wheeler. Roads in Alaska's Bush were little more than tracks in most instances and without roads there is no reason to own a car or pickup.

She motioned for the other officers and the EMTs to grab a second four-wheeler over by the flight service station.

Burke watched his team out of the corner of his eye as they departed for town. He continued answering the flurry of questions being fired at him. When the questions grew repetitive, he reminded himself of the importance of giving his officers time to set up a command post and continued to answer them as completely as possible. He was displaying a patience that even he didn't recognize.

The team itself was taken aback by the devastation that had been wrought upon Larsen Bay. Where houses once stood there were only splintered remains. Only a few buildings were still standing. Fortunately, one of them was the school.

As they pulled up in front of the school, Dornier put her skills as a savvy politician to work. Flashing her best smile and using her firmest handshake, she introduced herself to the principal, who had come to the door to meet them. After introducing herself, she used her sweetest tone to convince him to let her use the administration offices to set up a "communications center." Without delay, the officers unpacked their equipment, charts, and plans in the principal's office.

The EMTs went immediately to the nurse's station and set up an emergency triage center.

Just as they were finishing up their work, Burke arrived escorted by the mayor of Larsen Bay.

The mayor was wondering why two state commissioners were in a small town like Larsen Bay immediately following a massive earthquake. But with the citizens of Larsen Bay consumed by their own grief, he didn't bother asking—at least not yet.

Burke instructed the mayor to form a small committee to make a list of supplies the community would need to get by for the next few weeks. After sending the mayor on his way, he signaled for Dornier and the four members of the hunt team to adjourn to the principal's office to discuss their plan.

Without knowing exactly where the survivors made landfall, it was difficult to know where to begin. Kodiak Island was far too big to simply set out on a random search for the fugitives.

"It's obvious we can't just start out blind. Let's send out the helicopters to search the beaches for any rafts or debris. Maybe that will give us a clue on where to begin," Burke said.

"We're going to need some serious luck," piped in Officer Marston.

"Luck is something we've been rather short on lately," quipped Dornier.

Governor's Office, Juneau, Alaska

"Thank you General," said Governor Malloy hanging up the phone. He was grinning after concluding a most informative conversation with his good friend. Pressing the intercom button, he summoned his chief-of-staff, "George, come into my office."

"What's up Governor?"

"Have a seat, George. I think we may be having some good luck for a change."

"What makes you say that?" Roberts responded gruffly.

Ignoring Robert's sullen reply, Governor Malloy informed his chief-of-staff that CIA Director Colin Clarke had reliable information on the situation involving the escaped prisoners, both on Adak and on Kodiak. CIA satellite data showed a small boat with a single occupant heading west just south of Kanaga Island and NSA listening posts had picked up radio traffic from the fishing vessel Neptune. Apparently, the Neptune's captain had radioed his wife and told her that they had dropped off two correctional officers in Larsen Bay. The captain said the officers would be heading up the Karluk River Valley in search of two prisoners and a someone named Joy. And last, but not least, Admiral Quinn, Chief of Naval Operations, had advised General McCarthy that the Fast Frigate USS Billings was in hot pursuit of that Russian submarine.

"Damn," said Roberts slapping his thigh and displaying a rare smile, "This is good news, Governor. Now it's time to get busy."

"I trust that you know what to do George?"

"Damn right I do," Roberts growled forcefully.

Rick Malloy didn't ask for an explanation. He knew that while Roberts was a sourpuss, he always got the job done.

Roberts returned to his office and placed an immediate call to Captain Anderson at Malloy Super Max. Toby Church was heading west. Next he went to the basement and radioed Commissioners Burke and Dornier to tell them that two DOC officers were on the trail of Inmates Lincoln and LeDue and a civilian hostage named Joy. The fugitives were heading south—up the Karluk River Valley.

While his chief-of-staff passed the word to Anderson and Dornier, Governor Malloy called The White House. The president was out of the office. He left a message.

Next Governor Malloy placed a call to Admiral Quinn in Washington, DC. He wanted the latest information on the Russians. But before he could finish dialing, the phone rang.

"Hello. This is Governor Malloy."

"Governor, this is Marc Anderson, uh, I'm sorry, Captain Anderson from Malloy Super Max."

"That's okay Marc, what can I do for you?"

"Well Governor, Mr. Roberts just gave me the information about Toby Church's location."

"Yes," replied Governor Malloy. He was a little annoyed at having his thoughts interrupted at this particular moment.

"Well, Governor, my search team is heading east. I hate to call them back for a red herring. I was wondering if you could get the Air Force to send a reconnaissance flight over the area and see if they can't confirm the sighting?"

"I can do that Captain, but I don't think it's necessary," Malloy replied firmly.

"Are you sure Governor?" Anderson felt uncomfortable challenging such an important person, but how could he be sure it was Church the satellite had spotted?

"Yes, I'm quite sure. I suggest you recall your team right away." Rick Malloy was used to giving orders.

If the Governor was that confident, Anderson didn't feel like following a hunch. He would turn Carlos Banderas's team around. "Thank you very much Governor."

But before the governor could hang up, Anderson asked for one more favor.

"Yes, Captain," replied Governor Malloy. *I don't have time for this.*

"Could you get a message to the Navy that we found their SH-60 helicopter on Great Sitkin Island? Both pilots and the crew chief are dead."

Governor Malloy sighed heavily. He squeezed the bridge of his nose harder, trying to make his grief go away. He didn't even know these young men, but still he found himself fighting back tears. "Yes, Captain, I can do that." He felt drained of all energy. He had never been any good at dealing with death. All his life he'd managed to avoid the issue, but as governor that simply wasn't possible. Silently, he hung up the phone.

After taking a short walk down to the docks to clear his mind, Governor Malloy returned to his office and placed his call to Admiral Quinn. He was impressed by the Navy's resolve to stop the Russians. But he was disappointed they only had one frigate assigned to the task.

"Well Governor," retorted Admiral Quinn somewhat testily, "we couldn't exactly conduct a naval exercise in the area without showing the Russians our hand. We have several ships steaming at full speed across the Gulf of Alaska this very moment. They will be under the command of Commander Englemann. However," he continued more calmly, "I dare say that none of us expected one of the greatest natural disasters in history to take place on the day we transported the nation's most famous traitor since Benedict Arnold to the far reaches of the earth."

"Point well taken Admiral," answered a hopeful, but worried Governor Malloy. "I didn't mean to say the Navy was derelict in its duty."

"No offense taken Governor, but you must realize this is a delicate mission. We weren't sure of the Russian's plans and one frigate was plenty of support to place a covert operations team on Adak Island. With two SH-60 Seahawks . . . uh, pardon me, with one SH-60, the Billings is more than a match for the Russians. And with Margaret Englemann in command the odds are in our favor."

Cape Amagalik, Tanaga Island, Aleutian Islands, Alaska

Except for flocks of sea birds scattering into the bright blue sky and a few foxes scurrying away through the windswept grass, Toby Church found the old airstrip at Cape Amagalik on Tanaga

Island deserted. He breathed in the fresh salt air, finding strength in his newfound freedom. The magnificent sight of Tanaga Volcano towering 5,000-feet above the shore was inspiring.

Church was secure in his belief he had eluded any search team with his clever backtracking. Like a man in a shower, he sang bawdy tunes while he searched the collapsed Quonset huts and hangars for extra fuel and other useful items.

Scattered around the airfield were military aircraft, abandoned and rusting, their windshields broken and jagged, their engines missing, and their fuselages riddled with holes caused by decades of ferocious weather. At the far end of the runway, near a large mound of dirt, lay the rusting hulk of an old Consolidated Catalina PBY. Bright orange streaks of rust stained the once proud ship. The tires were flat and gray with age. On one side, the landing gear had collapsed making the plane list to one side. Only the wingtip sticking into a sand dune kept the derelict from falling completely over. During the war it had been painted in dark blue and gray. Now the color was faded into a dull dark gray with a peeling white star near the hatch, which was open and hanging precariously by its bent hinges.

Seeing the relic brought back childhood memories of visiting air museums with his dad, who had been a flight engineer on a Navy P-3 Orion during the Gulf War. These were some of his fondest memories. He remembered the many hours he had spent with his mother sitting on the couch looking at the book filled with pictures of Naval aircraft as they waited for his father to return from a long patrol.

With youthful exuberance, he climbed all around the skeleton of this once proud veteran. He crawled into the cockpit and sat down in the pilot's seat. Grabbing the yoke, he tried to imagine what it was like to fly 12-hour patrols over the North Pacific in search of Japanese warships. Coming back to his senses, he resumed his search for supplies.

Rummaging through the lockers in the tail of the aircraft, he came across an old M-1 Carbine and a magazine with 30 rounds of armor-piercing ammunition. *Most useful in an emergency*, he reminded himself. Gingerly, he checked the weapon's action. The rifle was rusted in spots, but it had been well oiled and wrapped to protect it from the elements. It must have been overlooked when the airbase was abandoned. The leather strap was still intact, although it was brittle from all the years of disuse. Tipping the rifle up towards an opening in the Catalina's roof, he looked down the barrel for any obstructions. It was clear and he could see light at the end of the barrel.

Taking a piece of cloth from a large rag, he dipped it in oil and using a piece of wire, he carefully ran the cloth down the inside of the barrel. It came out covered in blackened rust. He repeated the procedure until the cloth came through clean. Gently loosening the strap, he swung the rifle over his shoulder and climbed back outside.

He congratulated himself. Pulling back the action, he inserted a round into the chamber. Hoping his luck would hold and that the ammunition was still good, he took aim at the side of an old hangar and pulled the trigger.

With a satisfying 'crack' the carbine found its mark. He grinned with satisfaction. Armed with a handgun and now a rifle, his chances for survival had just markedly improved. Out of habit he looked around to make sure no one had heard him shoot. He laughed. "You damn fool," he said to himself and loudly, "you're all alone out here. Quit being so nervous." Still, after so many years on the run and in prison, it would take a long time before he would truly be convinced that an enemy wouldn't appear unexpectedly.

Over the next hour, he combed the airfield for gasoline. Whenever a gust of wind made a door slam or a wall creak, he would get nervous and spend a few minutes checking that he was still alone. He hated feeling this way, but he knew that if he got careless, he could end up going back to that hell of Malloy Super Max.

While most of the fuel had turned to turpentine with age, he did manage to salvage enough of it to fill his ten-gallon can. Satisfied there was no more fuel and convinced that no edible food remained in the abandoned mess hall, he headed back down to the beach.

Carefully, he placed the rifle and his scavenged supplies into the skiff, picked up the anchor, and launched the boat into the rolling surf. He started the engine and pointed the bow of his boat due west. One hundred miles across the waters of Amchitka Pass lay Amchitka Island. If his map was correct, there were lots of roads on the island. No villages were shown on the map, but with that many roads, there had to be people living there.

Malloy Super Maximum-Security Prison, Adak Island, Alaska

"Banderas, Anderson, do you copy?"

Carlos throttled back so he could reply to the radio summons. "Copy Captain. Read you loud and clear. Go."

"Church has been spotted heading west past Kanaga Island. Return to Adak."

"Are you sure?" Carlos answered warily. *Heading west? That doesn't make sense.*

"Yes," said Captain Anderson, "US intelligence satellites have spotted a small boat with a single occupant in an orange suit at that location."

Carlos swung their skiff back around. They were well out in Fenimore Pass when the call had come in. It would take them several hours to return to Adak.

Ben Williams tried not to look smug. However, his pride in guessing Church's move was dampened by his frustration at being so far behind in the chase. He fought off the urge to say, "I told you so."

Carlos ordered Ben and Travis to examine the charts once again. Perhaps they could glean just where Church was headed and why.

Meanwhile, Carlos was beating himself up for not listening to Ben's advice. *I should have trusted Ben's instincts. After all, hunting is 95 percent luck and five percent skill.*

Clearing the outer sally port, Sgt. Knight and his team entered the secured perimeter of the prison. They were bone tired. It had been a frustrating day. They hadn't found any sign of Church on the island.

Bill Knight rang the buzzer outside Main Control and wiped the mud from his pants. He was anxious to speak to Captain Anderson. He'd heard the radio traffic with Lt. Banderas. He was tired and sweaty. They had spent hours traipsing over the island looking for any sign of the fugitive. He was anxious to get caught up on the latest news. It was hard to be patient while he waited for the officer to open the inner security door. He strode across the room and knocked on the window.

"Welcome back Bill, come on in," Anderson said, sweeping his hand across his charts. "We've got a fix on Church."

Knight watched Anderson run his finger in a circle around the islands to the west of Tanaga Island. "You think he's heading west from Tanaga Island?"

"Yep," Anderson said grinning. "I think he stopped off at the abandoned airstrip at Cape Amagalik to rummage through the buildings for supplies and probably fuel. And I think he's going to head over to Amchitka Island in the hopes of finding a bigger boat to steal, or maybe an airplane."

Knight wasn't so sure. "I don't know Captain. That seems just a little too easy to guess. Maybe he's not headed to Amchitka at all."

Anderson was taken aback by that response and a little offended at having his deduction questioned. But as soon as he saw the evil grin on his friend's face, he knew he'd been had. "Well, I haven't thought this out completely, but all the facts would indicate that Amchitka is his goal."

As Bill Knight listened to his friend's analysis, he couldn't help thinking about how much it annoyed him when Anderson counted on his fingers to make a point. He shook off his feelings. *No time to get petty.* He began picking the dirt out from underneath his fingernails with a paperclip.

"First of all, he's in a skiff with a limited fuel supply. Second, Church is a skilled survivalist and he knows he's not going to get too far without better transportation. Third, we know he took the charts from that Navy chopper along with a compass. Fourth, he knows how to navigate and he knows how to fly a plane. All these signs make me believe he will try to get to Amchitka."

Enjoying his role as the pessimist, Knight countered, "Okay, I'll buy your guess he's going to try and land at Amchitka. But then what? Our search team is hours behind him. We don't have an operational airfield or any aircraft to get to Amchitka. There is no radio contact with any of the surrounding island villages, so we have to presume the earthquake and tsunamis wiped them out too. Just how are we supposed to stop him? Furthermore," he said with more ferocity than he intended, "how can we be sure he's headed for Amchitka? After all, he's got good charts and those charts show there aren't any settlements on Amchitka."

Anderson kicked aside a chair, letting his frustration come to a boil. Knight's points were all valid. His plan was riddled with flaws. He began pacing around his office.

Using a ruler and a calculator, Anderson tried to estimate how many hours it would take Church to reach Amchitka. Even if Amchitka wasn't his final destination, not even Toby Church was fool enough to spend the night on the open ocean in a tiny skiff. He would make land to spend the night. And if they were lucky, he would waste his time searching the island for a village or airstrip that didn't exist.

Sgt. Knight ran his hand over his chin. *How can we get to Amchitka Island before Toby Church?* Then it struck him—a totally outrageous idea, but one that he felt just might work. Another evil grin spread across his face.

Captain Anderson stopped pacing. "By that shit-eating grin Bill," he said with a smile, "I'd say you just came up with a plan."

"It's a wild idea and may not even have a chance." Knight removed his cap and ran his hand over his flattop. He set his cap down on Anderson's desk.

Anderson sat down and let Knight fill him in on the details.

Leaning back in his chair, Anderson said, "damned risky, Bill. Damned risky. But we don't have many options. It's probably the best shot we've got. I'll get on the horn to the Governor and see if he can get us what we need."

"You know, Marc," Knight said mischievously, "Banderas is going to hate us both."

Karluk Lake, Kodiak Island, Alaska

All through the morning, Ivan Lincoln had been driving his captives mercilessly. The longer they stayed in the open, the more he ran the risk of getting caught.

"Lazy bitches!" he yelled as he pushed Elizabeth in the back. "Come on you fucking bitches! Move!" he screamed as he kicked Joy in the back of the leg.

When this didn't work, he cut off the end of a willow branch and whipped them like cattle. With a hiss, the switch cut through the air, cutting across Elizabeth's back and Joy's thighs. Bloody streaks appeared through their clothing.

Tears ran down Elizabeth's face as she winced under the latest assault. She was still suffering from the previous night's trauma. Her legs burned with fatigue, her back hurt, and her intestines were cramping. *Why doesn't he just kill me?* Anything was better than this torture.

While the willow hurt, the beating only served to strengthen Joy's resolve to escape the clutches of this madman. She wasn't going to take it anymore. As Lincoln drew back to hit her again, she reached out and caught the branch in her hand. "Stop it!" she shouted defiantly. "We are not animals!"

"You stupid fucking bitch!" he shouted. He jerked the branch back out of her hand and punched her solidly in the chest.

With a thud, Joy fell backward onto the ground. Before she could react, Lincoln was upon her. Raising her arms to protect her face, she recoiled under a flurry of kicks and punches.

His anger spent, Lincoln relented. Grabbing her by the hair, he jerked her back to her feet. With a push, he sent her up the steep hillside.

Joy held her ribs. It hurt to breathe. *Maybe my ribs are broken?* She fought back the pain. She wasn't sure her lack of breath was from the beating or if it was related to the curious haze that was enveloping the surrounding mountains. Behind her, she could hear Elizabeth coughing and wheezing. A fine dust was slowly graying out the blue sky.

Lincoln fought against the burning in his lungs too. He was becoming confused and disoriented. He coughed to clear his throat. The change in the weather aggravated his temper.

"What the hell is going on?" he barked. Neither woman answered him.

"God damn it, you worthless bitches, I asked you a question. What is happening to the weather?" He snarled. Their silence was maddening.

Knowing that refusing to answer him was dangerous, Elizabeth took her best guess without bothering to turn around and look at him. "I don't know for certain, but given the geology of this part of Alaska, I'd have to say that a volcano has erupted somewhere. This is volcanic ash."

Lincoln ordered the women to stop. He pulled out his knife and cut a piece of cloth into strips. Laying the strips out on a damp rock, he showed them how to tie the cloth around their faces covering their nose and mouth.

Tying a knot in the back of the makeshift mask, Elizabeth made sure to dampen her cloth before slipping over her head. The moisture would help block the fine dust. She motioned for Joy to follow suit. She did not give similar assistance to Lincoln.

Within a few minutes the sky had turned dark under the advancing cloud of ash. Like a great grey blanket, the ash smothered the entire island. By the time they got their masks on, they were engulfed in a blizzard.

"Get moving," bellowed a coughing Lincoln. He motioned with his pistol for the women to begin moving down the ridge to the creek below.

Across the valley, Harry Ignustuk and Danny Sanders had lost sight of Lincoln's party after they began their descent into Alder Creek.

Danny was the first to notice the gray ash falling from the sky. Catching some of it in his hand, he examined it, looking skyward. Above him he watched the sun fade from sight. "Harry, I think we're in trouble."

Harry had been ignoring the fine ash falling all around. He didn't want to lose sight of Lincoln for too long. Harry coughed to clear his throat and nose. He attributed his difficulty breathing to the exertion of trying to move down the ridge and back up again as quickly as possible. Hearing Danny's warning, he stopped, taking notice for the first time of the gray ash falling all around them. "What the heck is this stuff?" he asked, looking to Danny for an answer.

"This stuff can kill you if you breathe in too much, Harry. And by the looks of the sky, I think we're in for one hell of an ash storm." Ever since childhood, Danny had been fascinated by science. He knew exactly what the fine gray ash was and he proceeded to give his boss a quick science lesson.

"Well, we can't stop moving. Any suggestions?" Harry asked.

Taking his handkerchief from his pocket, Danny dipped it in the cold water of Alder Creek and tied it around his nose and mouth. He motioned for Harry to follow suit. Unrolling his knit cap, he pulled it down over his eyes. Feeling with his fingers, he found the approximate location for his eyes. He removed the cap, took out his knife and cut two small eyeholes. Pulling the clear plastic wrapper off a package of food, he used medical tape to attach the plastic over the eyeholes. Without asking, he snatched Harry's knit cap from his head and modified it in a similar fashion.

After handing Harry his cap, Danny pulled his mask over his irritated eyes. Harry followed suit.

While the look was somewhat comical, it was effective. They would just have to suffer through the heat of having their heads and faces covered.

Knowing the situation would soon turn deadly, they filled every available water container. Soon every water source in the area would be contaminated.

Looking like two hoodlums up to serious mischief, they set off up the ridge on the other side of Alder Creek.

Since the masks limited their vision, they were forced to slow their pace considerably. Their only comfort was the knowledge that Ivan Lincoln was suffering, too. With at least one hostage in tow, he would be going even slower. Would he kill his victims out of desperation? He was unpredictable.

The ash fell like a heavy snow, mixing with the water-soaked soil, covering everything in a slippery slime. On both sides of the valley, hunters and hunted struggled to maintain their footing.

Matters were worse for Lincoln and his hostages. They did not have any way to stop the ash from irritating their eyes. It scratched the inside of their eyelids like fine sandpaper. Tears only served to create a slimy mud in the corners of their eyes, which burned with acid. Only by dipping their heads in swift flowing streams were they able to get some relief. The water was like ice. It made their heads hurt, but it was better than the ash.

Further complicating matters was the lack of light. Thirty minutes after the first sign of ash, it was no longer possible to see across the Karluk Lake valley. You couldn't see ten feet.

Harry wasn't worried. He was confident in his tracking and survival skills. If they kept moving in a southerly direction and if they kept their wits about them, they would eventually pick up Lincoln's trail. In some respects, he actually found the ash to be an asset in the upcoming search. Footprints were easy to see in this mess.

Lincoln also knew the ash would make it easier for him to be tracked. On the other hand, the ash would prevent any air searches—and if it fell long enough and heavy enough, it would cover their tracks completely.

Joy was in the lead. She concentrated on keeping her balance on the narrow mountain ridge, looking for an opportunity to escape. While she feared what Lincoln could do to her, she also knew he was just as preoccupied with keeping his footing on the slippery terrain. As unobtrusively as possible, she began opening the gap between herself and her captor. Her heart pounded hard inside her chest as tried not to attract attention to her plan to bolt for freedom. While she felt sorry for Dr. LeDue, she knew she had to save herself. *If I get away, maybe I can get help and the police can capture him before he kills her.*

A few paces behind, Elizabeth noticed that Joy was picking up the pace. *She's getting ready to run!* She didn't want to be left alone with this beast. She wanted to shout for Joy to stay.

But before either woman could react, Lincoln came jogging up from behind. Pulling out his pistol, he called out, "Where do you think you're going, Bitch?"

For just a moment, Joy thought about making a run for it. *Now,* she thought to herself, *run for all you're worth.* But it was too late. He had caught wind of her plan and was too close for her to get away. Joy's heart sank.

Always keen to the reactions of his prey, Lincoln had noticed Joy moving slightly ahead of the group. He had allowed her to get just far enough ahead to let her believe she just might be able to make a break for it. He had watched carefully, waiting until the last minute before shattering her hopes by running up from behind.

Joy raised her hands over her face. He had his pistol out. *He's going to shoot me!* She closed her eyes and waited for the shot. Instead, he clumped her on the back of the skull with the butt of the pistol.

Clutching the back of her head, Joy fell to her knees.

"Don't ever try that again, Bitch," he growled in her ear, "or I'll skin you alive."

Joy held her head, trying not to cry. She didn't want to give the son-of-a-bitch the satisfaction. She could feel a lump rising on the back of her skull. It was moist. Blood.

Lincoln was in a fury. He was waving the pistol around and shouting. "Get on the ground! You worthless fucking bitches! NOW!" Opening his knapsack, he took out some rope and tied it around Elizabeth's ankle. He pulled her over to Joy. Grabbing Joy's ankle, he tied them together. Now it would be impossible for them to run.

He pulled them to their feet by their hair, motioning for them to continue down the slope towards Meadow Creek. Even through the storm he could see that the terrain leveled out by the lakeshore. Traveling there would be easier. They could make better time, possibly even rounding the end of the lake by early afternoon.

Harry and Danny were trying to maintain their balance in the slippery conditions as they slid on their hands and feet down the steep slopes above Thumb Lake. They were moving as quickly as conditions would allow, but they had to be careful not to injure themselves on the rocks jutting out of the ground or to stick the barrels of their rifles into the slime. At the bottom of a particularly steep precipice, they found flat terrain. Standing up, they set off in the direction where they last saw Lincoln and the women.

Even though the masks were hot and limited their vision, they thanked their lucky stars they were able to see and breathe in an environment rapidly becoming toxic to man and beast.

As the two groups continued moving, the ash storm increased in intensity. Animals, large and small, were desperately seeking shelter in groves of trees, caves and bushes. Agitated by the ash burning their eyes and nostrils, the great bears roaming the creek beds were actively searching for shelter from the storm.

Larsen Bay, Kodiak Island, Alaska

Michelle Dornier looked out the window of the school. She couldn't believe her eyes. *Late spring and it's snowing! My God, what kind of weather is this!* Putting down her pen, she walked outside and held her hand out to catch some of the flakes. *Strange,* she thought, *these don't look like snowflakes.* Closer examination revealed the 'snowflakes' weren't melting. Puzzled, she turned back around taking her sample back into the office. "Commissioner Burke," she called out, "what do you make of this?" She held out her hand, which was covered in gray ash. "Do you think it's from that volcano they told us about?"

Burke examined the dust and said matter-of-factly, "volcanic dust alright—must be from the Okmok eruption."

He walked over to the window. Even he was taken aback at the volume of falling ash. "Looks like it's going to give us a good dusting. Depending on the prevailing winds, we could see this pass in a few hours, or days. One thing's for sure," he said dejectedly, "our search teams aren't going anywhere for awhile. And the choppers are grounded until the skies are clear."

How can he stay so calm? Dornier still didn't appreciate that Alaskans live in the shadows of volcanoes every day. She stood transfixed as the ash slowly obscured the sun. Twilight settled over the village. "Guess we'd better prepare for some very panicky residents," she said with more confidence than she felt. "They'll surely be upset over this latest development."

"They'll be fine," Burke answered absent-mindedly. He didn't see this as a crisis. It was just Mother Nature showing them who was boss.

With cool resolve, Burke ordered his officers to bring survivors to the school, to check food and water supplies, to ration important items, to find tarps and cover the helicopters, and to prepare to settle in for what could be a rather long few days.

Without turning from the window Dornier asked Burke, "Do you think that Lincoln and LeDue will be able to survive this storm without shelter?"

Burke stopped in mid-stride. *Good question.* "Hard to say really," he answered thoughtfully. "If they find shelter, then they've got a pretty good chance of survival—if they have some food and water. If they don't find shelter, then they probably won't."

Dornier turned away from the window, settling back against the sill with her hands under her buttocks. She had more questions to ask and now seemed like a good time. "How will they die?"

Pausing for a moment, Burke replied, "suffocate I imagine. The dust will clog their lungs."

"Will we be able to find them? What about my two officers already on the ground?" she asked. She was worried about losing more good people to this disaster.

Burke held up his hands. "Slow down a little. Find them? Hard to say. Depends on how much ash falls. Your other officers? Well, let's just pray that they find a cabin or a cave for shelter."

Dornier walked out of the room. She found the thought of suffocating from this ash oppressive. Grabbing some blankets, and food, she got busy assisting her employees caring for Larsen Bay's survivors. It felt good to help—especially the children.

Dick Burke was a little surprised and not unimpressed with Dornier's apparently cool demeanor under this most recent calamity. *Maybe I've been underestimating her?* Still, he didn't like outsiders.

He walked over to the radio. He needed to tell Governor Malloy what was happening.

USS Billings, Gulf of Alaska

The Billings knifed through the rolling seas, her clipper bow separating the water into frothy spray. Gritty gray ash fell from the sky. Light reflecting through the clouds illuminated the seascape in an eerie orange glow. Everyone on board felt like they'd been transported to an alien world.

The plume of ash spewing from the gaping crater of the Okmok Caldera had delayed the launch of the SH-60. Commander Englemann could not take the risk. If too much of the silicon-based ash got sucked into the turbine engines, they would shut down—glazed in a thin sheet of onyx.

The officers groused about their luck. Without their most formidable anti-submarine warfare tool, stopping the Russians would be that much more difficult.

Commander Englemann was sequestered in her quarters with several of her officers. They were discussing the tactical situation, arguing about the pros and cons of launching of the Seahawk.

Lt. Surin argued it was imperative to get his team on the ground as soon as possible. He understood the capabilities of the Russian Spetsnaz. Any advantage given to the Russians would be difficult to overcome.

Lt. Commander Hastings, a former Naval aviator and geologist, advocated for a more patient approach. He understood the dangers of volcanic ash when ingested by a jet turbine. No matter how good the Russians were, there was no way to get to Dr. LeDue first if the helicopter never made it to Kodiak. Delaying the launch of the Seahawk for a few hours would give them time to see if the winds would shift.

Lt. Cowdrey, Hawk Two's pilot, was silent.

Englemann moved forward in her chair, raising her hand slightly to indicate her desire to close the discussion. She turned to her meteorologist. "Lieutenant, what do you think will happen to the prevailing winds in the next two hours?"

He pulled the corners of his mouth downward with his left hand. "My best guess, and I stress that it is a guess," he said in a staccato voice, "is that the wind will shift to the south, southeast in about an hour. We're expecting the arrival of that new Siberian Low I told you about. I predict it will move through the Gulf cutting directly across our path."

Englemann smiled at the Lieutenant's deliberate manner. "Given that your guesses are better than most forecasts, I'll take you at your word."

She then asked her chief pilot his thoughts. "Lt. Cowdrey, what do think of the situation? Do I order a launch or not?"

Because of his youthful appearance, many people found it hard to take Cowdrey seriously. However, he had an excellent reputation as a rough weather pilot—one of the reasons he had been assigned to the Billings for this mission. "I think this is a poor situation, but I'm willing to risk it. I think I can get Lt. Surin's team to Kodiak. And if the ash tapers off, I can search for the Russians."

Turning to her XO, Commander Englemann sought one final piece of advice, "Commander Hastings, what is your final opinion?"

Hastings pushed his Navy ball cap back off his forehead. Launching the SH-60 in a volcanic storm was very risky. He reminded everyone they'd already lost Hawk One. "I say we wait for an hour to see what the weather does."

Margaret Englemann didn't like going against the advice of her most senior officer. But her years of experience had taught her that sometimes you had to bet it all to win. Life was risky and so was command. "I'm going to lay my bets on the prediction the winds will clear our course in the next hour. I'm going to order the helo to launch."

She slapped her fingers on the edge of the table and stood up. "Lt. Cowdrey, fire up Hawk Two. Lt. Surin, ready your Marines for an immediate launch. Commander Hastings, call engineering and get me another knot or two of speed."

Next she looked around the room, making sure everyone understood what was expected of them. "Commander Hastings, load the Seahawk with one Mark 50 torpedo and several sonobouys. Ready the Billings' Mark 46 torpedoes. Lt. Cowdrey, you are not to launch any weapons without my authorization. Is that clear?"

"Aye, aye, Skipper," Lt. Cowdrey replied.

"Meeting adjourned, gentlemen. God Speed."

The men and women of the Billings went to work preparing the SH-60 Seahawk helicopter for its mission. Lieutenants Cowdrey and Martin began their pre-flight inspections, ensuring there was a full load of fuel on board, all survival gear was properly stored and ready for use, and all the electronics were working.

Below decks, Lt. Surin gathered his maps of Kodiak. Sergeants Ramirez and Ali ran through their checklists, conducting final weapons checks, and making sure they had extra cleaning fluid for their rifles. They exited the compartment, heading for the waiting chopper topside. Each man "checked his gut" as they climbed the ladder.

Up on the flight deck, Lieutenants Cowdrey and Martin had finished their final pre-flight checks. When Surin's men were aboard, Cowdrey spooled up the powerful turbine engines. Soon the air was filled with the sound of rotor blades chopping through the heavy sea air. When the engines reached full throttle, the flight deck officer dropped his flags signaling Hawk Two to lift off.

Cowdrey pulled upward on the collective control by his left side and lifted the SH-60 off the launch pad. The Billings sped out from underneath them. Stepping on the rudder pedals, he moved Hawk Two over the starboard side, staying close to the waves. Next, Cowdrey moved the cyclic, making the helicopter's nose drop slightly. Hawk Two accelerated past the Billings. Lt. Surin and his men watched the Billings fade from sight. Up ahead, the dark ocean blended into the ashen sky. There was no horizon.

Commander Englemann and Lt. Commander Hastings were on the bridge, watching with baited breath as Hawk Two sped by, disappearing into the gray sky.

Lt. Cowdrey and Lt. Martin were monitoring their engine readouts very carefully—looking for any sign of trouble from crystallization or overheating as Hawk Two raced over the waves at over 120 miles per hour. They hoped to avoid flying into a deadly cloud of ash. Ditching in these frigid waters was not a very pleasant prospect. Before they knew it, they could see the shadow of Kodiak Island looming in the distance.

Using the GPS navigation system, Cowdrey started the search by conducting a flyover over the last known position of Malloy 1. Failing to see any debris in the water, he swung the nose of the Hawk Two towards Kodiak Island. He was piloting along the most logical route the survivors would have taken to shore. Within a few minutes, Hawk Two was hovering over Sevenmile Beach.

Sgt. Ramirez was the first to spot the abandoned inflatable. He tapped Lt. Surin on the shoulder, pointing to the footprints in the mud.

Lt. Surin keyed his headset so he could speak to Cowdrey. "Ramirez just saw a boat on the beach. Put us down here."

Cowdrey watched Surin point to the raft. "I'm not going to set the runners on the ground," he said to Lt. Surin, "just in case the prisoners are hiding in the bushes. Prepare for an assault egress."

While Hawk Two hovered, Lt. Surin, Sgt. Ramirez, and Sgt. Ali rappelled to the ground. Once the men were safely on the ground, Lt. Cowdrey pulled up on the collective, making Hawk Two climb high above the beach. Dropping the nose and pivoting to the west, he headed back towards the western entrance to Shelikof Straits. Lt. Martin radioed back to the Billings—they had located a boat and Surin's men were on the ground. Hawk Two was on its way to drop sonobouys across the straits.

Lt. Cowdrey followed the shoreline. He flew west about 20 miles before turning his aircraft north, northwest cutting across Shelikof Straits. Stopping every two miles, he hovered above the ocean while the crew chief dropped a sonobouy into the ocean. Thirty minutes later, Hawk Two took up station above the straits so Chief Neilsen could listen for the approach of an enemy submarine.

Back at Sevenmile Beach, Lt. Surin and his team had determined that Dr. LeDue and two other people were heading inland, in the general direction of Karluk Lake. They were puzzled as to why the fugitives would not head to the nearby community of Larsen Bay. They must be trying to cut across the island and head for the town of Kodiak on the far Southeastern shore of the island. Lt. Surin's team put on their gas masks, covered their rifles with their ponchos, and set out in pursuit of the fugitives.

Akula Class Submarine Putin, Shelikof Straits, Alaska

"Helm, come to periscope depth," ordered Commander Ivanshenko. After running hard for almost a day and a half, the Putin was entering Shelikof Straits. Ivanshenko was betting the Americans were aware of his presence in the area and that they would try to stop him from surfacing to dispatch his covert operations team. He scanned the surface through the periscope. All he saw was the shoreline being obscured by falling gray ash. *It's too early to be dark outside.*

He asked Lt. Commander Vatutin to come take a look through the scope, waiting for him to conduct a 360-degree sweep of the area.

"Why is it dark outside Commander?" Vatutin asked without removing his face from the eyepieces.

"It must be the ash from that volcano."

"So soon? There should be plenty of daylight left," answered a perplexed Vatutin. He pulled his face back from the periscope.

Ivanshenko shrugged his shoulders, "The eruption must be bigger than we think."

He went back to the periscope and did another slow 360-degree turn. *This is most frustrating. I need to fix our position.* "Lieutenant, what's on the radar?"

"Not much Commander. There's a lot of interference. I can make out the large landmasses, but something is jamming the radar," the young officer responded with concern. He glanced at Ivanshenko for reassurance.

Seeing the distressed look on the officer's face, Ivanshenko walked over to take a look at the radar. It was a jumbled mass of signals. He cursed under his breath. *The ash is causing the radar to malfunction.* "Run a systems diagnostic check to make sure the equipment is functioning properly."

"All systems are operational Commander. No malfunctions," came the reply a few minutes later.

"Are you sure?" growled Ivanshenko.

"Positive Sir."

"Vatutin, sound general quarters. Helm, prepare to surface. Reduce speed to ten knots. Radar, pay attention. Let me know immediately of any contacts, surface or air. Join me topside once we break the surface." He pointed to Vatutin and the young lieutenant.

The Putin's dark gray hull surged out of the icy depths, breaking the surface. Ivanshenko spun the lock on the hatch and pushed it open. Icy water spilled into the boat and down the sleeves of his rubber slicker.

Climbing the ladder, the officers took up positions on the conning tower. The smell of sulfur immediately overwhelmed their senses. Gritty gray ash was falling all around.

Ivanshenko wiped his hand along the rail. He noticed how it turned to a gray sludge. It was like sandpaper on his fingers. "This may be to our advantage," he yelled to Vatutin over the wind. He grinned broadly. *Maybe our luck will hold. This storm is perfect for cloaking our approach to the island. We might even be able to put Major Golkin on the island before nightfall. All I need to do is fix my position.*

Confident that the Putin was cloaked from radar detection, he kept the Putin cruising on the surface. It was important to verify his bearings on his charts by triangulating his position. Unfortunately, conditions were not cooperating.

"Commander!," the lieutenant shouted, "American helicopter at 11 o'clock!" He had the binoculars pressed to his eyes and was pointing excitedly in the direction of the approaching helicopter.

"Shit!" Vatutin and Ivanshenko exclaimed simultaneously. "Clear the bridge!" Ivanshenko barked while shoving Vatutin and the lieutenant down the hatch in front of him. He pulled the hatch closed, hit the dive alarm and shouted, "Helm, take us deep!

Engineering, give me 15 knots, bring the reactors to 85 percent. Navigation, give me our current position and plot a course to the west. Helm, fifteen degrees down on the dive planes, make our depth 300 meters."

Men were racing around, hitting switches and pulling levers to flood the ballast tanks. As the Putin took on weight, it angled down towards the obsidian depths. The Putin disappeared beneath the waves just as Hawk Two streaked overhead.

If Ivanshenko was going to have a chance of shaking the American helicopter, he needed to get his submarine between some cold-water layers. Grabbing the chart table with both hands as the angle of the dive increased, he continued issuing commands. "Helm, 20 degrees down on the dive planes. Sonar, keep giving me status reports. Engineering, give me flank speed. Everybody pay attention!" he ordered in a steady, but firm voice.

"Commander," the sonarman said, "the American helicopter is circling overhead." He held his headphones with one hand, while fine-tuning his sonar with the other. "I have sonobouys in the water."

Commander Ivanshenko ordered the helm to reduce speed and for all unnecessary equipment to be shut down. "Sonar, find me a thermocline to hide in. Rig for silent running."

"Commander. There are several objects entering the water."

"Torpedoes?" asked Commander Ivanshenko.

"No sir," the sonarman replied, "I don't hear any screws. Nothing."

"What do you think it is?" Vatutin asked. This was most unusual.

"Don't know," Ivanshenko replied absent-mindedly. He was trying to figure out what objects the American helicopter had dropped in the water.

Boom! Boom! Boom!

The sonarman ripped his headphones off in pain. He cursed while rubbing his ears vigorously.

"What the hell was that?" someone blurted.

"Quiet!" growled Ivanshenko. "Everyone remain calm. They weren't depth charges. Too small."

Vatutin was relieved. "It's an old tactic that everybody uses," he said to the crew. "Drop small charges in the water to harass your enemy. Harmless, but annoyingly effective. Any ideas, Commander?" he asked.

"Matter of fact, yes," replied a smiling Ivanshenko. "Helm, all stop. Let's see how long their fuel lasts."

The Americans were dropping small explosive charges to harass the Putin. Far below the waves, however, Commander Ivanshenko knew that the Americans would not have enough fuel to stay on station for very long. And when the helicopter left, he would move off to another location.

Hawk Two, Shelikof Straits, Alaska

After dropping Lt. Surin and his team at Sevenmile Beach and placing sonobuoys across the entrance of Shelikof Straits, Lt. Cowdrey had flown Hawk Two to a location where the prevailing winds were keeping the ash storm at bay. As he fought to keep Hawk Two steady in the blustery wind, the crew chief was listening for the approach of the Russian submarine.

Lt. Martin wore his night vision goggles, keeping a lookout for ships moving on the surface. The ash storm had rendered their radar useless.

Cowdrey was hoping his fuel would allow Hawk Two to stay on station long enough to locate the Russians steaming into the straits. He would not be able to patrol indefinitely. Soon, they would have to head back to the Billings.

While Lt. Cowdrey calculated his fuel reserves, Lt. Martin caught sight of a submarine breaking the surface 15 miles to the southwest. In a day filled with ill fortune, once again Cowdrey had demonstrated his knack for being lucky.

At the same time, the crew chief picked up the sounds of a submarine blowing its ballast tanks. "No doubt about it Lieutenant," the chief called out, "it's the Russian."

Cowdrey ordered the hydrophone to be raised and swung the nose of the helicopter in the direction of the submarine. "Tallyho!" he shouted, accelerating his helicopter towards the hulking gray mass in the distance.

As Hawk Two raced through sky towards the Russians, Lt. Cowdrey was surprised—not only were the Russians running on the surface, but they had yet to spot him. Lt. Martin reminded him the Russian's were probably having radar problems too.

About five miles from his target, Lt. Cowdrey could see the distinctive lines of the Putin. An officer standing on the sail was pointing in their direction. They had been spotted. He smiled at his success in surprising his foe. He could see the officers scrambling off the sail as the submarine began to disappear beneath the waves.

Before the submarine disappeared completely, they were on station, hovering above the rolling waves.

"Chief. Drop a couple of sonobuoys in the water. Let's make em' sweat," Cowdrey ordered over the intercom.

"Buoys away, Lieutenant."

"Great Chief. Prepare a few of those small charges to drop on top of them. Set their depth at 100 meters. That should shake them up."

While Lt. Cowdrey harassed the Russians, Lt. Martin sent a message back to the Billings. They had made contact with a Russian Akula Class submarine near the entrance of Shelikof Straits.

After concluding his radio report to the Billings, Lt. Martin did a systems check. He tapped the fuel gauge to make sure it was reading correctly. They were running low on fuel. He made a quick calculation. "Lieutenant, we have to head back. We're low on fuel."

Lt. Cowdrey gave up the chase and turned Hawk Two west. They all hoped they had calculated their fuel requirements correctly. Otherwise, it was going to be a long, cold swim.

Governor's Office, Juneau, Alaska

Governor Malloy was agitated. *Why haven't I received any reports from Commissioners Burke and Dornier?* He picked up his tea. *Cold.* He found it increasingly difficult to concentrate on other tasks when he desperately wanted information on this most important quest. Setting his pen down, he got up and walked into the hallway outside his office. He needed some fresh air and some more hot water.

The hallway was a beehive of activity. Special assistants and commissioners were racing up and down the blue-carpeted hallway. Despite the outward appearance of chaos, however, things were running smoothly. Under the gruff, but disciplined control of his Chief-of-Staff, George Roberts, agencies were responding to the myriad of emergencies. An emergency response center had been established in the basement of the Capitol. The deputy director of the Alaska State Troopers was coordinating the efforts of state and federal agencies. General McCarthy of the Alaska Command had been a Godsend. When Governor Malloy called him with the request for a C-130 mission to Adak, he had gotten right on it, despite the strain being placed on his resources.

Governor Malloy stepped back inside his office and went to his phone. He needed his friend's help again. *Perhaps the General can get in contact with Larsen Bay?*

True to his promise to call back in an hour, General McCarthy said in jest, "Rick, you just don't get this unlucky everyday."

"You can say that again General. What's the word?" He tried not to get upset at being teased.

"Well, Rick, this is what I can tell you. Satellite data shows the plume of ash from Unmak Island has made its way to Kodiak Island. You're probably not receiving any communication from there, because the entire island is engulfed in a silicon ash blizzard."

Governor Malloy was unable to think of anything to say. *When are we going to get some good news?*

"My meteorologist predicts the prevailing winds will move the plume off Kodiak and to the south in a few hours. When this happens, I'm sure your commissioners will call in a report. As to how much ash is going to fall, that's anybody's guess. But given the magnitude of the eruption, I think it's safe to say they're going to get a pretty good shellacking."

"What about the C-130 mission to Adak," Governor Malloy asked.

"We launched a C-130 about 30 minutes ago. It will take them about four hours to arrive at Adak. Make sure your people are ready."

"You know General, I'm still not sure how you guys are going to pull off this Adak mission with Mitchell Field still closed, but I guess I'll just have to trust you know what you're doing."

"Don't worry Governor. It's no different than the time I took you bear hunting in the Talkeetna Mountains and you got lost. I got you out of there without anybody knowing about it. My people know what they're doing."

Rick Malloy laughed. He was certainly glad General McCarthy was efficient and discreet. He never would have lived it down if the press had learned of that little outing.

Malloy Super Maximum-Security Prison, Adak Island, Alaska

"We're going to do what?" Carlos exclaimed. He was reacting to the plan being proposed by Sgt. Knight and Captain Anderson. He couldn't believe his ears! *Has everyone suddenly gone mad?*

"Calm down, Carlos," Captain Anderson said placing his hand on Carlos's shoulder, "I know you're tired and I know you're not a spring chicken any more. But, we've got to head Church off—before he gets his hands on a boat or a plane."

Carlos stared at Sgt. Knight, trying to fathom the desperation driving this idea. "Jesus, Bill, I haven't jumped out of an airplane for over 20 years. And you know that Ben is even older than me. The only one young enough and stupid enough to agree to this idea is Travis." Carlos thrust his thumb in the direction of Corporal Nelson. "Sorry Nelson, no offense intended," he interjected as an afterthought, "but this idea has pain and suffering written all over it." He began pacing the room. "Just how do we know Church is headed for Amchitka?"

"That's enough, Lieutenant," Anderson said more forcefully. He directed him to sit down on the couch. "A CIA satellite spotted a small craft in Amchitka Pass. It had a single passenger wearing an orange survival suit."

This was their only option if they were to beat Toby Church to Amchitka Island. Anderson knew that once Carlos had some time to think, he would come to the same realization. "Carlos, we don't have a lot of time to argue," he continued. "I need you, Ben Williams and Corporal Nelson to gather your gear, go with Sgt. Knight to Mitchell Field and wait for the Hercules to make its drop. It should be here in 30 or 40 minutes."

A scowling Carlos responded, "Yes sir." Then he turned to Sgt. Knight. "I sure as hell hope you know what you're doing Bill."

Putting on his best face, Bill Knight tried reassuring the trio that his plan was sound. "Relax Lieutenant, I'm sure it will work.

Just remember to bend your legs when you hit the ground." His attempt at humor failed.

"Malloy Super Max this is Hercules alpha, alpha seven, seven five," came the call over the radio.

"Roger, seven, seven, five, this is Captain Anderson at Malloy Super Max, go ahead."

"Roger, Captain Anderson. We are 25 minutes north, northeast of Mitchell Field. Is your team ready?"

"10-4. They are waiting at Mitchell Field. Drop zone is marked with red cones. Pick up zone with orange cones."

"Very good Captain. Please inform them to stand back from the drop zones in case the wind throws the supplies off target. We will drop the jump gear to your capture team first. While they are suiting up, we will circle around and drop the food. Tell your men to be quick and get the balloons in the air."

"10-4. We'll be ready."

"Sgt. Knight, SS."

"Go for Knight."

"Herc reports 25 miles north, northwest. Will drop gear to team first, then supplies for prison, then back around to pick up team."

Throughout the prison, officers were listening to the radio with great interest. Originally, Anderson had thought to conduct all radio communications on a separate channel, but he knew that would be fruitless, because the officers would scan the channels and figure out where to listen in anyway. Besides, it would do everyone good to have something to focus on during the next few hours.

Inside the cellblocks, prisoners were betting on the outcome of the manhunt. Officers tried to limit the chitchat between cells, but even in a super maximum-security prison, stopping all communication was impossible. And these types of prisoner exchanges often revealed shifts among the inmate factions.

In every prison there are cliques. Toby Church had led the White supremacists. On the other side were the Blacks, the

Hispanics, the Asians, and the Homosexuals. None of them got along. This internal racism forced the prison to provide separate recreation and dining periods for each group to curtail stabbings and fights. Right now, Toby Church's allies were pulling for him to make good his escape. The other groups were betting on how he would die.

Down on Mitchell Field, Sgt. Knight, Lt. Banderas, Corporal Nelson, and Officer Williams were keeping a sharp eye out for the approaching C-130.

"There it is," Nelson said, pointing out over Kuluk Bay. Four trails of black smoke poured from the engines as the plane descended from 30,000 feet with its powerful landing lights shining brightly.

As the men waited for the C-130 to make its first drop, Sgt. Knight again explained how they were to get into the jump suits and how he would inflate a balloon, before releasing it into the sky. He used his hands to illustrate how the C-130 would come in for a low-level approach, catch the rope running from the balloon to the suit harness, and snap them up off the ground. Once airborne, he explained, they would be reeled into the C-130's cargo bay. This would be repeated four times—once for each man and once more for their weapons and rain gear.

From the cockpit, the pilots could see the orange and red drop zones outlined next to the runway. In the rear of the plane, the crew chief and his men prepared to drop the supplies. The sound of a hydraulic motor announced the opening of the cargo bay door. The airmen waited for the droplight to turn green—their signal to push the equipment out of the airplane.

The instant the light turned green, the crew chief shouted, "Go! Go, go, go! Come on men, push!"

The airmen shoved the crates filled with harnesses, balloons, and helium tanks out of the aircraft's cargo bay. As the crates exited the rear of the plane, a small parachute deployed to slow their descent. With amazing accuracy, the cargo landed neatly within the drop zone.

Carlos and his men shielded their eyes from the sun, watching the supplies fall from the rear of the aircraft. When the crates hit the ground, they ran over and pulled them apart with hammers.

As the Hercules circled back around to drop food and medical supplies, Sgt. Knight helped Banderas, Nelson and Williams wiggle into the snug coveralls. He double-checked to make sure they were secure in their suits and harnesses, before clipping the rope with the deflated balloon to the shoulders of each man's harness.

Taking a helium bottle, Sgt. Knight inflated the first balloon, which was attached to Lt. Carlos Banderas. Filling it to capacity, he let it go. It rocketed into the sky.

Carlos held on tightly to his shoulder straps, watching with trepidation as the big cargo plane swung around over the south end of the bay. It banked steeply, heading directly toward the bright orange balloon, which was now floating high above the airfield. Squinting, he could make out the long antennae jutting from the nose of the transport like a giant snake's forked tongue. "God help me," he half prayed, half cursed under his breath as the antennae grabbed the rope and the balloon rolled across the top of the cockpit.

The sound of the wind being knocked out of Carlos's lungs was all the other men heard as he was jerked into the air.

The harness pinched his groin, making him wince. But he couldn't take time to hurt. He was fighting for air as he was being dragged through the sky at over 150 miles per hour. The wind sounded like a freight train. It tore at his goggles and sucked the air out of his lungs. He felt like he was suffocating.

Back on the ground, Bill Knight smiled sheepishly at Ben Williams. They watched the C-130's crew reel Carlos on board through the rear cargo door. "That looked fun, Bill," Ben said sarcastically.

"Looked kinda painful to me," commented Corporal Nelson adjusting the straps between his legs.

Knight and Williams just smiled at Nelson's comment. Everyone shared in the memory of being kicked in the testicles.

"Get ready," Knight yelled as the plane came around for another pickup.

Thirty minutes later, the airlift was complete.

Bill Knight watched the transport disappear as it flew west over the island.

"That looked exciting," remarked Captain Anderson walking up beside Sgt. Knight.

"Kinda painful too," chuckled Sgt. Knight grabbing his crotch. "But it went off without a hitch—no pun intended." He tried not to laugh. "They should be over Amchitka is less than an hour."

"Let's hope their jump goes as well as their pickup." Better than anyone, Marc Anderson understood the dangers these men faced. Too many good people had died already.

It had been years since Carlos had flown in a C-130. He had forgotten about the deafening noise inside the cargo bay. It was too noisy to talk. "Get into your parachutes!" he yelled over the drone of the engines.

With the assistance of the airmen, the correctional officers put on their parachutes, shouldered their rifles, checked their ammunition bandoliers, and made sure their packs were filled with food and rain gear.

Just as Carlos was finishing his equipment check, the crew chief tapped him on the shoulder, pointing to the cockpit. The pilot wanted a few words with him.

The cockpit was much quieter. The flight engineer offered Carlos a cup of coffee and an overturned milk crate for a seat between the pilots. "Welcome aboard Lieutenant. I'm Major Brille and this is my co-pilot Captain Swanson. I thought you'd like to have a look at potential drop sites before we choose one for you."

"Thanks," Carlos answered, taking a sip of the piping hot coffee.

"Major," said Captain Swanson, "look out the port side." He was pointing to the wake of a small boat racing across the choppy waters of Amchitka Pass.

"Looks like your man is headed straight for Amchitka," the pilot said. He invited Carlos to take a look out the window.

Carlos breathed a sigh of relief. It was comforting to know they were once again on the trail of Toby Church. "Yeah, that's him alright," he said. "One smart son-of-a-bitch. Dangerous too. We'll need to make sure he doesn't see us drop over the island.

He's probably spotted us by now, although I doubt he'll be expecting us to parachute onto the island." Carlos hoped he was right.

"You'll only parachute if the runway is broken up Lieutenant," answered the co-pilot. If the old World War II airfield were still intact, they'd land. If not, they'd have to jump. He admired their courage at braving a parachute jump. "We'll fly to the far west of the island and try to make him think we didn't see him. Then we'll head on to Shemya before flying back to Anchorage."

"Good idea," Carlos replied, grinning for the first time. "We need to keep him guessing. He's got a pistol. He's a skilled survivalist and has no qualms about killing anybody that gets in his way.

May I use your radio to call in our sighting?" Carlos asked.

Captain Anderson was elated at the news. They'd spotted Church! *Maybe the CIA isn't so bad after all.* He dialed the Governor's office in Juneau. He was anxious to inform Governor Malloy of the first good news in two days.

Flying directly over Amchitka Island, the pilot reduced airspeed so they could get a good look at the terrain and the abandoned airfield. It was a shambles. Not only had years of neglect seen the tarmac riddled with potholes and grass, but the earthquake had buckled the runway in several places. Landing was impossible. Carlos and his team would have to jump.

The pilot circled the C-130 over the west end of the island, while the crew chief opened the rear cargo bay door. Outside the wind was howling. They were circling a grassy meadow. It looked smooth from this high up, but they all knew it was littered with rocks and holes. They were anxious. No one was looking forward to the prospect of jumping from a perfectly good airplane.

Averaging only three miles wide and about 65 miles long, Amchitka Island is a windswept, grass-covered rock of rolling hills and ridges. Its beaches are a haven for seals, sea lions and walruses. Sea birds abound on the island. There is also a healthy population of foxes, which feed on the bird eggs. An old road runs the length of the island's spine—a relic from World War II, the Cold War and US Department of Energy's desire to experiment with underwater nuclear detonations. Much of the terrain is a spongy bog, filled with mosquitoes in the summer and frozen solid in the winter. With each step the ground tries to swallow your feet.

During the thawing of relations with the Soviet Union in the late 1980s and after the collapse of the Soviet Empire in the early 1990s, Amchitka lost its importance. The garrison of scientists and soldiers left for good. Only derelict vehicles and Quonset huts from those turbulent days of conflict remain.

The crew chief yelled above the din of the engines and the rushing wind, giving them their instructions. "Count to ten, pull the cord and let yourself float down! Don't lock your knees when you hit the ground! Roll on impact. Get to your feet as soon as possible to prevent being dragged!" He noticed that Corporal Nelson was especially white.

Carlos watched the jump light, waiting for it to change from red to green. His throat was parched. *Green.* Closing his eyes, keeping his legs straight and his body stiff, he hopped from the rear of the aircraft. As he counted to ten, he could feel his stomach turning over. *And some people get a rush from this.* "Ten!" he shouted. Excitedly, he pulled the ripcord. With a whoosh, the parachute deployed, jerking him to a sudden stop. "Damn!" he cursed as the harness pinched his testicles again. He swore he was going to kick Bill Knight in the nuts when he got back.

Now that he was drifting slowly toward the ground, Carlos found the courage to open his eyes. He repeated the crew chief's instructions. *Hit and roll. Hit and roll.* The ground was coming up very fast. He hit with a thud, let his knees buckle and rolled. Before he could get to his feet, the wind grabbed his parachute, dragging him along the damp, tussocky terrain. With a burst of energy, he scrambled upright. *Whew! I made it.* Working quickly, he released the chute from its harness and gathered it up in a ball.

All the while, he watched Ben Williams and Travis Nelson float to the ground. They both landed without incident.

They waved as the C-130 made a final pass over their position. Saluting from his cockpit, the pilot bid farewell to Lt. Banderas and his men.

With a roar, the C-130 accelerated. Black exhaust trailed from its four mighty engines as it climbed higher into the sky heading out to sea.

Carlos picked up his pack and rifle and started walking up the trail to the east. "Okay guys, saddle up, we've got a lot of ground to cover. I want to make it to the top of that ridge so we can see where Church makes landfall."

Shouldering their packs, Ben and Travis set off at a brisk pace just a few yards behind Carlos. They were still feeling heady from their jump. Down on the beaches, they could hear the sounds of sea lions grunting. The skies were filled with thousands of birds.

Until today, most of the visitors to the island had come to view the wildlife. Amchitka Island is an internationally famous bird sanctuary and site of the Alaska Maritime Wildlife Refuge.

Ben Williams couldn't help thinking about how sad it was that Amchitka's greatest claim to fame was being the site of the US Government's bizarre attempts to create a man-made harbor on the island using nuclear bombs.

For several hours they slogged their way over the spongy terrain alternatingly stumbling and slipping and soaking their feet. On more than one occasion one of them would slip off a tussock and land on his hands and knees further adding to their discomfort. It was late afternoon by the time they reached the crest of a spiny ridge that ran the length of the island. They settled in to watch for Church's arrival. It wouldn't be long now.

Carlos decided they would follow Ben's plan—he wasn't going to ignore Ben again. They would allow Church to land unopposed, work around behind him and disable his skiff. Then they could take their time tracking him down. There were no boats on the island and the only aircraft on the airfield were rusting derelicts from the Cold War.

Amchitka Pass, Alaska

With his skiff bouncing over the small waves of Amchitka Pass, Toby Church was thoroughly enjoying his freedom and the sea. He had forgotten just how much he missed being outside, unfettered by chains, movement bells, clanking gates and iron bars. The salt air and the glistening snow-capped volcanoes were invigorating. His thoughts turned to home.

It seemed like an eternity since he had been a young man in high school, playing football, dating girls, and making his parents proud. Then it was off to college. He remembered how disappointed he was when he failed to make the varsity football squad. Without football, his life had seemed so empty. He sought solace by attending the meetings of various groups around campus. He found his calling at a meeting of the Pure Nations. That was where he discovered the reason he hadn't made the football squad—*I didn't fail to make the team—it was that Nigger coach and the Kike President who filled the team with mud-people and Jew-loving whites.* The twisted logic of the Pure Nations had found a home in his shattered ego.

Church loved the twisted camaraderie of the racist world of Neo-Nazism and ultra-nationalism. But he also felt that the Pure Nations and the Ku Klux Klan were not committed enough to the elimination of the sub-human races in the United States. What the organization needed was less talk and more action.

That's why he had broken off from the Pure Nations to join the splinter faction, Reich America—an organization dedicated to destroying all their perceived enemies. Initially, the group had been comprised of only a handful of resentful youths. Marching on campus and holding weekly meetings, they were seen as a fringe group with little hope of surviving. This all changed the day they pulled off the Cleveland car bombing, which killed a half-dozen people. In a few days, Toby Church and Reich America were known nation-wide. He smiled as he remembered those headlines.

Fleeing to their hideout in Southern Illinois, Church and his followers evaded the FBI's manhunt with the help of racist sympathizers. Hiding in safe houses and using aliases, they made their way to Montana's remote Bull Mountains.

Church had been amazed by the amount of support he garnered from disaffected citizens and other fringe groups. Having started out with very little money, the ragtag group of radicals was soon flush with cash from selling drugs—an activity that served their dual purposes: fund the operations and create addicts among America's racial poor.

Reich America used its money to purchase weapons and high-technology gadgets designed to infiltrate banking systems and attack even the most secure industrial sites.

Followers formed satellite groups throughout the country. Church directed the operations of these satellite groups from his lair in the mountains. That's when he met and fell in lust with Penny Monroe—*the bitch who led me into the Fed's trap.*

The drone of a C-130 high overhead snapped him out of his daydream. Looking north, he spotted the transport glimmering against the bright blue sky. His throat grew tight. He licked his lips and throttled back to cut down on his wake. *Maybe they haven't spotted me? Maybe they're not even looking for me? Maybe they're out here dropping off supplies to villages destroyed by the earthquake? Maybe.* But he knew he was too important a prisoner. The plane was probably combing the seas for him.

He didn't know that he'd already been spotted by one of the CIA's KH-11 spy satellites orbiting high above the Earth.

When the giant transport continued westward without swinging in his direction, he let out a sigh. *They didn't see me.* Still, he took the precaution of covering his orange survival suit with a gray tarp. He scratched at the double-lightning bolt SS tattoo on his neck out of nervous habit.

Up in the distance, Amchitka Island appeared through the haze. He pulled out his chart and laid it in front of him. Running his finger along the shoreline, he searched for a village. Nothing. All that was on the island was an airstrip, a wildlife refuge, and a bunch of roads. He reassured himself again that with so many roads there had to be people.

He chose a small cove just west of Ivakin Point on the Northeastern shore to make land. It was close to several roads, but still far enough away to make his approach hard to detect.

Church inventoried his supplies—compass, pistol, jacket, rifle, ammunition, food, and clothing. He retraced each step of his plan in his mind. *First, leave the boat on the beach and comb the island for a settlement. Then steal a bigger boat and head further west. Of course, if the boat is big enough I just might head southeast and try and make it to Canada. If I can get there, they'll never find me. I'll disappear into the wilds of the Pacific Northwest. Then I'll relocate my organization closer to my brothers in the Pure Nations. And this time, I'll keep my zipper zipped.*

Church slowed down as he came around the north side of Ivakin Point. At the head of the cove was a gravel beach. Hundreds of sea lions were sunning themselves on the beach, but he was sure they would scatter when he came ashore.

To his surprise, the sea lions did not race back into the sea when he beached his boat. Those nearest to him charged off to the sides to avoid his approach, but overall they seemed pretty indifferent about his presence. He did notice, however, that a couple of the bulls were taking a more than curious interest in him. He paid heed to the bulls' grunting and movements. *Good God! They're as big as a Volkswagen bus!* He picked up his rifle just in case.

He pushed the anchor chain into the gravel and tested it to make sure the sea lions couldn't dislodge it. Next he grabbed all the gear he could carry. Gingerly, he moved through the mass of barking mammals away from the beach and inland. He knew enough about wild animals not to startle them.

Just then one of the bulls decided he was tired of this intruder. With surprising speed, the sea lion charged. Church scurried up the grassy cliff.

Daylight was fading fast. He hurried up the hillside, looking for a rock outcropping or cave to spend the night. *Tomorrow I'll find a road and a bigger boat.*

Karluk Lake, Kodiak Island, Alaska

Ivan Lincoln, Elizabeth LeDue and Joy Frank had managed to struggle through the ash storm to the forest service cabin on the Northwest shore of O'Malley Lake. Amazingly, the cabin had survived the earthquake. There were a few places where the roof had separated from the logs, but overall it had rode out the shaking fairly well.

Lincoln led them on a beeline to the shelter across the lowlands on the lakeshore. He stopped just short of the cabin and began circling it to make sure it was unoccupied.

Carefully he searched the ground for footprints or other signs of human habitation. Satisfied that no one was around, he slithered up to a window to check inside. It was empty.

Lincoln led his captives inside, where they took off their makeshift masks and ran their fingers through their hair, shaking the dust to the floor. Everyone was coughing.

Lincoln took a big swallow of water, rinsing the ash from his mouth. He didn't bother passing the canteen to his captives. *No use wasting water on the dead.*

Taking Elizabeth by the wrist, Lincoln led her and Joy over to the corner of the room, where he handcuffed them to the bed frame. Next he went over to the woodstove and used the kindling to start a fire. Both women were amazed that he would take the chance of lighting a fire and risk bringing attention to the cabin. Lincoln, however, was confident no one would be moving in this storm. He was going to take the opportunity to dry out his clothes, eat some hot food, and get some sleep.

Soon the woodstove was radiating heat and the temperature inside the room began to climb. Outside the ash was falling so hard a person could barely see 20 feet. Lincoln gazed out the window, keeping lookout for the police. At the same time, he sliced up some of the meat from the mountain goat they had found earlier in the day. Pulling a frying pan from the cupboard, he threw a slice of fat into the pan and set it on top of the woodstove. The smell of cooking flesh filled the air.

Rummaging through the cupboards, Lincoln found several cans of vegetables. He pulled a can of peas from the shelf, cut the top off with the end of his knife and set it on the stove.

The aroma of cooking food made Elizabeth and Joy salivate and their stomachs growl. Lincoln tormented them by making them watch him eat. He made loud chewing sounds and smacked his lips in delight.

"Aren't you going to let us eat?" Joy said defiantly.

He looked up from his plate. Juice ran from the corner of his mouth. He smiled.

What kind of a beast would taunt a person like this? How could a human being take such delight in another person's misery? Trying to ignore the growling in her stomach, Joy looked away from Lincoln's feast.

Elizabeth sat limply on the floor. She had laid her head against the bed railing in an effort to get some rest. Her legs felt like rubber. Her eyes burned with grit. The knife and willow cuts on her back and neck stung. Never had she felt so lost and alone—not even during her trial and sentencing. Her chest heaved. She thought about all the friends she'd lost.

To escape this hell, Elizabeth started daydreaming about the days before her world had come crashing down. Memories of her ex-husband made her smile. *Was it really ten years ago that we first met?* He was so handsome in his Navy dress whites and she was glowing in her slinky sequined evening gown. As they chatted through the evening and danced to the music of the small band, several people had commented on what a dashing couple they made.

It was a fairytale romance and wedding. Soon they were moving among the social elite of Washington, DC—Gary, an up and coming Lt. Commander posted at the Pentagon, and Elizabeth, the new head of the CIA's biological warfare development program. They were on all the invitation lists, including several functions at the White House.

Where did it all go wrong? She searched her mind for answers. *Did we simply grow apart with Gary on the road so much and me working so many hours? Did we stop loving each other once romance turned into routine?* She wondered where and what he was doing now.

Was it my failing marriage that pushed me into the arms of Sasha? If only Gary had loved me more and kept up the romance. Maybe I wouldn't have been so ready to take Sasha to my bed. How could I have been so blind not to see that Sasha was setting me up? But by the time she realized he was working for the Russians, it was too late. If she revealed her affair to her superiors, she would be ruined. She refused to risk falling from the limelight the way her father had after his bankruptcy.

Sasha had been very crafty. He knew she would do anything to prevent being exposed, including providing him with the base formuli for some of the CIA's most promising biological weapons. He'd used her and now she hated him.

Having food pressed against her lips brought Elizabeth out of her dream world. She opened her eyes. Joy was pressing a small piece of gristle into her mouth.

"Here, eat this. It's not much, but it'll help," Joy said kindly.

Although the meat was tough to chew, both Elizabeth and Joy had never tasted anything so good. The natural salts and fats from the gristle-laced meat coated their starving taste buds. They savored every bite. There weren't many.

After stoking the fire, Lincoln lay down on the mattress and drifted off to sleep.

Joy snuggled up against Elizabeth. They soon fell fast asleep.

Several miles away, Harry and Danny had managed to find shelter in a rock outcropping just above Thumb Lake. They had blocked off the entrance to the shallow cave with tree branches and one of their ponchos. It wasn't much, but it kept them free from the ravages of the silicon dust. They could breathe with relative ease, eat and drink, and they were fairly warm.

"Sure hope this ash storm moves on soon," Danny commented peeking out from behind the poncho. "If it doesn't, we might end up being buried alive," he commented only half in jest.

"Never seen anything like it before," answered Harry, "and I certainly hope never to again." The falling ash blurred out the surrounding terrain. The blizzard reminded him of the storms he'd endured as a boy living on the Arctic Coast.

"Do you think that Lincoln and the women have found shelter? Or do you think we'll find them dead in a few days, buried under this mess?" asked Danny.

Harry thought carefully before answering. "Hard to say. But my guess is that Lincoln, being the lucky SOB that he is, has either found a cave or a cabin in which to hide out. Once this storm lets up, it should be pretty easy to pick up the trail. It's not like you can walk in this stuff and not leave footprints."

Danny leaned back against a rock, hoping the wind would stay calm. If it started to blow, all this dust would eliminate any footprints. And it would make movement almost impossible.

"Looks like night's beginning to fall," Harry said looking out from the corner of their shelter. "Let's get some shuteye. Maybe in a few hours the storm will pass, and if we're lucky the sky will be clear so we can set out in the dark."

Danny had a puzzled look on his face. He was perplexed by the suggestion that they set off at night to continue their pursuit of Lincoln.

Seeing Danny's confusion, Harry said, "Lincoln won't move at night. He'll settle in figuring that nobody is after him. He's also betting that he has at least a two-day lead on any search party. Tracking at night is a skill you learn living on the Arctic Coast. In the summer, there's plenty of sunlight, but in the winter, you get used to tracking in the dark. As a boy, I got pretty good at it. We've got to make up some time. You need to learn to trust this old Eskimo." Harry flashed a rare smile.

Talking about his youthful days in Kaktovik reminded Harry of the good times he had had with his family during the long Arctic summers. They had lived a subsistence lifestyle, following the caribou herds across the Arctic marshes. His father believed it was important for his children to gain an understanding of how their ancestors had lived off the land. Robert Ignustuk taught his children how to fish for arctic grayling, trap ptarmigan, and rabbits, and pick berries. He also taught them how to hunt for seals among the ice floes from their boat. During the winter, his father would take them trapping for Arctic Fox and if the occasion arose, they would track a Polar Bear, even though they were no longer allowed to kill them.

These were times Harry remembered with great fondness. However, he also remembered his parents lecturing all their children that the way of the Inuit was disappearing and that to survive in the world, they needed to go away to college. After his siblings died in that tragic boating accident, his parents had focused all their energy on helping him go to college.

And now here you are. He said a silent prayer for the souls of his departed brother and sister, settled down with his head on his pack and drifted off to sleep. When the storm broke they would have to move hard and fast. He would need all his wits and energy to catch Ivan Lincoln. He wished that his beloved Malamute Max were still alive. He could use a good dog right now.

Like Harry, Danny was thinking about family and friends as he drifted off to sleep. He thought of his girlfriend Patty and their two-year old son, Brandon. He prayed they had survived the earthquake. Living in a cabin near Moose Pass south of Anchorage, he knew that if they were hurt, it would be difficult for them to get help anytime soon. He also thought about his parents back in San Diego. He smiled as he remembered the looks on their faces when he announced he was quitting his job with the police department, divorcing his wife and moving to Alaska to be a prisoner transport officer.

Danny's father had assumed his son would follow his footsteps—work for the city police department for 20 years, get married, raise a family, and retire near the folks. Both his parents were flabbergasted when he announced his plan to escape the trappings of civilization for the untamed wilderness of Moose Pass, Alaska. It took them weeks to even find it on the map. It was no more than a wide spot in the road. But after a few years, they came to Alaska to visit him. Danny seemed happy, and that's all that mattered to them. Nevertheless, they still hoped their son would come to his senses when he retired and move back closer to home.

Alaska was a far cry from where he had grown up as a black kid in a predominantly white suburb. And even though he was the only black person living in Moose Pass, he felt more at home there than he did in San Diego. To the other residents of Moose Pass, Danny was just another Cheechako looking for his home in the wilderness.

At first Danny couldn't understand why the locals had accepted him so readily. But after his first winter, he found out that to survive in the Arctic you have to rely on your friends and neighbors. The color of your skin means very little when it's 30 below zero and the snow hasn't stopped falling for two weeks.

Danny shifted on his butt. He couldn't get comfortable. He kept expecting Ivan Lincoln to sneak up on them. He wanted to believe that Lincoln would be holed up in a cabin or a cave somewhere, but he just didn't trust inmates. In his experience, they were always scheming and manipulating.

Outside, the ash continued falling like a mid-winter blizzard. Danny peeked around the poncho, wondering if they really would be buried alive.

Lincoln slept hard for several hours before waking up. He felt refreshed. His stomach was full and he felt good about being in control of his situation once again. His thoughts turned to the women in the cabin. *Which one will be my treat tonight?*

Twisting deep within Lincoln's psyche was the memory of his uncle, choosing one of his children or his nephews to sodomize after a long night of drinking. His entire childhood had been spent hiding from this sexual predator, and succumbing to his abuse whenever he couldn't find a hiding place quick enough. All the while, his mother, a victim of the epidemic alcoholism in Alaska's rural communities, stood stuporously by—oblivious to her children's brutalization.

Lincoln grabbed Elizabeth by the hair, untied her leg and released the handcuff. Pulling her to the side of the bed, he yanked off her coveralls, bent her over and exacted his vengeance. *Soon, it will be time to make her pay. Then it'll be the young one's turn.*

Elizabeth did not resist. Despite her terror, she remained silent, sparing Joy the horrific nightmare of Lincoln's predation. She bit her lip in pain, as he sodomized her. She could feel him making shallow stabs in her shoulders with his knife. He kept telling her how he was going to kill her.

She wished he would cut her throat like he said. *Death would be a blessing.*

Joy was sleeping deeply, dreaming about her mom cooking dinner at home in Connecticut. She hadn't felt Lincoln take Elizabeth. Her mind's eye was focused on playing chess with her Dad, while the aroma of lasagna wafted in from the kitchen—her Mom hollering a question about who wanted garlic toast with their meal and who wanted red wine.

Slowly, the sounds of Lincoln raping Elizabeth roused Joy from her slumber. She could hear him growling, and by the smell that filled the room, knew he was sodomizing her. Quietly, she cursed Lincoln and said a little prayer for Elizabeth. Joy was afraid. *When is he coming for me?*

Larsen Bay, Alaska

The citizens of Larsen Bay were wandering around the school gymnasium—still in shock from the loss of so many loved ones and so many precious memories. Outside, the storm grew in intensity. But despite the increasingly frightening atmosphere, no one complained, not even the children. Instead they accepted their situation with stoic bravery.

Michelle Dornier moved among the people with food and words of encouragement. Touching a shoulder here or giving an embrace there, she displayed a compassion that few would expect from a woman of such political power. Even Dick Burke was surprised at how well she was handling this latest setback. He had figured she would have been hysterical by now.

A few of the more suspicious people questioned why two state commissioners and two helicopters full of state troopers had come to Larsen Bay. They weren't buying the cover story that Governor Malloy was simply ensuring they got the help they needed. There were too many cops and only two medical people. Adding to the intrigue was the presence of two correctional officers. Things simply didn't add up.

Reacting to the rumors beginning to circulate amongst the survivors, the mayor had pulled Dornier and Burke aside to their office. "Okay, I'm sorry that I have to ask you again, but just why are you here?" he asked with searching eyes. "People are beginning to talk and it doesn't make sense that two important people like you, along with all these officers, would be sent to little old Larsen Bay."

Burke and Dornier glanced at each other, waiting to see who would speak first.

Burke started to blurt out the truth in all its ugliness, when Michelle Dornier raised her hand interjecting, "Look Mr. Mayor, you're right. We weren't just sent to Larsen Bay to handle the earthquake. We were sent here to make sure that the people of Larsen Bay are safe."

She motioned for the mayor to sit down, and handed a tray of food to Burke, who looked at her somewhat puzzled until she grabbed him by the shoulders, turned him towards the gym and gave him a little shove with an admonition to get busy helping the survivors. Sitting down next to the mayor, she used her best political-speak to break the news to the mayor that two fugitives had escaped from a transport plane near Larsen Bay. They were there to coordinate the capture of the prisoners and to make sure the people of Larsen Bay would be protected should the need arise.

The mayor was unhappy about this news. However, there was nothing he could do to change things. "Well, I guess you're doing the best you can with an impossible situation. I'll leave you to your work and for the time being I will let the rumors run. If I try and tell everyone what's up right now, it will just cause panic.

Some of our more vocal people will wonder why you're not out in the middle of this horrible storm trying to catch them by nightfall." He smiled to take the sting out of his words, picked up a food tray, and headed out into the gym.

Dornier let out a huge sigh and sat down on the edge of a desk. This had been an incredible two days. Never in her wildest dreams did she ever envision that she would be working in an isolated Alaska outpost, weathering a volcanic ash storm, and coordinating the manhunt for two notorious criminals.

Her mind skipped through memories as she sat watching the ash fall outside: how she had struggled to pay her way through college, the long hours of studying followed by the late-night shifts at the local pizza parlor, her first job in corrections, her promotions, her marriage, and finally the shock of having her husband inform her that he was in love with another woman and wanted a divorce.

Quietly at first and then louder, a little voice told her she did have the wherewithal to handle this situation and to come out on top. She needed to stop being intimidated by Burke's belligerence, stand up for herself, admit her limitations, and be willing to make a few mistakes to get the job done.

Slapping her hands on her thighs, she rose to her feet. *We'll just have to wait until the storm passes.* She prayed they wouldn't have to dig out of several feet of volcanic ash.

Across the gym, officers Marston and Price were helping the EMTs care for the injured. Major Calhoun and Trooper Abelsen were rationing food, clothing and water. Over in the corner, the gruff, seemingly unapproachable Commissioner of Public Safety was reading a bedtime story to the children. On his lap was a young Koniag girl of about four. She was holding his hand and resting her head on his chest. Michelle Dornier noticed that he didn't look so tough right now.

USS Billings, Gulf of Alaska

Shouting "Clear!" from his side window, Lt. Cowdrey fired up the twin turbine engines of the SH-60. Once again, he was going to risk flying through volcanic ash. Luckily for him, radar showed that the bulk of the storm was south of Kodiak Island and not over Shelikof Straits.

Commander Englemann stood on the deck, watching as the rotor blades became a spinning blur. Snapping a salute, Lt. Cowdrey pulled up on the collective and lifted the helicopter off the deck. Englemann turned around and headed for the bridge.

"Captain on the bridge."

"Helm, change course to zero nine two. Increase speed to 32 knots," Englemann ordered as she moved to her chair.

A few minutes later the Billings' clipper bow was slicing through the water as the gas turbines churned the water into a respectable rooster tail off the stern. Dall Porpoises raced alongside the ship, darting in and out of the bow's wake. Their antics brought smiles to the sailors' faces.

Throughout the ship, men and women checked and double-checked their weapons, communications, and tracking systems. The Chief Machinist's Mate was pacing up and down the engine room, fussing over how hard Commander Englemann was pushing his turbines. The Billings was a new ship, but they had been running hard for almost a full 24-hours. Even the best-maintained equipment was subject to failure when pushed too hard for too long and the Skipper was taxing the systems pretty damn hard. He didn't know how long the air filters would stand up to ingesting silicon ash. But the Chief was never one to complain. After 22 years in the Navy, he took immense pride in his engines and kept them in tip-top shape.

Besides, he owed Commander Englemann a lot. After tearing up a bar, stealing a patrol car and making the military police chase him all over North Island two years ago, he had found himself facing an ignominious end to an otherwise respectable career. He remembered distinctly the cold stare she had given him the day she came to pick him up at the brig. He also remembered her warning that no matter how good a machinist he was, she would not be there to save his butt if he screwed up again. He wasn't about to let her down.

On the fantail of the Billings, the crew had donned gas masks to help them breathe in the ash-choked air, while they loaded the depth charge racks. Below decks, Lt. Commander Hastings watched the crew prepare the Mark 46 torpedoes—just in case they were needed.

With a range of 8,000 yards and a speed of 28 knots, the Mk 46 was not fast enough to catch an Akula Class submarine, but if the Russian made a mistake or timed his turn wrong, the 98-pound warhead would make short work of any submarine, except a Typhoon.

In the Combat Information Center (CIC), radar and sonar operators checked their equipment. They had already downloaded the acoustic tapes from Hawk Two's tracking of the submarine. Since each submarine has its own unique sounds, a tape of the acoustic signature would make tracking easier. They could now detect the submarine through the noise of volcanic rumblings, surf, whales, dolphins and tides.

After weaving through holes in the ash storm, Hawk Two was again on station, hovering over the Shelikof Straits. Dangling beneath the fuselage were the MAD (Magnetic Anomaly Detector) and the hydrophone. Adjusting his instruments to filter out noise, the sonarman listened for the acoustic signature of the Akula moving through the water and watched the screen for magnetic fluctuations signaling the passing of a submarine. "Nothing yet, sir," he reported to Lt. Cowdrey.

Slowly, Lt. Cowdrey began flying a box-shaped search pattern based on the assumption that the Russians had the same coordinates for the crash site as they did.

"There she is!" the sonarman shouted as he fine-tuned the dials. "5,000 yards to the south, southeast—right off our one o'clock position. Speed 12 knots, depth 30 meters and running steady."

Keying his radio, Lt. Cowdrey called the Billings. "Bloodhound, Bloodhound, this is Hawk Two, over."

"Roger, Hawk Two, read you loud and clear."

"Bloodhound, we have contact. Repeat, we have contact. Initiating pursuit, over."

"Roger, Hawk Two. What are the coordinates?" came the excited reply.

"Coordinates are 57 degrees 45 minutes North and 154 degrees 45 minutes West. Speed 12-knots. Depth 30 meters."

"Copy Hawk Two, we are one hour out. Attempt to drive quarry west."

"Roger Bloodhound."

The nose of the SH-60 dropped slightly as it sped off to give chase to the Putin. Cowdrey was going to take up station in front of the oncoming Russians. He ordered the Crew Chief to drop sonobuoys in the water with active pinging—a wakeup call for the Russians.

Entering the water with two small splashes, the sonobuoys immediately found their mark. The familiar metallic "bwong" echoed back off the metal hull of the Putin. Lt. Cowdrey had just announced his arrival.

Akula Class Submarine Putin, Shelikof Straits, Alaska

No one had to announce the presence of sonobuoys in the water. Everyone onboard the Putin heard the familiar gong as the sonar signal bounced off the hull.

Reacting instinctively, Commander Ivanshenko barked orders, demanding to know the source of the pinging and if sonar was picking up any propellers in the water.

"No propellers in the water, Commander."

Ivanshenko quickly deduced that the American Seahawk was back to harass them.

"Helm. Five degrees down on the dive planes. Execute a slow 360-degree turn. Engineering, slow to eight knots. Let's lose them in a thermocline."

With smooth precision, the Putin's sailors responded to Ivanshenko's commands. The Putin was going deep. This would make tracking more difficult. Under the cold thermal layers of water, the acoustic and magnetic signatures of the submarine would subside markedly as they decreased speed. Commander Ivanshenko knew he couldn't outpace the American helicopter, but he could hide. All he needed was a cold, dense layer of water at a respectable depth. Unlike the helicopter, the Putin didn't need to go back for fuel. She could stay down here for weeks. *Come nightfall, I will surface and launch Major Golkin's team.*

Satisfied that he had taken his boat to a depth sufficient to block the broadband and narrowband searches of the American's sonar, Commander Ivanshenko brought Lt. Commander Vatutin and Major Golkin to his cabin to discuss a new strategy.

"Tea gentlemen?" he asked, pouring each of them a steaming cup. He motioned for them to join him around his table as he moved his chessboard over to his bunk.

Never one to hold his peace, Major Golkin began, "Commander, isn't it possible to shake off this pesky American helicopter and get me and my men on shore?"

Lt. Commander Vatutin tried not to sound patronizing as he displayed his gold-toothed smile, "No offense Major, but shaking off the American helicopter won't be easy, and if my hunch is correct, her mother ship—probably a frigate or cruiser—will arrive pretty soon. I think it's obvious by now that the Americans know what we're up to and had a pretty good idea from the start."

Ivanshenko and Golkin nodded in agreement. Vatutin continued, "We all know how important this American scientist is to both our countries. The Americans will do everything possible, short of sinking us, to stop us."

Ivanshenko rubbed his chin. He interjected, "I agree Vatutin, but I disagree over what actions the Americans are willing to take to stop us. Given the stakes involved and the fact that we are now well inside US territorial waters, I believe the Americans are authorized to sink us if we try to put Major Golkin's team on the beach."

Both Lt. Commander Vatutin and Major Golkin stared at Ivanshenko in disbelief.

Golkin was a veteran of covert operations. He had gone on several missions challenging the Americans, and not once had any shots been fired. There had been some tense games of cat and mouse, and on one occasion in the Balkans they had come close to shooting, but no one wanted to be the instigator of an international incident.

Vatutin sided with Major Golkin. He, too, had been involved in several Cold War chases in the waters off Petropavlovsk and the Kamchatka Peninsula when American missile boats had taken up station to practice their missile drills. Once, while tracking an American Trident submarine, their submarine had been "bumped" by a Los Angeles Class attack submarine, which had been conducting its own tracking exercise. Tempers had flared and accusations flew, but no one got shot at and no headlines were published.

Commander Ivanshenko had experienced many similar events, but he had a gut feeling that this time the stakes was higher. He was sure that if they slipped up, the game could turn deadly.

While Lt. Commander Vatutin and Major Golkin debated about what strategy the Americans would employ, Ivanshenko pulled out some charts of the area. *I have to come up with a quick solution. If I wait too long the American warship will be on my tail and with two foes, I will be hard pressed to accomplish this mission.* Suddenly, without looking up from the table, he dismissed Major Golkin. "Will you excuse us Major? I need to discuss some naval strategy with my executive officer."

Golkin was surprised by the request. *Why shouldn't I be included?* Ever the good soldier, however, he got up without showing his anger and left the cabin. He didn't even slam the door.

Ivanshenko turned back to Lt. Commander Vatutin. "I like the Major, but we can't forget he is working for the GRU," he whispered to his executive officer as a brief explanation before pointing to the chart of Kodiak Island. "Give me your best guess as to where two criminals would run if they came ashore here." His finger landed on Sevenmile Beach.

Vatutin looked at the map. Unlike city-bred Ivanshenko, Georgii Vatutin had grown up in the vast taiga of Siberia. Commander Ivanshenko was betting on his outdoor experiences to give him a place to hang his hat. "Well, Commander, I am not very knowledgeable about criminals, but if it was me, I'd head straight up this river valley, cross the island and make for the south side."

Ivanshenko raised one of his jet-black eyebrows. "Really? You wouldn't hug the shoreline and try to get to a village or town?"

Vatutin shook his head slowly from side to side. "No. If you stay on the beach it's too easy for someone to see you. Very little cover on the beach. If I were trying to escape, I would try and lose anybody following me in the wilderness and then make for the largest community in the area. That way I could walk the streets without anybody recognizing me. No, Commander," he concluded, "I think the criminals are headed up the Karluk River valley to this lake and pass, where they will turn east and make for the town of Kodiak."

Ivanshenko smiled at his executive officer, not only for his reasoning, but because his statements confirmed his own thoughts. He rolled up the map returning it to its cylinder. "Very good. I agree. Let's get to work."

Vatutin didn't bother asking about the plan. Ivanshenko wouldn't be able to give him any more than cursory details anyway. That was what set Ivanshenko apart from other Soviet and then Russian naval commanders. He avoided set-piece battles. He was creative and spontaneous. While this spontaneity was wonderful for accomplishing missions, it did little to endear him to the high command. In the former Soviet Union, innovative thinking was considered radical, and anything radical was dangerous. This was one reason why Igor Ivanshenko had been passed over for promotion year after year. The other reason was his willingness to disobey orders, just like he did when he rescued those Swedish sailors from their sinking destroyer after it collided with a Soviet spy sub in the straits near Stockholm.

"Helm, 10 degrees up on the bow planes. Bring us up to 15 meters. Once at depth execute a 180-degree course change. Engineering increase speed to 18 knots," Ivanshenko ordered as he returned to the control room.

Sailors at every station were taken aback by this abrupt change of course, speed and depth. The American helicopter was still harassing them. It made no sense to make more noise and come closer to the surface if they were trying to evade detection. Even Vatutin was perplexed by this strange set of orders. The new lieutenant stifled an urge to blurt out an inappropriate question. It was a running joke among the crew that the only reason the young officer wasn't thrown overboard by the Commander was because he could calculate course changes and target ranges faster than a computer.

Rising closer to the surface, picking up speed, and changing direction confused Lt. Cowdrey. *What are the Russians up to? Surely they're not giving up this easy?*

Ivanshenko was counting on this unorthodox maneuver to confuse his pursuers. *It's time to let the Americans believe they've won.*

Less than thirty minutes later, when the sonar station reported fast turning screws in the water approaching from the west, Commander Ivanshenko realized he had made the right choice. "Helm, five degrees down on the bow planes, maintain course of two four zero degrees. Engineering increase speed to 22 knots."

The active pinging from the American frigate echoed off the hull of the Putin, sending shivers down the crews' spines. They weren't out of the woods yet.

Sevenmile Beach, Kodiak Island, Alaska

After finding the abandoned raft on the beach, Lt. Vance Surin had led Sergeant Francisco Ramirez and Sergeant Tariq Ali up the western shore of the Karluk River. Code-named "Foxhound", Lt. Surin's special operations team was well equipped and trained to operate in hostile environments. With their weapons covered and wearing gas masks to filter out the deadly volcanic dust they had set off in search of their target—Dr. Elizabeth LeDue.

Their pace was hampered by the dust from the volcano's fallout and by the slippery mud. Night was falling by the time they made it to the site of the fugitives' first camp.

"Lieutenant," called out Sgt. Ali, "here's the remains of a small campfire and some trash. Looks like they spent their first night right here."

Surin picked up a piece of trash and kicked his boot through the dead coals from the fire, patting Ali on the shoulder. Sgt. Ali was one of the best trackers in the Marine Corps. A first-class sniper and a dogged hunter with incredible energy and physical stamina, Tariq Ali was determined to make his Egyptian-American parents proud. Joining the Marines at age 18, he had vowed to volunteer for the toughest duty available. He soon found himself assigned to Lt. Surin.

Lt. Surin unshouldered his pack, motioning for his sergeants to do the same. With the skill developed by years of practice, they soon had their perimeter trip wires rigged, set up their pup tents, and established a guard rotation for the night.

Lt. Surin retired to his tent, removed his mask, which was chaffing his chin and forehead, and switched on the radio. Apparently the prevailing winds were shifting, because the fall of ash was decreasing at a very encouraging rate. The Marines could make out the faint twinkle of the evening's first stars. "Bloodhound, Bloodhound, this is Foxhound, over," Surin said, keying the microphone.

"Go ahead Foxhound, this is Bloodhound."

"Foxhound has found the scent. There appear to be three, repeat three in the group. We are set up for the night. Off at first light. Over."

"Roger, Foxhound, we copy. Good hunting. Bloodhound out."

Surin exited the tent, calling Sergeants Ali and Ramirez over to discuss the next day's operations. Their job was to retrieve Dr. LeDue or at the very least prevent her from falling into Russian hands. He made sure they understood their orders to kill her if capture was not possible. However, with two other people in the mix, they were faced with a dilemma. They could kill the male prisoner. But the female civilian was a problem.

"It's pretty easy Lieutenant. If the Russians don't show up," counseled Sgt. Ramirez, "we simply take all three back to the Billings. On the other hand, if the Russians do show up, I don't think we have any option but to execute all three."

Lt. Surin did not react to Sgt. Ramirez's rather cold-blooded analysis. He had come to expect that kind of bluntness from this street-hardened kid from the barrios of Los Angeles. One thing about the short, stocky Francisco Ramirez, he was direct.

Surin and Ali had to agree with Ramirez. There could be no half measures. If they had to kill their quarry, they would have to make it look like the Russians did it. Each man pulled out his Russian-made 9mm Makarov pistol, which he carried for just such a contingency. Sergeant Ramirez unwrapped his Kalishnikov AK-47 rifle and stowed his M-16. Any investigation would confirm through ballistics that it was the Russians who had executed the fugitives.

Surin took the first watch as the blanket of night fell across the dust-encrusted landscape of Kodiak Island. Tomorrow they would push their hunt with renewed vigor. If they were lucky, Dr. Elizabeth LeDue would be back in prison by nightfall.

Outside the camp, a male grizzly sniffed the air. He'd caught the scent of food. He was hungry. It had been several days since he'd made a kill or found a carcass to scavenge. Plus, today's storm had disoriented him and made him more irritable than usual—a giant looking for trouble. Wrapped in thick dark fur, he was invisible in the darkness.

Lt. Surin never heard the giant bear approach from behind the alders. With terrifying acceleration the bear charged into the camp tripping wires and sending flares high into the inky darkness. The flares burned brightly, bathing the speeding monster in a green haze. Surin spun to his left as he shouldered his M-16, and took aim at the charging bear. The M-16 spit a line of bullets at the oncoming animal. Unfortunately for Lt. Surin, a .223-caliber M-16 has little effect on a 1,100 pound bear.

Dropping his rifle, he reached for his Makarov pistol. But before he could clear leather, the bear hit him like an NFL linebacker.

With a bone-crushing thud, Lt. Surin hit the ground. Fire shot through his right shoulder as the bear spun around and slashed him with his razor-sharp claws. As he tried to scramble away, the bear grabbed his foot in its jaws, lifting him off the ground. Surin screamed for help as the bear shook him like a rag doll. The bear tossed him to the ground and raked him with his claws a second time.

Sergeants Ramirez and Ali had shot up out of bed and grabbed their weapons at the sound of the flares going off. As they bolted out of their tents they were shocked to see a bear mauling a screaming Surin. Thinking quickly, Sergeant Ramirez grabbed his AK-47. Hollering for Surin to stay down, he fired several 30-caliber rounds into the animal. With a roar and a great expulsion of air, the bear staggered from the impact of the bullets. Grunting in pain, it rumbled off into the brush.

Sgt. Ali cautiously tracked the wounded beast through the dust and brush. He found it several hundred yards from their camp—dead. He examined the creature, marveling at its size.

"Are you alright Lieutenant?" Sgt. Ramirez called out, rushing over to Lt. Surin's side, medical kit in hand.

"Son-of-a-bitch," moaned Lt. Surin. He tried to raise himself up from his prone position. He could feel warm blood pumping from a gash on his right shoulder. He felt light headed. His chest hurt after being hit by a living freight train.

In the beam of a flashlight, Sgt. Ramirez saw three deep cuts on Lt. Surin's shoulder. Luckily, Surin's boot had protected his ankle from any serious injury. Ramirez applied pressure to the gashes. Next he gave Surin a shot of morphine and sutured the muscles back together. After applying generous amounts of antibacterial ointment to the area around the exposed muscles, he sewed the skin closed and covered the wound with gauze.

The effects of the morphine let Lt. Surin drift into unconsciousness. He would be sore the next day, but if Sgt. Ramirez knew the Lieutenant, he would be ready to march at first light. He probably wouldn't even call the incident in to Commander Englemann.

Coming over and squatting by his companion, Sgt. Ali announced the obvious. "Well, that was one helluva shootout. With the flares and the gunfire, I think they know someone is out looking for them now. How's the Lieutenant?"

"He'll be okay. The bear scored a good swipe on his shoulder, but I sewed him up. He's going to be sore tomorrow and we'll have to watch for infection, but we both know he'll be pushing us hard," Ramirez answered smiling.

O'Malley Lake, Kodiak Island, Alaska

Following the second rape of Elizabeth, Ivan Lincoln had once again bound her with the rope and handcuffs. He then settled in for a nice nap.

Joy took her into her arms in an attempt to comfort her.

Elizabeth found little solace in Joy's embrace. She was too traumatized. However, she did appreciate the kindness Joy showed her—it was nice to know she wasn't all alone in this terrible ordeal.

The faint echo of gunfire bouncing up the valley made Joy turn her head. Not believing her ears, she listened more intently. *Is that gunfire?* She shook her head straining to confirm her hopes. *It is gunfire*! A sense of hope displaced her despair. *Someone must be coming for us.* But something didn't make sense. *Why are they shooting their guns at night and who are they shooting at?*

Realizing that the sound of gunfire might rouse Lincoln from his slumber, Joy got to her knees and peered over the foot of the bed. Much to her relief, he was sound asleep. She couldn't believe it.

Quietly, she sat back down on the floor and placed Elizabeth's head in her lap. Silently she stroked her hair. Elizabeth didn't say a word, but when Joy promised not to leave her behind, she squeezed her leg to let her know she had heard her.

Joy tried thinking about happier thoughts. It had been a sunny day in New York City when she received the call from Captain Lind offering her a job on his boat. She was going to Alaska—the land of adventure and romance! Ever since she'd been a little girl, she had loved the tales of Jack London and Robert Service. She would watch all the nature shows on television about Alaska and the Arctic. The pictures of the Northern Lights drew her like a magnet. Like many people, she was caught up in the romance of the North.

When she arrived in Anchorage, the sun was glimmering off the summit of 20,320-foot Mt. McKinley 250 miles to the north. She was hooked. Her excitement grew as she looked out the window of the small plane as it flew down the Kenai Peninsula over turquoise lakes, meandering streams and endless forests. It was more beautiful than the pictures.

So much for adventure. Now she was handcuffed to a bed in a remote cabin in the middle of the wilderness, hostage to a madman. Right now she would settle for a quiet evening drinking hot cocoa with her parents in front of the fireplace. *Do they know I'm missing?*

Thumb Lake, Kodiak Island, Alaska

"Wake up Danny," Harry said, nudging his partner. "Listen," he said holding a finger to his lips and turning his head to improve the reception. "Gunfire. Lots of gunfire." He had a bewildered look on his weathered face.

The words gunfire snapped Danny out of his sleep-induced stupor. "What do you mean gunfire? Who in the hell would be out here in the middle of the night shooting up a storm like that?" he growled.

Harry tried to answer that riddle. "Beats the heck out of me, Danny. But I know what I heard. It's coming from the north end of the valley."

"Do you think they're ours?" asked Danny.

"Can't tell," Harry replied. *Has Lincoln doubled back on us and run into another search team? Have the fugitives run into a bear? Has a search team run into a bear?* Of course, neither he nor Danny knew that both the Americans and Russians were racing each other in a bid to be the first to capture Dr. Elizabeth LeDue.

For the next hour they discussed whether or not they should head back down the valley just in case Lincoln had doubled back. They decided he wouldn't abandon his race to the forest. The gunfire had to be department officers either dealing with an unruly bear or overreacting to something they thought they saw in the night.

Satisfied they had solved the riddle, they decided to sleep a few more hours and head out before daylight. The storm had cost them precious time. Harry wanted to get a jump on Lincoln and the other search team. The prisoners were his responsibility. He was determined to be the one to catch them.

Governor's Mansion, Juneau, Alaska

Governor Malloy put down his drink and retired to his upstairs office to take a call from a Mr. Frank in Connecticut. "Hello, this Governor Rick Malloy. To whom am I speaking?"

"My name is Thomas Frank, Governor Malloy. Thank you very much for taking my call." Joy's father was immensely relieved that his efforts to contact someone in Alaska about his missing daughter had succeeded.

"You can call me Rick, Mr. Frank."

"Ah yes, well, umh Rick, you see my daughter Joy went to Alaska this spring to work on a fishing boat—the Neptune. Well, I just spoke with the Captain of the Neptune, Mr. Alfred Lind. And you see, Mr. Lind tells me that my daughter was taken hostage by two of your escaped prisoners. He tells me she is somewhere on Kodiak Island. I'm wondering what you're doing to find my daughter."

I was wondering how long it would take for someone to identify the third person. Rick Malloy scratched his head, trying to come up with a good answer. "I've got a team on Kodiak searching for her right now." He omitted the information about the Russians and the US Navy—no need to upset him any more. "Rest assured Mr. Frank, my administration is committed to capturing the convicts and returning your daughter to you safe and sound."

Not quite satisfied with the answer he was getting, but knowing that he probably wouldn't get any more information, Thomas Frank left his telephone numbers and promised to email a recent photo of his daughter to Governor Malloy's office.

As soon as he hung up with Mr. Frank, Governor Malloy summoned his chief-of-staff to the mansion.

George Roberts knew just what to do. Hurrying from the mansion, he proceeded to his office where he retrieved Joy Frank's photograph from the computer. He placed a call to General McCarthy at Elmendorf, asking that the Navy be advised of the third person's identity. It was a young woman with a very concerned father.

After his call to General McCarthy, George Roberts went to the emergency command center in the basement of the Capitol. He needed to radio Dick Burke.

He informed Burke and Dornier that in addition to inmates Lincoln and LeDue, there was a hostage—a young woman named Joy Frank. It was imperative that this girl be returned to her parents unharmed. Their orders were to get that girl out of there without a scratch.

In the meantime, General McCarthy relayed the information about Joy Frank to the USS Billings and Commander Englemann. Commander Englemann relayed the information to Foxhound.

George Roberts had returned to the mansion, where he found Governor Malloy sitting in the small dining alcove. He sat down and they discussed this latest development and how it might impact the search for the two criminals. They knew that if any harm came to Ms. Frank, the level of scrutiny by the press, and probably a team of lawyers, would be intense. The prison on Adak could very well be in jeopardy. Given his impression of Mr. Frank on the phone, Governor Malloy did not believe that any amount of money would quiet him. He didn't blame him. He would be just as protective about his children.

"George, I want you to make sure this goes right," Governor Malloy directed forcefully. "I don't care if it takes a dozen troopers and half the Department of Corrections. I want those prisoners found and I want that girl back with her parents pronto. No screwups, no bad shootings, no nothing. I want this taken care of. Am I making myself crystal clear?"

"I'm on it," Roberts answered. He got up from the table. He was headed back to his office.

Once at the office he called Admiral Rourke of the Coast Guard. "Admiral? This is George Roberts. I need to come see you."

"Sure George. You know where I live?"

"Yep. See you in fifteen," he replied, putting down the receiver.

In less than 15 minutes, George Roberts was drinking coffee with Admiral Rourke at his home on Fritz Cove Road. He briefed the Admiral on the latest developments, and secured the Admiral's commitment to dedicate more resources for the search for the prisoners. However, Admiral Rourke informed Roberts that his command was already stretched thin. Resources were tight. He couldn't guarantee any more than ferrying his two SH-60 helicopters stationed in Juneau and Sitka to Kodiak. He would place them at the disposal of Commissioners Burke and Dornier. He would also dispatch a buoy tender to Larsen Bay with extra jet fuel.

Roberts thanked Admiral Rourke and bid farewell to the Admiral's wife. He headed home. He was exhausted. *Too many priorities and not enough resources.* No one knew the exact location of Lincoln and LeDue. *In the morning I'll order General Hornby to dispatch one of his Blackhawk helicopters to Larsen Bay with another team of State Troopers.*

George Roberts knew the people of Larsen Bay would not be happy to see an expansion of the operation in their community. He changed his mind about going home to bed and headed back to the office. It was almost midnight, but he needed to warn Larsen Bay that things were about to get really busy.

DAY THREE

Amchitka Island, Alaska

Dawn broke with an unusually brilliant display of blues and violets caused by the Sun's rays being filtered through the volcanic ash scattered high in the atmosphere to the east. Lt. Carlos Banderas and his team had been awake for several hours waiting for daybreak. They were hunkered down behind a small bluff, which shielded them from the biting wind of early morning. They did not start a fire to cook any food, because they did not want to risk giving away their position. Instead they ate smoked salmon, cheese and crackers, and drank water. It was hard to wake up without their morning coffee, but this was a small sacrifice if staying hidden helped them catch their elusive prey.

As they stood munching on their food they searched the surrounding area through their binoculars for any sign of Toby Church moving across the grassy terrain of Amchitka Island. Nothing. But they weren't too worried yet. It was still early.

"Ben?" asked Carlos, "any more ideas on how we should go about this hunt?"

Ben responded without hesitation. "Been thinking about it all night, Lieutenant. Church is one crafty and dangerous man. I think we stick to my original plan. The first thing we do is disable his boat so he can't get off the island. Then we can do a wide sweep and pin him on one end of the island."

"Sounds good to me," Carlos said as he shouldered his pack and picked up his rifle. "Okay, guys let's move out."

Travis and Ben followed Carlos's lead and picked up their gear.

Spaced at 10-foot intervals, the three officers moved out from their windbreak into the early morning light. Ben Williams was in the lead since it was his plan they were following.

Moving as quietly as possible, the three men worked their way across the undulating, spongy, treeless tundra. The only sound any of them made was when they would curse under their breath after breaking through the paper thin ice between the tussocks and soaking their feet in the frigid water underlying the grass.

The sun was well above the horizon when Ben motioned for everyone to stop and get down. He sniffed the air. Carlos and Travis watched in amusement.

Carlos trotted up next to Ben.

Ben pulled him down into a crouch and whispered in his ear, "Church is cooking breakfast, just down over that rise. By the smell of it, I'd say he's having sea lion." A grin crossed Ben's face. He was pleased with himself. He'd found Church. Just like he said he would.

They were all amazed that Toby Church was being so careless.

Toby Church had been awakened by the sunlight hitting his face. The sea air was fresh and clean and he was very hungry. Confident he had eluded his captors, he decided to have another hot meal.

He looked back towards his skiff far in the distance, making sure it had not been pulled out to sea in the night, or damaged by some of those cranky sea lions. Satisfied that it was still firmly in place, he settled down to cook over the small fire he had started with some driftwood salvaged from the beach the afternoon before.

Steam rose from the frying pan as the meat sizzled in the cool morning air.

"Any ideas on what we do now?" Carlos asked.

"I say we surround him," Corporal Nelson replied.

Ben didn't respond right away. He was thinking.

"Ben?" Carlos asked, hoping that his friend would have a solution or an alternative to their plan. Church's guard was down and now was a perfect time to surprise him.

Finally Ben spoke, "Surrounding him might work, but if he gets away and back to his boat, we'll never catch him. We've got no way off this rock for a couple of days. By then he'll be long gone. I still say we disable his boat, take our time and make sure we catch him."

"Okay," Carlos answered, "but just how do I get around him without being seen?"

Travis pulled out his binoculars and scoured the terrain. "Down there," he said pointing, "There's a ridge just below Church's position, which should hide you all the way to the beach."

Carlos took Travis's binoculars and surveyed the terrain himself. Handing the binoculars back to Travis, he said, "Very good. You two move into flanking positions and wait for me to work my way around Church to his boat. I'll disable it and then come up on him from behind. I'll call for his surrender and you two make sure he doesn't get away."

Cautiously, Carlos made his way down the ridge. After about 10 minutes of strenuous effort Carlos was poised just above the rocky beach where Toby Church had left his skiff. All around were sleeping sea lions. Some of the cows were slowly milling about. The youngsters were trying to find their mothers for breakfast. *Damn,* he thought, *just how am I going to get to that boat without the whole island knowing about it? The minute I step out into the middle of this herd they're going to begin barking and charging around.*

He looked over his shoulder at Ben and Travis on the hill above his position. He communicated his predicament with a shrug of his shoulders and moving his hand like a sea lion barking. Both officers responded with shoulder shrugs. No one knew how to breach one of Mother Nature's best alarm systems.

"Come on Carlos," he said to himself, "there's got to be a way."

Watching from above, Ben shook his head from side, partly in amusement at the situation and partly in frustration.

Carlos waved his arm, motioning for Ben and Travis to come down the hill and join him.

As Ben and Travis came alongside Carlos, Ben said, "we could rub you down in seal oil and maybe they wouldn't notice? Of course, they may keep you in the harem."

"Very funny Ben," Carlos said with a smile. He appreciated Ben's sense of the absurd and his ability to diffuse tension with his quick wit. That was one of the reasons why Ben was a popular officer at Malloy Super Max. "But be serious."

"Look Lieutenant," said Ben calmly, "if we want to disable his boat, we're going to have to risk having those sea lions raise a ruckus and give us away. Even though this may take away our chance of surprising Church, it will still leave him stranded on this rock. Then it will only be a matter of time before we hunt him down."

"Fair enough Ben. Still, I'm going to try and get to the boat without stirring them up. Maybe they'll ignore me," he said without confidence.

Carlos proceeded to the edge of the small overhang just up from the beach. With slow, steady movements he lowered himself down among the great mass of moving blubber and bad breath. *Whew, what a smell!*

Step by deliberate step, he crept through the herd of sea lions. Much to his surprise they seemed to ignore his presence. *Maybe I will make it down to the boat without them going crazy.*

It seemed like an eternity before he finally made it to the water's edge and the skiff. Working quickly, he removed the engine cover and pulled off the distributor cap and cut the spark plug wires.

The boat was now useless unless Church intended to row across the Pacific.

Carlos looked back on the herd of sea lions. He hoped they'd let him back through without raising a fuss. This time, however, he was upwind. He climbed out of the boat and took a step towards shore. At that instant a tremendous clamor arose from the herd. Bulls that had been lounging lazily in the morning sun, suddenly came charging in their awkward undulating motion toward him, flashing their razor sharp teeth. These 2,000-pound animals were dangerous. The chance of sneaking up on Toby Church was ruined. Carlos beat a hasty retreat back off the beach—a very aggressive male in hot pursuit. The speed of the legless mammal was impressive.

As Carlos sprinted through the herd and away from the bull trying its best to take a piece out of his ass, he motioned for Ben and Travis to move quickly back up the hill. *Maybe Church hasn't spotted us?* He thought hopefully.

While Carlos was dismantling his skiff, Toby Church was chewing on a crispy piece of blubber, thinking about the next phase of his plan. He was going to hike to the highest ridge and follow its rocky spine the length of the island. This would give him the best vantage point from which to survey the island and spot any habitations or vessels.

Just then, the sea lions's barking shattered the morning's tranquility. He jumped to his feet, shielding his eyes from the morning sunlight. He cursed when he saw a man with a rifle running up the beach towards two other men, who were standing on top of the small cliff overhanging the beach.

Stuffing the rest of the blubber into his mouth, he grabbed his rifle and the rest of his gear. In just a few minutes, he was racing away from his pursuers. *How did they find me?*

Coming to a ridge top, he stopped to catch his breath. Then it hit him. *It must've been that C-130 Hercules. There is an airfield on the island.* The airfield wasn't on his charts, but that didn't mean it didn't exist. He knew from experience that the government often hid secret installations from the public by not putting them on the map. He felt strong. He loved a good chase. And now he was sure there was an airbase on the island. *I'm getting off this desolate rock.* He had a new plan.

Dropping his gear into a rock outcropping for later retrieval, he doubled back in the direction of the pursuing officers.

The minute Lt. Banderas broke into a run up the beach, Corporal Nelson saw Church stand up and look in their direction. "He's seen us," Travis whispered to Ben.

Ben grabbed Travis by the elbow and began pulling him along at an amazing pace for a man his age. Ben knew it was important not to lose sight of Church. He was too dangerous. If they lost sight of him he could set up an ambush. Besides, he was going to be the one to nab Toby Church. His aim had been off in the tower. *This time I won't miss.*

But Church was too fast. He disappeared over a ridge.

Church trotted down the old asphalt road. It was important to move quickly without wasting energy. This was no time to panic. The officers would be quick to join in the pursuit. He was betting they would expect him to double back to his boat. *He was doubling back all right.* This time, however, he wasn't going to try and get off the island in a little aluminum boat. He had a better idea.

Church took up a position in the middle of a outcropping of rocks and waited for his pursuers to come running up the slope. He checked to make sure a round was chambered in his rifle. His throat was dry. He took a small drink of water. *I'm not going back to prison.*

Ben Williams followed Church's footprints in the marshy turf, leading Carlos Banderas and Travis Nelson up a narrow path, which had been etched into the ground years ago. Several times, he motioned for them to keep their spacing. It was dangerous for everybody to bunch up—it would make them easy targets.

As they approached the crest of the hill, Carlos motioned for them to spread out in a vee formation. With a wave of his arm, he ordered them to move in Church's direction. By placing one officer on the crest and one on either side of the ridgeline, he hoped to catch Church trying to sneak back to his boat.

The crack of a rifle shot broke Carlos' concentration. Looking left, he saw Corporal Nelson lying on the ground.

The bullet slamming into Corporal Nelson's chest spun him around. He crumpled to the ground. The last thing he felt was a strange burning sensation just over his right lung.

Suddenly the air surrounding Carlos and Ben erupted in gunfire. Ben dropped into a prone position and returned fire with his M-16 rifle. He could see the muzzle flash from Church's position behind a small outcropping of rock about 100 yards to the west. Dirt and grass flew into the air as bullets thumped into the soft ground just in front of him. He didn't flinch. Instead he continued returning fire. He wanted to time his shot and catch Church looking over the rocks.

While Ben kept Church pinned down, Carlos crawled on his knees over to Corporal Nelson. "You alright Travis?" Carlos asked. He reached out with his left hand, feeling Nelson's pulse. It was very weak. *He's wearing a ballistic vest. This doesn't make sense.* Running his hand over the young man's face, neck, pelvis and legs he couldn't feel any wounds.

"I think so," came the feeble reply, "but my chest burns and I feel dizzy."

Confident that Travis was just stunned from the impact of the bullet and that his vest had stopped it from penetrating, Carlos focused on keeping him calm. "You'll be just fine Travis. Good thing you were wearing your vest. Guess this is your lucky day," he said trying to make the young man smile.

Suddenly Carlos realized that Travis was not okay. His face was turning ashen. A small trace of blood seeped out of the corner of his mouth. He checked Travis's pulse again. It was getting weaker. Opening Nelson's coat and then his shirt, Carlos noticed the hole where the bullet had penetrated the vest, dragging shards of fiber and cloth with it as it slammed into the flesh. He ran his hand under the backside of the vest. There was no exit wound—the bullet had shattered inside Corporal Nelson.

Immediately, Carlos pulled the straps loose to remove the vest. Travis winced in pain. "No, no, don't bother Lieutenant. Am I going to die?"

"You're not going to die!" Carlos barked. "Stop talking like that!" Taking Travis's coat, he placed it under his head. "You just hang in there," he coached. "I've never lost an officer in the line of duty and by God, you don't have permission to be the first!"

A small tear ran down Travis' face as he summoned the last vestiges of strength. "Lieutenant?"

"Yes, Corporal, what is it?"

"Please tell my wife and son I love them."

"You can count on that Corporal."

Nelson coughed, spewing blood-filled spray into the air. Then he convulsed.

Carlos watched the light fade from Nelson's eyes. He hung his head in grief and swore an oath to even the score with Church. *This is the last person he's going to kill.*

Having suppressed the fire coming from Church's position, Ben squirmed sideways over to where Lt. Banderas had covered Travis' face with his coat. Only then did he realize that Nelson was dead.

"For the love of God Carlos, wasn't the kid wearing his vest?" Ben asked, while keeping a wary eye on Church's position and his rifle against his shoulder.

"Yes, Ben, he was wearing his vest, but not his trauma plate. Church must have a rifle."

"Well, I think he'll retreat," Ben said confidently. "I managed to give him another haircut. He's probably thinking about getting back to his boat right now."

"No Ben, I don't think that's his plan. If he wanted to get to the boat he wouldn't have ambushed us. I think he figures on killing us. That way he can take his time to escape," said a seething Banderas.

Noticing the grief in his long-time friend's eyes, Ben took a few moments to reassure Carlos that the shooting was not his fault. There was no way they could have known Church had a rifle. Furthermore, nobody would have expected him to get into a firefight with three well-armed officers.

Ben's words fell on deaf ears. Carlos blamed himself for Travis Nelson's death. He should have suspected Church might find a rifle as he ran through town during his initial escape. He should have foreseen the desperation of this very dangerous criminal. He had a hundred reasons why he should have outfoxed Church and saved Nelson's life. And he dreaded having to radio the bad news back to Malloy. It would be Captain Anderson, not him, who would make the phone call to Travis' family. *It's my job. I'm responsible.*

"What do we do now?" Ben asked. He was growing anxious lying on the ground exposed to the elements and enemy fire.

Carlos took a few minutes to think about a new strategy. *We could rush his position, but he's pretty well dug in. We could retreat. Church does have the tactical advantage right now.* "I'm thinking we retreat. Church is dug in and we'll be hard pressed to flush him out of that hole now that he's got us in his sights."

"I agree." Ben knew that now was not the time to press Church. They had time on their side. He wasn't going to get off the island.

"Pick the kid up, Ben," Carlos ordered. He rose to one knee and pointed his rifle at Church's position just in case the fugitive stuck his head out from behind the rocks.

Like a father caring for his child, Ben wiped the blood from Travis Nelson's mouth and picked him up, cradling him against his chest. "Come on Lieutenant," he said motioning with his head. "Let's get this boy back down the hill. He deserves a proper burial. I'll not leave his body out here to be picked over by scavengers. And when were done with that, we've got a job to finish."

As Ben moved down the hill, Carlos walked backwards, always keeping Church's position in his sights.

From his lair, Church watched Ben and Carlos move over the crest and down the hill. Their retreat was confusing. If it had been him, he would have pressed his attack. He leaned back against a rock, trying to figure out what they were up to now.

Carlos and Ben moved cautiously. Time was on their side. Church was no longer trying to run. They were sure he would try to set up another ambush. In a strange way they were happy that Toby Church was no longer running. It gave them the scenario they needed to even the score.

The sun was high in the Arctic sky as they dug a temporary grave to protect Nelson's body from being eaten by scavengers. They removed their caps. While keeping a sharp eye out for Church, they said a short prayer for Corporal Travis Nelson. Ben found a large piece of driftwood and attached his badge to it, marking the grave.

Carlos took a deep breath. It was time to make the dreaded radio call to Captain Anderson.

Malloy Super Max Prison, Adak Island, Alaska

Unable to censor open channel radio communications, Captain Anderson took the only course of action possible. "Sgt. Knight, this is the SS. Lock down all posts and have all officers assemble outside of Main Control in 15."

"10-4 SS. All posts this is Sgt. Knight. You heard the order."

After all the stress his employees had been under for the past 36 hours, Anderson dreaded having to break more bad news to them. However, he knew he had to get the information out quick. Otherwise people would gossip and the original story would get so distorted that it would be unrecognizable.

Captain Marc Anderson took a deep breath before exiting Main Control into the hallway filled with officers. Speaking in a firm, calm voice, he told them about the death of Corporal Travis Nelson. The hallway grew quiet. A few officers wiped away tears. Silently, they dispersed back to their posts.

"I hate this job," Anderson sighed as he went back into his office. He had never really gotten to know Nelson, but he felt the loss deeply anyway. Nelson was a young officer with a bright future and a family. Anderson was not looking forward to the phone call he was about to make—to Nelson's wife.

Speaking through her sobs, Nelson's wife asked how her husband had died. Anderson let her know her husband had died bravely and that his last words were how much he loved her and their son and how much he would miss them both. "Thank you, Captain. I know this has been tough on you too," she said courageously. "And please let everyone there know how much Travis liked working with them. And Captain, Travis would have wanted you to know how proud he was to work on your shift."

Up until this moment, Marc Anderson had been doing a pretty good job of maintaining his composure, but Sabrina's last comment brought tears to his eyes. Now, more than ever, he regretted not getting to know the scruffy redheaded Corporal better.

Their conversation ended with Marc Anderson promising to bring Toby Church back into custody, dead or alive, and with Mrs. Nelson extracting a promise from him to hold a proper memorial service for her husband at the prison.

It took a few minutes for Anderson to get control of his emotions. It was always the same when he had to deal with someone he knew dying. It had been that way ever since his 15-year old son had died of Leukemia. Reverently, he twisted the bracelet he wore on his left wrist. His son had given it to him on his 40th birthday.

A quiet knock on the door interrupted his thoughts.

"Come in," Anderson replied absent-mindedly.

Father Androvsky, the saint in this horrible crisis and the town's Russian Orthodox Priest, continued knocking lightly as he opened the door. "Captain?" queried the bearded Androvsky, "may I come in?"

Rising from his desk, Captain Anderson welcomed the priest with a warm smile and a strong handshake. "Of course Father, you know you are always welcome."

Father Androvsky placed his hand on Anderson's shoulder. He had just learned of the tragic death of Corporal Nelson. He knew this was an unneeded burden for the already overtaxed Captain. Taking Anderson by the elbow, he led him over to the map table, where they knelt and prayed for the soul of the slain Corporal and for the welfare of his family.

After finishing the Lord's Prayer, Father Androvsky rose from his knees. With so much still to be done, there was little time to grieve. He took advantage of his audience with Anderson and began listing off the tasks he wanted to accomplish. He wanted to organize the survivors into work crews to clean up the devastated community. He wanted to use the motor grader to repair the runway so supplies could be flown into Adak. He wanted to put people to work collecting the debris and sorting it into usable and unusable piles. They would burn the junk and salvage the rest. "It's time," he said in his quiet, but authoritative manner, "for the people of Adak to quit mourning and get on with living."

Captain Anderson approved Androvsky's plan. He notified maintenance that as soon as the perimeter road was fixed, the grader was to begin working for Androvsky.

The maintenance crew at Malloy Super Max had worked wonders over the last day and a half. The outer perimeter fence was once again standing and secure. The crew was busy replanting the poles and stretching the wire on the inner perimeter fence and would have that task finished by tomorrow. The kitchen was open. The perimeter road would be usable by the morning. There were still a lot of loose ends, but for the most part, the prison perimeter and buildings were secure.

While operations at Malloy were returning to normal, the officers and staff were anxiously awaiting any news of Corporal Joan Steiger. Captain Anderson had been informed that Dutch Harbor was a shambles. No one had reported a small plane carrying two injured passengers arriving anywhere in the vicinity. No one in Anchorage had any news and neither did the department's central office in Juneau. Marc Anderson was questioning his decision to send CO Blaine Smith off on that damned fool medical flight. He was sure they were all dead.

USS Billings, Shelikof Straits, Alaska

All through the night, the Billings had been zigzagging across Shelikof Straits pinging away with her active sonar. Lt. Cowdrey and Hawk Two had been brought back on board so that the crew could get some rest before renewing their search. After tracking the Putin when she was running shallow, they had lost the Russian submarine when it went deep and silent. The last known heading was west.

Bathed in the artificial light of the Combat Information Center, Lt. Commander Hastings was frustrated. The sonar scope was filled with false contacts. "Damn it Sonar," he bellowed, "clean out your ears and give me a good target to hunt!"

"We're trying sir," the sailor answered sheepishly, "but with all the thermoclines and biologics, we're getting a lot of clutter on the scope."

Must be getting tired. "That's okay, sailor. Just try to get me a fix on that Russian." Hastings knew the crew was as tired and frustrated as he was. He left the CIC and walked back up to the bridge.

As they passed the entrance to Uyak Bay, Hastings ordered the Billings to come about and begin a search pattern back down the straits. *Maybe the Russians have doubled back and headed back out to sea?* He looked out at the dawn breaking over the eastern horizon. The weather forecast was for scattered rain showers with winds from the south-southwest at 20 knots. It was going to be an unpleasant, bumpy day.

"Captain on the bridge," came the call as Margaret Englemann entered through the hatch.

"Good morning Brad," she said with a smile.

"Morning Skipper," he replied. He was surprised to see her in such a good mood.

Commander Englemann motioned for Lt. Commander Hastings to join her at the chart table and update her on the night's events and the search results. He pointed out how he had conducted his search, the number of hits they had investigated and the results of each chase. He gave Englemann his best estimate. "If I had to guess Skipper, I'd say the Akula doubled back and headed back out into the Gulf of Alaska. That's why I brought us about 180 degrees. We are now heading west."

Margaret Englemann stared at the chart. *What are the Russians up to? They could be heading into Uyak Bay, but that would risk being spotted by a fishing boat out of Larsen Bay. They could be lurking under a thermal layer waiting for us to move off to a distance where they could surface and launch their team? Or, as Lt. Commander Hastings is guessing, they could have headed back out to sea?*

Logic dictated that the Russians were lying deep and waiting for her to move off. However, she couldn't discount the notion they had turned around and were heading back to the Gulf of Alaska. After all, this was the direction they were headed when Hawk Two lost contact.

Setting her Texas A&M mug down on the table, she said, "Brad, I think there are two possibilities. One, the Russians are cruising around beneath us at four or five knots running silent and waiting for us to move off. Two, they have headed back out to sea and given up the chase. The problem with two is that I don't believe they'd give up that easily."

Before Hastings could answer, she went into action, issuing orders. "Helm, come to a full stop. Sonar, cease active pinging and put some passive sonobouys over the side. Commander Hastings roust out Lieutenants Cowdrey and Martin and get them up to the bridge. I have a job for them."

"Aye, aye, Skipper," he said, still wondering what she was planning.

The Billings was wallowing in the waves, trying to locate the Russian submarine with hydrophones, passive sonar and the magnetic anomaly detector. The hum of the Billings' turbine engines could still be heard by the sonarmen, but they could use their equipment to filter out this background noise. All ears were tuned to picking up the broadband noise of a submarine's propeller turning in the water or the narrowband noise of the submarine's power plant.

"Lieutenants Cowdrey and Martin reporting as ordered."

"Ah, good morning gentlemen," Englemann said with a smile. "How are you feeling after a few hours rest?"

"Fine Skipper. Thanks for asking," answered the good-natured Martin.

"Come over here," she said, "I have a plan." She waved them over to the chart table and used her finger to trace around the western tip of the island and over to the east along the Southern coast. "I want you to keep a lookout out for any sign of a submarine surfacing or surfaced in one of these remote bays. Be patient," she cautioned, "and put your hydrophone in the water at the entrance to these bays. The Russians may have doubled back to the west, but I don't think they are ready to give up their mission just yet. My gut tells me they will try and put their Spetsnaz team on the ground at the head of one of these secluded bays."

After being dismissed, Lieutenant Cowdrey assembled his crew on the fantail of the Billings. He explained Englemann's orders and instructed them to take their stations. In a few minutes, the blades on Hawk Two were slicing through the air. He twisted the throttle, lifting Hawk Two off the bobbing deck. They headed out over the waves in search of the elusive Commander Ivanshenko and his Akula Class submarine.

Back on board the Billings, the only sounds being received by the sonar were the squeaking conversations of dolphins, killer whales and humpback whales, and the faint thush, thush, thush of a large fishing trawler at the far eastern end of Shelikof Straits.

Lt. Cowdrey was flying a set search pattern near the shores of Kodiak, stopping occasionally to lower the hydrophone into the water. It was tedious, but necessary work. No potential landing site could be overlooked. Coming around the tip of Cape Alitak, Cowdrey brought Hawk Two to a stop in the middle of the entrance to Alitak Bay. The hydrophone was lowered into the water and the crew listened for the telltale sounds of a propeller. With a subtle twist of the dial, the sonarman grinned. "Lieutenant."

"Yes, what is it?" Cowdrey answered absent-mindedly. He was concentrating on keeping the helicopter level in the gusting winds.

"I've got a single screw turning in the water to the northeast. I estimate they are making ten knots, running about 20 meters below the surface. It's the Russians, sir!"

Cowdrey looked down at his chart. The map showed three different bays branching off Alitak Bay—Moser Bay, which leads into Olga Bay, Deadman Bay, and Portage Bay.

"Which bay do you think they're in?" Lt. Martin asked, twisting around over his seat, holding the map for the sonarman to see.

"Can't tell Lieutenant," he replied while looking closely at the chart. "The signal isn't that clear. All these deep fjords make it hard for me to triangulate. There's a lot of echoing in these narrow passages."

Lt. Cowdrey turned the controls over to Lt. Martin. He examined his choices. *Moser Bay gets very narrow before it enters Olga Bay. Not even the bravest or most foolhardy Russian Commander would chance getting caught in that narrow entrance. Portage Bay is too far south. If I was in charge of the mission, that would be my last choice. The most logical choice for the Russian Commander is Deadman Bay.*

Extending 35 miles into the interior of Kodiak Island and surrounded by snow-capped 2,000-foot mountains, Deadman Bay is wide enough to maneuver a submarine. And it would allow the Russians to put ashore within about 15 miles of Karluk Lake. Cowdrey was sure that this is where the Russians were headed.

"Martin," Cowdrey ordered, "call the Billings. Let them know we've found the Russians. Chief, raise the hydrophone."

Climbing to a few hundred feet above the water, Lt. Cowdrey accelerated Hawk Two up the entrance of Alitak Bay in the direction of Deadman Bay.

"Bloodhound, Bloodhound," called Lt. Martin, "this is Hawk Two, repeat, this is Hawk Two."

"Go Hawk Two, this Bloodhound."

"We have contact with target. Currently in Deadman Bay on the southwest corner of the island."

"Acknowledged Hawk Two. We are making steam."

Commander Englemann ordered the Billings to get underway. The frigate came alive with activity as sailors rushed back to general quarters. With the rough seas, it was going to be a bumpy ride.

Just as Hawk Two flew into Deadman Bay, Lt. Martin caught sight of the Putin slipping beneath the waves. He knew they'd been spotted.

The sonar man was the first to spot the wake of the Russian's zodiac heading for the beach at the head of the bay. "There they are, Lieutenant!" he shouted, pointing excitedly.

"Damn, you've got good eyes," Cowdrey commented as he dropped the nose of the helicopter and added thrust. He wanted to get over the Russians as quickly as possible. *Maybe I can turn them back before they land.*

He was wrong. The Russians landed on the beach before Hawk Two could get there.

Flying over the Russians at just over 150 miles per hour, Lt. Cowdrey could make out six men in camouflage heading inland—Russian special forces—Spetsnaz.

Lt. Cowdrey started flying in circles around the Russians soldiers. He changed his mind about this tactic when he saw the flash of gunfire erupt from the barrels of several rifles.

"God damn," blurted Lt. Martin, "they're shooting at us!"

Cowdrey pulled up on the cyclic, making Hawk Two climb. This was no time to risk the Billings' only remaining ASW aircraft. Besides, he didn't have authorization to exchange gunfire with Russian soldiers.

"Skipper!" came the excited call from the signalman, "Hawk Two reports the Russians are on the ground and shooting at them!"

Akula Class Submarine Putin, Deadman Bay, Kodiak Island, Alaska

Lt. Commander Vatutin stood on the bridge of the Putin, admiring the magnificent scenery around him. Emerald green mountain slopes, topped with crystalline snow arched high into the overcast sky. It reminded him of his home in Petropavlovsk on the Kamchatka Peninsula. "Commander?" asked Vatutin, "do you think we lost the Americans?"

Ivanshenko took a sip of his coffee. "I'm not sure. I'm surprised at how easily we shook off their helicopter, but I'm learning to respect the commander of that frigate. She keeps guessing my strategy. I don't think she'll give up looking for us quite so easily."

Over the years Ivanshenko had grown to respect the prowess of American commanders. Even with his stealthy Akula, he had had limited success eluding detection. His job had become even tougher after the Soviet Union fell apart and the national economy collapsed. Maintenance on the submarines and all naval vessels suffered. They also put to sea far less often. This severely hampered training for his crew. All these factors aggravated the disadvantage they already faced against the US Navy.

Still, Ivanshenko was feeling good about losing the Americans. He was pleased with his decision to double back on them and come into Deadman Bay. He returned Major Golkin's salute as the boats pulled away from the Putin. Commander Ivanshenko was preparing to clear the bridge to submerge for the day, when the call came over the intercom.

"Conn, Sonar! Aircraft approaching from the southwest!"

Radar had just picked up Hawk Two.

Ivanshenko sprang into action. "Clear the bridge! Flood all ballast tanks! Dive!"

Immediately, the crew went into action. The Putin began moving forward as the crew engaged the propeller and opened the ballast tank intakes. Ivanshenko scanned the skies. He grimaced at the sight of the approaching helicopter. There it was—an American SH-60 Seahawk helicopter approaching at a high rate of speed. He cursed under his breath, as he stood on the bridge, watching Major Golkin and his men race for the shore.

Ivanshenko jumped down the ladder and closed the hatch above him. "Dive officer, make your depth 20 meters. Helm come about 180 degrees and make your speed 21-knots." It was time to get into deeper water and lose the Americans one more time.

Looking back over his shoulder, Major Golkin could see the black dot racing towards the Putin. He knew in an instant it was the Americans. "Son-of-a-bitch," he cursed. *Maybe the Americans haven't spotted us.* He hoped they would busy themselves with harassing the Putin. Hope turned to disappointment as he watched the Seahawk shoot over the top of the Putin without even slowing down. They were heading straight for his position.

The small inflatables ground to a halt on the boulder-strewn beach. Major Golkin shouted at his men to disembark as quickly as possible and run for the small trees lining the creek. He was gasping for breath as he made it to cover. He looked up at the circling American helicopter. The Americans couldn't stay overhead forever. Unfortunately for Major Golkin, his combat experience didn't translate to his men and his order to hold their fire came too late.

Private Rudenko was the first to shoot at the Americans. Before either Major Golkin or Captain Petrov could react, the other team members began firing too.

"Idiots!" Golkin screamed as he ran among his men hitting them on the sides of their heads. "You fucking idiots! Cease fire! Do you realize what will happen if we shoot down an American helicopter?" he yelled at the top of his lungs.

None of them dared look him in the eye.

Major Golkin continued his tirade, bellowing at his men. If they wanted to guarantee they would never make it back to Russia all they had to do was shoot down an American helicopter.

Finally, his anger spent, Major Golkin calmed down. He told them this was no time to get careless. Both sides knew what the other was up to, but the rules of the game meant that neither side exposed the other. And this was the most important part—no one fired any shots unless there was no alternative!

Satisfied that his men understood his instructions, Major Golkin told them to retrieve their gear. In the meantime, Captain Petrov and Sergeant Korkov placed small explosive charges in the inflatables. They started up the engines and headed them back out into the bay. The explosives would pierce the rubber hulls, sinking them into the murky waters. They had no need of these boats now that the Putin had been spotted and they needed to dispose of any evidence of their visit to Kodiak Island. Ivanshenko would now proceed to their alternate rendezvous site.

As they watched their boats sink beneath the waves of Deadman Bay, the Russians suddenly felt isolated and alone. Things were not proceeding very well. They had been forced to make their insertion during daylight hours and the Putin was now heading back out to sea, where they were sure the American frigate was waiting to pounce.

Major Golkin, however, took it all in stride. He was too experienced to allow these events to unnerve him. He was a firm believer in the axiom, "a battle plan never survives after the first contact with the enemy."

"Let's go," he shouted, "we've got a long day ahead of us!"

Shouldering his pack, he led his men along the creek, inland. Using information from the intercepted American radio traffic, Major Golkin had deduced that the prisoners were somewhere in the Karluk River Valley. He suspected they would be trying to get to the town of Kodiak, where they would have a better chance of getting off the island. All his team had to do was reach high ground and move to intercept the escaping prisoners. A bear had injured one of the American soldiers last night. He was betting they would be moving slower than normal. He'd lost the element of surprise, but he still had the edge in terrain and tactics. He intended to use these to his best advantage.

The Putin was cruising at 21-knots beneath the unfamiliar waters of Alitak Bay. Ivanshenko had to get out of the bay before the American frigate could close the gate and pin him inside. If he failed to escape into deeper water, he would be unable to rendezvous with Major Golkin.

"Screws in the water Commander," came the call from the sonar station. "It's the American frigate. She's running hard, turning the corner at Cape Alitak."

Studying the chart, Ivanshenko noted the Billings' position and plotted his course accordingly. "Increase to flank, take us down to 100 meters."

"Sonobuoys in the water, Commander!" the sonarman called out.

Hawk Two was laying a string of sonobouys across the entrance to the bay.

Ivanshenko called the American's bluff, ordering the Putin to make full speed toward open water. He knew the Americans could hear his submarine. Russian engineers had yet to solve the rhythmic vibrations that emanated from an Akula class submarine at high speed. Still, it was a small sacrifice for being able to go over 33-knots submerged.

As the Putin raced towards the frigate, Commander Ivanshenko had to ask his sonarman to repeat his warning. He didn't believe his ears the first time.

"That's right Commander, I said torpedo in the water."

Unbelievable?! The Americans are shooting! And I'm stuck inside the mouth of Alitak Bay!

The Putin's sailors sweated as they listened to the pinging of the Mark 50 torpedo trying to locate its prey. With a speed of over 40-knots and a 500-pound warhead, the new Mark 50 was a formidable weapon. However, its high speed limited its range. If you could keep the distance open, it would run out of fuel.

"Helm, come about 180 degrees, launch countermeasures! Bring the reactor to 110 percent!" Ivanshenko ordered. He was going to head at full speed back into Alitak Bay. His charts showed a reef in the middle of the bay. He had to get on the other side of that reef before the torpedo. "Time to impact?"

"Eight minutes at this speed," Vatutin answered from his weapons station.

At almost 40-knots, the 13,000-ton submarine surged through the dark waters of Alitak Bay. Commander Ivanshenko ordered a steep dive the moment they cleared the reef.

"Launch countermeasures," Vatutin ordered, just as the Putin cleared the reef and dove.

Spinning cylinders of compressed gas were released into the sea. Their spinning action simulated the sound of a submarine. Sometimes a torpedo would take the bait.

Pressure inside the submarine increased as the Putin charged down into the depths of the bay. Men tried to equalize the pressure in their heads by opening their mouths and popping their ears.

The American torpedo sensed the Russian crash dive and altered its course accordingly.

The sonar man waited anxiously along with the rest of the crew for the torpedo to explode on the reef. A minute passed and still there was no explosion. Then to their chagrin, they heard the torpedo clear the top of the reef, its sonar still pinging in search mode. It located the Putin at a range of 1,500 yards.

Realizing his ploy had failed, Ivanshenko ordered the Putin to come hard to port and then hard to starboard, launching countermeasures between the turns. He was stuck in the narrow confines of a bay with a high-speed torpedo bearing down on his submarine. Time was running out. He ordered the Putin to conduct an emergency surface. "Blow all ballast, 20 degrees up on the dive planes." He was going to race to the surface before the torpedo crashed into his boat. Maybe he could get his crew off the submarine before it sank back into the icy depths of Alitak Bay.

As it breeched the surface, the front half of the Putin arched out of the water before it came crashing back down again. Huge waves rippled out across the bay.

"Torpedo closing fast," came the sonarman's running commentary. "Range 1500 meters, 1000 meters, 500 meters, 100 meters."

"Sound collision!" barked Lt. Commander Vatutin.

The sweat-drench crewmen closed their eyes hanging on to whatever was handy as they waited for the dreaded explosion. Some men were praying, while others were cursing the Americans and the men who had ordered this mission. Commander Ivanshenko was going over the abandon ship drill in his mind.

With a bone-crushing thud the torpedo struck the Putin from underneath. Like a hammer hitting a large metal plate, the sound reverberated throughout the submarine. There was no explosion! The torpedo was a dud! A cheer of relief rang out. Men started hugging and laughing.

Ivanshenko was puzzled. Why hadn't the torpedo detonated? He had little time to question their good fortune. The American frigate was still out there. "Helm come left to course two four zero," he ordered. "Take us to periscope depth. Maintain flank speed."

Ivanshenko peered through his periscope, searching for the American frigate. Then he spotted her. Right in the middle of the entrance to Alitak Bay—perfectly poised to intercept the Putin regardless of any angle he took to escape this trap.

At this moment Ivanshenko realized that the torpedo was not a dud. The American commander had not armed the warhead. It had been launched to give the frigate time to get into the middle of the bay. Laughing, he took off his hat, bowing at the waist towards his worthy opponent.

O'Malley Lake, Kodiak Island, Alaska

Ivan Lincoln had roused Joy Frank and Elizabeth LeDue before dawn from their fitful slumber, throwing each of them a morsel of food to help them march through the long day. He felt great. He had slept well. Even though the surrounding countryside was covered in a fine gray ash, he knew the drizzle falling outside would keep the dust from choking their lungs.

Joy had slept fitfully. Her body was stiff and sore and she was hungry. Her mouth was chalky and the gritty. She longed for a long, hot bath. Her stomach growled. The tiny meals were hardly enough to keep a person going. With all the stress and physical exertions she needed thousands of calories. It was obvious that her captor did not intend to keep either her or Elizabeth around for very long. She had to escape today.

Only with the greatest of effort was Elizabeth able to move. The small punctures all over her back burned. Debilitating cramps seized her bowels whenever she tried moving. She fought back the sudden urge to defecate. She was not about to give that animal the satisfaction of humiliating her further.

"Excuse me," Joy said forcing herself to look Lincoln in the eye, "but could you let us up to go to the bathroom?"

Lincoln grunted. Reluctantly, he came over and unhooked them from the bed. Before they could rub the red creases out of their wrists, he handcuffed them back together. "You can go outside the door. If you try to get any farther than that, you're both dead," he warned menacingly.

Joy was shocked at how weak Elizabeth was. "Come on Elizabeth," Joy said quietly, "you've got to get to your feet. You've got to move or he'll kill you."

Somehow Elizabeth found it within herself to rise to her feet. Grimacing in pain, she shuffled alongside Joy, exiting through the cabin door. She thanked Joy for her kindness, while apologizing for her inability to control her bowels.

Joy was overcome with emotion as she took a pail of water and a rag and washed Elizabeth's wounds. Tears ran down her face as she watched Elizabeth grimace under her ministrations.

Growing tired of this display of compassion, Lincoln ordered the women to get ready to move out. He had a lot of miles to cover, and he had no intention of letting two lazy bitches slow him down.

Joy squeezed Elizabeth's hand. Today promised to be a long hard day of hiking in the muck. The light drizzle was turning the gray ash into a slick gray mass of ooze, lubricating everything around them. Joy tried boosting Elizabeth's spirits by whispering in her ear that she'd heard gunshots last night. Someone was coming to rescue them.

Elizabeth found little comfort in Joy's words. Right now she was living a nightmare. But being returned to custody meant a lifetime behind bars. She didn't have the energy or heart to tell this wonderful young woman that neither option was very palatable.

Throwing them their gear, Lincoln motioned for them to leave the cabin and head towards the small stream running from the mountains into the lake. The drizzle soon soaked their clothing. It was going to be a long miserable day.

As they walked in the freezing muck beside Falls Creek, Lincoln ordered them to head towards the saddle in the mountains directly up ahead. They had to get deeper into the interior—to the forest. There he could shake off any search team.

High above the mountain valleys, helicopters from the Alaska State Troopers and the Coast Guard were flying back and forth over the mountainous terrain in a box search pattern. Inside each chopper, officers were watching the tangled vegetation below for any sign of human activity.

Because of the ash, the helicopters could not risk landing if they spotted the fugitives, but they could radio in their last known position. This would allow the ground teams to make best use of the terrain to cut off the prisoners' escape.

The rumbling of a helicopter flying up the Karluk River Valley sent Lincoln scurrying under the branches of a grove of alders with the women in tow. His worst fears were confirmed. The cops were out looking for him in force. He would have to lighten his load. He should kill them both right now. But something was stopping him—he wasn't finished with them just yet.

Thumb River, Kodiak Island, Alaska

Harry Ignustuk and Danny Sanders had been moving up the Thumb River drainage since before dawn. Harry still believed that the gunfire they heard last night was not Lincoln trying to escape back down the Karluk River. He still believed Lincoln would push deeper into the interior of the island.

When Danny asked him about his hunches, Harry could only say that he was running on gut instinct. It didn't make sense for Lincoln to double back. That was not his style. Harry couldn't explain the gunfire last night, but he was willing to bet it didn't involve Lincoln.

Harry had hunted a lot of bears in his life. Without exception they would make for their home terrain before they would turn on you. He couldn't shake the feeling that Lincoln was going to do the same thing.

As they moved in and out of the alders and willows, up in the distance they could see the 2,000-foot rise marking the head of the Thumb River Valley. Once they made it to the top, Harry hoped to catch a glimpse of Lincoln and LeDue. *Lincoln has to be heading east.* To the west, they could hear the search helicopters getting closer.

Glancing over their shoulders, they spied the approaching helicopters. They stopped hiking and waved their arms as the helicopters began circling. They pulled out their badges, holding them above their heads. One of the helicopters hovered above them.

Harry and Danny were surprised to see PTO Karen Marston lean out of the helicopter door. She was holding a handheld radio and motioning that she was going to drop it to them.

Danny nodded, holding his hands out to make the catch. The impact of the hard plastic hitting his hands made him wince, but he didn't drop the radio. He handed it to Harry.

Harry wasted no time turning on the radio and keying the microphone. “AST, AST, this is Prisoner Transport Officer Harry Ignustuk, over.”

“Hello Officer Ignustuk, this is PTO Marston. How are you doing?”

Harry smiled. “Real good. I’ve got a good hunch on where Lincoln and LeDue are headed. We’re going to head up this river valley and try to catch sight of them. Over.”

“Roger that,” replied Marston. “We are unable to land due to the ash. We will proceed with our search. That is a short-range radio. Whenever you see us, be sure to check in. We won’t be able to reach you if we can’t see you. Over.”

PTO Marston could now report back to Commissioner Dornier that they had located her two surviving prisoner transport officers. They were on the fugitives’s trail.

Harry raised his fingers in a ‘V’ for victory. The pilot replied with a “thumbs up” before taking off to resume the search. Harry and Danny watched the helicopters peel off and thunder back down the valley.

Shouldering his pack, Harry said, “Well, I guess we’d better get moving again.”

Danny picked up his pack and fell in behind Harry.

It was a strenuous trek through the tangled brush and over rocky terrain. It took several hours to reach the saddle in the mountains. Reaching the crest, they stopped to catch their breath and take a drink of water.

To their right was another peak jutting 1,200 feet above their current position. They had to get to the top of this higher peak before they could see more of the surrounding countryside.

Danny took a deep breath, steeling himself for what was sure to be a hard climb.

Thirty minutes later, they were standing on the summit of this unnamed peak gazing out over the wide river valley that fed Dog Salmon Creek fifteen miles to the west. To the south, they could just make out the waters of Deadman Bay. To the east they had a clear view of the valley as it forked into two shorter valleys that terminated in steep cliffs—a perfect place to see anyone who tried to double back around them. They unpacked their gear, pulled out their binoculars and settled in to wait for Lincoln to make his appearance.

Meadow Creek, Kodiak Island, Alaska

Despite being mauled by a bear, Lt. Surin had proven his mettle when he had awakened Sergeants Ali and Ramirez stating his intention to get a jump on Dr. LeDue.

All through the early morning, they had moved at a blistering pace. They knew they were on the right trail when they came upon the carcass of the dead mountain goat. The clean slices where Lincoln had cut off chunks of meat were evidence of human scavengers.

A bright crimson dawn was breaking over the eastern horizon. Lt. Surin was glad for sunrise. Now they would be able to spot their quarry from a distance. He took a moment to rest. His arm throbbed. Fresh blood soaked through his uniform. And even though the bear hadn't punctured his foot, it still ached. All this activity was counterproductive to proper healing. *But we have to keep moving.* He ignored the throbbing and changed the bandage.

As Surin cared for his wound and Ali examined the carcass, Sgt. Ramirez scanned the surrounding countryside with his binoculars for any signs of the fugitives. He spotted a small cabin at the head of the valley near O'Malley Lake. "Lieutenant," he said, motioning for Surin to grab a set of binoculars and look in the direction of O'Malley Lake, "I see a small cabin down in the bottom of the valley about 7 clicks away. I bet they spent the night there."

Surin agreed. He ordered his men to begin hiking down to the cabin.

As they descended the slippery slopes, Lt. Surin instructed his men about how they were going to approach the cabin from the southwest. They would space themselves about 30 feet apart and creep up on the site. He would take point. If there was any shooting, they were not to return fire, but move back. There was a civilian in the group. It wouldn't look very good for any of them if she bought a round in a firefight. Instead, they would throw smoke into the cabin, and flush their quarry into the open. They could shoot the male. They needed to capture the females.

The sound of search helicopters flying up the valley rendered all of Lt. Surin's plans null and void. If there were any fugitives inside the cabin, the helicopters would put them on their guard. If the fugitives were gone, the helicopters would push them under cover. Surin cursed. *Sometimes technology can be more of a liability than an asset.*

He ordered his men to duck into the rocks to avoid being seen by the helicopters. Everybody didn't need to know that the Marines were on Kodiak.

The helicopters were getting closer. They could hear one of them hovering above the dead goat. Their footprints would be visible in the muck around the carcass. Only an idiot could overlook them.

Using the terrain as camouflage, the Marines blended into the environment, moving deeper into the canyon where they found boulders to hide them from the prying eyes of the helicopter search team. The helicopters couldn't land. There was too much ash.

As the helicopters moved off, Lt. Surin motioned for his men to move out once again in the direction of the cabin at O'Malley Lake. He knew the chances of finding the fugitives still there were slim, but maybe they would get lucky.

Lt. Surin led his men along the top of the ridges so they could keep a lookout for anyone moving below them, doubling back or heading off to the west. They covered the five miles from Meadow Creek Canyon to O'Malley Lake in short order.

Once they reached the valley floor, Lt. Surin spaced his team in thirty-foot intervals. Weapons at the ready, they moved forward into the thick brush surrounding the cabin. Surin took the lead position, moving swiftly up to the side of the cabin. Peering carefully over the lip of the bottom windowsill, he looked inside. Nothing. It appeared empty. *Still, it might be an ambush.*

He motioned for Sgt. Ramirez to take up a firing position at a forty-five degree angle to the door.

Sgt. Ali was lying hidden in a position where he could provide cover fire.

Moving in a crouch around the side of the cabin to the front door, Lt. Surin came to a halt at the spot where Dr. LeDue had relieved herself. With his knife he poked through the bloody rags that littered the ground. *Where did these come from? Is one of them wounded? Injured from the crash? Has someone been killed?*

He slung his rifle and moved to the door. With his Makarov pistol held in the guard position, he slowly grabbed the door handle. With a quick twist he flung the door open and took a quick glance around the corner. Empty. The smell of cooked food lingered in the air. The room was still warm. They weren't too far behind.

Surin signaled to his men that the cabin was vacant, motioning for them to fall in behind him. Rising from his crouch, he followed the footsteps leading away from the cabin and up Falls Creek.

About a quarter mile from the cabin Lt. Surin signaled for his men to halt. He was looking at the tracks of a very large bear, paralleling those of the fugitives. For a moment he couldn't fathom why a bear would be tracking the prisoners. Then it dawned on him—blood.

"Apparently we're not the only ones out hunting today," Surin said quietly. He pointed out the tracks to his men and counseled them to keep a sharp eye out for bears. They slowed their pace. He'd already learned his lesson about Kodiak grizzlies. He looked at the pink patch of blood under the patch on his shoulder. They continued moving up the valley. Lt. Surin was confident the prisoners would be in custody by the end of the afternoon.

Without stopping to rest or eat, they hiked as silently as possible through the eight miles of thickets lining Falls Creek Valley. This was dangerous. This was ideal terrain for an ambush—human or ursine. The thick, tangled brush made movement difficult and the stress of keeping a constant lookout for the fugitives sapped their energy.

After hours of strenuous effort they reached the top of the saddle at the head of Falls Creek Valley. With his binoculars he scanned the terrain below their position. Surin was disappointed that he couldn't locate the fugitives. He was surprised at how fast the prisoners were moving.

The Marines were now looking out over the same valley being watched by Ignustuk and Sanders. They could see human footprints leading into the alders along the Dog Salmon Creek, but from there they weren't sure.

Deadman Creek, Kodiak Island, Alaska

The Russian soldiers had been moving at double-time pace all morning up the broad valley east of Deadman Bay. They had almost 18 miles to cover before they could be in a position to observe the numerous river valleys branching off Karluk Lake.

Despite being almost twice as old as the youngest team member, Major Golkin prided himself on being more robust and stronger than any other man in his squad. During training he would taunt the younger soldiers about how they couldn't keep up with an old man, or shoot better than an old man who needed glasses. It was his way of motivating them. He knew the horrors of combat and wanted to spare them from learning their trade the hard way.

Golkin wiped the sweat from his brow. He was pushing his team hard. They had a lot of ground to cover before nightfall. He ignored the burning sensation in his thigh. It was an old wound and often plagued him when he pushed himself too hard. However, he was used to pain.

Throughout his long military career, Major Josef Golkin had fought in the jungles of Southeast Asia, the high desert mountains of Afghanistan, and the deserts of the Middle East. He knew how to survive and how to use every kind of terrain to his advantage. On two occasions he had been wounded—once when serving as a military advisor in North Vietnam, when he had stepped into a booby trap set by the Viet Cong; and once when caught in an ambush in a high Afghan mountain pass. These lessons were not lost on him. Both times he had let his guard down and trusted information provided by others.

He took a deep breath to help dispel the pain in his leg. Looking over his shoulder he could see his men moving up behind him. He stopped for a moment to give them a chance to catch up. He pulled his map from his shirt pocket and examined it again. He liked to commit things to his memory. Maps could be lost or hard to read at night.

As he surveyed the surrounding terrain, Major Golkin went over his strategy in his mind. He was counting on several things: that the fugitives would move as quickly and as carelessly as possible, that they would fall into his flanking maneuver, and he would capture his prey without firing a shot.

Once the prisoners were in his grasp, he would move quickly to rendezvous with the Putin. At any point along the way, he could dispose of the excess prisoners and make it look like the Americans did it—his team was carrying NATO-issued Beretta 9mm semi-automatic pistols.

The mission to kidnap Dr. Elizabeth LeDue was of vital strategic interest to Russia. He intended to succeed. Even though the Americans knew he was on the island, they didn't know his exact location and they had no idea of how good he was at his job. *Well, they will find out soon enough.*

The sound of helicopters pounding up the mountain valleys to the west did not deter him. Their presence did, however, force his men to remain hidden in the willows, slowing their pace more than he liked. Of course, he would have preferred moving in the treeless terrain on the hillsides, but that was not an option.

Before resuming his march, Golkin reminded his men to make noise as they moved through the brush. This would prevent them from surprising any bears. It was better to make a little noise than to have to shoot a charging bear. The echo of a rifle shot in these canyons would carry for miles.

By early afternoon, the Russians were strategically positioned on the hillsides at the head of the valley overlooking Dog Salmon Creek. Major Golkin had split his team into two squads. He commanded one squad positioned on the northern-most hillside. Captain Petrov commanded the other squad positioned on the southern hillside.

Major Golkin applied some bug cream to ward off the voracious biting flies. Next he pulled out a candy bar—it would be a long wait.

Larsen Bay, Kodiak Island, Alaska

It had been a long night of caring for Larsen Bay's survivors. Commissioners Burke and Dornier were sitting next to the radio listening to the reports coming in from the three search helicopters flying a zigzag pattern over the Karluk River Valley. So far the results were disappointing. The only good news was the sighting of PTOs Ignustuk and Sanders.

It was during the late evening of the previous night when the true nature of their presence in Larsen Bay had become common knowledge. Needless to say, there were more than just a few upset citizens.

The citizens were frightened because they had two dangerous fugitives loose near their community and they were furious that the governor had only sent a small team to search for them.

Angry comments from several of the most vocal residents failed to ruffle Michelle Dornier. She had deflected their arguments by pointing out that Larsen Bay was a priority to Governor Malloy. After all, she told them, in this time of crisis throughout all of Alaska, he had dispatched a team of desperately needed troopers, correctional officers, and medical personnel to Larsen Bay. There was a supply ship on its way from Kodiak. The governor had sent two department heads to manage the search. All these things, she pointed out, were evidence of the governor's concern for the safety of the people of Larsen Bay.

After she had calmed the mob, Dornier enlisted the support of several of the women from the community. With their help she managed to shift the survivors's focus away from the manhunt and back to picking up the pieces of their shattered community.

Burke had to admit that, despite her ignorance of Alaska geography, Commissioner Dornier did have a way with people. He was beginning to appreciate her talents. He would handle the nuts and bolts of hunting down two dangerous criminals while she handled public relations and the media. Then it hit him: *Governor Malloy had probably known all along that we would end up complimenting each other's qualities.* He smiled.

Amchitka Island, Alaska

Toby Church was moving west along the spine of the island, plotting his next ambush. By now he realized Amchitka was devoid of any airbase or settlements. He was stuck on an isolated rock in the middle of the ocean with two officers in hot pursuit. He needed to put distance between himself and his pursuers.

Clouds rolled in from the southwest, announcing the arrival of a storm. Soon it would engulf the tiny island. Waves driven by the howling winds crashed into the shore, spraying white foam high into the air. The wind pressed the tall grass flat against the hillsides. Kittiwakes and gulls frolicked on the updrafts before seeking shelter in their nests in the rock cliffs.

Church shielded his eyes from the pelting rain, looking out to sea. Whitecaps stretched as far as the eye could see. They etched a path across the darkening waters. He cursed. He was so close to escape, and yet so far. He tugged on the collar of his coat, trying in vain to stop the wind from cutting through him like a knife.

Church started walking again. Time was running short for him to make a quick escape on his boat to another island. Soon the wind would whip the sea into a tempest of 10 to 15-foot waves. He had no desire to navigate his tiny craft in heavy seas. To the northeast, he could see the 4,000-foot summit of Anvil Peak on Semisopochnoi Island. *Maybe there's a village on that island?* Far to the west he could see the top of Kiska Volcano on Kiska Island. It was too far to try and make it in an open skiff during a storm. He would have to find a place to hide out until the storm passed. For the first time since escaping he felt depressed—his five years at Malloy Super Max prison had taught him that storms in the Aleutians rarely pass quickly.

Church spied the remains of an old pillbox on a hillock overlooking Chitka Cove. It would provide some shelter from the battering wind and rain. He slithered into the crevasse of the rocks and crumbled concrete, and pulled out his navigation charts. Now that he was out of the wind and rain, he studied the map for any signs of a village, a harbor, an airfield, or another island.

Semisopochnoi Island lacked any markings at all. It was a grassy, uninhabited rock in the middle of nowhere. Forty-five miles to the west, Kiska Island was laced with a series of roads and even a harbor. There were no indications of any settlements, *but with a harbor and roads maybe, just maybe, there is some civilization there.* Thinking back on the lessons learned in his high school history class, Church recalled his teacher, Mr. Seymour, telling the class how Japan had invaded America during World War II. He remembered Mr. Seymour telling how the Japanese had landed troops on two islands in the Aleutians—Attu and Kiska. *Surely, the military must still maintain a base or station on this remote chunk of real estate.*

Secure in his belief that Kiska held the next key to his flight for freedom, Church laid out a plan to waylay his pursuers and get back to his boat. Once there, he would again brave the challenge of the ocean to sprint for freedom.

After paying their respects to Corporal Nelson, Lt. Banderas and Officer Williams had formulated a new plan to drive their prey into a corner of the island. They agreed that if Church refused to halt or surrender they would catch him in a crossfire.

With steady determination they began hiking up the tussocky hillside. The wind was driving the rain in stinging pellets. It was damn uncomfortable, but they were tough. They ignored the weather. It was too dangerous to pull up their ponchos to cover their heads. The hoods obscured their vision, making it easier for their quarry to sneak by them or ambush them from the side. They had to make do with their baseball caps.

"Keep a sharp eye out for that son-of-a-bitch," Carlos cautioned. "And remember, no matter how badly we want to kill this piece of shit, if he gives up, we have to take him back."

Ben refused to commit to an answer. *I let him get away on Adak. He isn't going to get away again.*

Deep in his heart, Carlos knew that Ben had no intention of taking Toby Church alive. He felt the same way. His statement only served to give them both "plausible deniability" when the internal investigation into his escape was launched. Carlos knew Ben blamed himself for letting Church get away at Malloy Super Max and he knew they both felt responsible for Corporal Nelson's death. Carlos told himself that if they spotted Toby Church, he would give Ben the first opportunity to bring him down.

As they approached Chitka Cove, Carlos spotted a small outcropping of rocks and crumbled concrete very similar to the one where Church had ambushed them previously. He raised his hand, signaling for Ben to stop.

Ben dropped to the ground in a prone position and crawled over to Carlos, who had also taken up a prone shooter's position facing the old pillbox. "Do you see anything Lieutenant?" he whispered. He tried to ignore the chill as the spongy terrain soaked his pant legs.

Carlos searched the area in front of them.

Ben watched to make sure Church wasn't sneaking up on them from behind.

"Not a damn thing Ben," Carlos cursed quietly.

Ben lifted his nose into the air, sniffing deeply. "He's up there somewhere Lieutenant, I can smell him."

"How can you be sure?" came Carlos's puzzled reply.

Without taking his eyes off his binoculars, Ben stated matter-of-factly, "the wind is just right and he hasn't bathed in a couple days. I can smell him. Sweat, sea lion blubber, and cordite from his rifle."

Ben released the safety on his rifle and positioned himself so he could block the wind buffeting his rifle. In moments like these, he hated the M-16—its light bullet was easily deflected by wind. Right now he would have given anything for his trusty 30.06 and its 180-grain bullet. Ben sighed. *It's too late to bitch now.*

Carlos was the first one to catch a glimpse of Toby Church moving among the rubble. He reached over, tapping Ben on the shoulder and pointing in the direction of the lowest crevasse. Keeping his rifle aimed, he watched Ben slide around to get into a better firing position. He was torn between his own desire to kill the man who had murdered two officers and his duty, which required him to capture an escaping convict alive, if possible.

Settling in behind a small outcropping of rocks about 15 feet away, Ben looked back at Carlos. He gestured for permission to open fire.

"I just can't let you shoot him without giving him the chance to give up," Carlos whispered loudly. "You and I both know the policy. If we're called to testify, we can't lie about what happened here. I'm going to move off to the right to cut off his escape and then call out for him to give himself up." Carlos pointed to a small grassy knoll where he intended to take up position.

Ben knew Carlos was right. He didn't like it, but they had to go by the book—for now. He nodded and then asked, "how long will we give him to surrender?"

"If he doesn't stand up and raise his hands over his head the moment I order him to surrender," Carlos said coldly, "shoot him."

Policy said that you only had to give an inmate one chance to halt or surrender. It did not give a response time for the inmate to surrender. If they ended up shooting Church, they would be able to, in good conscience, testify that they had afforded him the opportunity to surrender.

Carlos took up a firing position behind a small boulder about 30-yards to Ben's right and just down the hill from Church's hiding place. It wasn't much protection, but it was better than nothing. Wetting his lips and swallowing to make sure his voice would not break when he shouted the order, Carlos placed his left hand alongside his face and shouted, "Toby Church! This is Lieutenant

Carlos Banderas of the Alaska Department of Corrections! Throw down your weapons and come out with your hands above your head!"

Carlos' voice resonating above the howling wind, took Toby Church by surprise. He dropped to his knees and grabbed his rifle. His mind raced. "Fuck." He was surprised at how quickly they had caught up to him.

After checking to make sure there was a bullet chambered in his rife, Church peered cautiously around a block of concrete to catch a glimpse of where his captors were positioned. The sound of a bullet ricocheting just above his head made him duck back behind the rubble. However, he had caught a glimpse of an officer lying behind a small boulder just downhill from his position. Considering where that bullet hit, he surmised that the other officer was just up the rise to his right.

Church looked to his left and calculated how long it would take him to sprint down the hill to the next crop of rocks closer to the beach. He would have to cross about 50 yards of open terrain. He didn't relish racing into the open with two men bent on killing him. Still he didn't have a lot of ammunition left and he had lost the element of surprise.

Patience, thought Church, *patience. These bastards don't know how much ammo you have left. You're stuffed down here among the rocks, out of the wind and most of the rain. They, on the other hand, are stuck out in the open in the wind and the rain. In a few hours night will fall and you can sneak out of here.*

Church settled in for a siege. He popped around the corner of a boulder and fired several shots at Carlos. He'd given his answer to the call to surrender.

Realizing that Church had no intention of surrendering, Carlos crawled back over to Ben's position. He was disappointed Church hadn't run for it.

"That's one cool cat," Ben said with grudging admiration. "I guess he's going to try and outwait us."

Carlos looked up at the overcast sky. Darkness was several hours away. If they allowed Church to stay holed up in the rocks with them stuck out in the open, exposed to the elements, Church would have the advantage. They had to come up with a plan to flush him out. His pants were soaking wet too. If they weren't careful, hypothermia would set in and they would both die.

"Any ideas on how to flush him out of those rocks?" Carlos asked.

Ben shook his head no. He had no ideas for getting Church out into the open without getting one of them shot or killed. The open terrain of Amchitka is a double-edged sword—it allows you to track an adversary for miles, but it also prevents getting close undetected. Ben tapped Carlos on the shoulder and started crawling backwards away from Church's position. He motioned for Carlos to join him in this tactical retreat. He wanted to get out of range.

The two men spent the next hour discussing how to flush Toby Church out of his hiding place. Carlos played the Devil's advocate, while Ben brainstormed.

While his adversaries pondered a solution to their dilemma, Toby Church evaluated his situation. He only had ten rounds of rifle ammunition left. It was too windy for his pistol to be of much use. He needed to get back to his boat. He couldn't gamble on finding another boat on the island. He would have to wait until nightfall before moving out. He could put into action the night assault drills he had learned at his headquarters in Montana. Night would even the odds. It was a risky plan, but there weren't a lot of options left.

A wicked grin crossed Carlos' face. *Brilliant. Simply brilliant. It's perfect!*

Ben stared at him with great curiosity.

Carlos took his canister of OC (Oleo Capsicum—Pepper Spray) from his utility belt.

"You can't use your OC," Ben blurted out. "You'll never get close enough to paint him. And in this wind, it will disperse in an instant."

"I don't intend to paint him," Carlos retorted coldly, "I'm going to lob this little hummer right into his little hideout."

Ben looked askew at Carlos. OC wasn't a grenade. *How is this going to work?*

Carlos elaborated on his plan. "Did you ever shake up a can of soda pop or beer and then throw it to the ground?"

Ben nodded yes.

Carlos pulled out his knife. "Remember how it spun around wildly spraying liquid in every direction? Well, I'm going to use my knife, poke a little hole, right here in the side, cover it with my finger, and toss this lovely little canister like a grenade right into Church's foxhole. When it hits it'll spin wildly and spew its contents in all directions. I may not get a clean paint job, but he just might jump up so you can shoot him."

"That just might work," Ben crowed.

They went into action.

Taking an extra magazine of ammunition from Carlos, Ben crawled through the wet grass to a spot about 20-feet down the hill from Carlos' original position. From this angle he would be able to send bullets into the outer entrance of Church's rocky den.

In the meantime, Carlos circled back down around the bottom of the hill, making sure to remain out of Church's sight. He needed to get into a position where the howling wind would carry the canister towards the rocks. Once he was sure he was out of sight and couldn't be seen approaching Church's position, he crawled to the crest of the hill overlooking the old pillbox.

Taking out his knife, Carlos placed the OC canister on the ground, put the tip of the blade on the side and hit the butt of the knife, puncturing a small hole in the can. With a hiss cayenne pepper began spewing from the hole. Being careful to keep his head away from the spray, he placed his thumb over the hole. He signaled Ben that he was ready. He crept closer to the rocks.

At Carlos's signal, Ben took aim at the entrance to the rocks and fired off several rounds, which ricocheted harmlessly into the sky.

Rushing up to about fifteen feet from the rocks, Carlos drew back his arm and lobbed the pepper spray canister through the air. Just as he predicted, the canister tumbled as it flew towards its destination.

With all the gunfire, Church knew the officers were up to something, but there was little he could do with bullets flying all around him. He checked the magazine on his pistol getting ready to pop up in between the incoming rounds to return fire. He looked up just in time to see a small red aluminum cylinder spinning through the air towards him. He jumped to the side to avoid the projectile, watching in disbelief as it hit the ground and continued spinning.

In an instant, the area inside the rocks was filled with the burning, choking mist of cayenne pepper. Carlos's aim had been perfect. Church tried to grab the spinning cylinder and in the process took a full shot of spray right across the chin and mouth. Shouting obscenities, he instinctively jumped back from the mist.

This was all Ben Williams needed. Seeing Church's shoulders and head rise above the rocks, he fired several quick bursts.

Like a finger of fire, the bullet ripped through Church's shoulder. Crying out in pain as the second bullet grazed the back of his neck, Church spun around firing wildly with his pistol. He fell to the ground, grabbed the canister, and tossed it back out of his hole in the direction of his attacker. He couldn't breathe and his eyes were on fire! In a panic, he bolted from the safety of his rocky lair.

Pistol in his hand, Church took off running in a zigzag motion down the hillside shooting in Ben's general direction.

Carlos jumped to his feet taking aim at the fleeing felon. He fired several shots. It was no use. The wind was too strong and the bullets too light to find their mark.

Carlos watched Ben race off in pursuit. He joined in the foot chase. Running up alongside his friend, he asked if he thought he hit him. Ben replied that he thought he'd hit him in the chest or shoulder on the first shot and maybe somewhere in the back on the second shot. From the lack of a blood trail they knew Church was either wounded internally or not very badly. They were regretting not bringing a hunting rifle.

Toby Church was rushing headlong down the hill towards the beach. The pepper spray in his eyes made it hard to see, but with each passing minute the burning grew less intense and his breathing eased. His stamina was being fueled by adrenaline and fear. Arriving at the cliffs overlooking the beach, he turned east and headed back towards his skiff at Ivakin Point. Blood was oozing from his shoulder, but he didn't have time to stop and take stock of his injuries. He could see Carlos and Ben following in the distance.

He took a deep breath and forged ahead. He was showing the resiliency that had earned him the respect of his followers. Whenever he set his mind on a goal, he achieved it. And now he set his mind on getting back to his skiff and out to sea.

Sitkinak Strait, Kodiak Island, Alaska

Throughout the morning and into the afternoon Commander Englemann had harassed the Russians with depth charges whenever they tried making a run for open water. Even though she had authorization to sink the Russians, she wasn't in any hurry to condemn 73 men to the deaths. She was playing an old Cold War game—harass your adversary until they are driven off. *Maybe I'll get lucky and shake some pipes loose and force the Russians to surface.* The Russian submarine commander was a formidable opponent. She was learning to respect his daring and cunning.

Beneath the waves, Ivanshenko's men were feeling the strain. He could overhear them grumbling about the "American Devils" and "Those Bastards." He didn't react to such comments. Instead he continued plotting potential escape routes. This was a game of chess and he was a Russian—chess is the national pastime.

Eventually I'll be presented with an opportunity to break into the open ocean. As long as the Americans weren't shooting live torpedoes, there would be no checkmate.

But this American commander was special—she had managed to outthink him at every turn, even when he tried some very unorthodox maneuvers. Bold, decisive and flexible—the American was proving more than a match for him.

"Commander?" asked Lt. Commander Vatutin touching Ivanshenko lightly on the shoulder, "may I have a word with you?"

Ivanshenko looked up from the screen and stared into the worried face of his executive officer. "Go ahead Vatutin, what's on your mind?"

"Commander, the crew is beginning to wear thin. With all this depth charging and maneuvering, they're beginning to make mistakes. If we were in a war sir, we would be dead."

The words, "if we were in a war," struck a chord in Ivan Ivanshenko's head. *Maybe that's the piece of the puzzle I'm missing?* Then it dawned on him. He smiled, turned back to his charts, and calculated a new solution.

"Commander?" Vatutin asked, "Why are you smiling?" As Ivanshenko's Executive Officer for the last three years, he had come to understand his commander and to respect him. On more than one occasion, he had seen Ivanshenko pull a proverbial rabbit out of his hat and extricate the Putin from a seemingly impossible situation. Ivanshenko reminded him of his Uncle Peter, a mining engineer in the Donets Basin. Uncle Peter could overcome almost any obstacle with his ingenuity. Perhaps it was all those days spent roaming the mineshafts with his uncle that had prepared him for life on a submarine? It didn't matter. All that mattered was that his commander was one of the very best in the Russian fleet. And whenever he saw a smile cross Ivanshenko's face during a battle, he knew a solution had been found.

Ivanshenko motioned for Vatutin to join him at the chart table. He said, "You gave me the answer to our problem. Look here on the chart." He pointed to the location of the Billings and the two points on either side of the bay's entrance. "The American frigate is in perfect position to cut off any run to the open sea. We dare not get too close to their depth charges or we could very well find ourselves a rusting hulk on the bottom of the bay." With a flare for the dramatic, Ivanshenko raised his eyebrows, his eyes flashing bright with mischievousness. "The solution to our problem is not in plotting our escape, but in how we've been approaching our adversary." He punched his open palm.

Vatutin shook his head in confusion.

Ivanshenko slapped Vatutin on the shoulder. "Don't you see it? The Americans are winning, because they're approaching this situation like a war. They are willing to risk sinking a Russian submarine inside their territorial waters. We," he exclaimed while poking himself in the chest, "on the other hand have been trying not to incite an international incident. Well, two can play this game.

Helm bring us about to course one nine five, increase speed to 15 knots, and bring us to periscope depth. Commander Vatutin, proceed to the torpedo room. Disarm three of our torpedoes. Load two of the forward torpedo tubes and one of the stern torpedo tubes."

Inside the Billings' Combat Information Center, Lt. Commander Hastings took note of the Russian's change in course and speed. "Skipper, this is Commander Hastings. The Russian is making another run."

"Copy that Commander Hastings, you know the drill. Helm, bring us about to course zero two two, increase speed to 20-knots. Prepare to drop depth charges. This time I want the charges to detonate under the sub. Let's push them up to the surface if we can."

Margaret Englemann loved a good fight. *This Russian sure is stubborn.* Of course, she had to admit, she would be doing exactly the same thing. *How was my morning report to Honolulu received?* Earlier in the day, she had reported to CINCPAC that she had the Russian cornered. There had been no reply, even though she included her decision to depth charge the trespassing Russians.

The lack of response could mean many things. Either they thought she was doing just fine, or they didn't want to validate her decision in the event a scapegoat was needed. She was sure several policy wonks back in the Pentagon were rushing around trying to come up with a set of orders.

She shook her head to clear her thoughts and returned to the task at hand. She needed to time her run so she could switch course at the last minute. The Russian was probably going to try a quick turn or a deep dive to shake her pursuit. If she guessed correctly, she would be able to drop her depth charges in the path of the oncoming sub.

"Skipper! Periscope in the water," called out the helmsman, "off our port bow."

Through her binoculars, she saw the periscope's wake. She called down to the CIC, asking for the exact depth, course and speed of the Russian sub. She ordered the Billings to turn to starboard and increase speed to 23-knots.

To the untrained eye, it appeared that the two warships would collide. However, Commander Englemann was cutting her angle precisely and just as the stern of the Billings cut in front of the Russian sub, the crew fired four depth charges.

Columns of water spouted from the sea as the depth charges hit the surface and sank into the depths. The Russian sub continued running at 15-knots just below the surface. With a thunderous roar, the depth charges detonated in quick succession making the surface boil with foam.

"Come right to course one nine five," Englemann ordered. She picked up the phone to ask Commander Hastings whether or not the Russian was turning back into the bay.

"Aye Skipper," he replied. "He's coming about to course zero one zero and increasing speed."

"Keep reading the ranges out to me Brad." *That was too easy. It doesn't make sense for the Russian to try the same maneuver he had tried just a few hours ago.* Something was afoot. She could sense it.

As the Russian sub reached a range of 1,000 yards, Commander Englemann's suspicions were realized.

"Torpedo in the water!" Hastings cried over the intercom.

"Helm! Change course to two nine five and make flank speed. Deploy the Nixie! Engage Prairiemasker," Englemann ordered.

The Billings began picking up speed as it zigzagged away from the Putin to the northwest. Commander Englemann continued ordering course changes in an effort to throw off the guidance systems of the Russian torpedo. The Nixie was sending out signals designed to attract an enemy torpedo, while the Prairiemasker was generating a ring of bubbles around the hull to obscure the frigate's exact location.

As the Russian torpedo cut through the water at a little over 30-knots, Commander Ivanshenko ordered the Putin to come about 180 degrees, dive and make flank speed into the open ocean. The Putin churned through the icy depths, accelerating to over 33-knots. Sailors cheered as the sonarman announced the American frigate was sailing away to the northwest.

Commander Ivanshenko smiled at this small victory. He had timed his approach just after the American frigate had taken her helicopter back on board for refueling. This would give him at least 20 or 30 minutes to make his escape. He intended to take his boat into deep water before turning left and heading southeast through Sitkinak Strait. To add to his ruse, he intended to launch one of the experimental long-range decoys. This new invention mimicked the sounds made by a submarine running at high speed. Hopefully, the decoy would draw the Americans off to the west. This was its first combat test. If it worked it would give him even more time to increase the distance.

"Get that helicopter back in the air," barked Commander Englemann. She was upset at herself for getting caught with the SH-60 on the deck when the Russians made their run. She was also upset for not figuring out that the Russians would use the same trick she had pulled. By the time they had dodged the torpedo, they were several miles north of the entrance to Alitak Bay.

She did not relish trying to play catch up once more. She waited anxiously to hear Lt. Cowdrey announce lift off.

On the frigate's fantail, sailors were working feverishly to refuel and rearm of the SH-60. Lt. Cowdrey was discussing his battle plan with Commander Hastings. Time was of the essence. If the Russians went deep and then silent, it would be hard to find them. And the changing tide would greatly increase the amount of underwater background noise.

Commander Ivanshenko ordered the Putin to level off at 200 meters and rig for silent running. Standing over the sonar station with a set of headphones over his ears, he waited for a pod of whales to begin singing again before he launched his long-range decoy. With a whoosh, the decoy shot from the forward torpedo tube. The entire boat shuddered from the expulsion of compressed air.

"Decoy away," whispered the sonarman, "running hot and fast at 22-knots."

"Helm," Ivanshenko whispered, "reduce speed to nine knots and change course to one one zero. Take us through Sitkinak Strait."

Hawk Two was hovering above the waves a few miles from the entrance of Alitak Bay. Lt. Cowdrey and the crew listened intently for any sound of the fleeing Russian sub. The sonarman stared at the sonar scope. They did not hear the Putin launch its decoy.

"Lieutenant. I've got a contact running due west at about 22-knots at 100 meters."

"Great work, chief," praised Lt. Cowdrey. "Bloodhound this is Hawk Two, over."

"Hawk Two this is Bloodhound, go ahead."

"Bloodhound, I have a contact running west at 22-knots and 100 meters. A little quiet for an Akula, but with all this background noise, it's the best we've got."

"Roger, Hawk Two. Bloodhound copies. Take an intercept course. We are making steam and will take up a chase position."

As the crew chief lifted the hydrophone out of the water, Lt. Cowdrey dipped the nose of Hawk Two, accelerating the helicopter in the direction of the Russian decoy.

Several miles to the east, Commander Englemann plotted a course to fall in behind what she believed to be the Russian submarine. But at the same time, she ordered her sonar stations to listen for the Russians doubling back either to the north or the south. She wasn't willing to believe that the Russian commander had given up so easily.

Governor's Officer, Juneau, Alaska

"This is serious Admiral," said a surprised Governor Malloy. "Your commander is depth charging the Russians?" *Has everyone in Washington lost their mind?*

"That's correct Governor," stated CIA Director Colin Clarke. "We have absolutely no intention of letting the Russians get their hands on Dr. Elizabeth LeDue. The President is committed to this mission." The chill in his voice was unnerving—especially over the phone.

While sympathetic to their cause, but still concerned about his officers, citizens, and young Joy Frank, Governor Malloy tried to convey to Director Clarke, Admiral Quinn and General Sheridan the delicacy of the situation in Alaska. "Just how far do your orders permit you to go Admiral?" he asked. "Are the Navy and the CIA ready to spill blood, perhaps a lot of blood?"

Admiral Quinn put down his coffee cup. Preventing Dr. LeDue from being taken captive by the Russians was a matter of national security. Therefore, the commander of the USS Billings was free to exercise any command decision necessary to accomplish the President's directive. While he appreciated the Governor's position, his special operations team would not let the Russians off the island, even if it meant killing the Russians, the prisoners, and anyone else caught in the crossfire.

Governor Malloy resigned himself to the situation. President Bainbridge was a man of commitment and decisiveness. It was pointless to advocate for de-escalation in the interests of saving Joy Frank or any other innocent civilians. Instead, he argued for additional military resources for the manhunt on Kodiak. Ms. Frank's father had just flown into Juneau to meet with him. He was going to want answers about what was being done to rescue his daughter. He wasn't going to like hearing that she was not part of the calculation. Governor Malloy needed Admiral Quinn and General Sheridan to give him something to placate what was surely going to be an angry citizen—a man sick with worry and someone not bound by the rules of confidentiality.

"Governor," replied Admiral Quinn, "I can tell you that I have several warships running at flank speed to rendezvous with the Billings. For security reasons, I cannot give you the specifics on which vessels or how many, but you can tell Mr. Frank we intend to keep the Russian Spetsnaz on the island. I feel confident my force will be sufficient to neutralize the Russian submarine."

Admiral Quinn had a reputation for honesty. Governor Malloy accepted his answer. "Thank you Admiral. I appreciate you letting me know a little something about what's afoot. I can't say that I like it, but I'll take what I can get." With that he hung up.

Joy's father had arrived in Juneau the night before and had been waiting impatiently for his appointment with Governor Malloy since eight o'clock in the morning. Thomas Frank was everybody's ideal dad. He was a devoted husband and father. Joy was his first child and the apple of his eye. When she had dropped out of Columbia to head north to "find herself" he was very concerned. Joy was a strong girl, but she'd never been exposed to hard work or the wilderness. He'd told her Alaska wasn't summer camp. She didn't have his experience of working in her grandfather's welding shop, where the work was dirty and dangerous, and the hours long.

Thomas Frank had driven himself to make a good life for his children. So when Joy made her announcement, he called up his old college buddy Albert Lind in Homer, Alaska and asked him if he'd take her on his boat. He knew Albert would work her hard, but watch over her like his own daughter. It took some of the worry off his shoulders.

"Mr. Frank?" said Governor Malloy's secretary as she entered the lobby, where earlier she had served him coffee and a few pastries, "The Governor will see you now." She motioned for him to follow her back through the security station and into the Governor's office.

Governor Malloy was studying the map on the wall. He extended his hand. "Mr. Frank, I'm Governor Rick Malloy. Pleased to meet you."

Thomas Frank was impressed by the firmness of Governor Malloy's handshake and the direct way he looked into his eyes. "Thomas Frank, Mr. Governor. Thank you for meeting with me."

"Kari," instructed Governor Malloy, "would you please bring us some lunch? I want to have a nice long talk with Mr. Frank. Please hold my calls." With that Governor Malloy shooed his secretary out of the room. Turning back around, he gestured for Mr. Frank to take a seat on the sofa nearest the map on the wall.

For the next hour, the two men talked candidly about the situation on Kodiak. Governor Malloy tried to answer as many questions as possible, but he did not have a lot of information and he couldn't reveal much of what he did know. By the end of the conversation, Governor Malloy had grown to respect Joy's father for his commitment to his daughter and his willingness to travel to Kodiak to help in the search. Thomas Frank came to appreciate Rick Malloy's candor. He believed Governor Malloy when he told him he was doing everything within his power to rescue his daughter from the clutches of that madman.

After exchanging parting compliments, Governor Malloy escorted Mr. Frank down the hallway to the elevators. A firm handshake sealed their agreement—Governor Malloy would continue to work on finding Joy and Mr. Frank would give up his plans to travel to Kodiak—for now.

"George," hollered Governor Malloy, coming back down the hallway, "come in here. I need you to bulldog something for me."

"Yes Rick," Roberts answered closing the door behind him.

"George, I just finished a heart to heart discussion with the father of that young woman currently being held hostage by our prisoners on Kodiak. She, and I emphasize this George, she is the dearest thing in that man's heart. I for one do not intend to let him grieve over her. I don't care if the Joint Chiefs, the CIA, or the President thinks she's expendable. She's not expendable to me."

Governor Malloy instructed him to fly to Larsen Bay with another helicopter and the State Troopers K-9 unit. "You take my plane to Anchorage. Get out to Kodiak pronto."

As soon as Roberts departed his office, Governor Malloy placed a call to President Bainbridge. *Joy Frank may not be critical to national security, but she's important to her family.* He was going to make sure the president understood his position.

Russian Pacific Fleet Headquarters, Vladivostok, Russia

"Any word from the Putin," asked Admiral Voroshilov staring out his office window overlooking the harbor.

"No, Admiral," replied Captain Gromyko. "Not a word since she reported receiving the distress signal from the American transport plane."

Once again, Voroshilov regretted his failure to abort this mission. He had told the high command there were too many dangers inherent in this mission. He had warned them that if they were caught or exposed, the Americans would have a perfect opportunity to embarrass Russia once more.

But he was in the minority. *Those fools in the SVR, GRU, the Army, and even my own boss Admiral Bulgakov, support the plan.* Admiral Voroshilov had resigned himself to putting his best attack submarine commander in charge of the mission and hoping for the best. Ivanshenko would be going against the odds. Given the American's ability to intercept Russian communications and decipher them, he had bet the Americans would know something was afoot before it ever happened. Furthermore, no one at the meeting in Moscow had wanted to face the grim reality that his submarine fleet, not to mention his surface fleet, was barely seaworthy. Reactors were not being maintained, equipment was not being serviced, and morale among his sailors was at an all time low.

"Maybe we should find a younger, more enthusiastic man to command the Pacific Fleet?" Admiral Bulgakov had criticized. Bulgakov had made it clear that if he didn't order the mission, they would find some lackey who would, so he had swallowed his common sense and submitted to their madness.

Ivanshenko was their only hope. *The man is a maverick and is very good at irritating Moscow, but his crew is devoted to him and he keeps his boat in better condition than any other commander in the fleet.* Voroshilov never bothered digging too deep into how Ivanshenko always managed to get spare parts for his submarine—he didn't want to know, just in case Ivanshenko got caught.

As he lit up another cigarette and sipped his tea, he found himself becoming even more annoyed at being left out of the meeting with Prime Minister Kirov and Foreign Minister Kremenek. He was sure they had not been told the whole truth. Otherwise they would not have given their approval. He was sure that General Chernikov and the others had sold the ministers a bill of goods. The military was looking to bolster its image during this time of economic upheaval.

And now I'm to report in person to the Prime Minister and brief him on the mission. I have no news! He did not relish the ten-hour flight to Moscow, nor the meeting where he would tell the prime minister that the Putin was deep inside American waters off the coast of Kodiak Island. Once again he would be left holding the bag and all the "salesmen" would disappear into the woodwork. If the Putin were lost at sea, the prime minister would face a political crisis. Families would demand answers to their questions about sons, fathers, and husbands who had failed to come home.

He gulped down the last of his tea and ordered Captain Gromyko to have his car meet them out front.

He offered his aide a cigarette before they entered his Chaika sedan and asked, "Alexander, did you order Captain Frunze to call me if they hear from the Putin?"

"Of course, Admiral. I've instructed our men to stay at their stations 24-hours a day and to call us in Moscow if there is any news."

Over the past three years, Captain Gromyko had come to read his boss's moods. The Admiral did not fear politicians or even his superior officers. But when Voroshilov played with his cigarette, instead of smoking it, he was very worried. Gromyko hoped they would receive some communication from the Putin before they arrived in Moscow.

Kodiak Island, Alaska

Harry Ignustuk was the first to catch sight of Ivan Lincoln and the two women moving in the valley below amid the tangled growth of alders and willows. He tapped Danny Sanders on the shoulder and pointed down into the valley.

It took Danny a few moments to catch sight of the trio. "Got 'em," he said vehemently. "We got you, you son-of-a-bitch! Let's move out."

"Not so fast," Harry cautioned grabbing Danny's arm. "They have company and we do too."

Danny looked at him like he was crazy. "What do you mean, they have company and we do too?"

"There," Harry whispered, pointing, "just behind them in the alders about 300 yards back. You can see him. Big old guy, that one is."

"What old guy?" asked a puzzled Danny. Then he saw the giant bear moving stealthily behind the fugitives. It was huge! "Holy crimeny!" he exclaimed in disbelief, "That bear is stalking them. Look at the way he's sniffing the air."

"More than that, Danny," Harry said, once again tapping Danny on the shoulder, "we might have some help in catching these guys. See those three men on the ridge to our right? And if you look real hard at the ridge line directly ahead of Lincoln, you can see several more people hiding in the bushes."

"Who do you think they are Harry?"

"Haven't got a clue. But it doesn't really matter if they help us catch Lincoln and LeDue, now does it?"

A smile broke across Harry's usually unexpressive face as he thought about bringing an end to this manhunt.

Danny noticed that whenever Harry smiled his eyes became slits.

While they picked up their gear, Harry explained how they would cut down into the valley, intercept the three men in camouflage on their right, and link up with them. "Keep a sharp lookout for any more of those damn bears," Harry cautioned. With their packs on their backs and rifles at the ready, they set off.

At almost the same moment as Harry and Danny spotted the Marines, Lt. Surin and his men caught sight of the Alaska officers moving down the mountain. "Looks like we got company," said Lt. Surin. "And I think they know we're here."

Sergeants Ramirez and Ali spied the two officers on the far ridge. They were guessing these two men were from the Department of Corrections, because they could see their light blue uniform tops under their jackets.

"What's the plan, Lieutenant?" asked Sergeant Ramirez.

"Well, looking at the terrain down below us, I don't know how we're going to avoid contact with them. Do we try and avoid contact? Or do we link up with them and try to use them to our advantage?" He hoped they had an idea.

This was quite a dilemma. On the one hand they wanted to keep this mission as covert as possible. On the other, the ultimate goal was to prevent Dr. LeDue from falling into Russian hands. All three of them fell silent as they pondered the possibilities.

It was the stocky Sergeant Ramirez, who spoke first. "If our prime directive is to bring Dr. LeDue back into custody, then I think we need to join up with these two and pool our resources. I mean, we know the Russians have us outnumbered and we can use all the help we can get."

Sergeant Ali jumped into the conversation, "I agree Lieutenant. What can it hurt for them to know about the Russians? They have the same job we do."

Surin agreed. He ordered his men to pick up their gear and led them down off the ridge on an intercept course with the Alaskans.

About five miles to the east, Major Golkin and his Spetsnaz team were watching the movements of the two groups of Americans descending from the ridges to the west with great interest. He counted five men—three military men dressed in camouflage and two "police officers" dressed in light blue. All of them appeared to be well armed. Helicopters flying up and down the mountain valleys further complicated the situation.

Major Golkin looked around at his men. Gregorii Petrov was an able and experienced leader. He could be counted on to carry out his duties with precision and lethality. Sergeant Timoshenko came from a long line of military men, who had served the Tsars and the Bolsheviks. He knew his business and spoke the best English in the group. Privates Korkov, Rudenko, and Balzan had been with his team for less than a year. Their inexperience worried him.

Through his binoculars, Major Golkin watched the Americans heading in his direction. The two blue-shirted officers had been pointing in the direction of the wooded valley directly in front of his position. It was obvious they had spotted something moving across the valley. *It shouldn't be too long before the fugitives will come out the woods below my position. They will have to go north, south or right over us.* His instincts told him they would head directly towards him or follow the river downhill to the sea. Either way, his team would be in an ideal position to intercept them and make off with their prize.

Moving with the skill acquired in years of clandestine operations, Major Golkin went to each of his men and explained his plan. Barring any unforeseen surprises, they would soon have Dr. LeDue in their clutches and retreat to rendezvous with the Putin.

Ivan Lincoln was frustrated at the women's slow pace, but he couldn't bring himself to kill them yet. It had been two years since he had last enjoyed himself with a woman. He felt compelled to complete the subjugation of Elizabeth LeDue before he executed her. He loved it when bitches begged for their lives.

He picked up a sharp branch and poked Elizabeth and Joy in the back, prodding them to move faster. Each stab of the stick sent sensations of fire shooting through Elizabeth. The previous night's attacks had drained her strength. Tears of despair and pain rolled down her cheeks.

Being poked with the stick only served to increase Joy's loathing for Lincoln. He was a beast. She imagined how she would get even with him after she escaped.

Lincoln never heard or saw the Kodiak Brown Bear creeping up from behind. With an explosive "whoof" the bear launched into a sprint, breaking tree limbs off, making the air echo with the crack of snapping branches and the thundering of his weight on the ground.

Lincoln pivoted in the direction of the charging bear and reached for his pistol. In a rush to pull the pistol from his waistband, he put his finger through the trigger guard too soon. The pain of the bullet piercing his thigh delayed his reaction. Before he could react, the bear was on him.

Throwing its 1,300 pounds forward, the bear hit his victim just below the solar plexus, knocking the wind out of him and sending his pistol flying off into the creek. Launched with crushing force, Lincoln flew back into the branch of an alder tree, breaking several ribs and his left shoulder blade. Dazed, but still conscious, he rolled up into a ball, playing dead in a vain effort to stop the bear's attack.

Unfortunately for Lincoln, the old boar was not about to stop.

Lincoln screamed as the bear bit him and raked him with his razor-sharp claws all along the neck, back and legs. With each bite of the bear's gaping jaws, he felt its teeth puncture his flesh.

All Joy saw was a blur of dark brown fur and the feel of the ground shaking under the bear's weight. She heard Lincoln's pistol shot just before the bear slammed into him, filling the air with the sound of cracking bones and air rushing out of his lungs.

The women froze. As they stood transfixed by the bloody scene a few yards away, they wondered if they would be next on the menu.

"To hell with it," Joy said. Pulling at Elizabeth's handcuffed wrist, she led them headlong through the brush. As she ran, she glanced back over her shoulder. The bear had no interest in them. Joy ignored the stinging slap of the branches on her face and arms as she steered them up out of the trees and into the open. Once in the clear, she urged Elizabeth to time her steps so they could get as far away from the bear as possible. "Come on Elizabeth," Joy shouted, "now's our chance. Ignore the pain and get moving. I can't run and drag you behind me."

Elizabeth gasped for air. She wasn't young anymore. "Can't breathe," she grunted, "must catch breath, must rest."

"No resting!" shouted Joy, "Get your butt in gear and let's get out of here!"

"Look!" Elizabeth wheezed. She pointed at the six men running down the ridge to the east. "We're saved." With that Elizabeth tried to get Joy to slow down.

Joy, however, began pulling at her handcuff even harder. She had no intention of becoming bear bait, just when she could see the end of their ordeal. "Run damn you, run!" she barked at Elizabeth. "We haven't come this far to end up being eaten by a bear!"

In the woods behind them they could hear Lincoln's screams. Joy smiled. *How does it feel to die, you pig?*

A few miles back, Harry and Danny had just linked up with Lt. Surin and his team. They were discussing their strategy for flanking the prisoners, when Lincoln's pistol shot echoed across the valley.

"What was that?" Danny asked in surprise. He looked around for an answer.

"Sounded like a gunshot," replied Sergeant Ramirez.

"From where?" asked Sergeant Ali.

In unison, all five men pulled their binoculars out of their cases and scanned the valley for clues as to who and why someone was shooting. But the brush and trees along the river were too dense and their efforts to see what was happening were thwarted.

"Damn," cursed Lt. Surin, "what's happening?"

Harry put his hand to his ear, telling everyone to be quiet. "Bear. Sounds like the bear is attacking something."

"Are you sure?" questioned a skeptical Surin.

Ignoring the inference that he couldn't possibly know what was going on, Harry said, "We saw a bear stalking them. Let's go." Harry didn't have time to tell Surin how his father had taught him to use all his senses on the hunt. If you didn't you could end being eaten by a stalking Polar Bear.

Harry paused to raise his binoculars, focusing his attention to the east. "Take a look on the ridge directly to the east, about 1,000 feet up. I think we have company. Probably the Russians you were telling us about."

"Faster," Surin barked as they jogged in the direction of melee. He could see two figures emerge from the brush. "There they are!" he shouted pointing to Elizabeth LeDue and Joy Frank, who were running for all they were worth.

"Looks like they're handcuffed together Lieutenant," replied the eagle-eyed Sgt. Ali. "The bear must be attacking the male prisoner."

"Looks like the Russians are going to get to Dr. LeDue before we do," Danny commented between gasps. He watched the women moving towards the Russians. "They probably don't realize those guys are Russians. They probably think they're with us."

Reacting to a rapidly deteriorating situation, Lt. Surin laid out a quick plan. He turned around and led his men back into the brush. He was hoping the Russians had not yet spotted his team. He ordered his men to move out in single file down the trail. So they could cover more ground, they would skirt the edge of the heavy brush. But, he reminded them, it was imperative they keep the brush between them and a direct line-of-sight with the Russians. He stared at the powder blue shirts being worn by Officers Ignustuk and Sanders. He ordered them to cover their uniform tops.

Danny objected, "We need to get up there now!"

"Don't be a fool," Ramirez replied. "Those Spetsnaz would have no qualms about killing us. We don't need to make it easy for them. We're too late to get to the women first. We'll have to intercept them on the trail."

"Ramirez is right," Surin said, "we need to be smart and plan our attack."

Up on the ridge, Major Golkin had taken immediate notice of the gunshot echoing from the valley below.

He quickly assessed the situation. Several miles to the west he had been watching the five Americans moving towards his position. This led him to conclude that the prisoners were moving in his direction too. They wouldn't know he was Russian. Now was the time to intercept the prisoners, even if it meant exposing his position to the Americans at the other end of the valley.

He passed the word to move out at double-time down the mountainside. He reminded Captain Petrov that his priority was to capture Dr. LeDue. Once they had her, Petrov was to take Sergeant Timoshenko with him and move off to rendezvous with the Putin. He would stay with the other men and fight a delaying action.

The Russians were almost at the base of the mountain when they saw two women emerge from the woods. They were running very closely together and in a very strange manner. This didn't look right. He signaled for his men to halt and raised his binoculars. He could see Dr. LeDue and a younger woman running side by side. Their wrists were handcuffed together.

"Shit!" he exclaimed. He motioned for Petrov and Timoshenko to come over to him. "See those two women," he said pointing to the valley below. "They're chained together. I don't know who the other one is, but we have a problem. What are we going to do with the other woman?"

"Couldn't we cut them apart?" Timoshenko suggested.

Golkin shook his head. Cutting them apart was going to be necessary no matter what they did. "Of course we'll cut them apart, but then what do we do? If we leave the younger one behind she'll tell everyone we were here. She's not an American soldier. She will love talking to the newspapers and television reporters. It would be quite a story. How I saw the Russians kidnap an American scientist."

"Could we use one of our American pistols and shoot her?" suggested Captain Petrov.

"No, I don't think that's wise," Golkin responded. "The American soldiers are too close. Take her with you. We can sort out what to do later."

The bear was resting in the bushes a few paces away from the ravaged body of Ivan Lincoln. It planned to feed on his carcass for several days.

Slowly, Lincoln opened his eyes. His body was numb from the pain. Warm blood was seeping out of the puncture wounds along the back of his neck, shoulder blades, and thighs. There was no sensation below his left knee. *Did the bear pull my leg off?* His head hurt. With each breath, his broken ribs sent shots of pain through his torso.

Lincoln knew that bears often wait in hiding for their wounded prey to move before launching another attack. He had to think of a way to escape. He blinked to clear his vision and looked around without moving his head. He could hear the creek running in the background. Up ahead he could see the edge of the forest.

Unless someone came along to rescue him, he was going to bleed to death. *I can't die like this. Why did the bear attack me and not the women? After all, they would be the most heavily scented and the blood from that bitch's wounds should have drawn the bear like honey.* Then it hit him. *I forgot to wash that whore's scent from my body this morning.* Being upwind of the bear and at the back of the group had made him the perfect target.

Still he clung to the belief that his pursuers would rescue him from the clutches of this animal. He might end up being scarred and imprisoned for life, but he would be alive. *And who knows, maybe my wounds will make me look even more intimidating.*

Any hopes of surviving evaporated when he heard the bear rush out from behind the thicket. Grabbing him by the shin, the bear sprinted from the woods, dragging him along like a rag doll. Branches slapped at his arms, torso, and face, lacerating him and cracking bones with each violent impact. Lincoln screamed as the bear sank its teeth deeper into his shin, crushing the bones.

The giant bear thundered across the grassy tundra, its prey dangling from its mouth. Lincoln's limp body bounced off rocks and clumps of grass. His head slammed into a rock, splitting it and spilling his brains in a long bloody trail.

As they jogged down the valley, the Americans tried to catch a glimpse of the bear they knew to be lurking in the woods. At the same time, they were keeping vigil for the Russian soldiers.

Moments later they were startled by screams so loud they echoed down the valley. They were mesmerized as they watched the bear bolt from the woods with Lincoln firmly clenched in its crushing jaws. It galloped across the grassy field with Lincoln flopping along side, his screams splitting the silence. They were filled with mixed feelings as they saw Lincoln's head bounce high above the bear's back and then back down. A bright red plume flew through the air. The screaming stopped. A few moments later, the bear and his meal had disappeared from sight.

Danny smiled at Harry, holding his thumb up. The sick bastard was dead. One prisoner was accounted for. Now they could focus on capturing Dr. LeDue and freeing Joy Frank. Danny found morbid satisfaction in the painful and terrifying death Ivan Lincoln had just endured. *Perhaps,* he thought, *there is some justice. Still, it's not enough. Lincoln deserved a much longer and more excruciating death.*

Joy and Elizabeth were crying and laughing as they rushed headlong into the arms of the Russians. Major Golkin sat them down, motioning for Sgt. Timoshenko to cut them apart with his bolt cutters. He could see the bloody splotches on the back of Elizabeth's shirt. Private Rudenko gave them a drink of water from his canteen.

They all watched in fascination as the grizzly bear erupted from the woods with Lincoln in its jaws. Joy felt a sense of relief and vengeance as his brains flew through the air. It was over. Elizabeth felt nothing. She was too traumatized.

Before they could ask any questions, Sgt. Timoshenko ordered them to their feet and led them away. Captain Petrov was in the lead.

"Why are we going this way?" Joy asked plaintively. "Isn't there a helicopter coming to pick us up?"

"Just come with us," Timoshenko replied, in perfect English.

Lev Timoshenko had been in the military for almost 15 years. He had been assigned embassy duty in Washington, DC in the late 1980s, where his language skills had been finely honed. It was almost impossible to know he was not a native speaker. He even spoke American slang.

As they moved down the valley towards Kaiugnak Bay, Joy kept asking where they were headed. He refused to answer.

Somewhere to the east, they could hear the pounding blades of the Coast Guard helicopter. Both Elizabeth and Joy felt a wave of relief. Their salvation was at hand. When the two soldiers moved them into the woods under the cover of the brush, their spirits sank. *Something's wrong.*

"I demand an answer," Joy growled. "Why are we hiding from the helicopter?" She couldn't believe this nightmare wasn't over. She wrenched her wrist free from Sgt. Timoshenko, stood up and headed towards the clearing. Timoshenko swept her feet out from under her and drew his pistol.

Joy fell forward, hitting the ground with her hands and chest.

"Hey!" she shouted flipping onto her back in a challenge to her new captor. Staring straight into the barrel of a pistol made Joy rethink her next statement.

"Don't get any cute ideas young woman," Timoshenko said coldly. "If you try to run or make trouble, I will shoot you."

Elizabeth spoke for the first time. "Who are you? What do you want with us?"

Petrov evaded the question. "That is not important, Doctor. All that matters is that I am here to rescue you."

"I don't understand," she replied. Again she asked him more forcefully, "Who are you?"

"I am a friend. There is a submarine waiting to take us away from this place. You will be free and have a life filled with work and happiness."

Suddenly, Elizabeth realized the two men were Russian soldiers. She was overcome with emotions. She was grateful they were going to rescue her from a life behind bars. But she also felt like even more of a traitor for accepting their help.

When she had originally gotten involved with the Russian operative, it was out of a romantic interest, not because she wanted to betray her country. Still, Captain Petrov's kindness and willingness to risk his life to rescue her convinced her to cooperate for the time being.

Sgt. Timoshenko kept his foot on Joy's chest as he watched the orange and white Coast Guard helicopter fly its boxed search pattern above them. Even though he knew they could not hear him, he consciously made his breathing softer. He pulled out his silencer fitting it to the barrel of his pistol.

Joy began to shake. Thoughts of home, school, friends and family raced through her mind as she watched him finish twisting the silencer onto his pistol. *He's going to shoot me!*

As the helicopter moved off to the north, Captain Petrov and Sgt. Timoshenko breathed sighs of relief.

"Okay ladies," ordered Timoshenko, "let's get moving."

Joy didn't understand why they were taking her. Her heart sank as he pushed her along the path. She wanted to be home, safe in her room with her father bringing her a warm cup of cocoa.

Elizabeth tried to rationalize her situation. After being subjected to two days of terror, she was now on the run from the authorities, and caught up in an international incident. *Should I refuse to go with the Russians? Should I run with them? Will I really be free in Russia or will I become their prisoner? What are they going to do with Joy? Maybe if I refuse to go with them, they'll set Joy free?*

Harry tried to contact the Trooper search helicopter with his hand radio. "AST, AST, this is PTO Ignustuk. Over."

"Go for AST," the pilot answered.

"We are approximately 10 miles east of Dog Salmon Creek. We have made contact with the prisoners and what appear to be six, repeat six Russian soldiers. We need you to fly over our position and then locate the Russians. Over."

"Copy. We are headed in your direction. When we have you in sight, we will circle your position. AST out."

While Harry was communicating with the Troopers, Lt. Surin was reporting to Commander Englemann. He told her about Lincoln's death and that Dr. LeDue and a female civilian were now in Russian hands.

Commander Englemann reminded Surin he was to stop the Russians at all costs.

Larsen Bay, Alaska

The morning following the ash storm saw a flurry of activity as Commissioners Burke and Dornier coordinated the launch of the Trooper and Coast Guard helicopters. It was Major Calhoun who had talked both commissioners out of riding along. While he sympathized with their desire to get a bird's eye view of what they were dealing with, now was not the time to risk losing department leadership. This was a dangerous flying environment.

"Going to be a long day," Burke commented as they stood watching the helicopters thunder off towards Karluk Lake. For Dick Burke waiting was the hardest part. He wasn't a patient man.

"Oh don't be such a pessimist, Dick," Dornier said. She felt more confident. He was no longer putting her down all the time and was even asking her opinion. She was beginning to see through his brusque façade.

While Burke supervised the clearing of the airport of volcanic ash, Dornier returned to the school to monitor radio traffic and educate herself about Kodiak's geography.

One of the nation's largest islands, Kodiak is a sparsely populated emerald wilderness jutting out of the dark blue waters of the North Pacific Ocean, laced with countless mountains and valleys. Finding three humans in this expanse was going to be a real challenge. She promised herself that after this ordeal was over, she was going to visit all of the department's institutions and field offices. No longer would she be content to be an administrator: she was going to be a leader.

Twice during the day, the helicopters had returned to Larsen Bay and each time, Burke and Dornier were there to meet them.

Returning to the school after refueling the Coast Guard helicopter for the second time, Burke sought out the Mayor. "Mr. Mayor," he called from the entrance to the gym, "could I have a word with you please?"

"Be right there," he answered jovially, "just as soon as I finish changing Mr. Woolford's bandages."

Knowing it would be a few minutes before the mayor would be available, Burke headed into the administration office to speak with Dornier. "Afternoon Commissioner. Any word from the search teams or Governor Malloy?"

"Matter of fact," Dornier responded, removing the earphones, "we just got a call from Governor Malloy's Chief-of-Staff George

Roberts. He's headed to Larsen Bay with another search helicopter and your K-9 unit. They should be here in about two hours."

"Why in the hell is George Roberts coming here?!" bellowed Burke.

"Your guess is as good as mine Dick," Dornier replied calmly.

For the first time, Dick Burke noticed, Michelle Dornier didn't jump or twitch when he bellowed. *Maybe she's getting some metal in her spine.* "Something must have given this search an even higher priority," he conjectured.

"More than likely," she said nodding in agreement. "Look Dick," she continued, "it seems to me that you and I are just getting a handle on this situation. We don't need George Roberts taking over. He'll just set us back to square one. I think we need a plan to keep him out of our hair while we get this job done."

Dornier's seizure of the initiative took Burke by surprise. *This is another first.* "Go on?"

"When he gets here, I think we should sideline him with the Mayor and the survivors of Larsen Bay. They will be delighted that the Governor's chief-of-staff has come to their community. Roberts won't be in a position to brush them off—too much at stake politically." She looked at Burke to make sure he caught her drift.

Dick Burke smiled at her ingenuity.

She pulled Burke over to the map. "I'll keep Roberts here with me. You go with the K-9 unit and the helicopter to hook up with the others. Maybe you'll get lucky. I for one would feel better with you in command on the ground."

"Damn Commissioner," he said, "I like the way you think."

"Larsen Bay, Larsen Bay, this is AST One. Over."

Dornier picked up the radio and replied, "AST One, this is Larsen Bay. Go."

"PTO Ignustuk reports they have made contact with the fugitives. Over."

"10-4, AST One. Is there any more information? Over."

"Ignustuk reports that Inmate Lincoln is dead. Inmate LeDue and the civilian are not in custody. Over."

Burke and Dornier glanced at each other. *What the hell is going on out there?* "AST One, this is Dornier. Do you know status of LeDue and civilian? Over."

"Negative. Ignustuk believes they have been taken prisoner by Russian commandos. They are moving east. Ignustuk reports they are pursuing. Over."

"Damn!" exclaimed Burke. "The Governor isn't going to be happy if the Russians get Elizabeth LeDue off this island. We have got to do something." He went over to the map of the island. "Where is our team right now?" he asked.

"About seven miles south, southeast of O'Malley Lake," she answered joining him at the map to point out the approximate location.

Where are the Russians heading? He ran his fingers over the valleys and mountains. Burke's eyes came to rest at Kaiugnak Bay about 25 miles from the last known position of Ignustuk and Sanders. "Here," he declared hitting the map with his finger, "here is where the Russians will try and rendezvous with their submarine."

"Are you sure?" asked Dornier somewhat skeptically.

"No, but this is my best guess," he replied. "The bay is deep, the shoreline steep and it's the closest alternative to Deadman Bay."

"I agree. The Russians must be moving in the river valleys where there is cover. I think we should place a team here," she said pointing to the river valley running parallel to Kaiugnak Bay, "at the head of this valley. After George Roberts arrives, you go with the K-9 team and set up several checkpoints on the high ground to cut off any possible Russian retreat." She put pins into the map as she talked.

Burke had to admit he liked her idea. It was wise to remove himself from Larsen Bay when George Roberts arrived. They were too much alike and would end up shouting at each other.

The two commissioners left the administration office.

Dornier found the Mayor in the gym and told him about her plan. He was an easy sell. He liked the idea that his friends would be able to meet and discuss their needs and worries with the

Governor's chief-of-staff. He was the most important man to ever come to Larsen Bay.

Even after ground crews cleaned up the airfield, volcanic ash continued to swirl into the air as the Trooper Helicopter touched down next to the collapsed hangar. "Welcome to Larsen Bay, George," greeted Commissioner Dornier, extending her hand. "Follow me," she said, pointing toward the four-wheelers at the edge of the pad. "We can go back to our headquarters while Commissioner Burke oversees the refueling of the helicopter and briefs the K-9 team."

Before he knew it, Roberts was sitting behind the Mayor on a four-wheeler, bouncing down the road toward town, hanging on for dear life. Everything was happening so fast he didn't have time to protest being whisked away from the airport. Riding down main street, he was shocked by the devastation. "My God," he exclaimed, "if Larsen Bay took this pounding, I can't even imagine what Dutch Harbor looks like."

Arriving at the school, the Mayor led Roberts into the building and back toward the gymnasium. "It's important for you to let the people of Larsen Bay know just how much our governor cares about them," counseled the Mayor. "After all, we've never had a governor's chief-of-staff visit us. The people will be delighted to hear from you."

"But," stuttered Roberts, "I don't have time."

Ignoring his protests, the Mayor led Roberts into the gymnasium and into a throng of people.

George Roberts resigned himself to reality when he saw the worried looks of the people surrounding him—he was not going to get out of this meeting. Public relations were just as important at this juncture as real action. Putting on his best smile, he mingled with the crowd.

Aboard the helicopter, Burke instructed the pilot to head south over the Karluk River Valley and then to cut east towards Kaiugnak Bay.

Dornier stood in the hallway outside the gym watching with satisfaction as George Roberts walked among the people of Larsen

Bay. Talking, smiling, hugging, and otherwise being a perfect politician, he showed just why he was so valuable to Governor Malloy. She chuckled under her breath, squeezing the Mayor's shoulder before returning to the administration office to follow the developments taking place on the south side of the island. She was grateful for the time to prepare for Roberts. He was sure to be irritated when he learned that Burke had taken his helicopter and the K-9 team.

Amchitka Island, Alaska

Blood was running from the wound in Toby Church's shoulder. He held his coat up against the hole, trying to stop the bleeding, but it was impossible while his heart was beating so strongly. Burning streaks of pain shot through his chest and up his neck. "Must keep going, must keep going," he chanted. But the pain was too much. "You're never going to run all the way back to your boat bleeding like this," he said clutching his shoulder. "You've got to stop and bind the wound."

As he stumbled down a slight incline, he looked around for any sign of his enemy. No one. *Must have lost them for the moment.* Still, he knew they would not lose his trail for long. Coming to the bottom of a shallow ravine, he cut to his right, and ran up the other side to a rock protruding above the grassy hillside. He slid to the ground behind the rock, taking a few moments to catch his breath.

Using his glove as a pad and the rock as a platform, Church aimed his carbine in the direction of his pursuers. *Maybe I'll get lucky and hit one of them, even at this range.* Ignoring the pain, he pressed the butt of the rifle into his good shoulder. Blood continued oozing from his left shoulder onto the moss-covered rock.

Carlos and Ben heard the whine of a bullet passing over their heads just as they came up over the rise. Then they heard the report of the rifle. Dirt flew up several feet in front of them as they dropped to the ground. One of the bullets ricocheted over Ben's head. Another bullet whizzed past his leg.

"Don't move," Carlos ordered while pulling out his binoculars. In a slow, sweeping motion he scoured every inch of the terrain in front of them.

"He's one resilient son-of-a-bitch," said Ben with grudging respect.

Church was hiding behind the boulder, using the time he'd bought to dress his wound. He took a long piece of cloth he'd torn from the inside of his coat and tied it around the shoulder, covering the hole with a knot. He felt for an exit would, but there wasn't one. *The bullet is probably lodged in my shoulder blade. If I don't get to a doctor I'm going to die. Maybe the villagers will believe me if I tell them I've been out hunting and been shot by a hunter?*

With his wound bound, Church crawled backwards away from the boulder, being careful to keep his position hidden. Once on the other side of the ridge, he got to his feet and trotted along a worn trail that sloped down the hillside towards the beach.

"Can't see him," Carlos commented putting his binoculars away. "I think he was up behind that rock over there." He pointed to the moss-covered rock on the far side of the ravine. "I'm pretty sure he's gone now."

"Probably trying to buy time," Ben reflected.

"Whatever the reason, I think we'd better be a little more cautious from here on out, don't you?"

"Yeah, he's not going anywhere," said Ben smiling. "Let's go check out that rock. We might find out if I hit him back there."

With each man circling in a different direction, they flanked Church's now abandoned position.

"Got him!" Ben exclaimed with satisfaction examining the large bloodstain on the moss. "Got him good."

By the volume of blood on the ground and the moss, Carlos guessed that Ben Williams had hit Toby Church in the upper part of the chest or shoulder. It was a debilitating, but not immediately lethal wound. "Pretty good shooting Ben."

"Thanks."

They took up their pursuit once again. Carlos set out at a slow trot, following the footprints in the soft muskeg. Ben angled off to the right and up the hill. This time he wanted to get a shot at Church with the wind at his back and downhill.

For the next few miles, Church managed to keep up an almost superhuman effort. But he was growing weaker. He could feel his body going into shock. Only the hope of reaching his boat kept him going. Periodically he would catch sight of his enemy cresting the ridges far behind him. They didn't seem to be in too big of a hurry. He was confused. *Did they sabotage my boat?* He shook off this thought. It was too late to think about sabotage. He had to stay focused.

Cautiously, Carlos and Ben closed the gap with Church. They didn't intend to get ambushed again.

Cresting a ridge, Ben saw Church about 300 yards away. He went into action. "Halt!" he shouted above the wind.

Church heard the order, but ignored it and kept on running, picking up his pace despite the pain. He was getting light-headed. *I won't go back to jail.*

Dropping to one knee, Ben Williams took careful aim at the fleeing criminal. Holding the rifle steady in the stiff wind was difficult. Every time he'd get his sights on his target, the wind would buffet him, making him lose his aim. He tried timing his shot as his sights swayed across Church's back. He fired off three rounds.

One of the bullets ripped through Church's upper thigh sending him tumbling to the ground. He cried out in pain, clutching the back of his leg, and dropping his rifle.

"Got him!" Ben shouted in jubilation. His glee was short-lived as he watched Church roll through his fall and come back up to his feet limping, but still moving at a respectable pace.

Damn, thought Lt. Carlos Banderas, *he's one tough bastard.* He dropped to a knee and fired several times, but missed. The wind was gusting too hard.

Luck was with Church as he rolled through his fall and landed on his feet. His leg didn't want to work right, but the bullet had only hit flesh, passing clean through the muscle. There was very little blood. He used the burning sensation in his leg to feed his adrenaline to keep running.

Up in the distance, he saw his skiff sitting on the beach. He also noticed the large herd of sea lions piled up against the small cliff seeking shelter from the wind. *They're going to slow me down.*

Church stopped at the edge of the cliff and looked down at the mass of bodies wallowing around on the boulders. It was like a sea lion carpet—one big, noisy, smelly carpet of barking and growling flesh. Again he heard Ben yell "Halt" above the howling wind. Dirt flew into the air as the bullets fell short of their mark. The rifle's report echoed on the wind.

With one last effort, Church launched himself off the grass and down into the sea of moving flesh. He shoved against the massive bodies trying to clear a path through to his waiting boat. He never saw the young sea lion pup. All Toby Church heard was a loud bawl when he stepped on the pup's flipper.

A great roar surged out from the herd. Bull sea lions bellowed and cows began charging about. Before he could pull his pistol out of his coat, the mother of the distressed pup slammed into his wounded leg—knocking him to the ground. Rolling to the side, he cried out as his wounded shoulder collided with a sharp rock and his leg slipped into a hole in a jumble of mist-covered rocks. The sky above him disappeared behind a mass of brownish-grey fur. Toby Church could feel the pressing weight of stinking flesh suffocating him. He fought for air as tons of sea lion pressed down on him.

Carlos and Ben crawled through the grass to the edge of the beach on their bellies, keeping their rifles at the ready. They were expecting Church to ambush them again. He was nowhere to be seen. All they saw was a mass of undulating sea lion flesh.

"Where'd he go?" asked Ben.

"No damn idea," Carlos answered. "He's got to be around here somewhere. Even without being wounded he's not that fast."

It simply didn't make sense. They'd seen him descend to the beach. He was clearly trying to get back to his boat. Yet his boat was still there and they could not see any sign of him. It was as if he'd disappeared from the face of the Earth.

"Guess we'd better go down and check it out," Carlos said, rising slowly from his prone position. "Let's be extra careful, just in case he's hiding on the other side of the skiff or out in the water under it."

"Roger that, Lieutenant. However, I have to admit, I'm not real excited about trying to navigate through the middle of that herd. Do you think we should try and scare them into the water first?" The sea lions were clearly agitated and milling about nervously.

"Probably. How?"

Carefully, Ben slid down the embankment at the back of the herd. Raising his pistol above his head, he squeezed off two shots. The explosions echoed like a thunderclap among the boulders. Already agitated, the sea lions erupted in a cacophony of noise and charged down the beach in one great undulating mass. Most of them stormed into the surf, disappearing beneath the waves. Only the mothers with very young pups braved the shore unwilling to abandon their young. One in particular was hovering by her pup that was still bawling. He didn't appear to be injured—just scared.

From his position above the beach, Carlos spotted Church's crushed body. He was splayed across a boulder, blood running from his mouth. Their task was finished. "How the hell am I going to write this one up?" said a snickering Carlos Banderas. Somehow he would figure out how to word his report so everyone would know the nation's most famous Neo-Nazi was killed on a lonely island by a pissed-off mother sea lion.

They gathered up Church's body. Covering it with a plastic tarp from the skiff, they set up camp for the night and radioed their report back into Malloy Super Max.

Captain Anderson told them to set up a shelter, because it would be a few days before a boat could be dispatched from Adak to pick them up.

Night fell across the sea and the islands like a cloak of velvet. In the glow of a crackling driftwood fire they congratulated one another and paid homage to their fallen comrade, Corporal Travis Nelson. Above them the clouds parted briefly, exposing a sky filled with stars. It was as if Corporal Nelson were bidding them farewell and thanks.

Sitkinak Strait, Alaska

The Putin was rigged for silent running and cruising at a paltry five knots at 100 meters beneath Sitkinak Strait. Commander Ivanshenko was listening for any other warships. Sonar reported the Americans were far to the west and heading away.

"Don't you think we should increase speed, Commander?" asked Lt. Commander Vatutin.

"Not yet, Vatutin, not yet. This American commander is cunning. Once she realizes her mistake she'll head back in our direction. We will go to flank speed once the frigate turns around. Until then, we stay quiet and see how far she's going to sail in the wrong direction."

Lt. Cowdrey was piloting Hawk Two above the waves of Shelikof Strait, making for an interception point just ahead of the Russian decoy. He wanted a solid sonar signature on the submarine. *How is this Russian sub running so quiet at 22-knots?* Everyone knew that above 15-knots, a Russian submarine was very noisy.

As he brought Hawk Two to a stop, the crew chief dropped a sonobuoy into the water. Immediately, it began sending a signal. The sonarman listened through his headphones. *The target was too small to be a submarine. It must be a mechanical decoy! He'd heard the Russians had developed one. They'd been fooled!*

Lt. Cowdrey grimaced at the news. He relayed the information back to the Billings.

"Come about to course one five," ordered an angry Commander Englemann. "Make your speed two five knots and recall Hawk Two for refueling." She was furious at herself for falling for the Russian trick.

She was standing at the chart table, studying the straits and passages for the most likely route the Russian would take. She was kicking herself for biting on the decoy. *Did the Russian turn north and sail back into Shelikof Strait? No, he would not expect his team to traverse the entire width of the island for a rendezvous. Either the Russian will stay in the immediate vicinity or he will make for the South coast of the island.*

"Helm, come right to zero nine five degrees. Increase speed to 27-knots," she ordered. "Sonar keep your ears open for targets in Sitkinak Strait. Communications officer, this is the Skipper," she said keying the intercom, "have we heard from the battle group?"

"Negative, Skipper," the ensign replied. "No word from CINCPAC. And at last report the battle group was 500 miles south, southeast."

"Send a request to CINCPAC to dispatch a P-3 Orion."

"Commander, the Americans are coming about," came the call from the Putin's sonarman. "And they're picking up speed."

"Engineering, increase power on the reactor to 100 percent," Ivanshenko ordered. "Helm, take us to 200 meters and increase speed to flank. Lt. Commander Vatutin, keep a steady track on the American frigate. Lieutenant, keep your ears open for other vessels up ahead. The Americans may have another destroyer in the area."

As the 13,000-ton submarine shoved its way through the depths, its power plant was sending out subtle vibrations—

narrowband noises that are easy to track. But at flank speed the Putin had the advantage. As long as the Russians ran at full speed, the Americans would not be able to catch them. The real danger lay in the American Sea Hawk helicopter and its torpedoes.

As the frigate sliced through the waves, it slammed against quartering seas, showering the superstructure with spray. Vibrations shuddered through the ship. With the tide running hard through Sitkinak Strait, and a 20-knot wind blowing, it was an uncomfortable ride. Waves crashed over the deck. Sailors moving below decks hung onto anything bolted down. This was dangerous work, but for the most part they loved the thrill of the chase. This was stuff to tell your grandchildren—if you survived it.

"Skipper, this is Communications. I have a reply from CINCPAC."

"Very good Ensign. Bring it to me on the bridge."

The young ensign appeared a few minutes later. Englemann took the note, motioning for him to remain next to her while she read it.

TO: COMMANDER, USS BILLINGS
FR: CHIEF, NAVAL OPERATIONS, PACIFIC FLEET

USE ALL AVAILABLE FORCE TO PREVENT TARGET FROM ESCAPING. P-3 ORION ON STATION TOMORROW A.M. USS BARKSDALE, USS DONNER WILL RENDEZVOUS TOMORROW P.M. ASSUME COMMAND OF BATTLE GROUP. GOOD HUNTING.

Margaret Englemann smiled. "Very good, Ensign," she said. "Acknowledge the orders. And remember to thank the Admiral for his speedy reply. Send Lt. Commander Hastings to the bridge."

"You wanted to see me Skipper?"

"Ah, yes Brad," Englemann answered.

He noted her cheery mood. *What's up?*

She motioned for him to join her at the chart table. "I need your input. A P-3 Orion will be on station in the morning and in the afternoon we should rendezvous with the Barksdale and Donner. I will command the battle group."

Hastings pushed his cap up and let out a soft whistle. "Sounds like the old man is serious. Are we really going to sink the sub?"

"If the Russians get their hands on the prisoners, then yes, Brad, I will authorize the use of lethal force," she said coldly.

"You realize the Russians will shoot back," he said staring her in the eyes. "This Russian is no chump. Going up against an Akula is damn risky. They'll hang you from a yardarm if you lose," he said flatly. This was no time for sugar coating.

"I don't plan to lose."

"Bridge, Sonar," came the voice over the intercom, "I have a fast moving target 14 miles south southeast exiting Sitkinak Strait. Depth 200 meters. It's the Russian."

Englemann returned to her chair. "Commander Hastings, return to CIC. Helm, increase speed to flank. Sound general quarters." Picking up the phone, she called the engine room. "Engineering, I don't care how you do it, but get me 32-knots!"

"Commander," whispered Vatutin, "the American is increasing speed. They are about 23 kilometers behind us and coming on hard. Do you think they will shoot at us again?"

Ivanshenko thought carefully before replying. "The American will try to close with us in the next few hours. I think the American Commander has guessed my game. Will they shoot? Yes, I think they will shoot. And this time, Vatutin, I think the torpedoes will be armed."

Vatutin and several of the crew looked at Ivanshenko in disbelief.

Seeing the shock on their faces, Ivanshenko told them how Dr. Elizabeth LeDue was the world's foremost biological warfare scientist. Her knowledge would be invaluable to Russia and the Americans would not give her up without a fight. If Major Golkin's team succeeded in capturing her, the Americans would escalate the conflict. He was positive the Americans would attack.

Ivanshenko sprang into action. "Lt. Commander Vatutin, sound general quarters. Ready torpedoes for launching."

Commander Englemann and Commander Ivanshenko were embroiled in a lethal game of chess. Englemann hoped the Russian commandos would fail. Ivanshenko hoped he could shake off the American frigate before rendezvousing with Major Golkin. He'd never before abandoned a commando team and he did not intend to now.

Far to the south, the USS Barksdale and USS Donner were racing at flank speed through the heavy seas of the Gulf of Alaska. Their crews were busy talking among themselves. *Why were they in such a hurry?*

White House, Washington, DC

As he drove up to the East Gate of the White House, Russian Ambassador Potemkin was trying to guess what President Bainbridge wanted to talk about so suddenly. Not since the height of the Cold War had a request for a meeting arrived so unexpectedly or abruptly. The lack of diplomatic niceties in the request was most disturbing. And the Kremlin's silence did not improve matters. Potemkin had a bad feeling.

Inside the Oval Office, President Bainbridge was meeting with Admiral Quinn and General Sheridan. CIA Director Clarke was not present. President Bainbridge didn't want the CIA connected to this conversation.

During most meetings with Ambassador Potemkin, the President usually sat on the couch next to the fireplace, inviting the Ambassador to join him. This time, however, he sat behind his desk. A slight knock on the door announced the arrival of Ambassador Potemkin and his aide Sasha Akmatovka—the GRU's resident agent.

President Bainbridge walked around from behind his desk and extended his hand. "Come in, Mr. Ambassador. Ms. Akmatovka. I'm glad you could come on such short notice, especially concerning the serious nature of what we have to discuss." President Bainbridge locked eyes with Potemkin. He wanted no illusions about the nature of this meeting.

Ambassador Potemkin returned his gaze and hand squeeze. *What is going on?*

Returning to his desk, President Bainbridge motioned for the Russians to be seated on the other side of the imposing mahogany desktop. He interlaced his fingers in front of his chest and spoke in a serious tone. "Ambassador Potemkin, I have asked you here tonight to discuss a most serious matter. And I hope that by the end of our conversation my worst fears will not be realized."

Ambassador Potemkin glanced at Ms. Akmatovka. He hoped she knew what the president was talking about. However, her surprised looked told him she was in the dark, too.

President Bainbridge took note of their seemingly genuine surprise and puzzlement.

"I'm sorry, Mr. President," began Ambassador Potemkin, "but I haven't got the foggiest idea what you're talking about."

Making his face flush, a trick he'd learned in the Navy to motivate his junior officers, President Bainbridge feigned anger. "Don't pull my chain, Mr. Ambassador. Surely your government would not leave its most important Ambassador in the dark about its plans to violate American territory in a military action! That I refuse to believe!"

Potemkin was caught off guard by the president's uncharacteristic outburst. He sat silently, searching his mind for any reason for this outburst. Nothing. He couldn't think of a single bit of information that had crossed his desk in the last six weeks that would be of such importance to the Americans. He knew nothing of any proposed military actions in American territory.

"Mr. President," began Ambassador Potemkin in his best diplomatic voice, "I can assure you that I have no knowledge of any military action by my government on US soil." He held up his hand to indicate he was not finished speaking. "Furthermore, I do not believe that any such action has taken place." Holding the president's gaze in his, he paused, waiting for his patented diplomatic denial to find its mark.

President Bainbridge rose from behind his desk and walked slowly over to the map laid out on a small table just for this meeting. He invited his Russian guests to join him. Sweeping his hand over the map, President Bainbridge explained the situation to the Ambassador. "For two days, Mr. Ambassador, a Russian Akula Class submarine has been trespassing in American territorial waters off the Alaskan island of Kodiak. This submarine has landed a commando team here, at Deadman Bay. This commando team has fired upon a US Navy helicopter. And now I have a report from Admiral Quinn that your commando team has captured Dr. Elizabeth LeDue."

Believing that this disclosure would land like a bombshell, President Bainbridge watched GRU Agent Akmatovka to make sure she caught the name. "And now our intelligence is telling us that the commando team is trying to rendezvous with your submarine."

Pausing only briefly, because he didn't want to give Ambassador Potemkin an opportunity to protest, President Bainbridge proceeded to his closing statement. "And now, Mr. Ambassador I want an explanation of why your government has violated American territory, attacked one of our helicopters and is trying to kidnap an American citizen from American soil."

Ambassador Potemkin glared at his aide Akmatovka. Something big was afoot and he'd been left out of the loop. She held his stare. She had been left out of the loop too.

Breaking the heavy silence, President Bainbridge continued the meeting. "Mr. Ambassador, it appears your government has not informed you of this action. However," he said returning to his desk, "I am forced to register a strong protest that this action cannot—no—will not—be tolerated by the American people! I am giving your government exactly two hours to contact its submarine and order its withdrawal from American waters. If the submarine does not leave, I will order my battle group to sink her."

Sputtering slightly, Ambassador Potemkin tried to staff. "Mr. President, I do not think that such drastic action is necessary at this time. I think we can come to a diplomatic solution."

Unwilling to listen to any evasions, President Bainbridge assured Ambassador Potemkin he was not interested in a diplomatic solution. If the submarine left for open water, he would return the commandos without fanfare or press releases. If the submarine did not leave, he would order her sunk and would arrest and put the commandos on trial for the world to see. With that, he thanked Ambassador Potemkin for his time and had his secretary show them to their limousine.

After watching the Russians pull away from the White House, and after a quick check by the Secret Service for any bugs that might have been planted by Agent Akmatovka, President Bainbridge turned to his military advisors. "Well, gentlemen, do you think we'll get the desired result?"

The balding General Sheridan was the first to speak, spinning his drink between his hands. "That was a pretty strong presentation, Mr. President. As long as we're not bluffing I think we're in a pretty good position. However, if I know the Russians, they are probably going to bet we won't follow through with our threat."

"General," replied the President, "I can assure you my statements to the ambassador were not a threat, but a promise. I will not allow the Russians to take Dr. LeDue off that island—even if I have to bury 73 Russian sailors at the bottom of the North Pacific."

Clearing his throat before he spoke, Admiral Quinn stood up from his chair and walked over to the map. "You realize Mr. President, that even if the Russians agree to withdraw their submarine, they will probably not be able to contact her. She's submerged, and unless they have some new kind of communications equipment we don't know about, they will not be able to send an order for her to withdraw." He took a few moments to let that information sink in. Next he pointed out the obvious. "I'm afraid, Mr. President, you're going to have to sink that submarine."

Staring out the window, President Bainbridge replied, "I know that, Admiral. I just wanted to give the Russians a chance to save those men's lives if possible."

The Kremlin, Moscow

The corridor in the Kremlin was quiet except for the footsteps of Admiral Voroshilov and Captain Gromyko echoing off the marbled floors. Dressed in their dark blue uniforms, they were heading to the Prime Minister's office at the far end of the building. Despite the very early hour, several offices were busy with activity. Both officers found this unusual, even for the Kremlin. They looked at each other. Something was afoot—and it probably wasn't good.

Passing through the door, Admiral Voroshilov found himself in the Prime Minister's outer office. Seated across the room, drinking tea, was Admiral Bulgakov's aide-de-camp.

"Good morning, Commander Blucher," greeted Admiral Voroshilov, trying to sound more upbeat than he felt. "I'm surprised to find you here so early in the morning."

"Good morning, Admiral," replied the pudgy, but brilliant Blucher. "I trust your flight from Vladivostok was pleasant, and that you bring good news?" He shot a hopeful glance towards Captain Gromyko.

Admiral Voroshilov shook his head 'no' as he looked around the room for the coffee pot. He avoided discussing the situation by walking over to the table. He needed some food. The coffee was dark and steaming—a good Turkish blend. Three lumps of sugar and a good dollop of cream made the brew very tasty.

"Commander Blucher," called the Chief-of-Naval-Operations, Admiral Bulgakov, from inside the Prime Minister's office, "have you seen Admiral Voroshilov yet?"

"Yes sir," Commander Blucher responded. "Admiral Voroshilov just arrived. He's getting a cup of coffee."

"Well, just don't stand there! Send him in!" Bulgakov bellowed.

"Good morning Mr. Prime Minister," said Admiral Voroshilov as he entered the spacious office, closing the door behind him. "I presume by your presence at this most inconvenient hour that you have important news?" He looked around the room. Joining the meeting were the foreign minister, GRU General Chernikov and Army General Vasilof.

Prime Minister Kirov motioned for Admiral Voroshilov to make himself comfortable. A classmate of Voroshilov's at Leningrad State University's College of Engineering, Leo Kirov had a soft spot in his heart for his old classmate. He knew all the blame being placed on his old friend was undeserved, however unavoidable it might be.

"Admiral Voroshilov," began Kirov, staring at his friend with his light blue eyes, "do you have any news from your submarine?"

"No, Mr. Prime Minister," replied Admiral Voroshilov, making sure to hold his good friend's gaze. "We have not heard from the Putin since she radioed she was proceeding to the last known coordinates of the American transport." Voroshilov noticed how gray Kirov's hair had become since his election.

Kirov dipped his chin and exhaled deeply. He realized his military advisors had misled him. Still, he needed to keep up appearances. Rising from his desk, he put on his best scowl, ordering Admiral Voroshilov to give the assembled members a briefing of the known events over the last two days. He took up his seat next to the window, away from the noxious cigarette smoke.

Admiral Voroshilov started by piecing together, as best he could with his sporadic intelligence, what had taken place over the last two days. "In conclusion, gentlemen, I must admit I do not know if the Putin has accomplished her mission, failed, or is lost at sea."

Watching everyone's eyes dart around the room after his closing statement, Voroshilov realized they hadn't been up all night drinking and playing cards. Something had gone terribly wrong and they were expecting him to save them. He was being put on the spot. He turned to Prime Minister Kirov, looking for more information.

Seeing Voroshilov's confused look, Prime Minister Kirov began, "Last night, President Bainbridge summoned Ambassador

Potemkin to the White House. He informed Potemkin that the American Navy is pursuing one of our Akula Class submarines off the coast of Kodiak Island. He knows we have inserted a Spetsnaz team on the island and that they're trying to capture the American scientist. He told the Ambassador that if we don't withdraw the Putin from American territorial waters, he will order her to be attacked." Kirov's hands trembled as he spoke.

"What is going on out there, Admiral Voroshilov?" growled Admiral Bulgakov. "Your incompetence has placed the Prime Minister in a very awkward position."

Voroshilov was unmoved. Once again, Admiral Bulgakov was trying to place all the blame for the mission's current predicament on his shoulders. *Maintain your composure.* "Admiral Bulgakov," replied Admiral Voroshilov in his most saccharine tone, "you know as well as I that this plan had the blessing of all of the men in this room. If Prime Minister Kirov is in a precarious position today, it is because you did not invite me to the initial briefing."

Bulgakov bristled at Voroshilov's insubordination. His face turned red. "What do you mean by that?" he shouted, spraying the air with a mist of saliva.

Voroshilov's barb had found its mark. Carefully, he adjusted his tunic and touched his campaign ribbons. In a cool, rhythmic cadence he explained how excluding him from the meeting with the prime minister and foreign minister had led to certain facts being omitted from the briefing. He emphasized that Admiral Bulgakov had purposely failed to inform the prime minister about the mission's low probability of success.

Generals Chernikov and Vasilof sat next to the window, keeping silent. They hoped blame for this debacle would land on the Navy, thereby sparing them the wrath of the prime minister and the Duma (The Russian National Legislature.)

Trying to regain control of the meeting, Prime Minister Kirov pointed out he was not holding a meeting to assign blame. He was trying to find a solution to a very serious problem—one that held the potential to bring down his government. "Gentlemen, I don't care who said what. What I want to know is how do we get our submarine out of there and get our commandos back home."

The room was silent.

Admiral Voroshilov wondered why they paid these pompous windbags. Realizing no one had the courage to speak the truth, he decided he had to. As he refilled his coffee cup, he searched for a delicate way to relay such abysmal news. He couldn't think of any kind way to say what he had to say. "Mr. Prime Minister," he began in a somber tone, "I cannot think of a diplomatic way to say this. Unless the Putin comes to the surface, there is no way we can send a message to her to abort the mission. Given the fact that the American Navy is hunting her, I think it is unlikely Commander Ivanshenko will surface his boat."

Groans erupted around the room.

"I take it by this answer, Admiral," said Prime Minister Kirov above the grumbling, "that the Putin will be sunk by the Americans?"

"No, not at all Mr. Prime Minister," Voroshilov responded. He wanted to give his friend some hope in a hopeless situation. "Commander Ivanshenko is my best submarine commander. He is dogged and brilliant. He will surface to pick up the Spetsnaz team if he can shake the Americans. If he cannot shake the Americans, he will withdraw and return in a week or so to extract the commandos."

"So what do I tell President Bainbridge?" asked Kirov.

Voroshilov thought for a moment, before giving his old friend an answer. "Tell President Bainbridge you will try to send a satellite communication to the submarine and order it to withdraw. Tell him you do not expect the communication to be received. Ask him for ten hours to carry out this task before he authorizes lethal force. If after ten hours, the submarine has not withdrawn, you will work with him on a plausible cover story for the loss of the Putin." He lit another cigarette.

"I disagree," said GRU General Chernikov speaking for the first time. "I think we should warn the Americans not to attack our submarine and order the Putin to go on the offensive."

Hearing this, the foreign minister joined into the conversation. "Are you an idiot, General?" he snapped. "We have violated American territory, shot at one of their helicopters, and are trying to kidnap an American citizen. Just how do you propose to we justify more aggression?"

"It's not as if the Americans never violated our territory," General Vasilof reminded everyone. "Don't any of you remember their cable tapping operations in the Sea of Okhost or off Murmansk? This is a game of tit-for-tat, gentlemen. President Bainbridge is no more anxious to have this incident spread across the world than we are."

Good, thought Admiral Voroshilov, *one can always count on Vasilof to bring things into perspective.*

"Vasilof and Voroshilov are correct," concluded Prime Minister Kirov. "I will inform President Bainbridge that I will attempt to recall the Putin." Turning to Admiral Voroshilov, he asked, "Do you think we have a chance of recalling her?"

"Not a chance," replied Voroshilov flatly. "Our only hope is that Ivanshenko is as brilliant as I think he is."

Kodiak Island, Alaska

Commissioner Burke and Officers Marston and Price exited the helicopter on a ridge to the east and uphill from the Russians most likely path and spread out, taking up positions behind two rock outcroppings. Across the valley, Major Calhoun and his team headed for the top of the tallest ridge in the area—an ideal location to catch sight of the fleeing Russians in the valley below.

To the northwest of Burke's position, Lt. Surin and Harry Ignustuk were leading their men cautiously through the bottom of the valley towards the ridge where the Russians had first been seen.

"When you catch sight of the Americans, Korkov," instructed Major Golkin, "I want you, Rudenko, and Balzan to shoot over their heads." With his finger he emphasized his point and said, "I don't want anybody killed. Do you understand?" His eyes and tone were cold.

"Yes, Major."

"When the Americans return fire, you are to retreat. I will cover you from that ridge," he said pointing with the barrel of his rifle at the ridge from where they had just descended. "This should confuse the Americans as to our location and number. I will then make my own way to the rendezvous point." Before parting, he again emphasized in his most stern demeanor, "It is absolutely vital you do not kill any of the Americans or be captured. I am trusting in your skills."

"You can count on me, Major," Korkov responded proudly.

A few miles to the southeast, Captain Petrov and Sgt. Timoshenko were leading their captives along a game trail through the brush at the bottom of the valley. Overhead they could hear helicopters flying up and down the mountain passes. The light was growing dim. It'd been a long day. Come nightfall they would have to slow down.

Joy's legs ached. *How on Earth did I get caught up in all this? Should I try to run for it? Will they kill me if I run? How will I survive in this wilderness if I escape? Why is Elizabeth going along with all this?*

The willow branch slapping her across her forehead brought her back to reality. "Ouch!" she cried. She ran her hand over her forehead. A welt rose just above her eyes.

"Quiet!" Sgt. Timoshenko growled. "No talking, and keep your eyes open." He was annoyed with his captive. He pushed her in the back, motioning for her to close the distance with Captain Petrov and Elizabeth LeDue.

Captain Petrov turned to speak to Sgt. Timoshenko in Russian. "We're at the edge of the forest. From here on out we're going to be moving in the open. Do you think the Americans will spot us?"

"Hard to say Captain," Timoshenko replied thoughtfully. "By the sounds of it, the helicopters are moving off to the north and east. Now is as good a time as any."

"Let's go," ordered Captain Petrov. Gently, he pushed Elizabeth on the shoulder, pointing in the direction he wanted her to go.

Elizabeth stumbled out of the trees and into the grassy expanse that covered the steep hillside. Her legs felt like rubber and deep inside she struggled with feelings of shame for betraying her country. *But what options do I have?* She convinced herself that once they made it to Russia, the Russians would release Joy Frank. *Surely they won't kill an innocent American girl?*

Directly in front of Captain Petrov, on a hillside, high above the brush-filled valley, Karen Marston was waiting patiently behind the rocks. She had been the first to catch sight of the Russians emerging from the willows with the two women. "They're coming out of the woods Commissioner," she whispered.

"Where?" he asked anxiously.

"There," she said pointing, "down the valley at about twelve o'clock and 1,500 yards." In their camouflage, the soldiers were hard to spot, but Elizabeth LeDue's prisoner jumpsuit was very visible.

"Do we shoot them, or arrest them, Commissioner?" asked Officer Price.

"Good question," Burke responded. If they started shooting without giving a warning, he would be violating the very policy he'd helped write over 15 years ago. But in order to give an order to halt, he would have to expose his position. The likelihood of the Russians surrendering would be nil.

Karen Marston fidgeted. The Russians were getting closer. "Commissioner. They're getting too close for comfort."

Burke had no choice. "Marston," he asked quietly, "do you think you can wound LeDue without hitting any of the others?"

She looked down the slope at the grass swaying in the wind, checking its strength and direction. It was gusting and unpredictable. "Maybe," she replied, "if I can time my shot between gusts."

Burke made his decision. He tapped Officer Martson on the shoulder, signaling her to shoot LeDue. He ordered Price to move into a flanking position on the left, while he took up a firing position to the right. He was counting on Major Calhoun rolling up the Russians' left flank.

Marston had grown up shooting cans with her older brother on the windswept prairies of Wyoming. If she could hit a tin can in that wind, surely she could shoot a fugitive in the leg. She timed her breathing, waiting for the wind to die down. Exhaling slightly, she held her breath, and squeezed the trigger on her M-16 Assault Rifle. With a crack, the bullet went streaking towards its target. Before the sound of the shot could travel across the valley, blood spewed from Timoshenko's back. She'd missed!

"How the hell did I miss?"

Burke didn't say a word. He just groaned. *How am I going to explain this?*

A great "umph" erupted from Timoshenko's lips as the bullet hit him. The impact spun him around and to the ground.

Captain Petrov reacted instantly. He shoved Elizabeth to the ground, falling on top of her. Out of the corner of his eye he saw Joy bolt from the group and run down the hillside. Instinctively, he raised his rifle to shoot her before she could make her escape. But he couldn't pull the trigger. He had a daughter about her age.

"Keep your head down," Petrov ordered Elizabeth before crawling over to Timoshenko.

Timoshenko was lying face down in the grass, blooding spurting from the back of his protruding ribs, where the bullet had torn a gaping exit wound. He struggled to get to his rifle lying just a few feet away.

"Sergeant," Petrov commanded in his most calming tone, "be still. I'll get your rifle. Can you move or shoot?"

Blood-filled mist sprayed from his mouth when he tried to speak.

Captain Petrov realized he would soon be dead. He pulled out a cyanide capsule and placed it in Timoshenko's mouth.

Before biting down on the poison, Timoshenko reached inside his coat and took out a letter to his wife. He handed it to Petrov and asked in a raspy voice for a promise to deliver it to her.

Silently and with much regret, Petrov took the letter, nodding a promise to deliver it.

With a gurgle, Timoshenko took his last breath.

Cursing under his breath, Captain Petrov crawled back up the hillside to Elizabeth. He could see three people hiding in the rocks on the ridge above. Their lack of aggression was puzzling, given the favorable odds in this fight. Then he saw their uniforms. They were not soldiers. They were policemen. Their failure to catch him in a crossfire would be their undoing.

While the situation on the hillside remained static, Joy ran for all she was worth. She ignored the burning in her legs and lungs and barreled down the slope, gaining speed—too much speed. She tripped over a rock. With a thud, she hit the ground. Before she could catch herself, she began rolling over the bumpy terrain and down the grassy slope. Grunts erupted from her lungs as she bounced over the ground. Desperately, she tried to stop her descent. But without any branches, sticks or bushes to grab, it was a freefall. Luckily, there were few exposed rocks.

She bounced into a shallow depression and came to an abrupt stop. Her head was spinning. Her ribs hurt. Regaining her senses, she looked back up the hill to see if the Russians were pursuing her. *Was that a gunshot I heard just after the Russian soldier was knocked to the ground? Never mind,* she said to herself. *It doesn't matter. I'm free!*

Gingerly at first and then with more vigor she moved her slender arms and finely muscled legs measuring their movements, trying to gauge the extent of her injuries. Gaining more confidence with each movement, she decided she had some whopping bruises, but no broken bones. Tears of happiness ran down her muddy face as she realized her ordeal was over. Sobs racked her body as the stress from all she had endured came bubbling to the surface.

From the ridgeline high above the valley, Major Golkin was watching the Americans advance down the valley along the edge of the trees. To the south, he could see Sergeant Korkov disperse his men in a staggered arc. *Good placement—just right to catch the Americans in a crossfire.*

The Americans were moving as quickly as they could while being careful not to stumble into an ambush. Lt. Surin knew the Russians would be beating a hasty retreat, but he also knew from experience that the Spetsnaz liked to draw you into a chase and then turn on you when you least expected it—an ancient Mongol tactic everyone learned in command school.

Abruptly, Harry raised his arm. Everyone in the group froze. He sniffed the air, trying to identify the strange odor wafting in the swirling breeze. He couldn't quite place it. It wasn't a bear and it wasn't plants. He inhaled deeply. *Men—men who had not bathed in several days.* Human oils and sweat mixed with garlic and other strong spices—and cigarettes—heavy acrid odors from very powerful tobacco.

He motioned for everyone to kneel down and moved over to Lt. Surin's position a few yards to his left. "Lieutenant," he whispered, "there are several men upwind of us. Up there, beyond the woods, on the other side of the stream."

Surin, an experienced combat leader, looked at Harry with skepticism. He could hear nothing except the wind in the branches and the gurgling of the water in the stream to their right. "And how," he questioned cynically, "can you tell that?"

"Smell 'em," Harry said matter-of-factly.

Cocking an eyebrow, Surin scoffed. "Smell 'em? What do you mean you smell 'em?"

Harry didn't let the Lieutenant's barb get under his skin. "Been smelling game longer than you been alive Lieutenant. You can trust me and live, or ignore me and walk right into their ambush." Harry finished his point with a slight Eskimo smile and a twinkle in his eye.

Sensing there was more to this Eskimo than appeared on the surface, Surin decided that being able to smell an adversary was not outside the realm of possibility.

"Okay Ignustuk, I'll buy your nose. Just where are they and how many?"

"I'm good Lieutenant, but I'm not Superman," Harry answered flatly. "They must be to the south, probably lying in wait for us to cross the river. And," he said quietly, "I think we're being watched."

"Danny," Harry ordered, "get out your binoculars. See if you can't see someone up on the hillside to our left. From the same location where the Russians hid before."

Danny took out his binoculars and scanned the hillside. His heart was pounding. He loved the chase. This was exciting. "Can't see a thing Harry, not a damn thing."

Lt. Surin came up with a plan. Taking Danny Sanders with him, he started moving further uphill to their left, in an attempt to turn the Russians' right flank. At the same time, he sent Harry and Sgt. Ali downhill to execute another flanking maneuver on the Russians. To hold the Russians' attention, he sent Sgt. Ramirez directly across the stream through the woods to attack the Russian center.

Major Golkin watched the Americans disperse into their three groups. He was impressed. These were not ordinary American soldiers and policemen. They had sensed the trap and were moving to cut off the Russian retreat.

Raising his rifle, Golkin took aim at the two Americans moving up the hill towards him. He squeezed the trigger, firing a bullet into a large boulder just above Lt. Surin and Danny Sanders. Moments later the rifle report echoed across the valley.

Surin and Sanders dropped to the ground, rifles at the ready.

"Where the hell did that come from?" exclaimed Danny.

Surin looked up. He could see where the bullet had ricocheted off a boulder up on the hillside. "By the looks of that rock," he said pointing to the spot about 5 feet up the hill, "I'd say the sniper is on the hillside where we first spotted the Russians."

As soon as he heard the shot, Korkov ordered his men back down the valley. If Major Golkin was shooting, the Americans had sensed his trap.

Breaking from his hiding spot, Major Golkin intentionally stood erect. He wanted the Americans to see him. *Maybe I can draw them off?*

"Up there on the hillside," Danny said excitedly to Lt. Surin, pointing to the man moving quickly up the steep slope to the east.

"Ignore him," came Harry's gruff response. The minute he'd heard the shot he headed over to their position. "It's a ruse. The main body of the Russians is to the south. And," he continued, "I saw them retreating from their positions. We need to move now."

Lt. Surin agreed with Harry. The sniper was a decoy. If the Russians had taken Dr. LeDue and Joy Frank up the hill to the east, they would have spotted them. The only logical course for the Russians to follow was to retreat down the valley to the south.

"Let's move out," ordered Lt. Surin. "And keep your eyes open. I don't want any casualties."

As he crested the ridge, Major Golkin glanced back down the hill to see if the Americans had taken the bait. He was disappointed. Through his field glasses, he could see the five Americans moving into the woods along the stream. A few minutes later, he saw them exit on the other side—directly on the heels of Korkov and his men.

Captain Petrov was still lying prone on the slope of the mountain, thinking about how to extricate himself and his prize from the clutches of the Americans. He was in a pickle and he knew it. He was outnumbered. *But,* he reminded himself, *there are always alternatives. I will not surrender easily. The Americans are going to have to work for their victory.*

For Elizabeth LeDue this whole scene was surreal. Never in her wildest dreams did she imagine anything like this could happen.

On the hill above Captain Petrov and Elizabeth LeDue, Dick Burke was discussing his options with his team. None of them had a clear shot. In order to close the distance and surround their quarry, they would have to expose themselves. This would give the Russian an opportunity to shoot one of them. It was a stalemate.

Joy, on the other hand, was bound by no such restrictions. *Why didn't Elizabeth try to run when she had the opportunity?* "Don't forget," she said aloud, "Elizabeth LeDue is a criminal."

As she stood up, Joy caught sight of Lt. Surin's team far in the distance heading towards her from the north. *Are they Americans or Russians?* She was unsure of what to do. Her chest felt tight. She didn't want to be a prisoner again.

Looking around, she could see the Russians. They were heading towards her too. Even farther to the northeast was a lone figure moving parallel to her position along the top of the ridgeline. It didn't take a genius to know that events were about to heat up.

It was time to make a decision. She moved into a hollow to get out of the wind. She was going to sit tight and wait.

Larsen Bay, Alaska

"What do you mean, Dick Burke has taken a team to the far side of the island?" bellowed George Roberts. "I thought I made it clear. We were to have a meeting before any further action." He looked accusingly at Michelle Dornier, waiting for an answer.

Dornier kept her composure. Roberts had not given any specific instructions to either her or Commissioner Burke not to proceed with the search. Besides, she emphasized, it was important to act on the information they'd received about contact being made with the fugitives and Russians on the Southern side of the island. Now was not the time for recriminations, she argued, it was time to formulate a plan for handling Dr. LeDue once she was back in custody.

Dornier went over the plan to cut off the Russian retreat. Listing the alternatives, she pointed out how the most logical site was in Kaiugnak Bay. She explained how Commissioner Burke and Major Calhoun were going to insert themselves between the river valley and the bay.

Following her overview, she opened up the discussion of how, and where, they were going to transport Elizabeth LeDue. Should they take her back to Anchorage to face criminal charges for escape and murder? Or, since Alaska did not have the death penalty and she was serving life without parole, should they send her to Adak without filing new charges?

"She deserves to die for killing that fisherman," argued the Mayor.

"I agree with the Mayor," said Roberts, "but applying the death penalty would take a statutory change and would only apply to crimes committed after it became law."

"She could be put to death if they tried her under federal law," the Mayor countered. He was unwilling to concede his point. Murderers deserved to die.

"I understand your desire for revenge Mr. Mayor," said Dornier, "but you have to realize we are getting ahead of ourselves. First we need to catch her. Then we need to make sure she is securely behind bars. After all that," she said making a dramatic sweep with her arm, "we can debate the finer points of what to do with her. Don't forget that there is no statute of limitations on murder. And your argument about prosecuting her under federal law has some merit, although she was in state custody at the time. This is a problem our lawyers can argue about later."

"I suppose you're right," he conceded reluctantly.

"Now that we've settled that," said Dornier, changing the subject, "we need to discuss how to get Elizabeth LeDue to Malloy Super Max after we catch her."

Roberts was annoyed. *I'm being manipulated, but I'm damned if I know how to stop it.*

Dornier turned on her feminine charm, diffusing George Roberts' frustration. "I know you want to be out there hunting her, George, but if we're going to get Dr. LeDue to Adak, we need to get Larsen Bay's airstrip operational and made longer for the department's backup C-130. I need you and the Mayor to recruit some people to fix the runway. And," she said touching his forearm with her delicate fingers, "we need to coordinate a search of the town's ruins for any survivors."

Roberts gave up. He'd been outmaneuvered. Before she could come up with another idea, he took the Mayor by the arm and led him out into the gym in search of volunteers. They had a lot of work to do.

"I'll let you know about any new developments," Dornier shouted as she watched them disappear into a crowd of people at the far end of the gym.

"Base, this is Burke, over."

"Go ahead, Burke. I read you loud and clear," Dornier answered excitedly. *Maybe they've captured LeDue?*

"We have made contact with the Russians and Dr. LeDue. We are attempting to surround them. Dispatch helicopters to assist, over."

Michelle Dornier grinned—finally some good news. Affirming the message, she ripped off her headphones and ran outside. Jumping on a four-wheeler, she zoomed down the road to the airport. They had done a good job guessing the Russians' escape route.

Arriving at the airport a few minutes later, she leapt off the machine and raced into the small airport office. It was empty.

Looking out the window, she saw the chopper pilots refueling and inspecting their equipment. Near the middle of the gravel runway, George Roberts was working side by side with several other men filling in holes in the runway.

Jogging out of the office and over to the pilots, she instructed them to hurry up and finish with their refueling and inspections. They needed to rendezvous with Commissioner Burke, who had the Russians pinned down on the hillside. "Get moving. Now," she ordered.

Homer, Alaska

"But Dad," argued Joseph Lind, "you don't understand."

"Yes, I do, Son," Alfred replied as kindly as he could, "but your mother and I need you here to help put the house and pier back together. I'm sure those two officers will bring Joy back safe."

Maureen Lind looked into her son's eyes, placed her hands on his shoulders and squeezed. She understood what it was like to wait for news about a loved one. She had grown up in a fishing family and after being married to a Bering Sea fisherman all of her adult life, she had spent many long hours and days anxiously awaiting the return of her husband.

Joseph, however, was stubborn. "Dad, I love Joy. I need to tell her that I love her."

"Joseph," Maureen interrupted, "Joy knows you love her. She'd have to be blind not to see it."

"Besides that Joseph," Alfred argued, "just how do you propose to get to Kodiak? And if you get there, how do plan on finding her?"

Joseph hung his head and sat down with a thud. He knew his parents were right, but that didn't make it any easier. He was worried sick about Joy and terrified that he would never get to see her again.

Sitkalidak Straits, Kodiak Island, Alaska

Ivanshenko checked his watch. He was plotting the time necessary to sail into Three Saints Bay. Night would fall in about four hours. He needed the cover of darkness to execute his plan. The next few hours would be the most dangerous. When night fell, he would have to bring the Putin to the surface to make radio contact with Major Golkin. Once Golkin radioed in, Ivanshenko would have to navigate his boat closer to the shore. All of these maneuvers would expose the Putin to detection by the Americans. If he weren't both careful and lucky, he would find himself trapped once again.

Ivanshenko was worried. He could see the strain on his men's faces. They were at the breaking point. So was he for that matter. And now he had to make contact with Golkin and sail into uncharted waters under the cover of darkness. *Maybe it's time to retire*, he thought.

After instructing Lt. Commander Vatutin to keep the Putin stationary just outside Kaiugnak Bay, Ivanshenko retired to his cabin for some much needed rest. He sat down to his afternoon cup of tea and honey and began making his personal log entries. Putting his pen down, he went over to his bunk to get some rest. He needed a clear head to get them in and out of the treacherously narrow Three Saints Bay without getting caught.

"Where is she?" asked Commander Englemann pointedly.

"We've lost her Skipper," came the apologetic reply from Lt. Commander Hastings in the CIC.

She rubbed her temples. "Very well. Meet me in my quarters."

Lt. Commander Hastings knocked on the door, waiting to be invited into her quarters.

"Come in, Commander."

"Thank you, Skipper," he said peering around the edge of the door before entering. She was studying a chart of the area, which was spread out on her table. She looked very tired. He knew she was trying to divine just where the Russian submarine had disappeared over one hour ago. He joined her without saying a word. Only the smile on his face let her know he still had confidence in her abilities.

"Where did we lose her, Brad?" she asked tersely.

He placed his finger at the point marked 'Tallapoosa Shoal.'

She strummed her finger on her chin. Tallapoosa Shoal gave the Russians a lot of places to hide. With ridges and reefs and massive boulders, the Billings' sonar would be largely ineffective, if the Russian commander had brought his boat to a full stop and then bottomed her. She shook off this thought. *Not even this Russian would take such a dangerous risk.* Bottoming the submarine took the chance of breeching the hull or fouling the propeller.

Hastings watched her shake off an improbable thought. After so many years working with one person, you get to know their idiosyncrasies. Then he saw her smile. He asked, "What is it Skipper?"

She looked up and said, "Nothing Brad, just a crazy thought."

"Well?" he asked curiously.

"What would you do if you were in command of that Russian submarine?" Englemann often placed Hastings in this role. He had a talent for thinking like an adversary. *He's ready for his own command*, she reminded herself. She promised herself to personally recommend him to Admiral Quinn after this mission.

"If I were the Russian," he said, "I would figure I couldn't outrun the American frigate all day and make my rendezvous. I would have to shake off my pursuer. My crew would be tired. I would be tired. I would run to the shoals, order all stop in about 50 meters of water, and bottom the boat. Then I would wait for my enemy to sail past me and move off to a safe distance where I could run at three to five knots to my rendezvous under the cover of darkness."

A smile flashed across Englemann's face. That was how the Russians had ducked her pursuit. *He has bottomed his boat!* She had to admire the Russian commander's bravado. He was willing to take risks. This was the only way he could avoid detection in the narrow confines of the bay. Besides, the rest of the bay was too deep to bottom the boat.

Phoning the bridge, Englemann ordered the Billings to come about and take up station over the Tallapoosa Shoals. She also ordered Hawk Two to return to the ship.

Next she ordered the crew to plot all surface contacts in the area of Kaiugnak Bay and Three Saints Bay. She looked at her watch—they were about four hours away from nightfall. She cancelled general quarters. Division heads were given instructions to have their men rotate to chow, get some rest and report to their stations 30 minutes before nightfall. Finally, she ordered some food, asked for a status report on the USS Barksdale and USS Donner, and went to the head to freshen up before the tonight's action.

In the CIC, an officer was plotting the locations of three surface contacts. Two were circling outside the entrance of Kaiugnak Bay. The other one was circling just off the coast of tiny John Island near the mouth of Three Saints Bay. He knew these vessels were fishing boats. Their large radar signal relative to their length told him they had lots of poles and masts hanging from the superstructure for their salmon nets. He ordered a seaman to go topside and get a visual identification.

Beneath the waters of Kaiugnak Bay, Commander Ivanshenko was also tracking the two fishing vessels trolling above him. He was counting on them come darkness.

Malloy Super Max, Adak Island, Alaska

The news of Toby Church's death sent a wave of relief through the officers of Malloy Super Max. Lt. Banderas's radio report was a bright spot in what had been another stressful day at the prison.

While the citizens of Adak, under the exemplary leadership of Father Androvsky, had cleaned up the battered remains of what once was a proud community, the officers in Malloy were reeling from the news of the deaths of Blaine Smith, Joan Steiger, and Doreen Evers in the plane crash outside Cold Bay.

Marc Anderson took the news of Officer Smith's death particularly hard. After all, he was the one who had ordered him on that crazy mission.

"How ya' doing?" asked a concerned Sgt. Knight.

"Feeling pretty guilty," replied Anderson.

"Guilty?" Knight asked in surprise. "What the hell you feeling guilty about?"

"Jesus, Bill," growled Anderson, "I was the one who sent Smith on that damned-fool flight. I was the one who sent Travis Nelson on the hunt for Toby Church." He looked at Sgt. Knight like he of all people should understand his feelings.

Knight poured himself a cup of coffee and sat down across the desk from Anderson. "Command is not easy Marc, you know that. We were—are facing a crisis and you acted with the best information available. We are in the business of dealing with bad people. Sometimes people are going to die."

"I know that Bill. But it doesn't make it any easier," Anderson answered, running his hands over his face.

Knight slapped his hand against his knee and got up. "Never going to be easy Marc. But right now we have two officers on Amchitka Island, who are going to spend a cold night out in the rain and wind. We need to get them home. Time to stop feeling sorry for yourself."

Anderson knew he was right. He decided to make another call to Governor Malloy in Juneau. He hoped he would be home.

"Hello, this is Rick Malloy."

"Governor. This is Captain Anderson at Malloy Super Max."

"Good evening, Captain. How're you doing? What's up now?" asked Governor Malloy. *Why is Anderson calling me so soon after our last conversation?*

"Good news, bad news, Governor."

"Yes?" replied Governor Malloy cautiously.

Anderson told the Governor about the death of Toby Church on Amchitka. Then he told him about the deaths of Nurse Evers, and Officers Nelson, Steiger, and Smith.

"Kind of an ignominious end for Mr. Church, wouldn't you say Captain?" said Governor Malloy. While he was immensely relieved that one problem was solved, he was genuinely upset over the deaths of so many officers.

"Going to be a hard one to describe for the press, Governor," Anderson replied trying to suppress a laugh. *How do you tell the media that the nation's most notorious terrorist was killed by an angry mother sea lion?*

Hesitant to impose on Governor Malloy, but desperate for help, Anderson continued speaking, "Governor, I have favor to ask."

"Go ahead, Captain, I think you and your officers have earned one."

"Could you send a ship to Amchitka to pick up my officers and would you attend the memorial services for our fallen officers?"

"Already done Captain, and yes I would consider it an honor to attend the memorial services."

As he was hanging up the phone, Captain Anderson heard a call on the radio, "SS, this is Alpha."

What's up at this hour of the evening? "Go Alpha."

"Captain, there's a submarine coming into Kuluk Bay. It's approaching the remains of the deep water pier."

"I'm on my way." *What's a submarine doing here?* He wanted to get a look at this himself.

Winded after climbing the tower ladder, Captain Anderson held out his hand for the binoculars. He focused on the black mass moving across the bay. There it was—a huge black submarine flying an American flag.

"I'll be damned," muttered Captain Anderson. "Sgt. Knight, this is the SS."

"Go SS."

"Take a team of two armed officers and proceed to the old submarine pier. It looks like we have visitors."

Bill Knight and his men arrived just as the men of the USS Hammerhead were tying off their lines. They waved a greeting.

Up on the bridge, Commander Jones and his executive officer saluted. Their smiles turned to frowns of dismay as they saw the devastation caused by the earthquake and tsunami. Adak lay in ruins. Jones didn't recognize the town. He had put in here regularly as a junior officer during the Cold War.

"What brings you to Adak?" greeted Sgt. Knight, walking down the buckled remains of the pier. He took Commander Jones's hand in his, shaking it vigorously.

"Thought you might need some help."

"That we do," answered Sgt. Knight turning around to display the carnage with a sweep of his arm. "Let me take you to my leader," Knight said jokingly.

Captain Anderson welcomed the naval officers to his office. Following formal introductions, he invited them to make themselves comfortable. The conversation covered the events of the last two days.

"Can we speak confidentially Captain?" asked Commander Jones.

"Absolutely, Commander. Just let me close my door," Anderson replied rising from his seat and shutting the door.

"Captain," Jones began, "we just didn't drop in to see how you're doing." He was smiling, because he knew Captain Anderson was too smart to have bought that cover story. "Officially, we are here to deliver supplies. Unofficially, we are on a special mission related to the transport of Dr. Elizabeth LeDue to Malloy Super Max."

"Okay," interjected Captain Anderson, "but why are you here on Adak?"

"Quite frankly, I don't know why we were ordered here. But my orders were clear. Make port in Adak and render assistance."

Anderson knew why they were there. He sent a silent thank you to Governor Malloy for getting General McCarthy to ask the Navy for assistance. *Too bad they arrived too late to save Corporal Nelson.*

"Well Commander," responded Captain Anderson, "your assistance is most appreciated. Perhaps your doctor could take a look at a few of our more seriously injured citizens? And, if it's not too much trouble, I have two men on Amchitka Island who would like to come home."

Kodiak Island, Alaska

Slowly, Captain Petrov raised his rifle, whispering to Elizabeth to get ready to run back into the woods at his signal.

She looked at him like he was crazy. "What? Are you mad? The minute we move they'll shoot us."

"No they won't," Petrov growled in a hushed voice. "When I say move, I will open fire. You," he said emphasizing the word, "will jump up and run back to the trees. Once you're in the trees, I will follow."

"But they'll shoot you," she argued, "just like they did your partner."

He shook his head at her ignorance. She had no idea just how difficult it is to hit a moving target—a problem compounded by strong gusting winds.

Commissioner Burke and PTOs Marston and Price could see that the Russian was getting ready to make a move. "What's he up to," asked PTO Price.

"Don't know," answered Burke. *Where are Major Calhoun and his men? They should be arriving any time now.*

Moving up from the valley below, Major Calhoun was amazed at how far it was from their perch across the valley to Commissioner Burke's position. As a crow flies, it wasn't far at all. But on the ground it was a considerable distance. The rugged terrain made for very difficult hiking for him and his men. Only the dogs were moving without trouble.

Watching the men move up the valley didn't give Joy any sense of comfort. She couldn't tell which group was American and which was Russian. Her instincts told her to run, but her mind kept telling her that one of them had to be friendly. She wished Joseph were there with her. She was scared and he always made her feel better.

As the men got closer, Joy saw they were wearing blue uniforms. The reflection of a badge on a hat caught her eye. *Police. Thank God!*

She prepared to move. Then she heard shots echo across the valley. She fell to the ground covering her head with her hands. *I hate this place.*

Another flurry of gunfire on the ridge to the south sent Major Calhoun and his men scurrying for cover. There was at least one

Russian soldier still alive on the slope. They'd seen one of the Russians get shot. But he was unsure which female had bolted from the group. Calhoun decided it was time to act. "Let's go," he shouted above the wind, motioning for his men to start running towards the firefight. They let the dogs lead the charge.

"Run!" shouted Captain Petrov. He fired several short bursts to keep the Americans' heads down. It wasn't necessary to kill them—only delay them.

Springing to her feet, Elizabeth took off running down the hill. Blood was pumping through her chest and lungs. Although she was running as fast as she could, it still felt like she was moving in slow motion.

Driven by adrenaline, she never felt the bullet slice through her upper thigh. All she felt was the thudding impact of the bullet smashing into the back of her leg sending her crashing to the ground. Tumbling to the edge of the trees, she managed to regain her feet and scurry into the brush. A warm sensation running down her leg drew her attention. Blood soaked the leg of her pants. *I've been shot!* A wave of nausea swept over her. She sat down.

Captain Petrov was betting that either LeDue had made it back into the trees or she was dead. With a shout and several shots, he took off running down the hill in an erratic zigzag to the tree line. Dirt sprayed up around his feet as the Americans shot at him. He couldn't believe he made it to the bushes without getting hit. His heart was pounding and he was gasping for breath. As soon as he entered the alders, he spun around and got ready to return fire.

"Son-of-a-bitch!" Burke cursed as he watched the Russian soldier disappear into the trees. He couldn't believe it! LeDue had gotten away again.

"Don't feel so bad Commissioner," said a grinning Karen Marston, "I'm sure I hit her before she made it to the woods."

Before Burke or Marston could react, Price jumped up from his cover and started running down the hillside.

Burke shouted for him to come back.

The whine of the bullet passing his ear changed Kent Price's mind about charging the Russian position. He dropped to the ground and shimmied on his belly back up the hill.

Major Calhoun and his team were too late. By the time the shooting stopped they were just coming over the rise of the ravine where Joy was hiding. Calhoun was the first to spot her laying face down in the grass. Crossing over to the cowering female, he raised his rifle, ordering her to keep her hands in sight and slowly get to her feet. A Trooper searched her for weapons and pulled the picture of Dr. Elizabeth LeDue from his coat. "This isn't LeDue, Major. This must be the other woman."

Calhoun lowered his rifle and called off the dogs.

Joy breathed a sigh of relief. "I'm Joy Frank. Oh." She was unable to continue. Grabbing the Trooper, she embraced him with all her might.

Unsure of what to do, he returned the hug.

"We've got to get moving," Calhoun said. "Ms. Frank, you stay here. We'll come back for you in a little while."

"But why?" Joy said anxiously. She didn't want to be left alone.

"Because it's dangerous. We've got to catch Dr. LeDue before she gets away."

"Please don't leave me!" Joy pleaded. She clung to the Trooper.

"Don't worry," Calhoun said reassuringly, "we won't be long."

"Please, Ms. Frank," said a slightly embarrassed Trooper, "I promise we'll be right back." Peeling her hands from around the back of his neck, he held on to her arms, while gently sitting her down on his poncho.

Joy's heart sank as she watched them disappear over the ridge.

As they crested the rise, Major Calhoun motioned for his team to crawl on their bellies. He had no intention of rushing headlong into a firefight.

Slowly he peered over the top of the ridge. Up ahead he could see Commissioner Burke, PTO Price, and PTO Marston. Down the hillside, he could see the crumpled body of the dead Russian soldier. *Where are the other two?*

Calhoun sprinted up the rise to Burke. "Commissioner," he called out sliding down next to his boss.

Finally! "Where the hell have you been?" Burke launched into one of his famous butt-chewing sessions. Night was falling. The helicopters would have to return to base soon. They needed a plan. The Russians were getting away!

Calhoun cut off Burke's tirade. He'd been around too long to take a tongue-lashing from anybody. "Don't bark at me, Sir. Now isn't the time or place. We need a plan."

Calhoun recommended they launch a three-pronged advance down the hillside. He and Burke would take the center position, while PTOs Marston and Price would cover the left flank. The Troopers would cover the least likely direction of retreat on the right flank. The K-9 officers and their dogs would follow them in case they lost the trail.

Upon hearing the gunfire coming from the south, Korkov had his men pick up their pace. By the sounds of it, the Americans had intercepted Captain Petrov. Korkov planned to sweep up the American's right flank.

Coming to the edge of the trees, Korkov spied five Americans and two dogs above him on the ridge to his left. He was in a perfect position to spring a surprise assault. However, his orders were to avoid engaging the Americans. But he needed to relieve the pressure on Captain Petrov. Then he noticed the crumpled body of Sgt. Timoshenko. All bets were off. They were in a shooting war.

Korkov ordered Rudenko and Balzan to continue south, just inside the tree line. They were to make contact with Captain Petrov and help get Dr. LeDue back to the Putin.

Korkov began doubling back around to the northeast, staying just below the ridgeline and out of sight of the Americans on the hill above. He was going to move in behind and above them. From there he would be able to disrupt any attack they might launch against Captain Petrov. Up ahead he could see a small ravine. The depression would allow him to hide his movement.

He crested the rise and slid into it on his butt. He came to his feet about 10-feet away from Joy Frank.

Joy never heard him coming. She was still sitting on the Trooper's poncho, thinking about how good a shower was going to feel and how good Mrs. Lind's salmon chowder was going to taste. She was also thinking about Joseph Lind. *What would my parents say if I decide to stay in Alaska?*

Private Korkov's sudden arrival caught Joy completely off guard. Terrified at the sight of another Russian soldier, she jumped up to run, but it was too late. The muscular Korkov tackled her and held her down as he looked around for any sign of other Americans. With her face smashed into the ash-encrusted grass, Joy was unable to scream or move. To keep her still, Korkov had placed his knee on the Mastoid Process at the base of her skull—a painfully effective method of control.

Grabbing Joy by the hair, he pulled her to her feet. He couldn't believe his bad luck. He didn't need to be dragging this woman along with him, but he couldn't leave her behind. She might warn the others.

Joy struggled to free herself from Korkov's grasp. She grabbed his arm, trying to release his hold on her hair. At the same time, she spun around to kick him in the groin.

Korkov brought his knee up to cover his groin. As her leg crashed into his, he jammed his knee into her upper thigh.

Joy fell to the ground.

Angry at being attacked, Korkov kicked her in the face with the side of his boot, making her eyes blur and blood spray from her nose. Instinctively, she raised her hands to protect herself from any more blows.

In broken English, he said, "No fight. I kill. You come."

Joy got back to her feet, holding her swelling nose. Reluctantly, but without resistance she moved up the hill at Korkov's urging. Her face hurt. She began to cry.

High above on a ridge behind Burke's position, Major Golkin was trying to discern what was happening on the mountainsides to his right. Through his binoculars he could see Pvt. Korkov with the young woman moving below the ridge just north of the five Americans. He could also see the crumpled body of what appeared to be Sgt. Timoshenko several hundred yards below the Americans. He could not, however, locate Captain Petrov, the prisoner, or the other members of his Spetsnaz team. Anticipating that Korkov's strategy was to get behind the Americans, he set off at a jog. He would link up with Korkov and help him extract Captain Petrov from what appeared to be a tightening noose.

In the valley floor below Burke's position, Lt. Surin and Harry Ignustuk were advancing south, southeast in pursuit of Privates Rudenko and Balzan. To their left, they were catching periodic glimpses of Major Golkin moving on the ridgelines above them.

Harry had picked up the trail of Captain Petrov and Elizabeth LeDue. The muddy footprints showed where two men and two women had passed this way not too long before.

Lt. Surin ordered everyone to fall into single file and follow Harry.

It was Danny who caught sight of Korkov moving up the slopes to their left—Joy in tow. He trotted up to Sgt. Ramirez and tapped him on the back, pointing in the direction of the two people on the hillside.

Ramirez passed the information up the line. Everyone came to a halt.

It was time to go on the offensive. Lt. Surin dispatched Sgt. Ramirez and Sanders to pursue the fleeing Russian and his American hostage.

Sanders and Sgt. Ramirez set off to the east up the grassy hillside into the fading light.

Surin signaled for the team to resume their pursuit. There wasn't much daylight left and they needed to close the gap.

In the skies over Kodiak, the search helicopters were racing to get into position above the firefight. Even though the volcanic dust prevented them from landing, they could still be of use to Commissioner Burke and his men.

About three-quarters of the way up the mountainside they could see Commissioner Burke's team arrayed in an arc. To the north of Burke and moving up the hillside were a man and a woman. Down the hill from the man and woman, two men had emerged from the trees next to the creek. They were obviously pursuing their quarry up the hill.

Breaking formation, the Coast Guard helicopter headed for the man and woman jogging up the side of the mountain behind Commissioner Burke's position. The Trooper helicopter headed towards Commissioner Burke.

"Commissioner Burke, this is AST, over."

"Go for Burke."

"Coast Guard reports a man and a woman moving up the mountain behind you, over."

"Damn!" cursed Major Calhoun. "I shouldn't have left that civilian."

"Don't worry about that now," Burke advised Major Calhoun. "We need to concentrate on capturing Dr. LeDue. Then we can worry about young Ms. Frank."

"What if they kill her?" asked a concerned Trooper. She seemed like a good kid.

"They won't kill her," Burke said confidently. "It would be too messy. Too many witnesses."

Karen Marston wasn't worried about Joy Frank. She was concerned about the danger an enemy poses in your rear. She pointed out to that it wasn't wise to ignore the Russian moving up the mountain behind them.

Burke agreed.

"AST, this is Burke."

"Go, Commissioner."

"Roger the contact. Instruct the Coast Guard to harass the Russian and the woman on the hillside. Buy some time."

"10-4. AST out."

Down in the brush, Captain Petrov doctored Elizabeth's wound. Her stoicism and pain threshold were amazing. She didn't scream, cry or wiggle, as he squeezed antiseptic ointment into the bullet wound, before stuffing it with sterile gauze and giving her a shot of morphine. He cut two straight branches with his combat knife into roughly equal lengths. He used them to splint her leg. An elastic bandage tied the branches in place.

"There," he said smiling, "that should take care of you until we get you to the doctor."

She was grateful for his ministrations. "Why are you doing this?" she asked.

"Just following orders," Petrov answered. "I am proud to serve my country. My commanders think you are important enough to risk one of our best commando teams. Here, let me get you to your feet. We need to move." He helped her to her feet, supporting her with his shoulder.

With one last sprint, Privates Rudenko and Balzan caught up with Petrov, calling out in Russian so he didn't shoot them.

Captain Petrov was elated at the sight of Korkov's men.

"Welcome gentlemen," he said seriously.

"Where's Sgt. Timoshenko?" they asked in unison.

"Dead," Petrov said flatly. He still didn't believe that Timoshenko was dead. This whole mission was surreal.

Rudenko and Balzan looked at each other. "How?" Balzan asked angrily.

"American sniper."

"Shouldn't we go back for his body?" Rudenko asked.

"No," Petrov replied, "it will be dark soon. We need to elude the Americans. You know all of us are expendable." He understood their desire to go back for their comrade. The thought of leaving Timoshenko behind was repugnant. But he was a Spetsnaz soldier—he followed orders. He ordered the privates to cover the rear.

"Let's go," ordered Burke. It was time to implement Major Calhoun's plan.

The five officers fanned out and advanced down the hill. The K-9 officers and their dogs following close behind.

Above the tree-lined valley, the Trooper helicopter was flying a circular search pattern keeping a sharp lookout for any movement in the brush.

The moment the Americans broke from their cover on the mountainside, Privates Rudenko and Balzan began shooting. They were at extreme range and their shots fell short. But the dirt flying off the ground made the Americans dive for cover, giving them time to catch up with Captain Petrov. The K-9 officers retreated with their dogs back up the hill.

Seeing the Russian muzzle flashes in the trees, the pilot radioed this information to Burke. "I know they're shooting at us damnit!" Burke growled over the radio. "Try and find LeDue!"

Burke cursed. They still had over 500 yards of open ground to cover before they made it to the brush.

Meanwhile, Major Golkin had arrived unnoticed at a position high above Burke's team. It was a good sniper's nest. Aiming carefully, he fired a round, which struck just to the right of PTO Price.

"What the—?" Price blurted out as dirt flew up over his back and neck.

In quick succession, three more bullets struck the ground just to the rear of the Americans.

"AST, this is Burke! Is that Russian in position behind us?"

"Burke, AST. Coast Guard reports that is negative."

"Then who the hell is shooting at us?" bellowed Dick Burke over the radio.

Breaking off from his position over the valley floor, the AST helicopter ascended up the mountainside to locate the source of the gunfire.

Major Golkin watched the helicopter approach from below. Taking careful aim, he fired a single round into the right nacelle of the helicopter's engine. Smoke poured from the exhaust.

"Larsen Bay, Larsen Bay, this is AST. I am taking fire! Right engine hit, losing oil pressure! Returning to base. Over."

Dick Burke watched helplessly as the AST helicopter veered off to the north; smoke billowing from its right engine. With Russians in front and behind, they were in trouble. Major Golkin reminded him of his tactical error by firing more bullets into the ground behind them.

About two miles north of Burke's position, the Coast Guard helicopter was flying back and forth over Pvt. Korkov and Joy Frank in an attempt to harass and confuse the Russian. Korkov ignored the helicopter. With all the volcanic ash on the ground the helicopter couldn't land and with a hostage they couldn't shoot.

Hearing the radio call from the Trooper helicopter, the Coast Guard helo broke off its harassment. Ascending to a safe altitude, the pilot spotted the source of the sniper fire. "He's behind you about 250 yards up the mountain."

"Thanks," replied Burke, "now get out of here. It's almost dark. You can't help us now."

Dipping the nose of his helicopter, the Coast Guard pilot veered his chopper off in the direction the Trooper chopper had taken. Together they would return to Larsen Bay.

Pain shot through Elizabeth's leg as she limped down the trail. "Captain," she said through gritted teeth, "I don't think I can make it."

Captain Petrov noticed the beads of sweat on her face and her dilated pupils.

"Balzan, you big Cossack, get over here."

The bearlike Balzan hustled over to the waiting Captain Petrov. "Yes, Captain?"

"Give me your weapon," he ordered.

Balzan handed over his rifle. He understood what Petrov wanted. Turning around, he motioned for Elizabeth to climb onto his back. He placed her hands under his chin and grabbed her legs with his arms.

"I'm too heavy," Elizabeth apologized.

"No," replied the giant Balzan with a toothy grin.

Petrov shouldered Balzan's rifle and ordered his team to move out of the valley and up the hillside to the east. Twilight had fallen and it was dark enough to leave the safety of the brush.

Seeing smoke pouring from one of the American helicopters, and observing the other hovering high above the mountain, told Korkov that Major Golkin had caught up with them and was now laying down covering fire. Down below, he could see the two men who had been pursuing him up the ridge for the last half-hour. It was time to dump his hostage. Korkov stopped jogging and shoved Joy away.

She looked back at him in puzzlement. *What is he doing?*

He motioned for her to run to the men coming up from below.

Not waiting for a third invitation, she began hobbling down the mountainside. Her back tingled as she waited for the bullet she feared he would fire. The knot in her thigh was still there and her legs were cramping from struggling up the mountain, but she was determined to keep going.

Sgt. Ramirez and Danny Sanders wondered what the Russian was up to. *Why did he stop?* Then they saw Joy moving down the hill. She was hobbling as fast as anyone could. Unsure of what was happening, they dropped to their knees with rifles at the ready, just in case the Russian was using her as a decoy to ambush them.

Despite her exhaustion, Joy charged over a small rise, rushing into Danny's arms. He was caught off guard by the fierceness of her hug. He smiled at her youthful exuberance.

"You take her back," ordered Sgt. Ramirez, "I need to stay on the Russian's trail."

"Take her back where?" Danny asked. "I know it's not wise to drag a civilian into this mess, but it's just as dumb to send you off without a wingman."

Sgt. Ramirez reminded Danny that he got paid for taking these kinds of risks. Besides, he had to maintain contact with the Russians. There was no way they could keep up with Joy Frank in tow, and by the way she was clinging to Danny, there was no way she was going to be left behind again, either.

Danny shook his hand, bidding him farewell and good hunting.

Taking Joy in tow, Danny headed back down the mountain. There would be no rescue tonight, but they could find shelter and build a nice fire before it got too cold. *Heck,* he thought, *we might even be able to catch a fish.* Turning back around, he watched Ramirez disappear over the top of the ridge.

Lt. Surin was beginning to despair. Night had fallen. Even with night vision goggles, it would be almost impossible to track the fleeing Russians. Of course, he still did not fully appreciate the abilities of PTO Harry Ignustuk—a man, who had grown up hunting in winter darkness.

Surin ordered Sgt. Ali to break out the radio. He needed to report to Commander Englemann.

Major Golkin withdrew from his sniper position. It was time to rendezvous with the Putin. Using his compass and hand-held GPS, he headed for Three Saints Bay. The full moon, which made the gray landscape glow was a blessing. He was not worried about joining up with his men. They were all well trained. He just hoped that Captain Petrov still had Dr. LeDue. His team had paid a terrible price. Only her capture would make the sacrifice worthwhile.

Kaiugnak Bay, Kodiak Island, Alaska

Pulling in his nets just before nightfall, Tim Nederlander was grousing about the day's small catch. After twenty-five years of fishing for salmon in these waters, he was just about to hang up his nets for good. Each year the runs of salmon seemed to get smaller. He fired his boat's engines, preparing to get under way. *Maybe the fishing will be better at the head of Ugak Bay.*

The Putin was lurking just below the surface. Commander Ivanshenko was listening to the fishing boat fire up its diesel engines. *Perfect.* Just the cover we need to mask our submarine's noise. He prayed his luck would hold and the boat would head off in the direction of Three Saints Bay.

"Stay right in her prop wash, Vatutin," Ivanshenko ordered. "We'll use her to cover us. If," and he held up a finger, "she moves off in the right direction."

Pushing his throttles forward, Tim Nederlander steered his boat off to the northeast, unaware of the Russian submarine shadowing him 100 meters below the surface.

Commander Englemann took Lt. Surin's news with calm disappointment. No point in complaining. She didn't have time to dwell on the failures. With clear skies and a full moon, all the conditions favored the Russians. She prepared to make the most difficult command decision of her life. It was a lonely walk to the Ward Room.

"The Russians still have Dr. LeDue," Englemann told the officers assembled there. "By order of the President, we are to prevent the Russian submarine from linking up with the commandos. This is no drill people," she said gravely, "this time we will be shooting for real. And you can bet the Russians will be too." With those final words of admonition, she dismissed her officers to their respective divisions. She turned to Lt. Commander Hastings, "Brad, sound General Quarters."

Standing in the red glow of the Combat Information Center, Commander Englemann and Lt. Commander Hastings examined the navigation charts. Somewhere out there was a Russian submarine.

"What do you think Brad?" she asked.

Hastings stared at the charts, trying to guess the Russian's next move. "Well," he said thoughtfully, "I'd say he's going to try and use these fishing vessels as cover. I'm guessing he doesn't have accurate charts of the bays around here, and since he knows we're out here listening for him, he will be unable to use his active sonar to navigate. That means he'll creep up to a shoreline and come to the surface. He will try and use the terrain to cloud our radar and sneak into one of these two bays." Hastings pointed to Kaiugnak and Three Saints Bays.

"I agree," she replied. "Sonar, keep tuned for any unusual noises in the water. Radar, stay alert for any unusual surface contacts. Man the five-inch cannon and make ready for a night surface action."

Thumping along at 9-knots, the F/V Chiniak's old diesels provided plenty of cover for the stealthy Akula Class submarine. "This is beautiful," said a smiling Ivanshenko. The only question was how long he would stay in the wake of this most accommodating fishing boat.

White House, Washington, DC

Admiral Quinn rolled down his window to speak to the Marine on duty at the East Gate, "I'm here to see the President." After having his identification verified, he instructed his driver to proceed up to the residence. As they pulled up in front of the White House, he jumped out of his car, jogging up the steps into the building.

As he walked swiftly down the hallway to the president's private study, Admiral Quinn was going over in his mind the latest information relayed to him by Commander Englemann. He had never really believed the Russians would succeed in this damnfool mission. *Of course,* he reminded himself, *that was before the eruption and earthquake.* Three days ago he was prepared. The USS Billings and the USS Hammerhead were well placed to intercept the Russians before they could carry out their plans. Now, thanks to Mother Nature, they were in a very difficult position—one that had cost lives and by all appearances would claim even more.

The study was empty as the Admiral went inside. A Secret Service Agent informed him the President would be down momentarily. He took this opportunity to collect his thoughts. Looking out at the illuminated dome of the Capitol, he thought about how dangerous this situation had become.

"Mighty early to be up and about Admiral," said President Bainbridge entering the room in his favorite cotton bathrobe and slippers. "I presume we have news from Alaska."

"I'm afraid Mr. President, we are going to have some real shooting going on up there. I've studied the tactical situation and I don't think Commander Englemann has any options left."

"Any chance that the Russians have gotten word to their submarine to withdraw?" the President asked.

"I'm afraid not Mr. President," said Quinn shaking his head. "It was a long shot at best, especially with Commander Englemann riding herd on that sub for the past two days."

Accepting the inevitable, President Bainbridge went over to his phone and called his secretary. "Cathy, this is the President. I need you to come into work right away." He hung up the phone and grabbed a note pad, while Admiral Quinn made a pot of coffee.

Having just returned from the bathroom, Ambassador Potemkin had not yet fallen back asleep when the phone rang. "Hello?"

"Mr. Ambassador, this is Sasha Akmatovka."

"Yes, Akmatovka, what is it?" came the annoyed reply.

"Mr. Ambassador, President Bainbridge requests your presence at the White House again."

With a groan, Potemkin raised himself out of bed. Sometimes he hated his job, especially when Moscow kept him in the dark about a situation and he ended up being a messenger boy or a whipping post. Swinging his feet out from under the covers, he shook his head. Pulling on his pants and grabbing a shirt, he prepared for what he was sure was going to be an unpleasant meeting. "Try to get me the prime minister on the phone before I go, Akmatovka." He hung up the phone. He hoped she would be able to get through to the Kremlin before he left the embassy.

Potemkin had resigned himself to the fact that communicating with the Prime Minister had become more difficult ever since General Chernikov and Admiral Bulgakov had assumed their posts. He resented their interference in diplomatic affairs.

He arrived at the White House 20 minutes later and no wiser. Ambassador Potemkin put on his best diplomatic face. His job was to buy time and he was prepared to do just that.

President Bainbridge was waiting alone in his office, standing by the window looking out on the grounds. He invited Ambassador Potemkin in and offered him some juice, coffee, or tea, and a pastry.

"Just coffee, thank you. Mr. President," began Ambassador Potemkin, trying to gain control of the conversation by speaking first. "I do not believe you invited me to the White House at this very early hour to have coffee and cakes with you."

"No, Mr. Ambassador," replied the President, "I did not. I'm afraid," he said, turning back to the window to add dramatic effect to his next statement, "that circumstances have brought our two nations to a most serious crisis."

Potemkin sighed at the weight of those words.

President Bainbridge gestured for the Ambassador to make himself comfortable. "I regret to inform you, Mr. Ambassador, that within the next few hours my ships will sink your submarine."

"Surely," replied the Ambassador with his most heartfelt plea, "Mr. President, there is another course of action?"

President Bainbridge replied that he could not in good conscience allow a Russian submarine to penetrate American waters and kidnap an American citizen, let alone the most infamous traitor in American history since Benedict Arnold. Russia, he continued, had taken a bold risk and lost. He concluded by asking Ambassador Potemkin to forward his regrets to Prime Minister Kirov.

Thanking President Bainbridge for his courtesy, Ambassador Potemkin excused himself. *How am I going to inform Moscow of the President's decision to sink the Putin? What will that madman Bulgakov do now?*

The Kremlin, Moscow

Admiral Bulgakov was gazing out the Prime Minister's office window onto Red Square, admiring the last golden rays of sunlight reflecting off the multi-colored cupolas of St. Basil's Cathedral. He was eavesdropping on a telephone conversation. He could hear the tension in the Prime Minister's voice. Ambassador Potemkin was delivering bad news.

After the Kirov set down the receiver, Bulgakov turned around, waiting to be let in on the details. "Well, it seems the die is cast."

"Yes, Admiral it does," replied Kirov, taking a deep breath and rubbing his temples.

"Do we put our armed forces on alert?" he asked.

The very words made the Kirov stop rubbing his temples and open his eyes. "What? Are you mad?" he exclaimed. "Just how are we going to justify putting our armed forces on alert, when it was *our* submarine that invaded *their* territorial waters and kidnapped *their* scientist?" He was beginning to doubt the Admiral's sanity.

Responding to the Prime Minister's outburst, Bulgakov launched into a tirade of slights the Russian military had suffered at the hands of the Americans. The planned attack on the Putin was just one more example of America's disdain for Russian military might.

"You don't give Commander Ivanshenko enough credit," said General Chernikov entering the room. He had been listening to their conversation from the outer office. "Think about it gentlemen," he said didactically, "this mission was doomed to fail from the start, and yet here we are with our submarine deep inside American territory and our commandos in possession of Dr. LeDue. We just might pull this thing off." He looked hard at both of them. "Commander Ivanshenko only has to evade one American frigate and he's accomplished his mission. If he can get into deep water, he will lose the Americans." He ended his cheerleading session by pouring himself a cup of tea.

Admiral Bulgakov was speechless for one of the few times in his life. Prime Minister Kirov still didn't feel any better.

"General Chernikov is correct," interrupted the aging General Vasilof, who had just entered the office and was closing the door behind him. "We took a gamble and so far it's not gone too badly. If the Putin is sunk, we'll have to come up with a cover story for the folks back home, but if Ivanshenko makes it out with Dr. LeDue, we can deny the whole incident ever took place. The Americans will be boxed in. They can't tell their people what we did—too embarrassing."

Prime Minister Kirov walked over to the window. He decided he did not like international intrigue at all. He had no stomach for sending men on missions of speculative value. No one was even sure Dr. LeDue would cooperate once she was hidden away in the wilds of Siberia. And without her cooperation, Russia's biological warfare section would be no better off. He found the lies being bandied about his office repulsive. He didn't like lying, even in the interests of national security. Turning around from the window, he said sternly, "I think, gentlemen that from the beginning you did not properly inform me of the risks involved with this mission. I think you are wrong about the Americans. I do not believe they will sweep this incident under the rug. And now I find myself in the unenviable position of lying to the Russian people, either about the kidnapping of Dr. Elizabeth LeDue and a sinister plot the Americans are sure to expose, or about the disappearance of one of our submarines and its crew. None of you," he continued, pointing his finger at each one of them, "has to explain to the grieving mothers why their sons died."

Quietly opening the door, Admiral Voroshilov walked into the room and over to the window. Like Admiral Bulgakov, he stared at St. Basil's Cathedral in the soft evening light. It reminded him of Russia's former glory. *Russians,* he thought to himself. W*e are such a nostalgic people. How will Ivanshenko get himself out of this fix?* "Gentlemen," he said in his booming voice, "we all know that things have the potential to go terribly wrong. We knew this from the beginning. However, it is too late to worry about that now. We are in this noose and now we must wait to see if we all hang by our necks or if Commander Ivanshenko will make us all look like stars." With that, he turned and strode out of the room.

Kodiak Island, Alaska

Under the light of the full moon, Captain Petrov was pushing his men along the mountain ridges, east, towards the designated rendezvous point. Private Balzan was maintaining a superhuman pace. His legs burned from the exertion, but still he did not slow down. Private Rudenko was bringing up the rear.

Elizabeth LeDue was sleeping soundly. Not even the jarring of Balzan's trot could wake her. Her body had endured too much over the past few days. She had tried to stay awake, but the morphine and the rhythm of Balzan's gait had put her to sleep.

To the west and behind the Russians, the Americans were slowly closing the gap. Harry Ignustuk was straining all his senses to stay on the trail of the fleeing Russians. Every few minutes he would kneel, touch the trampled grass, examine the scrapes on the moss-covered rocks, and then resume the pursuit. The moonlight was helping him trace the Russians' path through the wilderness.

Lt. Surin was amazed at Harry's skills, but he still continued to use the night vision scope to catch glimpses of the Russians moving among the rocks and ravines. Never in a thousand years would Surin have thought it possible to track someone in the dark without the aid of night vision scope or a dog and yet this crafty Eskimo was doing just that.

Signaling a halt, Lt. Surin dropped to one knee. Using his night vision scope, he watched the three Russian soldiers moving away from them along the top of the mountain. "There they are," he whispered to Sgt. Ali, "just ahead and moving fast. Looks like one of them is carrying LeDue."

"Want me to take a shot?" Ali asked.

"Not yet," Surin replied. He wanted to get a little closer and wait for them to run into some terrain that would slow them down. This would give Sgt. Ali a better chance of hitting his target. He motioned for Harry to continue tracking. They set off at a slow jog.

Several miles north of Captain Petrov, Major Golkin had managed to catch up with Pvt. Korkov. Together, they were moving silently towards the rendezvous point. Korkov thanked his lucky stars for the bright moonlight. Major Golkin, however, was worried that too much light would expose them to ambush.

Sgt. Ramirez was about one-half mile behind Golkin and Korkov. Through his night vision scope, he could clearly see the two soldiers moving at a double-time pace over the undulating terrain. He was exhausted, but the thrill of the chase kept him going. This is what he loved about the job. Furthermore, he prided himself on being the most relentless man in Lt. Surin's team. It was a reputation he intended to keep intact.

Three Saints Bay, Kodiak Island, Alaska

Tim Nederlander moved his boat across the entrance to Three Saints Bay, altering his course to take him over to John Island. He wanted to say hello to his old friend and owner of the F/V Skookum. *Maybe Kurt had better luck with the Kings today.*

Twenty meters below the surface Commander Ivanshenko ordered a course change to keep the Putin in the prop wash of the fishing boat. He couldn't have asked for a better plan. He couldn't stop smiling at his luck. However, he tempered his glee with the realization that as soon as he got beyond the fishing boats and into Three Saints Bay, he would have to come to the surface and hug the shoreline. He didn't have accurate charts of the waters in this area. He couldn't risk grounding his boat by running submerged. He was hoping for a storm on the surface. This would help cover his approach into the narrow fjord. If not, the Putin would risk lighting up the American frigate's radar screen like a giant green bug.

Commander Englemann was standing on the bridge, sipping her coffee as she waited patiently for news from the CIC. At some point the Russian would have to come to the surface. Even if he did have charts of the local waters, he would have to blow his ballast and come up to retrieve his commandos. Then she would pounce. This time, it was for real. She planned to hit the Russian with everything in the Billings's arsenal.

As he slowed his boat, Tim Nederlander, a veteran of these waters, felt a giant swell pass under him. It had appeared out of nowhere. "What the?" he blurted in surprise as the wave rocked his boat. He looked out the window. He watched the freak swell advance under the FV Skookum and move into Three Saints Bay.

"What the hell was that?" the Skookum's owners shouted across the water.

"Beats the heck out of me!" Nederlander shouted back. "Never seen the like."

"Maybe," the old fisherman speculated, "it has something to do with that Navy destroyer over by Tallapoosa Shoal?"

The two crusty fishermen shrugged their shoulders and turned their conversation to more relevant topics—the fishing, the reasons why they had stayed at sea following the earthquake and tsunami, and where they were going to set their nets tomorrow.

Ivanshenko ordered the Putin to periscope depth. He wanted to take a look around. His throat grew dry when his periscope burst into the bright light of a full moon under a cloudless sky. "Damn!" he exclaimed.

"What is it commander?" asked Lt. Commander Vatutin.

"It's brighter than Moscow on May Day," Ivanshenko replied gruffly. "A full moon and no clouds. We're going to make one pretty sight once we surface. Only a blind man would be able to miss us."

Commander Ivanshenko's declaration made the crew nervous—just how, they wondered, would their brilliant commander accomplish this task? Sailing into an uncharted fjord, under a full moon, and unable to use their active sonar, the men of the Putin knew the odds against them had just increased dramatically.

Ivanshenko ordered the Putin to slow to two knots. He looked at the map of Three Saints Bay. About 15 miles long and three miles wide, Three Saints Bay is a classic steep-gorged fjord with one thousand and two thousand foot cliffs on both sides. Ten miles inside the bay, it makes a sharp turn to the west and terminates at the base of a steep 1,600-foot mountain. Rivers empty into the bay on each side of the mountain.

"Vatutin," barked Ivanshenko, "bring us to the middle of the channel and maintain periscope depth. Make your speed four knots." He looked back at his chart. *This plan just might work, if I'm lucky, and if the radarman on the American frigate is inexperienced.*

Bathed in the infrared glow of the CIC, Lt. Commander Hastings looked over the radarman's shoulder, watching for any telltale sign of a target coming to the surface in either of the two bays. For the moment, the only targets were the fishing boats, anchored for the night.

On the bridge, Margaret Englemann stood watching the moonlight dance off the water. She was calculating every possible scenario that could occur in the next few hours. The courage and skill of the Russian submarine commander was impressive. He had a knack for the unorthodox. She admired that kind of ingenuity and skill—a rare trait in the Russian Navy.

Then it hit her. Would this bold Russian risk running all the way into one of these bays submerged? It was improbable, given the dangers of navigating unknown waters, but he had proven himself before. Acting on her hunch, she picked up the phone ordering two experienced sailors to grab their night-vision binoculars and climb the crow's nest. One man was to watch Kaiugnak Bay and one was to watch Three Saints Bay. "Let me know if you see any unusually large waves slapping against the shorelines."

Kodiak Island, Alaska

As they came to the edge of the mountain leading down to the beach at the head of Three Saints Bay, Captain Petrov ordered his squad to take a minute to rest before descending the slippery slope. They were almost home—if the Putin had managed to make the rendezvous. Using his night vision scope he searched the bay for any sign of the Putin. And then just to make sure, he turned around and scanned the barren terrain for any sign of the Americans or Major Golkin. To his right, he could make out the fluorescent green shapes of three men moving over the undulating peaks in their direction. He guessed two of them were from his unit and the other one was American. He dispatched Private Rudenko to intercept Major Golkin and tell him about the American. The rest of the area appeared clear.

While he waited for Private Rudenko to link up with Major Golkin, Captain Petrov took the opportunity to catch his breath, drink some water and eat a small snack. He motioned for Private Balzan to set Elizabeth down and rest.

Groggy with morphine, Elizabeth took a drink from Private Balzan's canteen. Her leg hurt. *How much longer will this go on?* She took a bite of the candy bar offered to her.

The moment he saw the Russians come to an abrupt halt at the edge of the mountain, Harry motioned for Lt. Surin and Sgt.

Ali to halt and duck behind the rocks to their left. "They must be taking a break," Harry said sliding down next to Surin.

"Got any ideas?" asked Surin in a hushed voice.

Harry took his customary pause before saying, "I think it's pretty obvious they're trying to make it to that bay up ahead. Give me a few minutes head start. I will move to our right and down this slope to the valley below and work my way through the brush to the water's edge. While I move, you two lay down covering fire."

"That's a good idea Harry, but I want Sgt. Ali to go with you. It's better if two of you get behind them. I'll give you five minutes to get part of the way down the slope. That big Russian won't be able to move very fast with LeDue on his back. And," Surin said while watching the Russians through his scope, "it looks like one of them is heading off to the north to link up with those guys way over there." He pointed to his left, in the direction of Major Golkin.

Silently PTO Harry Ignustuk and Marine Sgt. Tariq Ali set off, retreating to the west before heading down the steep slopes towards the brush covered valley 1,600-feet below.

Ten miles away, Joy was lying on her back, basking in the glow of the warm firelight, staring up at the moonlit sky. Never before had the stars looked so bright or the moon so full. She wondered if Joseph was looking at the moon thinking about her. The smell of salmon cooking made her mouth water, although she was a little anxious the odor might attract a bear.

"How are you feeling now?" Danny asked.

"Better, much better," Joy replied with a sigh. She was so thankful for his kindness during their hike back to the river. Her legs had started cramping and he'd supported the bulk of her weight for most of the way. When he built a fire and boiled some water so she could wash her face and hands she was in heaven.

The sound of men approaching made Joy jump.

"Hello there," came the call.

It was an American. Joy sighed with relief. "Hello," she called back.

"Mind if we come in?"

"Not at all," Danny answered. He'd been expecting the other American officers to join his camp once they saw the fire. The Russians were long gone and there was no need to worry. Then he realized he'd forgotten to tell Joy to expect other officers. Danny apologized for not giving her a heads up.

Dejection was etched on the faces of Commissioner Burke and the other officers as they joined Danny and Joy around the fire. No one felt like talking. Even the dogs looked depressed. They immediately lay down at their masters' feet.

Danny broke the gloom by reminding them that Harry Ignustuk was the best tracker in the business. Harry, he said with conviction, had grown up hunting in the dark, treeless expanses of the Arctic. With this moonlight he would be able to stay on their trail all night long. Besides, they had rescued Joy.

Danny's comments made everyone's spirits rise. Maybe LeDue wouldn't escape after all. At least they were hoping that would be the outcome.

Three Saints Bay, Kodiak Island, Alaska

Hurrying down from the crow's nest, the sailor raced into the bridge. "Skipper. I think you should come and take a look at this," he said excitedly.

Margaret Englemann followed him to the crow's nest. Handing her the night vision binoculars, he pointed in the direction of Three Saints Bay.

"There," he said in a hushed voice, "watch the surf as it hits the shore to the north. Now," he said pointing towards Kaiugnak Bay, "watch the surf as it hits the shore to the west."

Slowly, a smile crossed her face. *Incredible!* She couldn't believe the Russian's bravado. He was using his passive sonar to navigate his boat at a snail's pace up Three Saints Bay. He was moving just beneath the surface. While his maneuver prevented a radar signature and limited her sonar contact, even the Russian commander couldn't stop his 13,000-ton boat from displacing all that water, sending large waves crashing against the shore. "Good job sailor!"

she said, handing him back his binoculars. Quickly, she returned to the bridge.

Her tone sharp, she ordered, "Lt. Commander Hastings, this is Commander Englemann. Report to the bridge immediately."

Hastings raced up from the CIC.

She motioned for him to join her at the chart table. She was beside herself with excitement. "Here Brad," she exclaimed thumping her finger down on the chart, "here is where he's headed!"

Hastings cocked his eyebrow. He trusted the Skipper's intuition, but he was unsure how she had come to that conclusion.

Seeing the skeptical look on Hastings's face, Commander Englemann explained how she had guessed the Russian commander would risk running submerged to his rendezvous point and how the displacement of water caused by his submarine would leave telltale waves on the shore.

Brilliant. He whistled in admiration, before asking her for her plan of attack. "Don't forget Skipper," he cautioned, "if the Russian launches torpedoes in this narrow fjord, it will be damn hard for us to get out of the way."

"That's the beauty of it Mister Hastings. I don't think I'll have to fire a shot."

Before he could ask her just how she intended to accomplish this, she ordered the Billings to make steam for 25-knots and set course for Three Saints Bay. "Trust me Brad," she said smiling. "But just in case, make sure the gun crews and torpedo crews are ready. And Brad, get Hawk Two ready in case we need her."

Kodiak Island, Alaska

Lt. Surin looked at his watch and raised his rifle. Aiming just to the left of the big Russian, he aligned his crosshairs on the center of Dr. Elizabeth LeDue's chest. *It's time to end this manhunt.* Applying steady pressure to the trigger, he exhaled just as the rifle recoiled into his shoulder.

Lt. Surin grimaced at his aim. He had only wounded her. *The woman has nine lives.*

Setting his rifle on full-automatic, Surin popped up from behind the rocks and squeezed off several bursts. He hoped to get lucky and hit one of the Russians, or at least prevent their headlong escape down the mountain.

Racked by chills caused by the morphine and shock, Elizabeth coughed just as Lt. Surin pulled the trigger. The bullet struck her just above the left shoulder. The impact spun her around. Searing pain shot through her back, arm and neck. She screamed.

Instinctively, Captain Petrov and Private Balzan flopped to the ground, searching the area for any sign of the sniper. Cursing in Russian, Captain Petrov crawled over to Elizabeth. "Be quiet!" he barked. "Stop screaming!" He applied pressure to the wound. Looking under her shirt, he could see the bullet had grazed her shoulder. It was a painful wound exposing a lot of nerves, but it was not life threatening.

Private Rudenko had been jogging at a good pace when he heard the report of the rifle echo through the mountain valley. He froze in place and dropped to one knee. "Major! It's me, Rudenko. Over here." He waved his arm, hoping the Major could see him in the eerie moonlight.

"Rudenko!" Major Golkin shouted back. "Where are you?"

"Over here," he shouted, taking out his flashlight and clicking it on and off as a signal.

Major Golkin led Korkov at a dead run towards Rudenko's position. "Who the hell is shooting?" he asked in between his gasps for air.

"I don't know," Rudenko replied. He took the point position leading the Major and Private Korkov back to Captain Petrov and Private Balzan. Finally, Golkin caught sight of the American soldier, who had been trailing them for the last few hours.

As they ran towards Captain Petrov's position, they could see the muzzle flashes in the darkness. The rapid 'twoof, twoof, twoof' of an American M-16 was being answered by the sharp crack of AK-47s.

Running up to Petrov's position, Golkin ordered, "Let's get down this mountain."

Picking Elizabeth up, Private Balzan headed down the steep mountainside. He wasn't really walking. It was more of a controlled slide. Petrov and Korkov were close behind.

Major Golkin and Private Rudenko turned to face the American gunfire. Sparks flew as bullets ricocheted off the rocks all around them. Scurrying for better cover, they crawled backwards towards a small outcropping of boulders situated on the edge of the steep slope.

Even though he was breathing harder than usual, the exchange of gunfire really didn't bother Golkin all that much. He understood that the chances of being shot in the dark at this range by an M-16 were pretty low. Rudenko, however, had never been under fire before and his heart was racing, his palms sweating, and his breathing was ragged. All this provided insurance to the Americans that only by sheer luck would they get hit by one of his bullets.

Once Golkin had led them safely behind the rocks, they began returning fire in earnest. All they had to target on were the muzzle flashes of the American M-16s. They took their best guess and returned fire. Golkin squeezed each round off calmly and deliberately. Rudenko was jerking the trigger and throwing his rounds wildly off target. Golkin didn't bother correcting him. He believed it was fortunate Rudenko was shooting so poorly. It would not be good to kill an American soldier on American soil. He made a mental note to pay special attention to Rudenko's training when they got home.

Gradually the Russians slid back off the ridge and down the slope to the next hiding place. In stages, Private Rudenko and Major Golkin were fighting a tactical retreat down the mountain.

They could hear Private Balzan cursing as he tried to maintain his footing on the tundra.

Elizabeth was clinging to Private Balzan's back. She held her breath as they slid down the precipitously steep slope. Her leg throbbed and her shoulder burned. At this moment, the moonlight reflecting off the waters of the bay was not beautiful. She just wanted this ordeal to be over. She had never really considered herself to be a criminal. In another place or different circumstances, she'd be able to appreciate the beauty of this island. But not now.

Sgt. Ramirez ignored the dirt and grass flying up in front of him as he ran in a zigzag pattern toward the Russian position. He raised his rifle squeezing off several bursts of automatic fire. He could tell by the exchange of gunfire that Lt. Surin's team was to his right. With him on the left, they had the Russians in a crossfire. And without any cover, it made just as much sense to charge their position as it did to drop to the ground.

The steady echo of gunfire told Harry and Sgt. Ali that the Russians were making a run for it. They rushed headlong down the slippery slope. They had to cover as much ground as possible before the Russians could get to the head of the bay.

Sliding to a stop at the edge of the trees, they turned left and ran along the edge of the forest towards the beach less than a mile away. Harry planned to hide in the brush and cut off the Russians' retreat. With Americans on all sides they would have no place to go.

Three Saints Bay, Kodiak Island, Alaska

"Shit!" the sonar man blurted out. He spun around, "Commander. I have a sonar contact moving in our direction at 25-knots."

"Damn!" exclaimed Ivanshenko. *How did the Americans spot us? Did they pick up our passive sonar signals? Perhaps. Are the narrow walls of this watery canyon amplifying the sound of our propeller?* He quit guessing. It wasn't important. Right now he had to come up with a plan for extracting Major Golkin and getting back out of this bottle.

"Helm, increase speed to 15-knots," he ordered. "Blow ballast and bring us to the surface. Lt. Commander Vatutin, assemble your men. Prepare to launch two boats to retrieve Major Golkin." Commander Ivanshenko hoped Golkin and his Spetsnaz team was waiting on the shore. This would be his only chance to get them off the island.

The Putin picked up speed, shoving aside the cold waters of Three Saints Bay. Ivanshenko was taking a huge gamble that there were no reefs or shoals in the middle of the channel. It would be impossible to stop the submarine in time if they were to stumble onto a reef or shoaling waters. Behind the Putin, the propeller churned the water into florescent foam.

Tim Nederlander was sitting in his galley, enjoying the first rest he'd had since sailing through Sitkalidak Strait a week ago. He was sipping a cup of Irish coffee, his favorite, absorbed in conversation with his old friend. He never expected to be tossed from his seat on such a clear night and calm seas. They rushed topside to catch a glimpse of what had caused such a disturbance.

Looking out over the moonlit sea, they saw the dark hulk of the Navy frigate churning swiftly through the water. *Why would a Navy warship be slicing at such a speed into one of Kodiak's narrowest fjords? Could it be related to that freak swell they had noticed several hours before?* "Must be another submarine exercise," he concluded turning to his friend, "although I'm surprised the Navy is out here on war games so soon after that God-awful earthquake."

"Submarine breaking the surface eight miles dead ahead," shouted Lt. Commander Hastings over the intercom. "She's picking up speed and moving away."

"Helm," Englemann ordered, "increase speed to 27-knots. Commander Hastings, order the gun crews to prepare for action. Launch Hawk Two."

Commander Englemann was driving the Billings hard. She had her game plan set, but for it to work, she needed to catch the Russian before he could complete his turn around the sharp curve in the bay.

Seals lining the shores were barking in distress as the waves generated by the Russian submarine and the Navy frigate slapped over the rocks.

As the Putin approached the head of Three Saints Bay, Ivanshenko was forced to slow his boat to navigate the tight turn. The Putin was not designed to run on the surface. Ivanshenko stood on the bridge, watching the radar, while Vatutin watched his men on the aft-deck preparing to launch rigid-hulled inflatables. With each minute the American frigate closed the distance. Before long the Putin would be in range of her 5-inch gun.

"Load aft torpedo tubes," Ivanshenko ordered. "Lieutenant, work out a firing solution on the American frigate and wait for my order to launch."

Margaret Englemann knew she was running a big risk sailing this fast into such a confined canyon. However, circumstances left her few options, especially if she wanted to avoid any more bloodshed.

"Shall we fire a warning shot over her bow?" asked Commander Hastings.

"Hold your fire Commander. I'm going to beat that crafty son-of-a-bitch to the end of the bay," she replied. She kept her eyes glued to the binoculars. "Helm, prepare to make a hard turn to port on my signal. Notify all hands to hold on tight!"

Kodiak Island, Alaska

From their perch at the top of the ridge, Lt. Surin and Sgt. Ramirez were the first to catch sight of the Russian submarine turning the corner. *How have the Russians managed to get this far?*

Surin and Ramirez prepared to head down the mountain in a full-scale attack on the Russians. Just then Ramirez shouted, "Look!"

Coming around the corner was the USS Billings. The frigate was listing heavily as the helmsmen put her over hard to port. Smiles broke across both men's faces as they realized the Billings would be able to position herself between the shore and the Russian submarine. There was no escape now.

Completing their descent to the boulder-strewn beach, the Russians couldn't believe their eyes as they watched the American frigate sail past the Putin.

Englemann had called Ivanshenko's bluff. He couldn't risk firing his torpedoes in the narrow fjord. If he missed the torpedo might track him and inside the fjord he could not maneuver. Besides, there were too many witnesses now.

"Drop your weapons and put your hands in the air," Harry shouted from the cover of the trees. He had his rifle pointed at Dr. LeDuc, ready to shoot her if they did not comply.

Major Golkin instructed his men to put down their weapons and surrender. For the first time in his illustrious career he had failed.

The chase was over. It was time to bury the dead and go home.

Commander's Quarters, USS Billings, Three Saints Bay, Kodiak Island, Alaska

Commander Margaret Englemann sat behind her desk, talking to her counterpart through a translator. "At first light, Commander Ivanshenko, I will dispatch my helicopter to retrieve the body of your Sergeant Timoshenko. Under orders from Admiral Quinn, the Billings will escort your submarine out to international waters, from where I presume you will sail for home."

"That is most generous, Commander," Commander Ivanshenko replied gratefully. "I thank you for allowing me to retrieve Sgt. Timoshenko. And," he continued, "I must compliment you on your tactical abilities. A lesser commander would not have caught me so easily."

Margaret Englemann thanked him for his compliment and assured him that his capture had not been easy.

After returning to the Putin, Ivanshenko informed Major Golkin that the Americans would retrieve the body of Sgt. Timoshenko in the morning. Major Golkin apologized for his failure.

"It is not you, Major, but I who have failed. I could not shake off the American frigate. If I had," he said, emphasizing his point with a slap on the Major's shoulder, "you, my most talented friend, would have found a way to get the good doctor onto my submarine."

PTO Harry Ignustuk was standing guard outside the Billings' infirmary, drinking a cup of coffee and eating a sandwich. Inside, the ship's doctor was treating Elizabeth LeDue's wounds. "Will she live doc?" he asked as the doctor emerged from the room.

"Yes." Removing his glasses the doctor looked directly at Harry. "Hard to believe she's such a notorious criminal isn't it?"

"Hmmm," Harry responded in typical Eskimo fashion, "hard to believe."

Unwilling to let the topic go, the doctor continued, "Something terrible happened out there. She has wounds all over her body, and in her eyes, you can see the fear."

Harry didn't reply. Something terrible did occur out there.

DAY FOUR

Larsen Bay, Alaska

Commissioner Michelle Dornier was in great spirits as Lt. Cowdrey brought Hawk Two in for a landing. Earlier in the day, the Coast Guard had retrieved Commissioner Burke and the others from their campsite and reported that an American frigate and Russian submarine were anchored at the head of Three Saints Bay. Now she could inform Governor Malloy that Dr. Elizabeth LeDue was back in custody.

"Welcome back, Officer Ignustuk," she said smiling, "and congratulations on a job well done."

Surprised to see the head of his department waiting for him in Larsen Bay, Harry was unable to think of anything to say other than thank you. Grabbing the other end of the stretcher, he helped the Navy corpsman unload Elizabeth LeDue and carry her over to the waiting blue and gold C-130 transport.

Danny Sanders was already on the transport, waiting and smiling grandly as Harry walked up the ramp of the transport holding one end of the stretcher. "Guess we'd better finish this transport," he said buoyantly. He moved in behind his partner to ensure the prisoner didn't escape again.

Harry found comfort in the routine.

Danny hit the switch, raising the pneumatic ramp at the rear of the aircraft. He was surprised that he wasn't nervous about flying again.

On the ground, the people of Larsen Bay were waving their thanks as they stood next to the stack of supplies flown in by the department.

At the other end of the runway, Commissioner Burke and his troopers were climbing into their helicopter. Burke was returning to Anchorage to take command of the earthquake cleanup program.

DAY FIVE

Malloy Super Max, Adak Island, Alaska

Captain Anderson walked down the hall, listening to Sgt. Knight brief him on the day's events. "Received a call from Commander Jones on the Hammerhead. They have Lt. Banderas, Officer Williams, and the bodies of Travis Nelson and Toby Church. They should be back here in a few hours."

"Haven't had this many dignitaries in Adak since the Cold War," commented Anderson. He was thinking about hosting Commissioner Burke, Commissioner Dornier, and their special guest, Governor Malloy. "Guess we'd better spiff up the place a little bit and get ready to greet them at the airport."

The black smoke billowing out of its four powerful engines let Captain Anderson and Sgt. Knight know that Malloy Two was on its descent to Mitchell Field. Not only was their relief shift arriving, but for the first time since she'd come to Alaska, Commissioner Dornier was coming to visit the department's most isolated facility. They buttoned up their jackets against the cool breeze blowing in off Kuluk Bay.

Governor Malloy's jet was already arcing in over Kuluk Bay on final approach. Looking out the window, Governor Malloy was dumbstruck at the devastation suffered by the town. He had experienced the same reaction visiting communities throughout

Alaska, although the worst hit was Dutch Harbor. *It will be weeks before we can even begin to calculate the damage.* On the hillside of Mt. Moffett, he could see the prison bearing his name.

Captain Anderson stood on the tarmac, preparing to issue a formal greeting.

As she descended the exit ramp, Commissioner Dornier swept up Captain Anderson's arm, walking with him over to Governor Malloy's jet. She was excited to be in Adak and proud to have Governor Malloy as the department's guest. However, she did make a mental note to wear a heavier coat next time she visited Adak.

They met Governor Malloy at his plane. Together they walked up the road to the prison. "You've done an amazing job here, Captain," expounded Governor Malloy. "With the capture of Elizabeth LeDue and the deaths of Ivan Lincoln and Toby Church, I can once again let our people know our prison system is secure. Commissioner, I believe you have something to say."

Dornier stepped forward, "Thank you Governor. Captain Anderson, it's my pleasure to promote you to Superintendent of Malloy Super Maximum Prison."

EPILOGUE

Over the next several months, the events surrounding the Great Aleutian Earthquake came into focus.

For his part, Governor Malloy took great pride in awarding medals of heroism to PTOs Harry Ignustuk and Danny Sanders, and Officers Carlos Banderas and Ben Williams. He also took it upon himself to personally extend his condolences to the families of officers Travis Nelson and Blaine Smith. He also issued an Executive Proclamation honoring their sacrifices.

Immediately upon receiving the news of Commander Englemann's victory, President Bainbridge called Prime Minister Kirov to inform him that the whole affair would be kept quiet. The tragic events surrounding the Great Aleutian Earthquake would be stored away in the annals of international espionage. Several weeks later he flew to San Diego to award a Presidential Unit Citation to the USS Billings and Commander Margaret Englemann. Along with Admiral Quinn, he attended the change of command ceremony for Lt. Commander Brad Hastings—the new Commander of the USS Billings. Commander Englemann was taking command of a new Aegis Class Cruiser.

Having been promoted to Admiral Bulgakov's position, Admiral Voroshilov had managed to protect Commander Ivanshenko from becoming a scapegoat for the whole LeDue affair. He convinced Prime Minister Kirov that the hawks within the military needed to be replaced by more open-minded men. Commander Ivanshenko politely declined an invitation to take over command of the Russian submarine fleet. His home was the sea and he intended to stay there.

It was another rare day of brilliant sunshine, when Michelle Dornier flew back to Adak. She never would get used to the vast distances involved with traveling in Alaska. She was there to preside over ceremonies in honor of officers Blaine Smith, Joan Steiger, Travis Nelson, and Nurse Doreen Evers and pinning Captain's bars on Carlos Banderas and, much to everyone's surprise, sergeant's chevrons on Ben Williams.

Thomas Frank found himself not in Hartford welcoming his little girl home, but in Homer, Alaska, walking his beautiful young daughter down the aisle. Waiting for her in his best blue jeans and wool shirt was Joseph Lind. It was a beautiful wedding, with the snow-encrusted summits of three volcanoes shimmering brightly in the background. Guests of honor included Harry Ignustuk, Danny Sanders, and the crew of the USS Billings.

Despite the trials she had endured in the rugged Alaska wilderness, Joy had fallen under the spell of the Great Land. Now her heart belonged to this rugged wilderness and the young man she had met that spring. She was home. And soon it would be time to set sail on the F/V Neptune once again—the salmon were running in Bristol Bay.